THE CALL HOME

ELI POPE

© US COPYRIGHT 2024 – Steven G Bassett

All rights reserved.

No portion of this book may be reproduced, stored in a retrieval system, or transmitted in any form or means including electronic, mechanical, photocopied, recorded, scanned, or other, with the exception of brief quotations in reviews or articles, without prior written permission of author or publisher.

Scripture quotations are taken from the Holy Bible, NIV®, MSG®, KJV®

This novel is a work of fiction. All names, characters, places, and incidents are either from the imagination of the author or used fictitiously. All characters are fictional, and any similarity to people living or dead is coincidental.

Cover Design – Steven G Bassett
Interior Formatting – 3dogsBarking Media LLC

Published by 3dogsBarking Media LLC

ISBN: 978-1-7358159-8-5

THE CALL HOME

DEDICATION

This story is dedicated to all those who have been faithful in following this saga of Billy Jay Cader. Thank you for your support and I hope you continue to follow my work.

ACKNOWLEDGMENTS

My editor Julie Luetschwager has not only fixed my many mistakes and pointed out changes that make me appear to be a smarter author than I truly am, but I also say thank you, thank you, and thank you. You've helped keep me inspired to move forward.

My Springfield Writers Guild members and fellow author friends, Malcolm Tanner, Antim Straus, and Drew Thorn, who share ideas, critiques, knowledge, and occasional beers. Thank you!

And my wife who puts up with the hours my head is buried in my other world. I love you and couldn't do it without you.

It truly takes a village to make it all work!

1
1986

Addison flung the door to Ethan's office wide open and very abruptly. Her face painted with fear and apprehension. She knew what she expected to see and was certain Ethan would need immediate medical attention. What she found was something totally unexpected. Her heart thundered inside her chest as the very hysterical gasp exited across her lips. "Oh my God!"

Ethan sat calmly at his desk, not even bothering to look up for a moment. His left hand propped his head up, a smoking revolver in his right, resting against his shoulder, barrel pointing behind him.

"You're alive! My God, Ethan... I... I thought... you... you...."

As Ethan slowly turned his head toward Addi, he lowered the revolver away from his neck and placed it on the desktop. Tears streamed down his cheeks; a sight Addi had never witnessed during her entire career working for him. Ethan's expression began to melt into a hollowness melting into despair. He attempted to slowly speak. "Addi... Addi... my dear... I... I... just... I couldn't bring... bring myself to... to... complete... the task at hand." His head twisted away from the shadows of the darkened side of the room and toward the window that gleamed light. "It appears that I am too much the coward to close this wretched case of mine." He close friends instead of coworkers. I do need a good friend, especially today."

Addison picked up her glass and walked over to the leather couch next to the pool table. She did fumble in her step for a moment, one heel almost curling under her ankle. As she slid back into the cushion, Ethan sat down in the chair beside her. Addison looked up overhead and above the conference area at the bull shark, which hung by wires—lurking above in the shadows. "I've always wanted to be a friend close enough to drink with you, Ethan. I just wasn't sure what my place was. It's a shame it almost took a bullet to find that out—isn't it?"

"Addi, Addi, Addi... you know I've always respected you. You are an incredible example of a woman filled full of intelligence and all wrapped up in a strong and very beautiful package. I mean this as the utmost of compliments. Hell... in my book... you've always been just out of reach for me. Far too smart and beautiful to get tangled up with the likes of my rather gritty character."

"Ethan..." Addison halted her sentence, as if planning exactly how she wanted to word her thoughts carefully.

After a few seconds of silence, Ethan spoke up quietly. "Cat got your tongue, Addi? I know you are aware that I can bite rather harshly, but I have no intentions of so much a growl directed at you—speak your mind, sweetheart, I will listen without rebuke."

"Ethan—I'm no foolish young girl just starting out in this big world like I was the first time I met you. I'm not blind to some of your ways and means, nor am I naïve of the way this world works. I've remained loyal and quiet all these years for reasons of my own. While at first, I held great concern and even a fear of you—I've seen that you are strong in your resolve with any situation you've faced. I've also seen that your response was not always done in what would be deemed proper... or even... legal..." Addison again paused as if to contemplate the proper way to continue. "I've trusted you, Ethan. I believe you know what is best. I know you've had... um... how shall I say this?" She smiled somewhat sheepishly but at the same time coyly. "Cravings of certain carnal desires in your past. Hungers I didn't understand at the time. But I sat back and remained quiet trusting you did the things required to keep your sanity and your plans on track. I knew you would succeed in anything you put your mind to. If I didn't retain that trust, I wouldn't be sitting here sharing a drink... heh hum... a man's drink, like I am—with you." She took another sip and then decided to throw the remainder down in another gulp. She slapped the empty glass onto the tabletop rather loudly. "But I never ever saw today coming. I sat outside your door for a brief time, wondering what happened to the aggressive, unforgiving, and relentlessly strong attorney I'd feared so many years ago. I felt I was watching a tall building in New York or some other big city—crumbling to the ground in slow motion without so much as an attempt to stand tall. I couldn't do anything but watch, lacking any knowledge of how to reverse its fall. And then that awful bang resounding through the closed door and throughout the office. My imagination having just enough time to picture you slumped over in the corner, a lifeless heap of brokenness and blood..." She sighed as she leaned up from the couch to pick up the bottle and pour another shot into both her and Ethan's glasses. Ethan took notice of her ample breasts practically spilling from the clutches of her blouse. "Do you have any idea what it took to grasp that doorhandle and twist it open, expecting to see the sight I just knew I'd find?"

"I have no idea, Addi. I'm beginning to draw a picture from your words though. I... I... don't know if I know how to respond?"

Ethan spoke in an uncommon, rattled tone. The softness in his voice overshadowed the strong and powerful fullness that was his normal timbre.

"I expected to find you dead, Goddamnit! You made me feel like I'd been wrong all these years... and that... that you were really harboring a coward within your fierce façade! I knew it was not possible, but...."

They quietly stared at one another as they each drew their freshly refilled glasses to their lips in unison and slowly sipped. Ethan then tipped his nose to the mouth of his glass and sniffed the aroma of the bourbon through his nostrils; he closed his eyes taking in the entire experience of the caramel-colored liquid.

Addison remained silent, watching without finishing the words of her previous thought. The moment suddenly stolen from her by the sly move of an experienced attorney. He was somehow a master at deflating an accusation or question directed at him. He'd held years of experience and triumphs doing the same kind of maneuver in court, and against people much stronger and full of resolve than her. Judges for God's sake. Prosecutors.

The wind suddenly sucked from Addison's sails as if she were a sleek-curved yacht racing to the finish and holding the lead—but seconds before crossing that invisible line of victory—hitting a dead calm. Her now emptied stark white sheets rustling and practically motionless, leaving her bobbing hull lifeless in the quavering bay. The once second place racer having snatched her wind while she watched helplessly as he raced past for the winning trophy with her stolen wind.

2

The queen bed seemed large enough at the beginning of the evening. Each woman turned away from the other, their heads nestled into each of their pillows. The neutral zone sandwiched between them, silently designated and comfortable for each. It would have been fine had neither been restless sleepers.

    This wasn't the case for Amy Jo. Her mind full of tensions from all directions when she carefully slid underneath the sheets at bedtime. Jay's letter sitting at home in the box on the mantle, tugging at her and the tension of her continued feelings for Georgie—who now lay within inches of her, pulling at her heartstrings. She could, in fact, feel the heat from Georgie's body as it warmed hers. It was almost too much for her to handle when it was piled onto everything else in her world. She had been through so much, but in this moment, the thing bearing the most within her mind, was the beautiful Hispanic woman who was now lightly snoring just mere inches behind her. It was driving her crazy. She knew it shouldn't, it was against the faith she was raised within, and she questioned if her grandfather and grandmother would hold these near nefarious feelings against her, if they were still alive. But can one really control such desires of the heart?

It didn't matter, Georgie didn't feel the same way about her. Amy Jo closed her eyes tightly together, lightly shaking her head into the pillow to rattle these thoughts from her mind. A deep long breath ending with a sigh, and all was clear. It had worked this time. Hopefully she could now sleep.

"Amy Jo?" Georgie quietly whispered.

Amy Jo quickly rolled over to her opposite side to face her friend's back turned toward her. "Yes, Georgie?" she quietly answered after clearing her throat. "I'm sorry if I woke you. I thought you were already asleep. I heard gentle snores." She giggled.

"Oh no, surely, I wasn't doing that. I'm so sorry!" Georgie answered as she too rolled over to face Amy Jo. When their eyes met, it suddenly became awkward. "Hey, Amy Jo...it's okay." She reached over and patted her arm. "What is the plan for tomorrow anyway?"

"Go to the beach and walk down to the fort... after breakfast of course!"

"Sounds like fun..." Georgie answered. "Hey..." She started and then hesitated.

"What, Georgie?"

"I was just thinking... were you thinking about the letter at home? Is that why you weren't asleep like I was?" Questioned Georgie.

There were a couple of silent seconds that passed between them. Amy Jo looked to the window at Georgie's back, the moon was shining through the clouds, showing in the upper righthand corner of the pane. It back lit her friend, highlighting the silhouette lying inches away from her. "No, not really. Not the letter itself."

"What do you mean, not the letter itself? I don't understand."

"I mean, I'm curious—very curious about the letter, but what is keeping me awake is wondering if he will ever try to show up to see me."

Georgie pushed her friend in the shoulder, almost knocking her to her back. "Oh, Amy Jo! Don't even say that! I hadn't even thought of that happening. Surely, he would not want to risk being caught—would he?"

"That's just it—I don't know. I wouldn't think so, but Jay isn't your average everyday criminal. He doesn't seem to hold the same fears as others. It's what has me awake and thinking."

"He wouldn't want to hurt you, would he?" Georgie asked in a worried tone.

"I don't think so. I just worry, that's all. It will all be okay. I think I can sleep now, can you?"

"I think so, I'm very tired. The truck ride wore me out today." Georgie said. "I imagine you are really frazzled, Amy Jo. If you roll over on your stomach...I could rub your shoulders and back muscles."

Amy Jo smiled. "That sounds wonderful—are you sure?"
"Absolutely."

Amy Jo rolled over, letting the sheet fall to her waistline as Georgie sat up and moved to her knees. Georgie moved closer and straddled Amy Jo's legs. As she began pinching Amy Jo's shoulders, she could hear her short moans of relief escape. She continued to dig deeper into her muscles, heating her back with her warm hands. "Is this helping Amy Jo?" Georgie scooted her body upwards until their hips were mashed together. "I can really dig in now," Georgie said as she wiggled into place.

"Oh, my Lord, yes, Georgie. Don't ever stop!"
Georgie giggled. "Oh, Amy Jo! You are crazy!"

Amy Jo began to roll over, so Georgie moved over off her buttocks. They both looked at each other for a second and then the moment became awkwardly quiet. Georgie leaned in close and began to quietly speak. "I think... I'd like to... to maybe try kissing you once more. I don't know...."

Amy Jo lifted herself up quickly to meet Georgie face to face. She started to lean in, and Georgie met her halfway. Before their lips met, Amy Jo began to whisper, "Are you sure you want this?"

"I'm not sure of anything anymore. I do know my whole body feels flush with heat and very jittery. I think that is some kind of sign, isn't it?"

Almost before Georgie finished her sentence, Amy Jo's lips pressed against Georgie's. After several seconds, Amy Jo pulled back, withdrawing her tongue back into her own mouth as she slowly opened her eyes. The two looked at each other and flustering smiles appeared simultaneously.

Georgie spoke up and asked, "Are you tired?"

Amy Jo answered, "Yes, I hate to admit it but I am."

How about we take this in small steps, is that okay?" Georgie questioned.

"Absolutely, Georgie, absolutely. You feel nice though."

"You do too."

The conversation paused. The room dimmed as the clouds overtook the moon on their race across the sky. Amy Jo cleared her throat and then in almost a whisper she asked, "Georgie—do you believe in love at first sight—or love only building with time being invested and nurtured?"

"Such a deep question, Amy Jo. I'm not sure there is just one answer." Georgie rolled her head to her left—so she could face Amy Jo. "I think if a woman gave birth to a child—the love with that child would be at first sight." She smiled in answer to Amy Jo's growing smile. "But between two people—I think it is infatuation, or puppy love at first. I believe true love, the kind of love that lasts a lifetime—grows and sometimes may not be noticed at first. Does that make sense?"

Amy Jo answered softly. "It makes perfect sense." Amy Jo kissed her finger and then lightly touched Georgie's lips before saying, "I just want you to know one thing."

"What is that, Amy Jo?"

"You are the only woman I've ever kissed or had any of these kind of feelings for."

"Me too, Amy Jo."

"Good night, sweet Georgie." She smiled again and then slowly turned to her sleeping side, her back to Georgie, goosebumps still prickling on her skin.

Sleep came quickly to both women.

3

The old Volvo rolled into Springfield at about 9 p.m. on Sunday. Joyce and Mitzi having taken turns driving, they drove straight through with nothing but potty breaks. Lots of time for conversations about everything in their lives. Ethan being a main topic and what they may find in Springfield, Joyce's new job about to begin, Darrell's new job with Ben and Gina—the list went on. They'd pretty much covered everything.

As the two came up through Arkansas, they hadn't expected the roads to contain all the twists and turns. In Florida, the drive was almost always straight as an arrow and flat. Both Mitzi and Joyce were ready to hit a bed and get some sleep. Dozing in a car seat was not quality sleep.

Tomorrow would bring a visit to the police station and anywhere else they could think of that may lead to possible reasons why Ethan had come back so different and guarded. Once they pulled into the hotel, they quickly took their bags in and settled in for the night. Mitzi sprawled out on the bed and turned on the television to unwind, the Channel 10 news was about to come on. Joyce was in the bathroom brushing her teeth and getting ready to lie down.

"Mom...you should come here...."

THE CALL HOME

"Still no solid leads on the probable double homicide that took place at a downtown warehouse and loft home owned by recently deceased founders and major shareholders of Gaynor Pharmaceuticals, Eldrich James, and Elizabeth Anne Gaynor. The Gaynor's daughter, Sarah, along with a co-worker Jaime Lynn Smith's bodies were both found shy of two months ago at the downtown building. The police have not released too many details as the investigation is still underway. The lead investigator, Detective Ray Gallum has stated 'The department is about ready to release some previously undetailed facts and findings, hoping to facilitate more leads.' More updates soon."

Joyce looked at her daughter with worn and tired eyes. Mitzi suddenly noticed the toll that all this Ethan business had taken on her. She'd aged what appeared years in the last two months. She'd looked so beautiful and young—full of vibrant life when she and Ethan became more than employer and employee.

Mitzi remembered not trusting him early on and even mentally and verbally sparring with him at that damned restaurant in Port St. Joe. The one where they'd first met Cali Lea Jenkins. The woman who had ended up shedding such bad light on Ethan. And now here they were, in Springfield, Missouri—almost 900 miles from home, playing the parts of Cagney and Lacey—investigating the man who was responsible for destroying her mom's dreams of love and happiness.

"Two months ago—that's about the time Ethan was here..." Joyce's tired eyes dimmed even more. "Surely—he... had... had nothing to... do... with any of... this. He isn't the... the murdering girls' type...."

"Momma—we really don't know what type he is at this point. He is smart, though—but very slimy. I smelled the dead fish in his pockets right away," Mitzi fired back.

"Oh, Mitzi. There you go again with your colorful adjectives and metaphors. Just remember, he's suspected of things—not convicted. I know I raised you to understand the difference."

"Mom! What do you need to make you realize how lucky you are to be away from him—you could be one of those girls for God sakes!"

"I'm too tired for this conversation. Let's at least wait until morning before we rush the posse out to hang him." Joyce said with callous as she turned and stepped back into the bathroom. "For the love of God, Mitzi, sometimes...."

"I don't want to fight, momma—and I know you hurt bad. But you can't go on living in denial of what's been laid out before you. You do believe Cali, don't you?"

Joyce again leaned out from the bathroom door. "What I believe is... is that I, for some reason, have been dealt a shit hand again when it was finally looking as if I might be a winner. I'm tired, Mitzi. I'm getting too old to have my heart run through the meat grinder. I've lost my job, my... my... future husband that I'd fallen head over heels in love with, and now I feel like I'm losing what tiny shred of sanity I've been clinging onto these last few months. I'm done! Pull me out of the damned oven and throw me under the sink water to put out the fire!" Joyce rested her head against the door jam and lifted her fingers to her face to ease the tears from her eyes with a shaky finger. "I need a good stiff drink, Mitzi. I'll never unwind and be able to rest unless I have a double-shot of something."

"They have a bar downstairs, Mom. Let's tidy up and head down. I could use one too."

A few minutes later, Mitzi and her mom were in the elevator riding down to the ground floor to the little quiet bar just off the lobby. As they peeked in, they saw about a half dozen other patrons scattered throughout. They headed over to a couple of overstuffed chairs with a table in the middle. It was next to a fireplace with gas flames licking at the cool air above. "This should help relax and knock the chill off at the same time, Mom."

There was a television on the wall near their seats. The Tonight Show was just about to start. Joyce glanced over toward the tv. "Well, at least some things are a constant in my life—thank God for Johnny Carson, he's always a good distraction from everyday crap." She glanced back over to her daughter and smiled. "That, and a good stiff double Manhattan."

"So, is that what you'd like me to bring to you, miss?"

The bartender walked up just behind Joyce's field of vision, and when he spoke, it slightly spooked her to jump. "Oh, my Lord!" Joyce squealed.

"I'm very sorry, miss! I didn't mean to startle you."

"That's okay—I think I may have just peed myself a bit, but I'll survive." She giggled slightly. "And yes, I'll have a good strong double Manhattan—and whatever my daughter would like."

"I'll just have a... oh... what the hell, I'll try a Manhattan also. I don't think I need to start with a double though." She smiled. One of us must lead the other back upstairs!"

"I'll be right back with those, young ladies."

As he walked away, Mitzi and her mom looked into each other's eyes and giggled. "I haven't been called a 'young lady' in quite some time." Joyce continued to chortle.

"You still have it goin' on, Momma. You still have a body that kills! Even Vio has commented about your ass." Mitzi responded back. "That, 'young lady,' is why you don't need to feel like life is over for you. You have that new job next week and still have the young men ogling over you. What more can you ask for?"

"I did tell you that he is based out of Tallahassee, didn't I?"

"Um, no..." Mitzi's mouth dropped. "That's a detail you left out! Are you moving there?"

"Still negotiating that fact. Mr. Bollard said he can fax my work to me until I'm ready to move up to Tallahassee. He said he'd like to either come down to Apalachicola or see me up there at least every other week to touch base face to face."

"Well, at least you have some time with Katie and us. My sweet little angel has become accustomed to seeing you on a regular basis. Me too, Momma. What are we gonna do?"

Joyce's eyes turned back to the Tonight Show as Johnny stood in front of the tall curtain rattling off the night's jokes. It was her way of avoiding the question itself, as well as the thought of it. She wasn't ready to face this upcoming future that was suddenly barreling towards her like a runaway freight train. So much was happening too quickly. Life had gone from the fears of Jay into the arms of her relatively new boss, Ethan. Life temporarily a romantic beach. Beautiful home alongside the ocean, a wealthy and generous attorney with fame and good looks that had flooded her with his attentions. And then one trip out of town, and boom. Her world exploded with cataclysmic damage leaving her all alone to figure things out once again.

She now surmised that either all men were snakes in the grass—or she held the poorest and most misinformed manner of choosing the correct ones. In her life, the only good thing that had come out of her first choice, Roy—was her daughter. Or so she'd thought. Now even that had been questioned and shattered like a crystal chandelier crashing to a marble floor. Roy hadn't been Mitzi's father. But how could this be? She'd never slept with anyone else after high school.

THE CALL HOME

Not after my wild teen days, anyway, which I, of course, failed to admit to Mitzi. No need to fess up to things that didn't matter anyway. None of those boys could be Mitzi's father. Far too long ago.

Without noticing, she began to shake her head back and forth in wonder of her thoughts.

"Mom? Our drinks are here—are you okay?"

"Yes, honey, I was just... um... deep in thought."

Mitzi tilted her head toward her mom's left—attempting to direct her attention to the bartender trying to hand her drink to her.

"Oh..." Joyce snickered. "I'm so sorry. My mind is off and running in the distance. We've had a long car trip from Florida. Straight through. About fifteen hours' worth, and it's now showing!"

"That's okay, miss. Totally understandable! I hope this helps knock that travel edge off."

"Honestly, young man, it will probably knock me on my ass." She giggled.

"Mom? Who are you tonight?" Mitzi blushed as she asked.

"Obviously a worn and frazzled woman in desperation of—this delicious drink and then—a bed to flop down into!"

Mitzi looked up at the bartender, "I'm sorry, she is never, ever like this. She is zoned out from the trip. I apologize." She blushed.

"No need to miss. Again, totally understandable. Just wave in the direction of the bar if you need anything. Anything at all." He turned to Joyce. "Miss, I just have to say, I can hardly believe that you are a mother of the young lady here. This is totally out of line for me to say—but, you are one hot lady, and she is lucky to be carrying on your genes. Enjoy the drinks. First one is on the house tonight."

As he walked away towards the bar, both ladies looked blankly at each other before coyly smiling and then morphing into audible giggles.

"You, miss... are... one... hot... lady. And your daughter is lucky to be wearing your genes...." Mitzi tried not to bust out laughing as she mocked the bartender's smooth moves. "Pardon my French, Momma—but when the fuck did, we drive off the map and where in the hell is this crazy ass town called Springfield? And I thought Apalachicola was batshit nuts!"

All Joyce could do was giggle and smile as she lifted the glass to her lips, sipping the tasty pain-nullifying liquid as it passed across her tongue. "Hmm, this is just what I needed."

Mitzi pulled a long sip from her glass and nodded in agreement. "Wow! This could be my new adult drink from now on, come on Doc—give me a script for this!"

4

Jay rubbed his neck. It was still very stiff from the punishment he'd been sentenced to by the Trusted 7, even though it had been a few months. He knew his situation had, however, turned out better than it could have. He could have hung by his neck until he died.

Of course, if he hadn't been judged by the T7 using the Mason jar judgment, he most certainly would have eventually been strapped into the electric chair, ending his existence much like a pig becomes someone's bacon and eggs breakfast; fried to a crisp.

He also knew his time could still be very limited in this world. There were several other things he felt he needed to take care of—wrongs that still required to be righted. Judgments already heard and sentencing passed by himself, but still awaiting the corporal punishment to be implemented. At that time, after those past indiscretions had been sanctified by his form of reclamation—then and only then would he be ready to release his heart and soul into whatever was true of the afterlife his maker would send him.

Pearly gates paved with gold and winged angels—or red-hot oceans filled with screaming souls begging to be mercifully extinguished of the singeing flames licking at their flesh. He

"Lloyd, go see what you can find. I'll stay here with Jay and talk about our next move."

"You got it, big brother." Lloyd replied.

"Be careful, Lloyd. Jay's right about you and I stickin' out. Don't take no chances."

It wasn't more than five minutes before the front screen door slammed with a pop as it snapped closed. Lyle walked back over and pulled the chair to the table as he sat back down. He looked over at Jay before beginning to start conversing again.

Clearing his throat, Jay squinted his eye a bit. Had Lyle been truly tuned in to the tension that was quietly residing in the room? Could he have sensed what I was thinking needed to be done? He wouldn't have sat back so comfortably into the old wooden kitchen chair so leisurely and unguarded if he had. After all, Jay wasn't a small man himself. He too had been a killer in his life. Several times over. He held no fears or uncomfortableness in ending someone's life. He was in fact, well-practiced at the act. At times, he'd even found solace in killing a person. Watching their eyes slowly dim into a cold gray stare.

He watched Lyle's demeanor sink into comfort, as if Lyle's words or insinuated threats had quelled any thoughts of Jay believing he himself oversaw this threesome of criminals. But what Lyle didn't take into consideration were the years of abuse Jay suffered being pushed down. All power held over him by his mean assed old man. He'd, after all, been dealt pain with the cruelest of punishments his entire life. He'd not taken kindly to Warden Willy's less than subtle threats, so was he going to cower to another wolverine just because he was bigger than he?

Jay continued to keep his eyes calmly pointed in Lyle's direction, showing no threat or concern at all. Let the acting begin! All the while his preparations brewed within.

THE CALL HOME

He thought to himself, how much better off would I be on my own. No loose ends to fuck things up. Yeah, I'd lived under my own charge my entire life. I didn't need nobody then and I sure as hell don't need these two hot-headed Goliaths to fuck things up for me before I got my personal business completed.

It didn't take too long for Jay to decide when the snake should strike. It needn't wait until the beast was asleep. The beast is already mentally at rest, satisfied he'd bettered me. Now he's revelin' in the aftermath of his false sense of security.

Jay began to slowly lean up from his resting position as he nonchalantly retrieved the scalpel he'd found inside the ambulance. It had been sitting on a shelf beside him as he began to gasp air back into his lungs. He'd been able to grab it in all the exhilaration of the escape. Neither brothers' focus on anything he was doing in the back; too busy as they drove the medical vehicle from the scene. He'd nonchalantly stashed the blade in his back pocket unknown for all this time just for such the need at just the proper moment. That moment was closing to its arrival time.

As he pushed his chair slowly backwards, in one smooth unthreatening collection of orchestrated moves, Jay stood up. He showed no apathy as he reached across the table and quickly forced the blade into Lyle's unguarded throat. He twisted the blade, then pulled it across his throat from one side to the other and then removed it. "Just like slicing a fat punk like Chubbs." Jay spoke aloud.

He then wiped the blade clean with his victim's shirt as Lyle sat gasping for air. Jay watched the blank look swirl within his fading eyes. The life slowly and quietly being ushered away, withering into the nothingness with no other than that of hushed gurgles and wisps.

After Jay wiped his knife clean, he unceremoniously tucked it back into his pocket. "Well, Lyle—I really regret the need to do such a thing, although I'll admit, I will take some pleasure in killin' your little smart-mouthed piece a shit brother when he gets back. I do wish you could hang on long enough to witness the performance." Jay smiled as Lyle's eyes stared with a look of horror, his mouth moving to try and speak.

"I wonder if he'll cry like a little frightened bitch?" Jay asked him. "By the way, if you see a round fat prick cryin' for his mommy when you reach hell—you be sure and tell Roy that Jay is comin' soon to kill him again."

Jay got up and opened the back door looking the area over before he walked outside. He noticed an old rusty shovel leaning against the wall several feet away. He walked over and grabbed it. Its handle old and weathered, likely spending most of its life leaned up outside in the weather, patiently waiting to be called out for a purpose. Jay picked it up and studied it, tapping it on the ground to assure the rusted metal shovel part was securely attached to its handle. He wouldn't want it to break free from the decaying wooden grip when being used. That could be most inconvenient. Satisfied with its ability to complete the task he was going to call on it to do, he carried it inside and set it against the wall beside the front door, just to the right. He glanced around to make sure there would be nothing in his path of swing.

Jay sidestepped back to the table and smiled at Lyle, who now lay slumped in his chair with tiny breaths barely noticeable, escaping his pursed lips. "You know Lyle, ole buddy, I do have one thought now when I think of you and your brother..." He took that intentional pause to draw the moment out before cutting the thought loose to be shared. "... you and your brother have shown me that all rubies—are not necessarily gems." He laughed at his pun. "That's a good one, ain't it?" He waited for any movement or response. "Oh well, we'll see what Lloyd thinks about that one when he gets back. I reckon he'll be a little 'disheveled' afterwards though." Jay smiled again. "I'm killin' myself here—how 'bout you? Oh wait, I am killin' you too! And soon your lil' brother."

It was late evening before Jay heard the footsteps coming up the porch stairs toward the front door. Lyle had been long deceased and would miss the second half of the show. He had just enough time to take his spot, shovel in hand, in a good spot where he could freely swing and give the shovel its best bite to Lloyd's face when he unsuspectedly stepped in. The plan played out as perfect in its deliverance as Jay had practiced the maneuver in his head.

The sound the shovel made when it connected with Lloyd's face was an odd crunching thud ending with hollow after-ring, much like a gong. Jay stood over Lloyd seeing the blood pooling around his thick head as it seeped steadily from the deep laceration across his forehead. Jay once again retrieved his blade and repeated the action he'd performed on Lloyd's older brother, Lyle. Lloyd had not cried as he might have suspected, yet he hadn't afforded him much of a chance. He wiped his blade clean again before stowing it away in his pocket. He surmised in this very moment, he was once again, solo, on his own. In charge and must rely on his own wits as he had so much of his past. Jay laid both brothers together on the floor and when he was satisfied with the pose he'd given them—he gathered his bag and left the Ruby's behind lying arm in arm like incestuous lovers in bed. Jay had an agenda that was brewing inside his head. He didn't have an exact timeline laid out, but he knew what he wanted to get accomplished before he was ready to re-relegate himself to either going back to prison life again—or facing his maker.

5

Tony lifted the glass to his mouth throwing its contents quickly down his gullet. "It's not fair, Sam." He said under his breath. "It should have been me. I'm the one whose life was expendable—not yours."

"Looks like you're ready for another round, Sarge." The bartender from Tony's watering hole suggested.

"Carl—" Tony lifted his head to his tall friend as he slid his now empty glass Carl's way. "It won't cure my ailment—but it's a damn good start. You ever have one of those nights? The one's that seem to dangle all your past haunts in your face at once. All raining down around you like a shitstorm of hammers and hand grenades. Just waiting to either explode into pieces or pound your fuckin' head in like a sixteen-penny nail."

"What? Surely you don't think I have the look of someone livin' the dream 24/7, do you?" Carl guffawed as his large hand snagged the empty glass and placed it in the bar sink as his other reached for a fresh one in a practiced display. "Tony, life is a bitch, and then you either marry one or you die lucky before you do. That's what my dad always told me. You just accept that fact and keep pushin' forward. Of course, a little liquid lubrication helps along the way every now and then. Loosens up the inner workings of one's head." He drew the neck of the Jack Daniels bottle to the glass and poured a little extra before sliding it back to Tony's waiting fingers.

"It's difficult to press forward—when I know that crazy fucker who killed my partner is still out there somewhere. Hell, Carl, he's probably 'livin' the dream' all the while Sam's wife and son are struggling to make ends meet. Grappling with the fact he's not ever coming home again." Tony lifted his drink to his lips before once again shooting the entire contents down in one swallow. His teeth tightened as his lips stretched toward his ears. The bite of Mr. Daniels being felt in a heated burn as it traveled downward, warming the center of his gut. "His boy, Clint, will never know his father, Sam. Too young to remember what a good man he was. A broken shell of a widow now, having to play both parts of parenting. It's just not right...."

Carl shook his head. "You need to talk to someone, you know—I'm happy to listen, brother, but you need somebody who knows the right questions to ask—the correct answers to give. This ghost is killing you, my friend. Slowly and methodically, and he doesn't even have to be here to do his damage."

"Don't go there, Carl. You're sounding like Chief Finny now." Tony rebutted.

"You better listen to your chief. The man probably speaks from experience."

"I don't need advice right now, Carl. What I need..." Tony lifted his empty glass to the air in the direction of the bar. "...is another one of these."

Carl stuck his hand out and clutched the glass in Tony's fumbling fingers. The sound of the bell hanging above the front door dinged and drew Carl and Tony's attention to it. A familiar face stepped through the doorway as the top of the doorframe struck the dangling bell again on its way back to the door jam.

"Gonna be a safe night at Charlie's Place this evening..." Carl smiled as he turned to grab a pilsner glass for Hank Robbins, Tony's partner. "Not just one, but two of the departments finest! Hell, I imagine I'm the only one not armed now." He smiled.

"Yeah, Carl, like you don't have a short douba barreled side by shide shotgun quick to grab." Tony slurred.

Hank walked up and tipped his head to the two. He chuckled as he grabbed up his glass of freshly poured beer from the tap. "A cold frosty mug of Hamm's waiting at the bar for me by the time I hit the footrail from the front door..." He shook his head back and forth as he winked at Tony. "Wouldn't my momma be proud as two peacocks fannin' feathers of me now!" The three chuckled as Hank drew his glass to his mouth. "Aw...now that is what makes the day worth the workin'."

Tony looked up from his stool at Hank. "Ever wonder if Billy Jay is enjoying a nice cold beer on a hot evening also? I mean, since Warden Wilkerson and his band of merry men just let him waltz out the front fucking gate in a chauffeured van with lights and sirens."

"Oh no, buddy boy—we are not drivin' down that road tonight. No way, no how." Hank answered as he sucked the suds from the newly growing mustache curled over his lip. "I'm gonna go sit at the other end of the bar if this shit is where the discussion was going when I came in." He glanced over at Carl and scrunched his eyebrows up as if to question Tony's mood.

"Okay, okay, okay already. I'm just thinking about Trisha and Clint today. She called to shack on me..." He slurred again. "Like she should be shecking on me—ha." He knew his speech was off a bit, but he looked up with a look of overwhelming guilt and ignored his screwed-up word pronunciations.

"Tony, we've talked about this. None of this is your fault. You know that..." Hank rebuffed.

"I shoulda' been the man at that door to greet that bullet. Not Sam—a husband and father..." Tony interrupted. He knew he should let it go as he felt the tear trying to force its way out of the tough façade he'd tried to keep up. "She called me today, damn it! She—called—me. That ain't right...."

"She's worried, Tony. Hell—I'm worried. The chief is worried. You gotta sit this one out for a bit. It's too personal. You know that. Your training is telling you that." Hank put his beer down on the bar top and turned to directly face Tony. He put a hand on each of Tony's shoulders and lightly squeezed. "None of us know when it comes. You don't, Sam didn't...but...but we trust each other, and we do what we do. No one person can be Superman and knock all the danger out of the way. This isn't Metropolis and we don't live in the comics. Come on Tony, you know all of this."

"I know that. But what if I were married and died in the way Sam did—and my wife called you because you were with me when it happened and should have been in my spot—well—well, then you'd know what this afternoon is for me when I gotta hear her crying and deal with her solemn voice in that damned phone call..." he somehow said without stumbling his speech this time.

The entire bar went silent. Part of that fact may have been that Tony's voice was louder than the juke box in the back room that sat blaring by the pool table. In fact, several faces peered from around the corner and over seatbacks to see what was happening. It was proof his words were above a normal conversation level. Especially for only 6:30 in the p.m. Usually the "arguing and fighting conversation volume" began after the supper hour, not before. It was obvious the telephone call had set the mood for Tony's lonely evening at Charlie's Tavern. He deserved a break though.

Hank was a new enough partner that he wasn't certain what course of action to proceed with. He didn't want to have to strong arm his partner out the door and home. Especially since he was his subordinate. Nothing like losing face and rank over a misunderstanding in a bar, even if it was afterhours.

Tony glanced over at Carl, "I need a shmoke, brother." He slurred.

Carl quickly stated, "You know I don't smoke. In fact, I've never seen you smoke either Tony."

"I said I want a fuckin' smoke! There's a first time for everything. Seems the appropriate time, don't it?"

Hank quickly stepped around Tony and headed toward the pool table room. Carl barely got a word out to Tony before Hank came back with a cigarette between his fingers, smoke rising from its lit end. "Here you go, Tony, damn thing stinks though. Just because you're a cop doesn't mean you have to play the tv show version of one smoking. You'd look better sporting a lollipop from your mouth like Kojak."

"I used to smoke..." Tony took the slender paper wrapped cylinder and placed the filtered end to his lips and sucked in. The end burned brighter with the orange glow as Tony started talking. "... back when I was married...."

Carl spoke up, "You were married? What kind of woman would put up with you?" He chuckled as Hank smiled.

"Pour me another Jack Black and I'll tell you all about her...." Tony's eyes glistened in the sparkle of the cigarette's glow. He inhaled another deep breath and then exhaled a large plume of smoke from his lungs into a ring that floated out and across the bar top. The burnt ashes grew on the end of the cigarette with each deep draw before Tony finally reached over to the ashtray and tapped it a couple of times causing the gray cylinder of spent tobacco to topple and fall. "I always thought Connie was too good for the likes of me." He looked up at Hank and Carl before lifting the smoke back up to his lips and inhaling a deep puff as if he'd never quit smoking. "Her old man hated me so bad. Didn't like cops. Told her all cops were either dirty and, on the take, or would end up dead leaving her a widow and in debt." He subtly snickered as if the memory came rushing back with clarity. "Yeah, he sure as hell didn't approve of me taking his daughter from him. Even though I had nothing but the best intentions for her."

Hank curiously asked, "How long were you married? You and this crazy Connie."

Tony grinned. "Two years. Short and sweet. I came home and found her in bed with the neighbor. Hell, she didn't even try to make any excuses. I guess thinking she was too good for me should have been a sign that my judge of character was off." He laughed. "And now I'm a detective...and Sam is dead. What the fuck does that tell you?"

Hank was quick to respond, "it says that everything doesn't always go to plan, Tony. It says that despite what you think about your abilities, you've proven over and over to be the best damned detective we've got. Chief Finney knows it—I know it, hell, the whole department knows it." Hank put his arm around his partner's shoulder and pulled him into himself. "Sounds like this Connie gal—was a real piece a work. Good to be shed of her." Hank finished.

Tony turned to face Hank squarely, "yeah, I believe you're right about that—but she had hidden talents..." Tony elbowed Hank in the ribs. "...yes, siree. Talents I could use tonight."

Hank guffawed along with Carl. "Yeah, I think we could all use those kinds of talented gals from time to time. Problem is—those magic moments come and go and for most of us—the only thing left behind is a memory from the good times and the bills from the bad."

Again, they all chuckled as if Hank's spoken observations were truth from the heavens.

6

"Hello, my name is Joyce Bonham, and this is my daughter Mitzi." Joyce hesitated with a pause that soon became uncomfortable.

"Yes, miss...?" The female officer questioned as she sat looking rather impatient as she waited for Joyce to continue.

"I'm sorry, I'm a little nervous and feeling somewhat out of place. We're from Florida—and we just arrived last night here to Springfield. I... um... my... my... fiancé... I mean, ex-fiancé... was here several weeks ago on business... and...."

"Yes, ma'am, I'm going to need you to get to the point, please, it's a busy morning."

"I'm feeling a bit foolish now, but he came home very different than when he left and..." Joyce nervously looked over to Mitzi, now feeling like a fish out of water.

"Ma'am, what my mom is trying to say is that Ethan Kendricks, her ex-fiancé, is acting all kinds of guilty about something. We were wondering if anything happened a couple of months ago that he may be involved in, in some way. We've just found out he is a pretty shady man." Mitzi stated, now feeling awkward and foolish herself. "I know this seems... crazy...."

"Miss, I can't really be of any help with the lack of any pertinent information you are failing to provide. We have crimes committed every day and without any facts about your mother's ex-fiancé—other than being 'shady'—I'm afraid we really wouldn't know where to begin. You understand, of course." The officer stated.

"Thank you for your time, officer. We'll just get out of your way and let you continue with your day..." Joyce answered as she reached out and tugged on her daughter's arm. Joyce looked back hesitantly as they exited the front door of the station. "Oh, my God! That was just embarrassing as hell! That woman thinks we're a couple of unintelligent and crazy women."

"Mom—you must admit, that's just what we looked like. Too much more time with her and they'd lock us up for observation!" Mitzi giggled but her bright red face gave her humiliation away. "This didn't feel this stupid as we talked it out on the way here."

"No, sweety, it most certainly did not. I'm afraid we've come all this way for nothing. Maybe Ethan..." Joyce was cut off instantly by her daughter.

"Don't you even say it, Mom. He is guilty of something. And you know it. Yes, we looked crazy and foolish just now, but we aren't just grabbing at straws that don't exist."

"Oh, honey. Maybe we should just turn around and go back home." Joyce sadly stated as she swung her Volvo's door open.

"Did you know where Ethan stayed when he was here?" Mitzi asked.

"No, but I remember he said it was near the downtown area."

THE CALL HOME

"Maybe we should drive around downtown and see how many hotels are near that area. Knowing him, it would have to be the nicest one. Might not be too hard to find." Mitzi said.

"We can give that a try. But if we don't find something very soon, I'm ready to just give up and go home. One way or the other, it isn't going to give me any answers that will lead me back to him." Joyce sadly answered. She started the car and backed out of the drive and pulled out onto Chestnut Expressway toward the tiny shallow skyline of Springfield's downtown area.

Joyce drove around the square in the center of Springfield and then began circling outward further as they looked for any hotels. It was looking like there really wasn't anything that matched what Ethan had told Joyce. "Probably just another lie he offered me." Joyce said as she gripped the wheel of her car tightly. "I'm such a fool. I don't know why I thought I deserved to find someone as perfect as he appeared to be."

Joyce slapped the wheel with her right hand as they drove down Walnut Street. Suddenly after about thirty or forty minutes of driving around in circles, they noticed an eight or nine story hotel building called University Plaza Hotel and Convention Center. "Bingo!" Joyce said. "This looks like a place Ethan would consider staying in a little town like this." Joyce swung the Volvo into a parking spot and looked over at Mitzi. "I don't know what the hell I'm doing here. I'm not a private investigator. I'm just a paralegal who is frazzled to the core, baby girl..." Joyce looked at her daughter and sighed. "... I was told that to be a paralegal one must be highly intellectual. While I have believed that of myself in the past when working with attorneys and matters of the law, I must admit that at this moment—I feel about as stupid as a pet rock..." Joyce turned and looked at the entrance to the hotel. "I need you to step up, Mitzi. I'm counting on your help with this if I begin to stumble again."

Mitzi leaned over and gave her mother a hug. "We got this, Mom. You and me. Cagney and Lacy." She smiled and they both opened their doors in unison. As they walked into the lobby, they stared up at the balconies that overlooked the atrium. "This is a pretty nice hotel for such a small town. I could see Ethan picking this one."

"Yes, this looks a little like the one he put me up in the first night I met him after we moved. This definitely is his style."

"May I help you ladies today?" asked the hotel worker.

"Well..." Joyce stumbled a bit. "I believe my husband stayed here about a month and a half ago and I was wanting to see if this is in fact where. I forgot the name he told me, but this looks like what he described to me. His name is Ethan Kendricks, my name is Joyce Kendricks, and this is our daughter Mitzi."

"Ma'am, I'm sorry, but I'm not allowed to give out names of guests who have stayed here." He paused. "I'm sure you understand."

Mitzi interrupted as she scooted up close to the desk. "My mom and I are very upset. You see, Daddy never came home after his business trip here to Springfield. We've driven all the way here from Apalachicola, Florida to see if we can locate him..." Mitzi turned up the sniffles and her eyes began to tear up.

"Oh, Mitzi honey, it's okay, sweety. We'll find him...."

The hotel clerk looked at both women more closely. "You seem like very nice ladies, but...."

"We... we... wouldn't say a word. We just want to know if Ethan stayed here on August 21st. He was here to see a client and he's not shown back up since." Joyce said as she comforted her daughter. "We don't want to get anyone in trouble, but anything you could do to help us...."

William began tapping keys on the computers keyboard. "Hmm. Hm huh. Okay. I see that he was here on that night. He checked in at 5:47 pm on the 21st, and... let me see...yes, he checked out at 9:16 am on the 22nd. He didn't stay the second night. His check in was on Skip's shift."

"That certainly helps us out. Could we talk to Skip today? It would help if we could see what his mood was, possibly."

William looked at the computer screen again as he typed on its keys. "It looks like he is due in for his shift in about an hour. We have a nice bar and restaurant if you'd like to wait there. I could send him in for a quick minute when he gets in?"

Joyce reached over and touched the young man's arm. "That would be such a great help, thank you—thank you very much, William. We'll do that, we'll get something to eat. I appreciate all of your help very much."

William smiled. "I'm glad I could do it. I hope you find your husband, and everything is okay."

Joyce and Mitzi walked over to the restaurant seating in the atrium. Plants were hanging down and the splashing of a waterfall quietly rumbled in the background. The open area ambiance was quite beautiful. A waitress came over and took their order. Two Pepsi-colas was all they asked for. "See, Mom, I told you we could manage this." Mitzi said.

"Well, we haven't really found anything out yet except that he did stay here one night, and I already assumed he'd come home early because he showed up Saturday instead of on Sunday when he told me he was planning to arrive. He already said he never met with his client because he overslept and missed the appointment. I thought that was very unusual. Ethan is always punctual, never late and most certainly never oversleeps, which is what he claimed. He said he must have had too many bourbons in the hotel bar."

"Well, there you go, Mom. Something we can work on. Let me have a picture of Ethan and I'll go to the bar and ask around if anyone remembers him."

Joyce opened her purse and pulled out a picture she'd taken of him sitting on his deck at home. "Here you go, Mitzi. Be careful!"

"Oh Mom, nobody is gonna kidnap me in broad daylight for showing a picture of a man to them," she laughed.

Joyce sat watching her daughter walk away towards Beethoven's, the bar entrance. Mitzi glanced back at her mom and smiled just before she walked through the door and disappeared. It wasn't but about ten minutes later that Mitzi exited the door and made her way back to her mom's table. Mitzi wore a look of doubt on her face. She barely got sat down before she began firing commentary to her.

"Mom! Nobody has seen Ethan here. One lady said that maybe someone from the night shift could have seen him. She suggested talking to Skip Connell, the night concierge, I told her we were already waiting for him to show up today." Mitzi sat down and sipped on her Pepsi before continuing. "She said if anyone knows anything, it's Skip."

"Did I hear my name?" The handsome tanned skinned man asked as he stepped up to the table from behind Mitzi. "Are you the ladies that have some questions for me about a past guest?"

Joyce answered, "Yes sir, that would be us. Pull up a chair if you'd like, would you like a drink or something?"

"No, ma'am, I only have a minute or two before I need to clock in. William was telling me about your predicament. I'm not sure I can help much, but I do seem to be the one with the best memory around here." He chuckled. "I guess that's how one gets to be the top manager!" He laughed again.

"Well, I appreciate you talking to us for a minute. I know this is maybe a little off base for you to do, but..."

"Ma'am, if someone is missing, I want to help all I can. I just need to be careful, that's all. I don't want to lose my job."

"We aren't going to publicize anything you tell us. I just want to know what happened to my husband, Ethan."

Mitzi slid the picture over in front of Skip and said, "This is him—" She gave him a minute to look it over before asking, "...does he look familiar?"

Skip scanned the photo for several seconds. Joyce could read it in his eyes that he did in fact recognize Ethan.

"Actually, I do remember him. He... um... he checked in and... uh... wanted to know where he could get a drink and find a good cigar. I told him about a cigar bar not far from here... within... within walking distance downtown. The Alibi Room down on Walnut and South Street." He handed the picture back. "I believe he was going to put his bag in his room and head straight down there. In fact, I'm certain of it. He sounded excited that Springfield would have a cigar bar."

"That sounds like something Ethan would look for. He hates flying and nothing unwinds him faster than a good bourbon and a fine cigar. Thank you, Skip. You've been very helpful."

"No problem, ma'am. If you are headed downtown to check it out, I will mention that you should call. The owner was recently found murdered in her home along with one of the servers and I'm not sure they are opened back up yet. Besides, it can get a little sketchy downtown in the evenings, so be careful."

Joyce glanced over at Mitzi and then back to Skip. "Murdered? What's the story? When did this happen?"

"A little over a month and a half," Skip answered. "In fact, I think it was the night your husband checked in here. Strange coincidence, huh?" Skips eyebrows raised. "You say he disappeared and never came back home?"

Mitzi locked eyes with her mom and gestured with her eyes.

Joyce looked back over to Skip. "Well, actually, I may have stretched that a bit—to get some answers. Ethan did come home. He was just a day early and has been acting different ever since."

"So, you conned me, huh?" Skip asked and then smiled. "If it weren't for the fact, you two ladies are nice looking—I'd probably be upset and kick you out."

"I'm sorry—really. I'm just desperate to find out what happened here with him, and no one has been able to help us out. The police looked at us like we were crazy."

Skip hesitated. "I don't blame you. If I could do more, I would. Like I said, you two seem very nice."

Joyce cleared her throat. "Huh hum, I... uh... I wouldn't mind hearing more about this murder if you know anything. We haven't heard anything about it."

"I really don't know anything other than what's been reported on the news. The latest thing they've released was about a watch they found at the scene. Some fancy wristwatch that was supposedly probably expensive. Other than that, they've been quiet about what they know."

"An expensive watch?" Mitzi asked as she looked at her mom.

"Yeah, a watch with some initials engraved on the backside. A.C. or something like that..." Skip answered. "Does that sound familiar to you?"

Joyce quickly answered, "No," and glanced back at Mitzi.

"Anyway, that's about all I know. The employee was found dead on the sidewalk as if she'd fallen or gotten pushed off the roof. The owner, a daughter of a dead rich guy who owned a pharmaceutical company, was found dead down in one of the old dude's cars in his collection. One of Al Capone's last cars. Strange stuff, huh? It's been on the downlow that they were both totally naked." Skip said softly. "These kinds of things never happen in this little burg. I guess we've made it up to big city standards now—murder wise, anyways!"

"We appreciate you spending time telling us what you know— and not being angry about not being totally honest." Joyce retorted.

Mitzi added, "So they think both girls were murdered and not just the one?"

"They aren't really saying, but like I said, they were both found naked. Some sex crazed maniacs, or something. Maybe gang rape is what I'm thinking. That's why I was saying be careful. They haven't brought anyone in for questioning yet—so I can only imagine he or they are still loose running around here."

"We will be careful, in fact, it may just be time to head back home to Florida!" Joyce replied. "If we stay and think of anything else to ask you—would it be okay to come back?"

"Yes, ma'am, anytime. I hope things work out with your husband, but if they don't..." Skip winked. "... I'm sorry, that was really in bad taste. You be careful."

Joyce and Mitzi paid for their drinks and then headed out the front lobby door, waving at Skip one last time. Mitzi turned to her mom, "See, Mom, you still got it going on. You don't need that sick killer...."

"Oh, Mitzi, you're truly preposterous!" As they opened their doors on the Volvo and climbed in, Joyce continued, "That's

Ethan's watch they have. His has A.C. engraved in the back also. And the fact that was Al Capone's car that one of the naked women was found in—the A.C. on his watch stands for Al Capone. Ethan had a weird admiration for him. He told me that was Al's wristwatch and he'd paid a bundle to own it. I just don't know what to do now." Tears began to seep from her eyes as she reached to slide the key into the ignition. "I'm thinking he may have killed those two women." She broke down and sobbed uncontrollably. "It could have been me, Mitzi! He could have decided to kill me!" Joyce continued to bawl, her mascara running down her cheeks. "What do we do, baby girl? What do we do?"

7

Addi tried to keep her composure as she slightly wobbled. She now felt the effects of the whiskey, and a warmth rushed from her face down to her—g-spot. She suddenly felt flush but urges she'd kept in check for years were now creating conflicting feelings within. She wasn't sure if Ethan had noticed anything different in the way she was acting. He'd never been more needy and attractive to her. She wanted to cure his ailing heart. Normally, she would have feelings of guilt since she knew how Joyce and Ethan had fit together. But Joyce had forsaken him. Joyce left him in a mental mess. My Lord, he'd almost taken his own life. I won't suffer guilt for reaching out and giving in to a man I've spent the better part of my life serving and admiring in his time of need. I'll do whatever he needs—anything.

Ethan held his crystal glass to his lips again and sipped from it. His eyes wore a tired look of despair that was becoming slowly glazed over from his self-prescribed elixir. He appeared weary from life as if it were slowly draining away in front of him. Addi grabbed the arm of the leather couch she'd let herself sink into, and slowly pulled herself up. Her legs felt numb and wobbly, but she stood straight and pushed the creases down and out from her skirt with the palms of her hands.

Ethan eyed her from the edge of his vision. He smiled slightly to himself as he appeared to notice her curvaceous body underneath her clinging wrapping. Addi had always felt she had nice form. Slender legs and firm breasts, maybe a bit of stomach pooch, but not too much. She always wondered if Ethan had ever taken notice. In this moment—she felt self-assured he indeed did. That thought forced the warmth in her south again and she suddenly felt moist with perspiration. It was time for her to make her move and let him know she was interested—and available. She sidestepped over to the chair where Ethan sat and as she bent her legs to lean in towards him—she toppled slightly and caught herself by plopping her right hand onto the chair he sat in, landing it between his legs. She looked over into his eyes and giggled. "I'm so sorry, I guess I'm not used to drinking this much whiskey this early." She smiled as she lifted her hand up, intentionally sliding her wrist against the inside of his inner thigh.

"Oh Addi, darling. Are you certain this is what you want to do?" He asked in his low sultry tone.

There was a moment of silence before Addi rotated her palm where her wrist had just brushed. "Are you sure you are ready for this?" Addi retorted with a low wispy voice.

"I must admit that you have hit a question I am not certain how to answer, miss Addi. My carnal interests are most definitely now very awakened from a state of... um... hibernation. This is a rather serendipitous happening."

Addi's face suddenly showed a bit of hurt within, but she continued to move her hand in ways of not showing retreat.

Ethan appeared to notice her look of rejection and reached for her hand. He grabbed it and held it tightly, but instead of removing it, he pushed it even closer to himself, nestling it tighter as his lips sought hers.

THE CALL HOME

They lightly pressed their mouths into each other's and soon their tongues entangled as their bodies heated to a boil with passion. Their clothes were quickly strewn across the floor of his office in no time, while they were tightly knitted together on the black leather chair.

Moving over to the leather couch, Addi was on her back staring at the giant bull shark which appeared as if it were hovering in the water just over her head. Circling like a true hunter as Ethan moved methodically on top of her. She enjoyed the moment even though it was mixed with the fright of being mauled by an apex predator. The encounter seemed to last forever, slow motion that could not be stopped or undone. She wasn't sure how she would feel when it was all over. Warm and happy, snuggling in—or cold and lifeless, feeling abandoned and left to bleed out. Does anyone ever know how these clandestine occurrences will end up when the climax comes to its end? Will I cling to him tightly in his arms—or slither away in shame with my clothes and shoes under my arms as the door quietly closes to the sound of his snores. I guess we'll see when done is done.

.

8

Georgie awoke to the sun shining through the split in between the curtains. She was toasty warm like nesting in a tightly woven cocoon. She moved her arm and felt another arm over her shoulder. It shocked her for a moment but then it came to her. She'd shared the queen bed with Amy Jo. She remembered the moment they'd almost shared together before going to sleep. Amy Jo kissing her own finger and then pressing that finger against my lips. What is happening? Why do I have goosebumps thinking about this? Is this wrong? These odd feelings I'm experiencing. I love my friend, Amy Jo, but....

      Georgie began trying to think back to the days of her teen years. Had she ever really held feelings for any boys in school? This is ridiculous! I don't need to try and justify anything. Just stop thinking about all of this! She began feeling cramped like she couldn't move, the walls began closing in on her. It was comforting and claustrophobic all at once. If she only knew what was happening between them. Friends or more? She stirred, feeling restless and not knowing how to react.

      She suddenly decided she couldn't stay still any longer. She began to roll over towards Amy Jo to her left. As she rolled, Amy Jo rolled simultaneously. It felt almost like an orchestrated dance move. Georgie's arm followed Amy Jo's body and wrapped over her bicep, her hand resting now on Amy Jo's breast.

Georgie's heart began to nervously pound. She could feel each pulse in her arm that now draped over Amy Jo.

Amy Jo began moving and stretching. She began to sit up and looked over as she slid out from under Georgie's arm. "Good morning." Amy Jo quietly spoke as she pushed her short brown hair back behind her ears and then rubbed her eyes with the fingers of her right hand. "How did you sleep? I hope I didn't crowd you— or God forbid—snore?" She giggled.

"No, no, Amy Jo! I didn't hear you snore! I thought maybe I was crowding you."

"I fell asleep quick and slept like a rock! The drive must have wiped me out more than I thought," she answered. She looked over at Georgie and only saw a silhouette of her outline because of the bright sun shining through the curtains behind her. She reached out and touched Georgie's arm. "I'm sorry if I... uh... freaked you out last night."

"Oh, stop it, Amy Jo. Seriously. I think we should just kiss again and see how we feel now. This worrying and talking about it is driving me crazy." Georgie became nervous as she started to get out of bed. "I'm going to shower quickly so we can go exploring on the beach. You know, see this fort your grandfather liked so much, okay?"

Amy Jo watched Georgie as she tossed the sheet off to the side and quickly walked toward the bathroom in nothing but her scant nightgown. "Sounds great—I'll take you up on your idea when you're done!" She laughed with a bit of hesitation.

"Could you start some coffee, please, Amy Jo? I'm going to need something to jumpstart me this morning."

"Sure will. It'll be ready when you come out."

*****

Amy Jo rolled out of bed with a new sense of urgency. She wasn't sure what was happening or what specifically was rolling around in Georgie's mind. But something felt very different this morning. She could feel a change in the air.

The coffee would need to be brewed extra strong. She heard the shower turn on which meant she had better get busy. She quickly made the bed and then headed out into the small kitchen area and found the coffee and filters. After loading the coffee maker, Amy walked over to the sliding door to the deck that faced the beach. Pulling the curtain back and sliding the glass open, she stepped out, allowing the sunlight to fill the room behind her. The morning breeze mixed with sounds of ocean waves and gulls, giving her a feeling of comfort, she'd long needed. Amy Jo wished she'd already stopped by the grocery store before checking in so she could fill the room with the smell of bacon and eggs like her grandmother used to almost every morning. She walked back inside and to the bathroom door. "Georgie, the coffee is on—I'm going to run to the store for some things for breakfast. Be right back."

"You don't have to do that, Amy Jo!" Georgie hollered.

"I want to! I'll be back soon, take your time." She quickly slid on the clothes she wore the night before and slipped out the front door to the truck. She was like that, once she got a thought in her head, she acted quickly with resolve. She could lounge around and procrastinate also—she was a woman of all traits. Her editor and friend, Malcolm, always teased her about being a human conglomeration of oddities all tied up in an eclectic but loveable package. It was one of her favorite descriptions ever given to

THE CALL HOME

explain her. She also knew it to be true. The thought brought a smile across her lips as she twisted the key to the right, bringing her grandfather's truck to life.

"It's going to be a beautiful day—I just know it," she said aloud to herself as she backed away from the cabin. In a flash she pulled out onto the highway and twisted the old radio volume up to a raucous level her grandfather would appreciate. Huey Lewis, The Power of Love was playing, and it sounded so good to her, she twisted the knob even further to the right, almost rattling the old speakers. "Yep, a great day indeed."

*****

Georgie toweled off and put on her shorts and halter top before heading to the kitchenette. The entire room was filled with the beautiful aroma of fresh brewed coffee. She poured a large cup and stepped out through the open glass and onto the deck, tempted by the beauty of the sun glimmering across the white fluffy tops of the gulf waters cresting waves. Sitting back into the ratan chair, she held the warm cup of coffee to her nose and took in its scent.

Georgie sipped her drink and watched as different couples strolled through the surf, some just side by side and others hand in hand. The sight of people enjoying each other's company stirred her emotions. The thought cascaded into her mind that she had never felt the kind of sentiments the couples below her appeared to be feeling. Closeness, sharing, and certainly goosebumps from the tingles of love and excitement surrounding them. She could only imagine what those sensations would be like.

Her thoughts evolved into the odd and rather uncomfortable but stimulating feelings she'd recently felt when with her friend, Amy Jo. Things seemed to be changing between them. Feelings she now struggled with.

The sound of kids playing with each other rose above everything else. Those sounds mixed with the seagulls conversing as they too seemed to frolic together, tearing Georgie's attention away from where her mind was beginning to lead her. She knew she had things to work out. Not only within, but with Amy Jo too. The awkwardness was getting in the way between them. They couldn't let this wall divide them and spoil all the time spent building their friendship. Would those other feelings be worth the risk? If they denied them, would each have passed up an opportunity to be truly happy? Would God accept them if they chose to follow these new urges and explore what could be? Was it wrong like society was telling them it was? What would my parents think?

This reflection immediately put a damper on any tickles and tingles she was beginning to feel. Like a flood of cold water splashed on a warm body. She was shocked into the reality of the complications any such relationship would create. They would have to sneak around and keep everything hidden. What would this do to each of us? What would it do to our friendship in time? It would most likely destroy it. Us. She had the sudden and urgent epiphany. It felt as if her creator himself sat next to her in the adjacent chair and revealed a truth at her feet.

Georgie sank in the chair she'd moments before enjoyed. Those warm soothing emotions, picturing herself and her best friend being one of those couples below holding hands and smiling—died in one hard moment of reality. The revelation now slapped her across her face. A harsh punishment for even daydreaming it. The dream perished before her coffee turned cold. Amy Jo would return any moment, not knowing the discovery she'd just realized. The thought of even telling Amy Jo suddenly felt cold fraught with a possible devastating outcome to their relationship. Was I being over-dramatic? Or would our friendship fizzle away this weekend by my wishy-washy feelings?

    Only moments earlier she'd felt excitement—now all she felt was the dread of Amy Jo's return from the store. All the refreshing morning scents of the ocean or aromas of a homecooked breakfast would not be able to erase the harshness of what was revealed to her as she sat in the morning sun staring at the horizon before her.

9

Tony's head pounded. He hadn't felt like this for a long time. He opened his eyes to a blurred haziness. "What the..." Each word drew another resounding painful boom within his brain causing him to stop speaking. He laid his head back down on the pillow. He lifted the sheet and peeked underneath. Why am I naked?

Tony attempted to coax his memory back to last night. He remembered Hank showing up. He also remembered Carl razzing him. And Connie... oh shit! Why in hell would I bring her into the conversation?

Tony's thoughts were interrupted by a loud thud in his bathroom. What the hell? He lifted the sheet again to double-check. Yep, stark-ass naked. I hope to God that's not Hank stumbling around in there. The absurd joke inside his head made him guffaw out loud.

"Are you awake out there? I'll be out in a minute...."

Holy crap—Tony's thoughts suddenly drew to Let's Make a Deal. He pictured himself standing uncomfortably next to Monty Hall while being asked, "Tony, will it be door 1, 2, or what's behind curtain 3?" He'd held no real choice. The door began to open slowly. Whichever door Monty would have chosen to name it, it was without a doubt going to be a surprise this morning. He was clueless who stood behind it, and he knew he wouldn't be able to trade its contents off for another door or curtain's contents.

"Here I come, Tony—ready or not...." The door opened all the way and revealed his prize.

"Terri? I mean, Officer Duncan?"

"Really? We're back to being formal. I would have thought after the things we did to each other last night—it might be more relaxed and casual."

"I—uh—I mean." Tony stuttered.

"Oh my God, you don't remember a thing about last night, do you?" Terri's shoulders slumped as she slowed her walk towards the bed with a new hesitation where Tony still lay in apparent shock.

"I'm sorry, Officer... I mean...Terri. I... I don't... I mean...." Tony continued to stutter as he massaged his temples with his left hand at the same time, he steadied his body upright in bed with his right.

"Well, this is about the most awkward morning-after that I've ever felt." Terri attempted to cover her nearly naked body in unpolished shame. "I know I've been trained to react to about every situation, but I'm at a loss of what to do in this moment of now obvious debauchery. And just so we're clear, Sergeant Rawlings—you—came on to me. You. I merely felt like a very lucky woman in the right place at the opportune time..." She hesitated. "I no longer feel that way." She dropped her hands attempting to cover her body parts she'd shared. "It's just a damn shame you don't remember this and what we shared—because I thought it was damn incredible. I was looking forward to much more." She walked closer towards him before bending down at the foot of the bed and collecting her clothes in a pile on top of her shoes. She quickly clutched her things close as she turned back toward the bathroom.

Tony watched Terri's small round butt cheeks wobble back and forth until the bathroom door slammed shut. He spoke aloud without thinking first, "If it's any consolation, Terri, I'd keep what came from door 2. I wouldn't trade even if Mr. Hall gave me that offer."

Terri opened the door abruptly, "What the hell does that mean? Salt rubbed deeper into the wound?"

"I wish I did remember. I know if I had, I wouldn't be watching you getting packed up to leave. I'd be inviting you back under this sheet to see where it led to."

Terri stopped in her tracks and glared back at Tony. "You know that's about the shittiest attempt at a recovery as I've ever witnessed. In fact, if I could, I'd cuff you right now—might even nightstick you a time or two."

"I'm sorry that I partook of too many shots last night. I truly am. I wish I remembered. I don't do this... very often—I mean, drink to my demise—or for that matter—bring a beautiful woman home with me." Hank swallowed hard. "Forgive me, I'm relatively new at this. I messed up and I know I don't deserve a second chance..." Tony cleared his throat, "...but I'm begging the court to overlook my stupidity and consider the fact I was indeed not myself last night. You should be able to see who I really am." He smiled. "I'm certain I'm much better than that bum last night you went home with."

Terri dropped her clothes where she stood and smiled. She then wiggled her way back to the bed. Before crawling back in she said one thing, "Tony—this is your one and only chance for redemption. Don't blow it."

"I have an answer for that—but I'm going to keep my mouth shut for now. He lifted the sheet open enough for Terri to wriggle back in.

Fifteen minutes later, Tony laid back into the pillow, sweaty and out of breath. He never questioned where his headache escaped to or when it left. He was suddenly thrilled that happenstance had worked its way into his life. The anxiety of Billy Jay Cader's effect on him and his partner's untimely exit from this world, now melted into warm tingles from a hot, sweaty body nestled tightly against his.

He gently pulled Terri's head towards his and kissed her moist lips. "I have no idea how I could have let this slip from my memory. I'm ready for another reminder though—you?"

10

Mitzi lay asleep in the passenger seat as Joyce steered the Volvo mile after mile southeast towards home. Her mind was all over the place. She glimpsed over at Mitzi as she lay quietly, her head on the pillow against the door. As a mother, she smiled momentarily when she noticed the tiny bit of drool seeping from her daughter's lips. She felt so fortunate to have her as a daughter. Joyce was happy Mitzi had found Darrell and that she now also had a granddaughter. Her life wasn't a total mess.

Should I wait until I start with Mr. Bollard and tell him about my dilemma with Ethan? She quietly thought to herself, Ethan, you son-of-a-bitch, how could you do this horrible thing? Why?

She of course unwillingly played different scenarios within her mind of what may have transpired the night of the horrible murders.

Two young girls, really? What could have led to their end?

Joyce couldn't help but relive some of the moments with Ethan, good ones that she shared with him. The one when she realized he was in love with her. When he'd compared the risk of laying his cards on the table of his feelings—with that of a poker player risking the odds. Lies? Were they—or did circumstance steal him away from his intention of good? How will I ever know? I can't face him alone ever again.

"Are you doing okay, Mom?"

Joyce glimpsed over at her daughter, "As good as possible, baby girl."

"Want me to drive? I'm wide awake now."

"I'm good for now. It's helping me clear my mind." She smiled a forced grin. "I'm just trying to wrap my head around this entire thing. I can't understand it."

"I can't imagine what is rattling around in your head. I'm sorry, Momma. You don't deserve any of this. First, Roy and now this...."

"I've been thinking about that. You know, the fact that Roy isn't your birth father, which totally baffled me." She looked over with concern. "I was pondering a weird possibility...."

"I'm wondering if it's the same one I've thought inside my head." Mitzi questioned.

"Well, Mitzi B—this may come to you as a shocker...."

"Mom! You hardly ever call me Mitzi B, anymore!"

"You're all grown up and you've gone and made me a grandmother. I figured it was time to let you be you." Joyce replied with a smile. "Anyway, do you remember I told you that Ethan had said something like—I'd been someone in his past, or something like that. It was the last time I was in our—I mean—his home. He was drunk out on his deck and was talking. I guess to himself. I wondered at the time if someone else was there, but I snuck back out undetected. Anyway, the way he worded 'us' now has me wondering if he'd..." Joyce hesitated as if she was rethinking her thoughts. "...or I guess I mean, we'd—known each other from the past. Roy was such a—prick—and he never really acted as if he cared for me or loved me after we married...."

"Mom, I think I know where you may be going with this." Mitzi reached her hand over and touched her mom's leg. "As much as it sickens me, I think I've wondered the exact same thing." She leaned forward a bit and turned so she could see her mom's eyes as she continued steering the Volvo down the highway. "You think that Ethan somehow slept with you way back then without you knowing it, don't you?" She squeezed her mom's leg and leaned even closer as if to whisper a secret. "You think that fucking creep is my dad, don't you?"

There was dead silence in the car except for the road noise and the wind. Her mom didn't even scold her use of foul language. It seemed as if Mitzi's words had swallowed up all the air and sounds within the interior.

"Mitzi—as much as I wish it wasn't possible, or even plausible—I'm having a difficult time coming up with any other scenario. I've never to my knowledge had sex with anyone before you were born except who I assumed was your father. Roy—except back in high school as an irresponsible..."

"I hate to say this, Mom, but—neither choice is one I would want to believe. I mean, at first, I kind of liked Ethan. I didn't trust him for some reason, but I was beginning to like him. He was at least making you happy. But Roy—while I never considered he wasn't my father; I never really was close enough to him to care one way or the other." Mitzi sighed. "I just hope I don't carry any traits of Ethan's if he..." Mitzi hesitated. "...he is, God forbid, my birth father."

"I'm sorry, baby girl. I know neither is a choice you'd pick yourself. And I'm sorry I said irresponsible in high school. You and Darrell are perfect together. Let alone that sweet angel of a little baby..." Joyce paused. "Change of topic—are you thirsty?

There's a little gas station coming up it looks like, and I feel like taking a potty break."

"Sure, but I think we need to continue this conversation and not let it shuffle off into nothingness."

"I agree, and we will." Joyce began to decelerate as the station became closer.

The weather was nice, so they sat out on a picnic table, which was next to the gas station just off to the left of the parking lot. Tall trees hovered overhead, and the limbs lightly blew in the breeze. They each tipped their bottles of Pepsi Cola as they both likely wrestled with the thought of going back to the previous conversation. Mitzi was the first to bring it up.

"So, we were saying...."

"Remember the rumors that Cali was telling us about Ethan and the principal, Charley, and—Roy," Joyce asked?

"You mean as we ironically sat at a picnic table like this one now?" Mitzi put the Pepsi bottle down on the wooden tabletop. "Yes, I remember that disgusting conversation."

"What if Roy, when we were newly married, drugged me and took me out to Ethan's? What if he—it makes me sick to even think of this, but—what if he shared me with Ethan? What if he drugged me like they did those poor schoolgirls like Cali, and performed some of their sick pleasures on me? It's the only viable answer I can come up with."

Mitzi slowly lifted her Pepsi back up to her lips and took a quick sip. "I hate to say it, Momma, but that has been what I've been thinking since Cali told us about Roy, Charley, and Ethan's sick games they played. But how could we get a blood test from him to prove it?"

"I don't know, Mitzi, but maybe my new boss, when I start, could figure it out." Joyce answered.

11

Amy Jo pulled into the parking lot of the cabin where she and Georgie were staying. She opened the door and saw immediately the open drapes and door out to the deck. She put her bag of groceries on the small kitchen table and walked over and peeked outside. "Hey, Georgie! I'm back. I'm going to scramble some eggs and cook some bacon—sound good?"

There was a brief void of sound. Georgie cleared her throat and answered, "Yes, that sounds delicious. Do you want some help?"

Amy Jo sensed an odd tone in Georgie's voice. "Um, no, I think I got it. Won't take too long, go ahead, and enjoy the morning sun." She wondered if it were intuition or her mind putting ridiculous thoughts in her head that didn't fit. But something felt different. The kiss that was offered earlier now felt a like a distant temptation melting like spilled ice cream on a warm summer's sidewalk.

Maybe it's just all in my head. "Leave it on its own to simmer," is what grandmother would tell me when I tried to put the cart before the horse.

THE CALL HOME

Amy Jo knew one thing in her life for certain at this moment. She seemed constantly rattled, and this wasn't like her. She was strong and independent. She was decisive and driven.

Who am I these days? I spent every weekend for months interviewing a convicted murderer and never backed away.

She knew where her weakness was coming from, yet she felt powerless to solve her dilemma. She didn't know where this sudden urge to build a relationship was coming from. She loved living and spending time alone. She always had. Malcolm had even questioned why she was still single and not pursuing a relationship.

Am I forcing this when I'm not truly ready? Was my mind pushing me into something I wasn't truly wanting?

She moved around the small kitchen busying herself with making breakfast. Amy Jo realized she more than likely either appeared to be an amateur at cooking or a cook that was totally preoccupied with anything but what she was doing. The bacon was now burning and filling the room with a smokey burnt aroma.

Georgie suddenly appeared in the small opening between the curtains partially obscuring the open patio door. "Is everything okay in here?" she questioned.

Amy Jo appeared completely frazzled. "No, Georgie—everything is not okay. In fact, it's completely fucked up—pardon my language." Amy Jo removed the smoking pan of bacon from the stovetop and slid the now dry eggs off the other burner. "Excuse me, Georgie, while I get this smoldering dead pig out of the cabin, so we don't get the firetrucks knocking the door down."

Georgie spread the curtains all the way open and slid the door as far to the left as it would go. She then stepped over to the bedroom window and opened it along with those on the opposite side of the room. She walked outside and found Amy Jo sitting in a chair, her head leaned over her legs, propped up with her hands.

"Amy Jo? Are you okay? It's just bacon, there's no need to be upset...."

"It's not the bacon, Georgie. It's my life—it's suddenly a damn disaster...."

"No, no it's not. You're just having a bad morning." Georgie replied.

Amy Jo lifted her head from her hands and looked teary-eyed into her friend's eyes. "No, Georgie, it's far more than that. I don't know what's wrong with me anymore. This isn't me—"

"No, Amy Jo, this person I'm looking at is not you. You never carry this kind of burden or tension."

"I know. Again, I'm just a friggin' train wreck. I don't know if it's the whole Billy Jay thing or...."

Georgie shook her head back and forth as she sat in the adjoining chair. "No, I don't think it's him. I think I know what it is." She stopped with pause and hesitation.

Amy Jo stared intently, "Okay, Doc, give me your diagnosis, please."

"It's me." She stopped. "It's you—it's this thing that has landed between us and is twisting our insides until they want to pop. I feel it too. It's crazy and it can't go on. It's going to make us sick or even kill us. At the very least destroy our friendship."

The awkward silence hung in the air between them.

Georgie finally broke the quiet stillness that had lasted at least a minute. A very long minute. "I love you, Amy Jo. I think I have since the first day we met. But I can't love you in the way you think you want. Our two worlds won't allow it. My parents, your friends, and co-workers—this world." She paused. "We can't go on like this and I... I... can't sneak around living a lie." Georgie sat down beside her friend. "Can we just go back to being good friends and forget this part? It was just a kiss. It's not that much of a thing to bury in our past, is it? It's not like we did anything that can never be undone."

"But I have these—these things pulling at my insides, Georgie. I'm an investigative reporter for my career. How do I just shut off that internal drive to research those feelings to see what they mean?"

"Because as your friend—and you are my best friend, in fact, my only true friend, and I'm asking you to stop. Please, before it destroys my only friend in the world." She sniffed, her nose beginning to run as she fought back tears. "I think that desire you have right now is the craving of a relationship. I think maybe you need that, but you are denying it. I can't be that relationship with you. Not in that way. I love you Amy Jo, but I don't have that part inside me. I tried to make it be there, I toyed with the idea, but...."

"I know that, Georgie. That's why I feel so bad. I think I knew it after that first night, but I'm selfish and I kept pushing. I'm a selfish bitch and I don't deserve a friend as good as you."

"Oh, Amy Jo. You do deserve a friend just like me. One who knows what's best even when you don't want to accept it. A friend who is willing to tell you, even though it's not what you want to hear." She stopped for a moment and sighed. "What was that one boy's name back in school that you said could maybe be the only boy you could ever love?"

Amy Jo looked up in question. "Cable?" she paused. "Cable Lee Johnson?" A smile came on from the familiar thought of him that she hadn't let wander across her brain for a long time. "I don't even know where he is now."

"You're smart. You just reminded me you are an investigative reporter. Who knows? Maybe he lives not too far away. Maybe he has never met the one who could replace you?"

Georgie smiled, which drew a small movement in Amy Jo's lip to stretch out into a small smile.

"I'm not gonna lie, Georgie—he was pretty hot to look at. But...."

"But nothing. You won't know unless you look. I think you need to do this for a distraction at least. I'm your friend, Amy Jo. I'm not going anywhere. I would love to see you happy—happy with someone who can love you like you should be loved."

Amy Jo sat up and leaned over toward Georgie into her open arms. As they hugged each other, Amy Jo leaned into Georgie's ear, "I love you, Georgie. And you will always be my best friend. I promise. Thank you."

Amy Jo sat back and caught her breath. It felt as if the freight train that had been bearing down on her for weeks had suddenly switched rails and went speeding past her side. She could almost feel the rushed wind as the cars flew past—but a feeling of rescue came with the blinding streak of the passing train. Relief of sorts. Out of danger. She could catch her breath without her heart racing out of control. She looked over at Georgie again. She noticed she was still a beautiful girl. Her eyes would always hold that dark brown beautiful color that mixed into her coal black pupils. She was gorgeous. But in this moment of hopeless failing and pressure, came an unexpected feeling of solace. It had come in the form of reassurance she would be okay. And it came from a friend brave enough to face her and tell her in a straightforward but kind way. She looked over and smiled. "I'm hungry, but I can't eat that mess I killed! Wanna go get some real breakfast before we go explore my grandfather's fort?"

Georgie smiled, "I thought you'd never ask!"

12

"It's not over—Chief! He's gonna come back. I feel it in my bones. The sick bastard is alive and out there. I'll lay dollars to donuts that Apalachicola hasn't seen the last of Billy Jay-fuckin'-Cader. He'll answer to the call home—the crazy ones always do. They return to the scene of the crime to see the damage they've done and relive the hideous glory of it, all while laughing in our blind faces. Well—Chief—I'm not fucking blind! Don't let him pull the wool over your eyes."

"Tony—let's hope you got this call wrong, maybe he instead made a wrong turn into the bogs—and became a big ole' gator's meal."

"Who killed the Ruby brothers then? They didn't kill themselves, Chief. And to leave 'em looking like lover's—"

"No, Tony—they did not kill themselves. Who knows how many enemies those two had on the outside? It doesn't mean Billy Jay did it. Nor that he is going back to the scene of his crimes. That's the movies, buddy, you know that. Besides, Tony, Warden Wilkerson said the Ruby brothers hung Billy Jay to aid in their escape! He was more than likely already dead on the gurney in the back of the ambulance they stole. They probably rolled him off in a ditch and left him for the buzzards and swamp creatures to finish him off."

Tony Rawlings, one of Florida State Police's best detectives rubbed his temples, gripping his forehead between his middle finger and thumb, massaging, and squeezing tightly.

"I hear you really tied one on last night. Care to talk about it?" Finney inquired.

There was a brief pause as Tony slowly lifted his eyes upward until he met his chief's. He shook his head slowly. "My loyal partner, Hank, throwin' me under the bus again, huh?"

"I wouldn't sum it up exactly like that. Hank is worried about you. We all are."

"Do you know what it feels like, Finney?"

"What? The pounding headache, the sour burn in your stomach aching to evacuate its contents. It's the price you pay for trying to kill your pain with a bottle. You know that too, Tony."

"It was supposed to be me, Finney—not Sam."

"Bullshit, and you know it! Why should it have been you who died any more than Sam? Tell me how you know that Tony...."

"I know because—Sam... Sam... left a beautiful wife... a.... a young son who's now fatherless... so... so a guy like me... with nobody... nothing... could go home every night to an empty house, refrigerator filled with nothing but beer, and a new partner who throws me under the damned bus to my damn boss. That's what I know, Chief."

"Take some time, Tony. You are officially on leave until I call you back. It's PTO, use it. You need a break—maybe have yourself checked out, talk to a...."

"Really? A fuckin' shrink? Come on, Chief, you can't take this case from me...."

"Case? Are you not hearing what's happening? There is no case. We got nothing. It's over. The DA says let it go."

Tony's face immediately became beet red. "But it's not over—don't let the department give up. It's not over! Mark my words, Chief. Mark my fucking words. It's not over...."

13

"I can't believe we're finally almost home, Mom." Mitzi couldn't sleep so she'd stayed up the last few hours, too hyped to wind down. "You sure you don't want me to drive again? I can't sleep—I'm way too excited to see Darrell and Katie! I bet she's grown three inches since we've been gone."

"I'm okay Mitzi. I'm wired too—only mine is anxious nerves about what to do. I'm almost sorry we went to Springfield. I just don't have the calmness in my body to be an investigator—not when I find out information that I really didn't want to know." Joyce glanced over at her daughter for some assurance.

"Mom, we did the right thing by going. You needed affirmation Ethan was indeed the snake we were told he is."

"I know, honey. I just don't know what to do now. Do you think he really had anything to do with those two girls' deaths?"

Mitzi looked at her mom's profile as she continued to watch the road ahead. "Yes—yes, I do. I think the sick bastard killed both of them. I have no idea why—but I think he did it. Why else would his watch end up at the scene?"

"What do we do now? We should have gone back to the station at Springfield and told the police." Joyce said quietly.

THE CALL HOME

"Mom! They practically ran us out of the station when we went to talk to them before we found out. We get a lawyer. Hell, talk to the one you're going to work for on Monday!"

"Oh my God, Mitzi—what a great first day on the job." Joyce began to play act the conversation like a scene out of a movie. "Well, hello, Mr. Bollard. I'm so glad to start my new job with you today. By the way, I believe my old boyfriend and almost new frickin' husband—you know him as Ethan Kendricks—most likely killed a couple of young girls over in Springfield, Missouri and we heard about some damning evidence of his that they are holding yet have no clue of who's it is. Well—guess what? It's Ethan's watch they found there. Of course, they don't know it yet because we failed to divulge this key information on account that they practically laughed us out of their station—" Joyce's voice fell away to a hollow hush. She twisted her head back to the passenger side of the car towards her daughter and spoke in an old man's voice as deep and gravelly as she could muster. "Well, well, Ms. Bonham—I uh... I mean... I... um ...won't be needing you as my new assistant... I ... uh... ended up filling that position with someone else. Someone—shall we say—a little less batshit crazy than the overwhelmingly scary-ass insanity you seem to possess..." Joyce smiled with sarcasm and then continued in an over dramatic voice, "... so, you do see why I have some hesitation with your plan don't you, Mitzi B?"

"I didn't know you were such a drama queen, Mom. The man is an attorney. We need an attorney. Would you rather just clam up, say nothing, and let Ethan get away with a double homicide after practically dragging you into his web of evil deceit? Maybe when we see him at Poppy's or at the grocery store...or the Coffee Caper, we can smile really big and say, 'Hi there Ethan—have you killed any other young women lately, or do you just do your sicko killing of young women in Springfield—you know, where you got away with it?'" Mitzi sported a wild-eyed look across her pretty face. "See what I mean, Mom?" she guffawed. "Talk to Mr. Bollard. At least ask him for a reference, I'm sure he'll then ask you why you need an attorney. You can slide into this touchy subject in a non-threatening way—like sliding a warm knife into butter."

"Um, Mitzi—" Joyce hesitated and then uncomfortably paused.

"Yes?" Mitzi asked as she rolled her eyes like she did back in school when her mom would ask her if she'd done her homework.

"I haven't actually told you, I imagined you'd figure it out and confront me, but...."

"Okay, Mom—what are you going to hit me with now?"

"You do know Mr. Bollard's practice is in Tallahassee—right?"

"Yeah, I know, I was wondering if your old Volvo was going to be able to make that drive every day, but it's done great on this trip."

"Um, Mitzi—it's a little over an hour and a half each way..." Joyce cleared her throat and reached for her cup of water held between her legs. "...you didn't really think I'd be driving back and forth every day—did you?"

Mitzi immediately jerked her head away from her mom's and to the side window where the scenery streamed by very quickly. She turned back as her now nervous looking hand began slapping her leg to no certain beat. "I'm losing you, aren't I? What about Katie? You can't leave your granddaughter!"

"Mitzi—" Joyce took another drink of water. "It's an hour and a half away. While that's a lot of time to spend every day back and forth—it's not too far for either you and your family to come visit—or me to come down to see you and your beautiful family."

"But—" Mitzi didn't have a rebuttal. Her voice went silent, only the hum of the Volvo's motor filled the interior. The mechanical tone of the engine mixed with the rush of wind blowing through the open windows and the tire noise against the road harmonizing and filling the void. The silence now suddenly seemed very loud and overwhelming. "How will you afford a new place? I mean, I could see if Darrell could get an advance...."

"Honey, sweetheart, I didn't bring this up to ask you for financial help. I've talked to James... I mean... Mr. Bollard—we've got it all taken care of for now."

Mitzi leaned forward and eyed her mother as she drove, "This isn't another kind of deal like with Ethan—right?"

"Mitzi B, my God! James is a very happily married man! He's as old as Ethan. And NO! I told him I wasn't sure how I could take the job since I'd used about all my savings moving down to Apalachicola. He's offered to help me with the rent at first. He needs help badly and he's heard good things about me. That's all it is. I'm done with men in that way anyway. They're nothing but lying trouble and pain for me—except for you, of course, you are such a worthwhile gift. I'm still never sorry about that. You are the best thing I ever did!"

"Yeah, too bad we don't really know for certain who gave me to you." Mitzi half smiled. "I didn't say that to be mean, Mom."

"I know, baby girl, I know."

14

Darrell and Katie were out on the porch with his mom, Cat, as Joyce and Mitzi pulled up into the drive. As they rushed up to see them, Kyle and Vio came out through their apartment door also.

"Looks like all your important people are here to greet you, Mitzi!" her mom said.

Kyle's friend, Jake then walked out holding a tray full of drinks in his hands.

Vio hugged Mitzi after Darrell let her go but before she could grab Katie from her grandma. "It's so good to have you back safe, girlfriend!"

"I know, it's great to be home!" She hugged Vio. "It's really good to see you, Vio. How you feeling?"

Vio smiled. "Good—actually—great!" She backed away so Mitzi could grab Katie. "I'm remembering things better...."

As Mitzi held her daughter up close and began kissing her cheeks, she turned back to her best friend, "I'm so, so happy to hear that. I love you, Vio." She reached back over and pulled Vio into her arm and gave her a squeeze. "You've had me worried, girl—and boy do I have some stories to tell you! Later though."

Vio nodded, "Sounds interesting, I can hardly wait!"

THE CALL HOME

While Mitzi held Vio close, she asked in a whisper, "How's Kyle doing?"

Vio leaned in, "He's doing better now that he has his new friend, Jake. Jake's been good for him. Kyle seems like he's craving to get better instead of beating himself up. And—" She snickered and leaned in closer, "Darrell's mom, Cat, and Jake seem like they are—hitting it off. They've both been over about every evening since you and your mom left."

Mitzi smiled as they pulled away. She put her nose on Katie's face and began baby-talking to her.

"Maaa...ma"

"Oh, my Lord! Did you hear that? She said momma!" Mitzi cuddled Katie even tighter as a couple of tears squeezed from her eyes. "My little girl said momma!"

Darrell put his hand on Mitzi's shoulder, "I don't wanna burst your bubble, sweetie, but she's been saying it since about the second day you were gone. I think she's missed you a lot!"

Everyone laughed and smiled, and Jake passed out lemonades to everyone as they all sat and welcomed Joyce and Mitzi home.

15

Ethan sat up from his leather sofa. He was in his office, and he was having trouble getting acclimated. *Had I drank that much?* He asked himself. Spying the coffee table in front of him, there were two glasses and an empty bottle of Weller's 107 along with another bottle of Maker's Mark— which was damn near empty.

"Lord, what have I occasioned upon now?" He began to attempt to stand up but settled back in after becoming aware of just what and whom he'd done. "Oh, shit." He looked down at his crotch. "My God, you little demon, you've really screwed the pooch this time." He spoke aloud. But internally, he held a horrible thought, I certainly hope this did not have any kind of an ending like in Springfield....

There was a shuffling of feet and the sound of a file drawer shutting on the other side of his office door. Addi. How am I going to face you this morning now? I've not only seen your beautiful pale white naked body, but... he straightened himself up in the couch as he heard and then watched the doorknob begin to twist... We shared such heated—well—we shared—he breathed a deep breath and smelled exactly what they'd shared. Sex together. The thought began to make his trousers tighten. The doorknob continued to twist, and he returned his attention to the widening space opening up to the outer office. She walked through the entry carrying a tray with a cup of what he assumed would be coffee. Her heels clicked across the hardwood floor drawing his eyes to look at her shoes before then following up her tightened calf muscles which flexed tightly with each step bringing her closer.

"Well, good morning, Ethan. I was wondering if I'd be waking you up. You do remember you have a ten o'clock meeting with Mr. Sumner, don't you?"

"Why yes, yes, Addi I most certainly do—now that you mention it." He coughed slightly. "I'm going to need you to call him and ask if he can meet me at Poppy's around eleven. We can have our meeting there if that's okay. I've got to get—cleaned up before I see him."

Addi walked over to him holding the tray with his cup of coffee.

Ethan wasn't sure if Addi would acknowledge their tryst last night or what almost happened before that tryst. He couldn't believe he'd actually contemplated the idea, let alone pulling the cold steel revolver from his drawer and actually resting its barrel under his chin. I'm not a coward, damn it! Words that screamed internally from his unmoving lips. It just wasn't the correct time. I have more to accomplish in life. And of course, there was what had happened afterwards—he smiled as he admired Addi's snow-white cleavage, reliving his growing memory of squeezing them firmly with his hands as she sat bouncing on top of him, riding him as if she were breaking a wild stallion. His trousers tightened again.

"Yes, Ethan, I don't believe you want to meet Carl with the smell of my sex on you. It may make for some—uncomfortable conversation, I would imagine. Although I do like the idea of you wearing my scent throughout the day." She winked and smiled as he took the cup from her hands.

Well, shit. There's my answer. I must have performed rather well. She's certainly not gonna let this disappear into the well of the forgotten.

She turned and began walking back toward the door. Her hips pushing tightly against the fabric of her skirt with each step. The image did not go unnoticed. Lord, I'm a very confused individual. Part of me wants to forget last night ever happened—yet another part of me wants to slip right back into the fold, so to speak. "Yes, Addi, that could make for an awkward meeting with that particular fragrance wafting overhead and between us. He smiled and Addi turned to catch him in a moment of smiling.

"I'll be in my shower, Miss Addi, so please hold any calls for the moment."

"Yes sir, Mr. Kendricks. You can erase my scent, but not the memory, I trust." The door quietly closed.

"These damned male parts are nothing but a damned curse." Ethan spoke aloud as he wrestled getting out of the couch without causing discomfort to his growing erection. "Mine seems to be as well trained as a drunken monkey in heat." He looked down at his trousers and guffawed as he strained to rise.

Ten minutes later the hot water was pouring over his head and shoulders as he soaped himself up.

*****

Addi walked to the front door and taped a note on the glass. She then snapped the key on the latch to the locked position. She glided back into Ethan's office and began peeling out of her clothes the minute she crossed the threshold and heard the shower. She quietly opened his bathroom door and tiptoed into the steamy room. Carefully opening the shower door, she slipped in behind him. She reached around while Ethan was lathering his face and began to give him a hand, concentrating on his lower anatomy.

"Oh, Lord!" Ethan said as he jumped and turned to see Addi's naked body standing behind him, her hand quickly gripping something she'd become familiar with last night.

"I hope I'm not disturbing you, Ethan, but I just couldn't resist locking the front door and making sure you were okay."

"I... um... well..."

"Cat got your tongue?"

"Well, yes ma'am it absolutely does—seems the kitty also has a growing surprise in one of her paws." He thought to himself as he began to rise to the occasion, yes—like a drunken monkey in heat...."

His quick shower turned into a half hour replay of last night, only with the added odd feeling of squeaky friction from the water. It also put Ethan on a tighter schedule.

*****

"Yes sir, I certainly did, Carl. And again, in the shower before I came—I mean, arrived here to meet you." Ethan began wickedly laughing at his little faux pas.

"Ethan—you are certainly a cocky dog of a different breed. But you do know how to tell a story that—wakes a man up. So, how is this new revelation going to work out for you now, though? It must—cause cogitation—when the hired help feels they can just walk into your private bathroom and shower without knocking. That may be a very difficult task to re-draw any lines of acceptable boundary crossing." Carl smirked.

"Indeed, it is. That is a bridge I will soon have to cross. But in the meantime, Carl..." Ethan smiled devilishly. "...this kitty has very neatly trimmed soft fur—and is definitely feisty with a tendency to play rough. It's as if the catnip has been genetically dabbled with."

"Someday you will pay, Ethan. That's all I'm going to say at this point. While I would love to spend a day in your shoes, I'm afraid they'd somehow end up buried deeply up my ass if I tried them on for even a minute."

16

Kyle and Jake were sitting out beside the smoker.

"That alligator tail is smelling wonderful. I'll be needing that recipe for the rub you put on it."

Kyle smiled. "I've just been playing around with different spices, and sea salt. I smoke this baby slow with mesquite after soaking it overnight in a mixture of liquid smoke, Worcestershire sauce and brown sugar."

"Sure was tasty the last time you had me over." Jake lifted his lemonade to his lips and sipped. "Vio makes great lemonade too." He smiled. "You two make a great couple, Kyle."

"Yeah, I just wish I could get out of this chair. I don't know how long I can expect her to stick around with me like this."

"Looks to me like she's planning on the full entire plan. She certainly looks happy."

Kyle's mood changed and he turned and stared at Jake. "I know I'm holding her back from the life she should be able to have—you know, with someone who can take care of her, can... uh... you know... satisfy those...."

"Kyle, as I see it, and this is me looking in from the outside—"

"I know what you're going to say, Jake."

"As I was about to say, looking in from the outside, I see a young lady who is crazy in love with a guy who seems to refuse to acknowledge it. Are you trying to chase her away and are you sure that you really want that?"

Kyle sat stiffly back into his chair, looking as if he was insulted at the insinuation. "Chase her away? Are you kidding me? Why in hell would I do that?"

Jake stared intently into Kyle's eyes. "Exactly—why in hell would you do that? Makes no sense."

"It's all my fault. I was so stupid that night. I wasn't thinking about anything but how much I loved her and how good she made me feel. That fuckin' car—" Kyle paused. "My mom told me when I was begging her to let me buy it—that it was a big mistake. Too much responsibility for a young kid my age." He looked away. "I hate it that she was right, and I didn't listen. I begged her like a spoiled child wanting a popsicle until she finally caved." Kyle wiped a tear and then turned back and looked intently at Jake. "...Why in the hell are you bringing all this shit up?"

Jake sat still, his elbows resting on his knees while one hand rubbed the other wrinkled hand as if it helped aid his seemingly unrelenting arthritis pain. Or maybe it just stirred his thoughts deep enough to allow them to gel together better. "Kyle—I wanna help you, son. I have a feeling you don't really have any kind of hold on your direction anymore for your life. You look lost, son. I want to help a lost soul navigate its way back before the forest closes in too tightly and the darkness overwhelms you. It can happen quick. That other world you're letting inside can keep you from finding your way back—it can happen so damn fast, let me tell you. I know."

"I think I like it better when we talk about pirate Tanner and the Indians, tales like that." Kyle rebutted.

THE CALL HOME

A smile washed across Jake's face. "I like those conversations too, but—a time and a place. When's the last time you did anything special for Vio? Totally off the top. A surprise—a serendipitous surprise."

Kyle scrunched his eyes together in thought. "Oh, man. I can't even remember. She's been so busy taking care of me and worrying about the bills and...."

"Exactly! You need to catch her off guard and remind her of the guy she fell in love with. The one before the accident. The one that is still inside you—lost—but still very much alive."

"But I'm not that guy anymore...."

"Bullshit, son!" Jake shook his head in disbelief. "You're taking the easy way out and trying to erase that guy—but he's still inside. He's trapped in the corner and hurt; he's withdrawn back in the shadows where he thinks no one can reach him. But he's in there. It's time to let him back out and experience life and love, Kyle. Start fresh. Show the girl your love for her hasn't left and that you're still strong and resilient. If you ever take another step again or not—you are destroying that young man that everyone around you still loves and remembers. Make it easier for them to remember—kick this poser's ass into that dark corner and reintroduce yourself!" Jake leaned forward and put his hands on Kyle's legs. "These things right here..." he squeezed both legs tighter until he saw Kyle felt his touch. "...these are not the only part of Kyle. They're not even the important part." He moved his hand up to Kyle's chest and thumped it, then to his head, grabbing the long strands of his hair into his fingers. "These are the important parts of that guy Vio still loves madly. Heart and soul—the wit and compassion still inside that you've buried and forgotten."

Kyle moved and wiggled in his chair as his gaze lifted to meet Jake's. There was a silence while Kyle appeared to take it in and sort through it. Those long strands of blonde hair glimmered in the sun's rays behind him.

The mesquite smoke swirled out from the smoker's stack while the breeze blew the sweet, tangy charcoal fragrance-filled clouds of slow-cooked gator meat around them.

Kyle's face began to grow a bright and genuine smile which began in the middle and quickly bloomed outwards toward each ear. "Thank you, Jake. I needed this." He reached over and patted Jake's hand. "I've been a stupid self-consumed punk who has been thinking only about me—myself—and I. I've almost let myself forget the girl inside who stole my heart and wrapped it up with hers. Thank you for waking me up before it's too late."

Jake reached inside his shirt pocket and pulled out a small roll of bills. He brought his hand down to Kyle's which still rested on his other hand. Jake poked the roll that was tightly wrapped with a rubber band around it, into Kyle's almost closed fist. "Here, son, I want you to surprise that girl to an evening out and dinner. Call and make reservations at that new restaurant—Apple on the Bay. Show her she still means everything to you, son."

"But I can't...."

"You, by-God can—and you will, son. I insist and I ain't takin' no for an answer."

Kyle looked up and into Jake's eyes, "I'm glad you stopped that day I foolishly wrecked my chair."

"Me too, son. Me too."

17

Vio pulled the door to Apple on the Bay open and stepped to the side so Kyle could wheel himself in. She wore her best outfit, making her appear like a Miami model. Her smile was what made her fashion work though. She wore it ear to ear as if she'd never let it out of the bag or been out on a date in her life. The fact was—she hadn't, not really, but tonight was making up for everything.

    She looked around the room as Kyle took care of letting the hostess know they were here. The interior looked so beautiful. It was nothing like the Coffee Caper, which she'd always loved. She'd never been inside a classy restaurant like this. There really was nowhere else like The Apple on the Bay around in Apalachicola. Part of her wished she could share the evening with Darrell and Mitzi—but a bigger part was thankful it was only Kyle and her. With the good mood he'd been in ever since he and Jake smoked the gator tail on the grill, she was hoping he might be willing to see what else they could do later. She grinned as little goosebumps and tingles shot through her body just imagining it.

    "They're getting our table ready, babe. It'll be just a second."

"Thank you for bringing me here, Kyle. It's lovely! I can hardly wait to see what's on the menu."

"I'm just sorry it's taken me so long to realize the life I was robbing you from by—you know—being so...."

Vio cut in, "Shoosh, it doesn't matter sweety. We're together and we will face whatever this crazy world throws at us. We'll always come out on top because we love each other." She leaned down and gave Kyle a deep kiss, pulling back slowly retrieving her tongue from his lips.

"This way please, we have your table ready. We've been able to put you out in our more private seating in our special bay window overlooking Apalachicola's most beautiful view of the Gulf."

"Oh my! It's gorgeous!" Vio exclaimed as she turned to face Kyle. "Thank you again, sweetheart, this is perfect, and it's not even my birthday or anything."

"We'll just have to make this a special night even though it isn't." Kyle winked at her.

"Your server will be right with you; can I get you anything to drink in the meantime?" asked the host.

*****

Earlier in the week

Kyle talked to Darrell about setting up the evening. Darrell was able to finagle the best table in the house for his best friend.

"Sure, pays to know all the right people!" Kyle joked.

"Kyle—for you buddy, I'd try to dim the moon if you asked. You say the word and I'm on it! I'm just glad you've dug outta' the hole you've been trapped in." He turned and faced his friend, "Seriously Kyle, I'm happy for you. You've had us all worried. Things will get better and better, you'll see."

"I'm still nervous." He looked down for a second. "These aren't the kind of wheels I wanted to drive the rest of my life...."

"Kyle! Vio doesn't care about that. It's you she cares about. Everybody sees it, my God, it's practically stamped across her forehead!"

"Thanks, brother. Between you and Jake, I don't stand a chance going back to feeling sorry for myself." He snickered. "Hey, I gotta another question—actually more like advice I need...."

"Fire away."

"After dinner—you know, I thought I'd see if she wanted to go for a walk down by the pier. Well, I'll go for a roll of course, she'll go for the walk...."

"Kyle—I know it's your brand of new humor, but I'd shitcan that act if I were you. No one who cares about you sees the wheels. Anyway, a walk by the pier—good idea. I remember a certain walk by the pier with Mitzi...." Darrell smiled at the memory. "Okay, back to your question."

"Sex...."

Darrell looked at his friend and raised his eyebrows. "Um, I don't think so, buddy. I mean—you have that whole surfer look going..." he acted as if he were looking him over thoroughly, "...but hell no!" He laughed loudly. "You're gonna have to talk to Vio about filling that need!"

Kyle wheeled a foot or two closer to where he could reach out and punch Darrell. "You asshole! That's who I'm talking about—I just don't know how to...."

"You guys haven't..." Darrell moved his fist back and forth a couple of times.

"No—not since the accident. We hit the spot at the beach... in the... driftwood pile... where you... you and Mitzi—you know. Anyway, that's why I was so juiced coming home that night. We were brand-new in love, dude. I mean—it was all in the air surrounding us. The tunes were cranked loud—I just felt so—so like, wow!"

"I know the feeling, brother. You need to recreate that feeling. I bet it wouldn't be too hard to do with Vio, she's been starving for you."

"But—I'm in this damn chair..." he shook his head. "...what girl wants to be with a guy who can barely get into the bed on his own?"

Darrell gave Kyle's arm a shove, "Vio, that's who." Darrell's face changed moods. "Do—ummm—things work down there? I can't believe I'm asking another guy this, but..." He stiffened his arm to stand straight up.

"Yes. It does what it's supposed to do. I just can't really feel anything in my legs. It's just gonna be awkward and...."

"Kyle—she loves YOU, dude. I bet she will be as nervous as you. It'll be like the first time again—you know, clumsy and nervous. But—she loves you."

There was brief silence between them.

"I'm glad I have you as a friend. I don't know what I'd do without you."

"Probably not have sex!" Darrell laughed hard and loud.

Vio and Mitzi walked outside, "Hey guys, whatcha doin' out here?"

Kyle and Darrell looked at each other and turned, speaking in unison, "Nuthin'!"

THE CALL HOME

Kyle continued, "nuthin' to see here' ladies, just two guys bein' two guys."

They all laughed together. Just like old times.

Mitzi asked, "You two ready for a couple more PBR's?"

"Yes ma'am, we certainly are," answered Kyle as he rolled closer to Vio and grabbed her hand, giving it a squeeze. "...Just like old times...."

18

Blending into the background isn't always the easiest thing to do. Looking as if you belong instead of drawing attention to oneself can be an art form. It's not something one usually gets schooled in from a university or trade college. It's a tact one learns out of necessity. When someone whose photo has been flashed repeatedly across the state's news channels and tacked up on grocery store windows and post office bulletin boards, can still slip into the shadows—that's a person to be wary of. Jay was exactly that kind of a man.

He could walk down a crowded sidewalk and say, "Howdy, and how are you doing today," and avoid the scrutiny of the woman he'd just spoken to. He could be charismatic, despite the tattooed arms and longer hair.

It'd been several months since he was locked away in solitary confinement at Lake Correctional, released back into the death row population and then hung by his fellow inmates using his own version of the Mason jar punishment. His two fellow escapees, the Ruby brothers, Lyle, and Lloyd, had recently paid their price for conspiring their plan of escape at his expense. They'd told him it was in their plan to "fake" hang him, in order to help him escape.

THE CALL HOME

What kinda' fool did those two damned liars take me for? One doesn't lynch a friend and watch him do the death dance to "help him out." In fact, they had hung him to help themselves out of incarceration. Used him like any old rusty tool from a toolbox. But they paid their final price. They never expected it, but their judgment came. Jay laughed a nasty howling growl. Indeed, it had.

"I still live, and those two traitors now swim in the lake of fire deep in the burning bowels of hell." Jay quietly said aloud to himself.

Jay imagined Lyle's and Lloyd's heads sticking up higher above all the other sinners of the world. Screaming and whimpering; the Ruby's abnormal heights of course forcing them to draw the attention of Satan himself.

"Yeah, Lyle—I hope you bump into old Roy while you're swimming down there. He'll be the one cryin' like a baby beggin' for his momma to send ice cubes to cool down his burnin' balls." A big grin spread across his face from cheek to cheek at the visualization.

Jay leaned over the small campfire he built. He stared at the bright glowing orange embers as he pictured the defendants, he'd personally sent to hell now suffering a fiery blistering heat. If one truly subscribes to such beliefs of heaven and hell, of course.

His stomach growled from hunger, but the sound and pang within his intestines landed just shy of drawing his attention and stares away from the flames licking up at the sky above. He continued his rants and cackles, bellowing out from his psychosis.

The time alone was again bringing back the familiar ravings of the lunatic he'd started becoming in New York. Nothing but time alone within his own twisted mind to console with. No one else present to break the mental feed of his internal disorder.

"I still have work to do..." he paused his sentence to erupt into an evil chuckling. "...Ethan-fuckin'-Kendricks..." his lip snarled, exposing his yellowed teeth. "...oh, the nasty crimes you're slated to be charged with and judged for. Guilty of tainting sweet young innocent girls with your fornicating perversions."

He then thought of Joyce and Mitzi. At one time he'd planned to have some fun with them at Ethan's beach lair.

I wonder if you two little tarts are still being sexually swindled and kept by Ethan, the rapin' predator? Wouldn't that be a shame if in order to rescue you—there was a small price to pay me back for my troubles?

His evil thoughts were the only meal he would be served tonight. There would be no charity from Ms. Cela Moses hands, dippin' warm soup into a cup to aid in filling his empty belly. Nor would any pages from her good book be able to calm his devilish thoughts tonight. Just his hollowed empty eyes reflecting the flicker of the yellow and orange flames in the night, dancing wildly within his dark black pupils that were empty of any humanity.

19

"Hey Tony—" Hank hollered from his kitchen. "Where's the food in here? You can't live on beer alone."

"I eat out when I'm hungry." He continued packing his bag.

Hank leaned in through the bedroom door. "So, where are you going?"

"The beach for a little 'r and r.' Since Finney is watching every move I make right now—I figure I may as well use some of the vacation I've accrued."

"How much time you got?"

Tony laughed, "You wouldn't believe me if I told you. I'm not taking it all. Just enough to satisfy him and enjoy a change of scenery."

"By change of scenery—you're talking about me, huh?" Hank laughed.

Tony turned around and looked Hank square, eye to eye. "Can I trust you?"

Hank smirked, "Well, hell yes—we're partners...."

"Hank—" Tony took a couple of steps his way. "I mean..." he moved one step closer making the two damn near on top of each other. "I'm dead serious. Can you be trusted?"

Hank stepped forward, closing the distance where their bodies almost touched. "I said—you can trust me. Do I need to fucking tattoo it on my arm?"

Tony smiled slightly and turned before taking several steps back to the bag of clothes sitting open on the bed. "I don't believe I've ever heard you speak such vulgar words." He laughed. "I'm going to Apalachicola—" he twisted his face back to Hank. "...that information goes nowhere. Especially Finney."

"That's a bad idea, Tony. Finney will blow an ass-seal if he finds out. Big trouble." Hank fired back.

"One—Finney isn't going to find out and two, it's my vacation time and I'll spend it wherever the hell I want. He can blow a seal's ass for all I care."

"But—if he's pulled you off the case, you're not officially able to investigate...."

"Finney said there isn't a case—it's been closed. I'm not investigating shit. I'm hanging out at a small Florida town on a bay and fishing, unwinding—resting my mental faculties, eating at local restaurants—Finney doesn't believe Cader is even alive. If he ain't alive, he can't show up in the little one stoplight town—now, can he?"

"Tony, I'm going to pretend I didn't hear where you said you were going. I don't wanna know anything else about it." Hank coughed, followed by clearing his throat. "I also want you to tell me you won't do anything stupid if by some long shot—a certain psychopathic killer happens to show up. You do know if he saw you, he'd try again to kill you. You will call me—right?"

"And put your career on the line? You'd really want that?"

"It concerns me that you'd even question it, Tony. We are partners—right?"

"I'm on vacation, Hank. I'm not on duty—if I'm going to have a vacation partner, she's gonna have nice long legs and sporting a golden-brown tan—and be nothing like my ex-wife. I sure as hell don't see this image when I look at you, buddy." Tony laughed and snatched up his bag after closing it. "I'd say—see you in a week and please feed my dog..." Tony winked. "...but I don't know exactly when I'll be back—and I've got no fuckin' canine—the ex took him along with half my pay in alimony...."

Tony gave a quick wave as he backed his copper colored Pontiac Le Mans with the white landau top out of his apartment building parking spot. The rear wheel chirped when he shifted into drive and gave the pedal a quick stomp.

Hank stood shaking his head back and forth. Tony noticed the sober flat look in his face when he peered back through his rear-view mirror as he drove away from the shrinking silhouette of his partner standing in the parking lot.

20

Darrell and Mitzi invited Joyce and Jake, along with Vio and Kyle for dinner. It was going to be their little last supper before Joyce headed to Tallahassee to start her new job with James T. Bollard.

"Mom, we want it to be special tonight. What do you want for dinner? Your choice." Mitzi asked.

"Well—" Joyce licked her lips and drew her hand to her chin as if in deep thought. "I sure have heard a lot of good compliments on the smoked gator tail that Kyle does...."

Vio smiled, "Yes ma'am, it's pretty darn tasty." She put her hand on Kyle's shoulder. "My man knows how to do a lot of things and that is one of his specialties!" She leaned down close to Kyle's ear before whispering, "Last night after dinner was incredible too—you sure know how to make a girl feel special." She raised her hand up and blatantly tried to display the new ring on her ring finger.

"Oh my God, Vio! It's beautiful!" Mitzi yelled before rushing over to her friend. "When did this happen? I can't believe I didn't notice it on my own!"

Joyce raised her hand to her mouth and took in a deep breath. "It's gorgeous, Vio—did you pick it out, Kyle? And Congratulations I presume!"

Kyle responded, "Ms. Bonham, it was my mother's. She wanted me to find just the right lady to give it to. I believe I've done that, ma'am. I feel very fortunate she said 'yes.'"

"Indeed, Kyle! You two have already made a great couple. I feel very happy you guys are so close to my Mitzi B. It makes it a little bit easier moving to Tallahassee knowing you are just a door away. Congratulations to both of you!"

Darrell stood holding Katie in his arms wearing a huge grin across his face. Mitzi glanced over at him and quickly gave him a punch in his arm when she noticed his coy smile.

"Darrell Lee Cader! Did you already know about this?" She looked him in the eye, and he grinned even bigger. "You did! Why—if you weren't holding my beautiful daughter—I'd...."

"That's right, I'm not stupid!" he responded.

Mitzi turned to Vio, "Okay, little miss sneaky, you have a story to tell me. I'm all ears right now!"

"I'll tell you when we go to get groceries for your mom's dinner for tonight." She turned to Joyce, "and I'll tell you tonight after I fill in my best friend!"

"I can hardly wait. Just tell me one thing. Where did he pop the question?" Joyce asked.

"Down alongside the bay, not far from the pier by one of the benches on the boardwalk. It was so romantic."

"Oh, Vio—I am so happy for you! Violet Jones! Mrs. Vio Jones—it has such a great ring to it!"

"I know, I've been saying it out loud to myself ever since! And Mitz..." she leaned in close so she could whisper into Mitzi's ear. "... we had... sex for the first time since the accident. It was incredible! I was afraid he'd never try again, but—wow!"

The two giggled as quietly as they could while they looked at her ring and whispered to each other.

21

"So, Amy Jo, what are you working on so diligently this morning? Just because you've wrapped up your book that's making such a splash and putting your name in the headlines—doesn't mean we don't have stories that need your attention!" Malcolm stated. "Did you dig any more up on those bank robberies over in Daytona?"

"I know, and yes, I've been excavating info on the Daytona Beach Bank robbers."

"Seriously, Amy Jo, how are you? You seem different these days. How goes—um—you know, the neighbor and you?"

Amy Jo smiled but guffawed quietly as she looked up from her computer screen. "We're just friends. That odd ship sailed."

Malcolm repositioned his head so he could see Amy Jo's face more clearly. "And you are okay with this ship sailing off?"

She looked up and rolled her eyes over to meet his. "Well, honestly..." she began to respond, "... when you don't totally have any control over a situation, you can cling onto the line and watch in pain—or you can let go and tread water until you're just too worn out to let it affect you."

"Sounds like you chose the wiser and jumped ship."

"Indeed, I'm still treading water but am taking heed of some advice the ship's captain gave me...."

"Sounds like a story here—one I want to hear more about. How about drinks later today after work?"

"Well, as long as you agree to stop 'digging' if I end up asking—and of course—you're buying!" she laughed aloud.

"Yes, on both accounts, now get on those Daytona robberies! I want something I can print before we leave!"

"You got it, chief!"

*****

Amy Jo walked over to the printer and picked up the copies she'd sent to be printed. She picked up the two copies and eyed them over. Johnson Bridge Builders was headlined across the top while line after line listed bridge projects the company was now working on and locations of the project sites. She smiled to herself before quietly speaking, "Cable Lee Johnson—I'm now officially on your case." She walked back to her desk, not being able to make the grin disappear. "I love a good story—and I'm going to do my best to dig in and write one."

22

Across the street from the Orlando Beacon News Building, stood a man who blended into the scenery of the sidewalk traffic. Just another body in the Orlando downtown. Passersby appeared to pay no attention to the older gentleman dressed in khaki pants and short-sleeved button-collared beach shirt. He looked like another tourist or window shopper as he turned to face the shiny reflective windows of the newspaper's two-story building. If one were to take notice of him, they may have seen his yellowed teeth behind his lips as his smile widened before turning slightly upward in the corners. He'd made it this far. Now he'd wait until she left work. That's what he hoped for anyway. He wanted to see Amy Jo again—before he made it back to Apalachicola to finish business. The thought made Billy Jay's grin widen even further. To the point his dry lips began to feel the sting of cracking.

He slowly stepped backward until he was able to lean against one of the shop's walls that lined the street where he stood. Pulling the brim of the brown fedora down lower over his brow, he turned so he could look at his reflection in the glass. His now freshly cut shorter hair and neatly trimmed goatee gave him an entirely new look. It wasn't until he saw the reflection of his arm as his hand reached to wipe the sweat from his brow, that he noticed all the inkwork on his aging tanned skin. These were images that could not be changed or erased as easily as a new haircut or beard trim. It was at this moment it appeared in his face that he realized he was a permanently marked man, no way around it. The pictures told the story of his tough life through prison tatts. Not very high-quality artwork at all, just sketches inked into his skin by other prisoners who deemed themselves artists.

His thoughts raced back to the night his colleagues strung him up from the pipe in the laundry room. Their images mixed throughout the group of other men, cons, who once had held respect and fear of him. Was I really any better than any of them? He asked himself. He guffawed. I hate these fuckin' moments where my weakness sneaks inside my head. Hell, yes, I'm better. I've been given the power of judgment. I've earned that much, goddamnit. And with that thought, he quickly dropped his hand from the reflection and pushed himself away from the wall before turning to blend back into the clusters of tourists walking in and out of t-shirt and souvenir shops. He'd come back later after he stole himself a car to follow Amy Jo home. Yeah, that's what I'll do. He told himself as his eyes turned dark again, his Mr. Hyde once again overcoming the Dr. Jekyll within.

Billy Jay was streetwise. He'd needed to be. He'd spent most of his existence living on either the street or keeping himself from becoming the fodder of another inmate or getting shanked. Jay knew how to survive. He moved a bit slower these days, woke up with aches and pains that hadn't seemed quite as predominant months ago when he slept on a cot instead of wherever he could find. Traveling became more difficult with age and meals more important now that he was back at being responsible for finding such things on his own instead of it being provided. Prison wasn't easy, but having meals cooked for you on a schedule, no matter how tasteless the slop was that they served, did make life easier. But he would keep his senses about him and not falter one step in surviving. Not until he was able to complete what he now saw as his final mission.

Two names were on the top of his list of those that had done deeds which needed judged and reprimanded. "Sgt. Tony Rawlings—and Ethan fucking Kendricks. Two vermin that need to be scourged and removed from this hellish world once and for all, and I'm the only man capable of such an important deed!" It seemed Billy Jay had forgotten where he was in the moment as he quickly was made aware from the quick stares, he began receiving from people walking around him on either direction. The groups of people began to give him a wider berth to pass as mothers drew their children closer to themselves and men watched with vigilance as they maneuvered between the women with them and him. It seemed Billy Jay was quickly slipping back into his previous world of mental brokenness, not they he was ever free of his delusions to begin with.

"Sorry, ma'am, I didn't mean to frighten the child—it's been a rough afternoon, and my mind is in overtime sorting out some family issues." He tipped the brim of his hat as he continued walking past. He knew he did not need any extracurricular troubles in Orlando. The one stop of pleasure before business was searching out Amy Jo Whitenhour, his one friend, at least at one time, and he needed to connect with a friend. Amy Jo in particular. He held special feelings for Amy Jo; she, after all, reminded him of another certain woman who also tugged at his heartstrings, even though his heart was normally tepid, if not stone cold. His heartstrings may be frazzled and tattered, as well as extremely short, but moments of humanity somehow snuck in and attempted to bring calm.

The merry-go-round of Billy Jay's life he always seemed to be riding, was still very much in motion. His life was also akin to a teetertotter that always swayed between its highs and lows. He lived in a constant battle of a three-ring circus; each part of his brain in one of those circular stages on the grounds, vying for the crowd's attention, cheering on whichever was holding the controlling reigns of his mind in a particular moment.

It was amazing such public outrageous ambiguousness hadn't brought the curtains down early on his craze-filled show long before this point in his life's performance.

Remaining the ringmaster of his own circus appeared sometimes a chore he seemed unable to take to task. He now recognized this from the outburst he'd unwittingly let escape. He would reel the tiger back into its cage and continue with the show he was setting out to complete.

He'd studied the different aspects of car theft. He knew to scout such things out instead of just spotting a vehicle and dashing off with it. He held skills of how to start a car without keys from his father's mechanic days. He'd learned what kind of car and what type of person to steal it from, on his own. Always look for an elderly person's car at their home. They didn't drive frequently, so they wouldn't miss it and report it as quick as someone younger who drove daily. Older people's cars blended better into the scenery also. Muscle cars, while more fun to drive, stuck out loudly when reported stolen. If one enjoyed car chases with cops—by all means, go for the hotrod. If instead you wanted to avoid run-ins with law enforcement, steal an elderly woman's Buick four-door in maroon or some other quiet-toned color that merges into the sea of the multitude of four-wheeled blandness.

It didn't take too long before Billy Jay spotted his mark. A light gold 1980 Buick Century. One couldn't find a more boring invisible car. Not only did the color blend, but there were tons of Century's' driving around in Orlando, home of the retired snowbirds who liked the comfort and reliability of a Buick. The little old man who just carried a week's worth of grocery bags into his little white house with the flowers on the porch before parking it inside the detached garage, was the perfect target.

"Bingo....," Billy Jay smiled. "The old fart even wears a fedora like mine..." he guffawed. "...neighbors won't suspect a thing seeing me back quietly from the driveway when the light of the television flickers from the living room window in a bit."

23

Four hours away from Orlando, Florida, Joyce walked into her new place of employment. James T. Bollard, a man of perhaps late sixties to early seventies, would be the new boss she would answer to. He was also the man her daughter had insisted she immediately bring up the trip they'd just returned from. Springfield, Missouri. The small midwestern town nestled in an area known as the Ozarks. A town where murder was not an everyday occurrence like it is in Miami or the likes. A double homicide was something very out of place from what she'd been told while visiting. Especially one involving two young ladies.

After parking the Volvo, she reluctantly made the trek up the short sidewalk to the front glass door. Grasping the silver looped handle, reading the name, Law Office of James T. Bollard, she began to tug as she sighed, "Here goes, you can do this, Joyce...."

"Good morning, Ms. Bonham!" she was immediately greeted. "I sincerely hope you are as excited to get started here as I am!" The well-dressed gentleman stated upon seeing her enter.

"Mr. Bollard, sir...."

"Now, Joyce, let's dispense immediately with the last name formalities. Yes, we live in the deep south, but we've already made acquaintances, so please, just call me Jim..." he smiled. "...I only answer to Jim with my closest friends and co-conspirators, which I assure you, you've already made that list!" he chuckled as he opened his arms for her to step into.

Joyce stepped nervously forward into his hug. It was friendly and professional, which set her at ease enough to reciprocate with a quick shoulder squeeze before backstepping.

"I must say, I've been impatiently waiting for this to happen. I hope you have felt the same."

"I'll have to be honest, Mr.... I mean... um... Jim. I've been nervous as can be. I hope I can keep up with the reputation you've somehow come to expect from me."

"Joyce—I've heard nothing but positive feedback when I've mentioned your name."

"Again, I hope to live up to such. I had no idea my name would even be recognized by anyone."

"Set your mind at ease, Joyce. We will move into this new setting gradually. I don't expect you to master my way of doing things on the immediate! I'm just pleased you accepted the offer and were willing to make the move so quickly."

"I... um... I do... have...."

A moment of uncomfortable silence began closing in on Joyce as she struggled to finish her sentence. She wanted to break into her quandary about her trip to Springfield and her fears and suspicions of Ethan, but the subject was impossible for her to just openly broach.

"Joyce, are you okay? You can just spit it out, I promise I don't bite, I can assure you. Your relationship with your past attorney bears no resemblance... you can be certain of that. I imagine he was a difficult man to please. I, myself, am rather easy. Painfully easy. My wife insists I'm the mouse among the lions."

He smiled briefly before he obviously took notice of her struggle. She saw it in his eyes and the look of compassion washing across his face.

"I haven't even begun my first day...."

"Joyce, dear, let's go into the conference room where you can sit, and we can talk a moment. I'll get us a cup of coffee." He led her to an open door where a large round walnut table sat squarely in the middle of the room. "You have a seat and calm your nerves, young lady. Everything is fine. Fine, indeed."

Joyce sat and reached inside her purse, which was nestled in her lap, pulled a tissue from the opening, and dabbed her eyes. Afterwards, she sniffled quietly and silently reprimanded herself. Damn it, Joyce. Be strong. Be honest. Just lay it all out on the table. This too shall pass.

24

Jake helped Kyle into his truck and then loaded Kyle's chair into the back. Kyle had pressed him several times about going to see his old Chevelle SS, or at least, what was left of it. Vio was unsure if it was a good idea and expressed that fact to Kyle. "You're doing so much better, honey. Can't you just put that night behind us and move forward? It's been long enough."

He answered her with, "Exactly, babe. I want to put it behind me and move forward. I wouldn't do this if I thought it wasn't going to be something positive. I love you. I need to see with my own eyes what brought me to this point in my life. I can't get past it until I meet it head-on, face to face. I'll come back better; I promise."

Jake looked over at his friend and smiled. His fingers reached to the ignition, and he inserted the key, giving it a twist, bringing the pickup truck to life. "You ready, Kyle?"

Kyle nodded in affirmation, "I'm ready. I'm a bit nervous, but I need to do this thing."

"I'm trusting you're not toying with me, Kyle. You are moving forward. There's no reverse on this ride you're on now. I won't allow it. You have too much good in your world to do anything but put that old demon to rest. Promise me, if this starts feeling anything other than good—you'll tell me, and we'll tackle it a different way."

"I promise, Jake. I'm not playing with matches; I'm putting an old fire out that's been slowly burning... singeing away at my psyche."

"Wisely spoken, my friend..." he pushed the clutch in and slid the gearshift lever to first gear and slowly released the clutch while giving it the fuel needed to pull out. "...and here we go!" The truck pulled away and Kyle looked up at the open door to his and Vio's apartment. He gave a quick wave and witnessed her concerned smile before he turned back toward the road ahead.

The ride wasn't too far. The salvage yard sat outside of the town of Wewahitchka, just about fifty miles northwest, inland of Apalachicola. They traveled through Port St. Joe on the way when Kyle noticed the little restaurant, Poppy's Net and Pasture. The name appeared to stir his brain as Jake glimpsed over at him. "I remember Mitzi and her mom talking about that place being a favorite of Ethan's. Hey, Jake. On the way back—I'd like to treat you to lunch at Poppy's. We can celebrate my facing demons and conquering them."

Jake glanced over and responded, "Kind of looks like a dive." He smiled. "I'll stop, but only if you let me buy!"

"Really? You're gonna argue this when you're already driving me to look at my battered baby?"

He nodded. "Yep, I reckon that'd be exactly what I'm doing. Of course, I'm driving, so I get to make the rules, friend!"

Kyle chuckled softly. "Yeah, you are driving, that's why it's taking so long to get there!" he looked over and smiled a devilish grin. "Come on, poke-along, how about a little extra feed to the horses under the hood!"

Jake just shook his head and the throttle remained without change.

Joe's Salvage appeared to be a large spread. There were vehicles of all years, makes and models along with every imaginable shape. Everything from almost new in appearance to twisted, mangled, rusted, and burnt to a crisp. No sooner than Kyle asked about his now retired baby, Joe immediately looked over the counter at the four-wheeled ride Kyle was now commanding.

"From the looks your Chevelle came in, you are one fortunate young man, son."

Kyle quickly retorted from mouth memory-muscle, "Yeah, fortunate—just one lucky little wheelchair-driving fool now."

Joe shook his head in reaction to Kyle's absurd response. "She's out to the left, fifth aisle and down almost to the end on the right—what's left of her anyway." He said smugly. "Musta been one hellova dinosaur that stepped out in front of you, son, takes a lot of self-control to keep the reins pulled in on a 454." He said in a snarky attempt to get a rise from him.

Jake was proud that Kyle didn't take the bait. With the banter coming on between the two, he was beginning to regret bringing him here, but Kyle seemed to shake off Joe's obtuse attitude towards him. It showed a good sign in his friend's personal growth. Kyle spun his chair around and wheeled up to the door, spinning backwards and pushing himself out into the parking lot. Jake turned to follow but after the door swung shut, he wheeled back around and leaned on the counter eyeing Joe.

"You might not know, but that young man out there has been through hell. He's suffered more than his share of guilt, let alone he most likely will never be able to walk..." he cleared his throat before continuing, "...so why in hell would you want to add insults to his already overwhelming injury? It's taken a lot for him to get to the point of coming here and facing his life-changing mistake. Why don't you be the man today and cut him some slack?"

Jake looked hard at Joe before turning and giving Joe his back as he headed for the door. Before the bell above it could ding, a humble voice stumbled over some awkward pauses, "Can you... uh... maybe... um... tell your... your... son that... I'm... I'm sorry for... being such an ass." Jake stopped and turned around to face him.

"I'll tell him. I realize we all have bad days, and we can take aim at the easy target. Thanks for stepping up to the plate and swinging—I appreciate it..." he smiled to himself. "I know my son will too." And he shook his head a couple of times with the warm grin he suddenly felt glide across his face. He suddenly felt like a proud dad who'd stood up for his son. It made him feel warm inside. His chest felt a flash of heat within. He thought to himself as he pulled the door back open, ringing the bell above his head, yeah, I guess Kyle kinda is my son now. My adopted boy.

"You ready to face your nemesis, son?" he asked as he reached over and patted Kyle's shoulder. "...by the way—Joe asked me to apologize for his dumbass attitude." Kyle looked up and grinned.

"Thanks. You didn't have to, you know."

"I realize that, but he needed to know how stupid he acted."

"Yeah, I suppose you're right."

They rounded the corner and continued down the aisle between the rusty boneyard of broken and twisted metal formal icons of engineering on either side of them. Shattered dreams of pampered carriages lost when circumstance brought their early demise. It was at that moment when the air felt heavy through thoughts of how accidents in life from sometimes poor decisions made in an instant could cause such carnage and pain. Something so violent a tragedy could take a bright red shell of Kyle's once cherished prized possession and twist it into something almost unrecognizable. Jake paused, remembering Kyle telling him how he'd begged his mother to let him have her. He would be respectful and safe. Jake looked at how the interior was scorched and torn, its form all mangled and smashed. He quietly turned his head and looked down. At first, he didn't notice the blonde-haired young man or even the empty look in his face. He observed the chair. The chair with the two big wheels and the two smaller wheels in the front. As his sight shifted upwards, his focus moved to his friend's eyes. He saw the sorrow, felt the pain of regret of his responsibility and the hurt of letting his word falter. The promise he'd broken to his mother that he'd be careful—he'd be safe and respect the power this automobile held under its hood.

It was amazingly fortunate he and Vio had survived the mishap. Then to later find out the rest of the outcome. A sheriff gunned down as they lie twisted and unconscious while a madman judged, sentenced, and then carried out an execution while they were minutes away from burning up in the aftermath. That poor boy. Jake was suddenly overwhelmed. He was swallowed up in that moment, full of compassion, as he watched the pain encompass Kyle's face as he looked upon the result of a single huge mistake he'd let himself make. It felt almost like Jake was there when it happened, able to feel what Kyle felt through watching his young friend's actions and anguish. Jake suddenly felt overwhelmed with a pain in the pit of his stomach.

*****

Kyle sat completely still; his eyes remained fixed on where the driver's side door used to be attached, the roof now smashed into the driver's seat to a point it would be impossible to sit behind the wheel. He struggled to lean in, one hand on each side of the opening as he gripped the crumpled rusted roof. He craned his neck to enable peering around the tattered black vinyl seat where he remembered Vio lay trapped behind him.

The night's events slowly scrolled through his mind. He faintly smelled the burnt fuel and paint. The scent almost diminished from time passed. He felt the heat radiating from the sunbaked metal. When Jake's hand touched his shoulder, he jumped and then pushed his head back out and turned towards him. There was a hesitation for a moment before words began exiting his lips. "Vio was lying behind me. I... I could... I could only see her arm. I called out... but... but... she didn't ans... answer me. I... I knew she must be dead. I... I couldn't move to reach... reach her. I couldn't save her. That's what I thought." Tears filled his eyes, but he continued, "...the car wasn't sitting... not like this... it was...upside down and I could... I could taste fuel in... in... my mouth. Someone was shining a light in my face. He came... from nowhere. He said he... he was gonna get... gonna get us out and call for help. That's when... when... that's when that fuckin' psychopath showed up. Jay. He started yelling at the sheriff. I tried to wiggle... to get free. I tried to yell... to tell Jay to help... help... get Vio out, but my throat burned... I... couldn't... my words... they were stuck inside... inside my throat..." he reached out and banged on the rooftop with both fists closed tightly. "...I tried... Ja... Jake. I couldn't... move... my words... wouldn't leave my mouth... the world started spinning and I heard loud pops... they kept sounding... and that... that laugh..." Kyle's fists slipped off the roof and onto his lap as his head dropped. His chin rested on his chest as he erupted in moans and groans. All he could mutter was, "It's all my fault. If I hadn't of... it's my fault. My heart... it was pounding... the music... love... adrenalin...and... Vio's hand on my...on my leg. She squeezed and asked me to... to slow down... and when... when I let up on the gas... the... the car... swerved and hit the... embankment and ricocheted back and... forth until it rolled. Over and over and over... I should... I should have died that night... for... for... for what I did...."

"No, son. That wouldn't have changed or solved a thing. You're both alive and that's what matters now. It's time to let go and lay it at the altar, boy. It's time to move forward." Jake knelt and wrapped his arms around Kyle, pulling him into his chest tightly. "What's done is done. Let it go, son. Let it go."

The ride back home was quiet. It wasn't long until Jake's truck slowed and pulled into the parking lot of Poppy's Net and Pasture. The two sat for several moments in the truck's cab letting what happened at Joe's Salvage settle a bit. Neither appeared to have any hunger for food, but Jake asked if he wanted to go in and have a beer to settle their nerves.

Kyle forced a smile and answered, "I could sure use a PBR, Pop. Can I call you that? It kind of seems fitting."

"Of course, you can, son. I'd be honored."

"Let's go, Pop. First one's on me."

"I reckon I could let you buy just one...."

Jake grinned. "That, son, is a good goal to work towards. Just remember...."

"I know if it happens it's a blessing. If it doesn't, it's no longer the end of my world. But...."

"I know. I'll be keeping that hope with me for you also. Always." He reached across the table and grasped his hand, giving it a strong squeeze. This too shall pass, son. Indeed."

"Mitz and her mom both use that same phrase."

When their bottles of PBR arrived at their table, they both lifted them to the air in celebration and clinked them together. In the corner a man sat, a fading look in his eyes. Kyle glanced over and refused to look away as if it would be defeat for whoever turned first. It felt odd to Kyle, but the magnetic hold refused to give him any release. In a brief moment, he felt a feeling of power inside. Ethan seemed to lose his resolve, unable to remain visually engaged and then he turned away, back to his table and conversation with the white-haired man. In that peculiar break in their connection, Kyle swore he saw Ethan's ego shrink. It brought a calm. It gave Kyle a feeling of purpose again. There was no explanation he could nail down in his head, but he suddenly felt very much—alive once again.

26

Jim Bollard walked back through the doorway carrying a round tray with steaming cups of coffee, one on either side of the pot. "Here we go, Joyce," he said as he set it down on the table and held a cup towards her. "You just take your time, and we can ease into whatever is ailing your heart at your convenience." He removed the other cup from the tray and held it up to his lip, blowing it to cool the liquid before sipping.

Joyce's eyes had dried, both from dabbing them with tissue and the time which passed while Jim was preparing the coffee. She still sat very uncomfortably poised in her seat as if she would bolt at any moment like a doe reacting out of instinct hearing the crack of a bullet leaving a rifle barrel. She too blew into her cup and took a sip from it before setting it down on the wooden table. She glanced around the room, imagining how many troubled clients with their difficult circumstances had been discussed while sitting in this conference room around this very table. *None could be as uncomfortable as the confusing pain I now hold inside.* She imagined. "I guess the only real way to confront what I'm upset about—is to just dive right in. Wouldn't you agree?"

Jim clasped his cup, turning it within his grip. "Sometimes, Joyce, doing just that, bypassing the dipping of one's toe to make certain the water temperature is indeed palatable—is the best way to proceed. I assure you, nothing said in this room between us will go anywhere further unless you allow it. I give you, my word. These walls hold many secrets absorbed within the brick and mortar."

She cleared her throat briefly before opening with something Jim both could, and could not, have imagined Joyce revealing. "I believe Ethan had something to do with the murder of two young girls over in Springfield, Missouri not too long ago." A twitch in her eye gave the first sign of another possible meltdown coming. "I think he killed those two poor girls. I don't know why or what the circumstances were surrounding such horror—but he hasn't been the same since he returned. And there was—a watch that never left his wrist—that was missing out of the blue when he returned. He won't talk about it, refusing to answer any questions and dismissing anything I bring up about his trip." Her eyes quivered and her head dipped down slightly. "I now know where that watch is." She lifted her face back to meet Jim's.

"Yes, I remember hearing about those poor girls. One was the daughter of a very wealthy couple that owned a pharmaceutical company. I was there a day after they found them."

"You were in Springfield?"

"Yes—to talk to Billy Jay Cader."

"That was who Ethan had made the trip for. He was going to try and offer him help with his defense."

"Seems none of that is needed anymore." Jim said as he watched Joyce's reaction. "So, about this missing watch, this wouldn't be the one that is supposedly Al Capone's, is it?"

"Yes! How did you know about it?"

"Oh Lord, Joyce—every attorney in southern Florida knows about Ethan's watch! He makes certain of it!" He chuckled.

THE CALL HOME

"I believe Ethan would sell his own soul to be reincarnated as that awful man, and he isn't afraid to let everyone know it."

"The Springfield police have that watch."

Jim's eyebrows raised in immediate question. "They do, do they? Now that is very interesting. Very interesting, indeed. Do they know it is Ethan's watch?"

"I don't think so. They would more than likely be down here to question him if they did, wouldn't they?"

"I would presume so. Does Ethan know that you know this information?" he asked with a concerned appearance that washed over him.

"No. I haven't talked to Ethan since I left him—and his firm. I haven't been back. In fact, I still have some belongings at his house, but I'm much too afraid to go get them."

"Yes, you most definitely do not want to return to his home, not without an escort. Many stories circulated about things he's been involved in. I would imagine he is suffering some consequences of losing you—and that damn watch." Jim's eyes twitched momentarily. "Ethan does not like to lose. Not cases, nor things he's acquired. He never has."

"He's made no attempt at contacting me. I think he is aware we are through."

"Let me mull all of this information over, Joyce. I don't believe any of this should be acted on too hastily. I must gather all the facts and lay a well-planned strategy. When dealing with a slithery serpent—one must cover all one's bases to avoid losing the reptile down a crack overlooked in the foundation or his fangs if he decides to strike.

27

Tony pulled his vehicle into the Gibson Inn's parking lot. He'd driven by the old Tanner house where Jay once lived upstairs on that fate-filled day he lost his best friend and partner, Sam Hayden. His emotions were kept in check, but the pangs of loss were just under the thin veil of that memory. He had attempted to push away any of remembering that day ever deeper and deeper into the shadows. He needed to keep his mind as clear as possible. Afterall, Jay also attempted to kill him that day too. He still held the scars left behind from the bullets permanently marking his body. He could still visualize the evil in Jay's eyes as he'd pointed his revolver and pulled the trigger sending the sharp searing pains into his flesh and muscle with the accompanying bang and sight of muzzle flash.

Recall. It could be a good thing, or not so. On one hand, that memory refreshed his resolve to reconcile his partner's murder. That was good. But to delve too far into that reminiscence could also aid in the dilution of his senses and attention to details that could prepare or save him from the unexpected. He'd been lucky the last time. Luck rarely revisits the same site twice. He wasn't normally an overly sensitive guy anyway, instead he had a more A-type personality who never let emotions bubble out.

Headstrong with persistence and determination. It's how he'd become one of Florida's top cops. He'd been held back on this case though and that fact angered him. He'd been removed, and now deleted from the investigation, even though he'd been instrumental in Jay's arrest and conviction. His testimony helped convince the jury of not only a guilty conviction, but also the demand of the electric chair for Billy Jay Cader. An indictment unfulfilled due only to Billy Jay's escape.

    He hated it when the murderous, psychopath's name even crossed through his thoughts, let alone when it remained and festered through headlines and news flashes forcing his senses to engage in the memory of Sam's death. There was only one way to remove his guilt forever, and that was to make sure the vermin was exterminated. Or at the very least standing back in line for such, waiting for that condemnation to happen. The chief may have been correct by invoking his being too close to the case from the beginning, but damn, he knew he was the correct choice to hunt him down. Tony also knew Jay somehow was able to elude death and recapture. He was still out there. He would kill again. He would answer the call to come back home. Killers always returned at some point to relive their experience. It's part of their make-up, their M.O. or modus operandi. It was scorched into their psyche. He wasn't a criminal psychologist by any means, but he'd dealt with enough sick bastards like Billy Jay to understand more than any professor with a doctorate in human behavior at some university who'd never come face to face to a killer. Lectures and study guides held no comparison to real life, and he trumped book smart education with practical experience. Life hanging in the balance kind of experience. The intimacy of loss of life. Tony couldn't understand why Finney refused to put stock in his interpretations of what Billy Jay was still capable of. His sixth

28

Jim sat back in his chair at the conference table, bringing his hands up to his chin in a fluid motion. His eyes held questions. Joyce could read it clearly through her blurred and teary vision. His wrinkled cheeks seemed to soften as he witnessed his brand-new employee's psyche become broken and vulnerable. All he could think inside his normally tactical mind was one thing. *Ethan Kendricks, you sick motherfucker.* The thought came in language that was not normally in his vocabulary, not now, not for many years. He'd heard plenty of the dark colorful language before and even spoken it occasionally, though seldom. In his line of work, defense, he'd been surrounded with people in pain, desperation, and at the end of their hope. Out of anger and frustration, lewd and sharp language was normal. Dark words hurled from hurt and sour mouths somehow gave comfort to the one who scattered them into the conversation.

He leaned back up to the table and reached his hand across as if to offer consolation. Joyce's hand slowly and shakingly maneuvered to meet his in the middle, allowing him to clasp it in his. "Pardon my language, Joyce, but I've found it does give a certain amount of relief to use such words at the proper time—and this indeed pulses in my veins as an appropriate moment. "Ethan

Kendricks is a good for nothing venomous snake in the grass. A calculating, predatorial and evil fucking viper..." his eyes darkened and now held a stern resolve within their dark pupils. "We are going to nail his slithery and wicked skin to an oak board and then hold it over the open flame before tacking it up on the wall for all to see. I've seen far too many people—women in particular—that he has used, abused, and left dangling in the wind to let this go on any longer. A damned line has been drawn in the sand, and we by God are gonna wipe it clean from the beach along with any memories he thought he'd leave behind in legacy." He leaned back again in his chair after releasing Joyce's hand. "I feel good now, how about you? Better? Are we on the same page, dear Joyce?"

She appeared unable to answer. She nodded her head in affirmation, but no words appeared able to escape her mouth, merely quiet sobs between the loud inhaling of heavy-laden breaths taken in.

"I want to assure you, Ms. Joyce—this case has moved expeditiously to the top of my pile. There will be no bill accrued nor expense reimbursement required. This case is one hundred percent gratis at this office's pleasure."

****

Joyce's sobs morphed into an uncontrolled release of tension and pain she'd managed to keep stuffed inside since her world unexpectedly fell apart. The matter of a missing watch was what could possibly bring down a town's living legend and powerhouse. A town's leader with a hidden reputation for sexual debauchery from his earliest days of adolescence. A man's obsession with another's world of likely the same type of mental temperament.

Alphonse Gabriel Capone, a maniacal gangster who ended up dying from syphilis. Did Ethan have the same strong and deviant sexual prowess as him? Joyce had no idea. She just knew the man she fell in love with was always obsessed with Al Capone and was very proud of owning his watch. She'd not thought much about it until it came up missing and later found in Springfield, Missouri. Ethan had avoided any mention of the watch which rarely left his wrist. And now turning up in a mid-sized town hosting a double murder of two young women who'd had sexual relations just before dying; a watch with A. C. engraved on its back found at the scene and her soon to be husband's identical watch absent on his return. It was now irretrievable, sitting in an evidence box with nothing but questions of where it came from. She knew the answer. Her question now was whether Ethan would die like his hero Al –diseased from a seedy lifestyle? Or guilt as he rotted in prison? Sex and murder. Was it even possible Ethan was capable of such? How could he have fooled her so easily?

Through her tears, her mind could focus on nothing else today. It was her first day at a new job, in a new town with a new start, yet here she was, back at the same root of her problem. She'd escaped what could possibly be a monster that may have done horrible things to her, her daughter—and all she could do was cry like a baby in front of her new boss and ask herself one question, *how could I be so blind and stupid?*

29

Vio had never felt more relief than when she heard the rumble of Jake's pickup when it pulled up in front of the apartment. She quickly opened the door and met them with a look of concern.

"I'm fine, Vio. I've put all that past behind me now."

She quickly moved close enough to lean down and hug him. She almost refused to let go, feeling as if the moment may change if she did. "I love you, Kyle." Sniffs followed her words as she pulled back to look at him eye to eye. "We'll make it past all of this together, okay?"

"Yes, and I know that. You're my focus... and of course working at getting my legs back if possible. I'm ready to quit feeling sorry for myself and do all I can to become as whole as possible."

"You would have been proud of him. He showed strong willpower today. This one is a survivor." Jake grinned.

"Thank you, Jake. You're a big part of steering him through all this transformation."

Darrell and Mitzi met them at the door.

"Hey, buddy, how you doing?" Darrell asked.

"Ben let you off early today?" Kyle questioned.

"I took the rest of the day off to take you guys out on Ben's boat! He finished my captain's training this morning!"

"Awesome! What a great day for it! Are you in, Jake?" Kyle looked at both him and Vio. "Vio?"

Jake looked at Vio for her approval.

"Sure, I can throw some snacks together and we have some beer for a cooler." She answered. "Just like old times!" She smiled before hesitating, realizing in the old times, Kyle wouldn't be chair-bound."

"New old times!" Kyle answered. "Let's do it!"

*****

The bay was calm as Darrell steered away from the dock. Mitzi stood beside him at the helm as he maneuvered the motor yacht out from the confines of moored boats and the water breaks toward the horizon. The wind blew through Mitzi's short hair as she held Katie in her arms beside her husband. It was just what she needed today. It was difficult knowing her mom was going through all the turmoil of what Ethan had likely done, her pain and fears of a new job while also being drawn away from Katie and her to continue her career. It wasn't fair. All the hell she and her mom had gone through since moving here. Her mom deserved so much more than the hard hand after hand this life kept dealing her. Mitzi quietly wished she had someone on the outside of her circle to talk to. Someone who wasn't closely involved in any of this Ethan crap. The guilt she was feeling at how well her life with Darrell and Katie was going, along with Darrell working for Ben and Gina. She was becoming closer to Gina though, because of Gina's pregnancy. There were still all the peripheral troubles tugging at her. Darrell's mom Cat, still having memory problems although Jake's interest in Cat helped. There was also of course Vio and Kyles's struggles—and the root of most all of it, was Billy Jay. The fact he may possibly still be alive and living without paying the price for what he'd brought down on everyone only added to Billy Jay's part in it all. The pain she knew Darrell was quietly living with, even though he wasn't blood related like he'd grown up believing. Yes, she needed someone unrelated to every bit of this bullshit to talk to and help her weed through it. But who? And would it really do any good? Of course, the final one on the list of woes was now moved up to the strongest concern—Ethan. Damn you, Ethan Kendricks. Damn you for what you've done to my mom... and of course... those two girls in Springfield. And who knows who else?

*****

By the end of afternoon as the sun slowly began its descent into the Gulf, the crew, and the boat slowly motored back. Ben and Gina stood dockside as Darrell masterfully pulled the boat back into the slip. Ben grabbed the lines and helped tie off as Gina watched. Her belly clearly showing the definition of being with child. Mitzi noticed her glow for possibly the very first time. She'd talked with her about her fears of Ben possibly not being the father. Yet another possible legacy of Billy Jay leaving his seed behind. A legacy that could end up destroying the woman who was now growing to be almost as good a friend as Vio.

Gina smiled and it gave Mitzi a feeling of joy yet mixed with the worry and conflict that her pregnancy brought. She was amazed at how Gina's husband, Ben, was handling everything. There are typically not too many men who held that kind of compassion, understanding, and forgiveness. She was certain the "not knowing" though, had to be wearing at his psyche, yet he never let it show. The man was as solid as a monument. Seeing the two of them together spurred the thought of a woman Mitzi used to feel close to not all that long ago. She held that same kind of compassion the two of them seem to share and she had helped both Darrell and her through so much, not all that long ago. Debbie Thomas, her school counselor from Apalachicola High. A woman who was instrumental in helping Darrell and her with finding out they weren't brother and sister. She was on the outside of the inner circle, yet very connected to Mitzi.

Mitzi suddenly felt a wave of relief come over her. *Yes! I will go see Debbie Thomas;* Mitzi told herself as she looked out amongst all the friends she'd made since moving here with her mom. So much has happened. Katie wriggled in her arms and cooed, bringing her attention to her daughter's sweet smiling face. Katie looked so much like her daddy it made Mitzi smile. Life could be good for her mom, just like Darrell and her's after overcoming their problems. And the way it appeared, Vio and Kyle were doing great too. This quirky little town that once angered her because of being moved here, had now become her home. She couldn't imagine living anywhere else.

As they all climbed across and landed their feet back onto firm ground dockside, Ben invited them all to share dinner at the Big Apple on the Bay, his treat.

30

The Buick drove nicely. It was smooth. As Jay drove, he began thinking of the risk he was taking by keeping tabs on Amy Jo in town. That feeling in the pit of his stomach came every time he met a cop either coming towards him or up from behind. He felt the target he was most certainly wearing on his back. One small slipup could cause his getting pulled over and end all of his plans. He continued to let those plans mull over in his thoughts as he steered the car towards the address he'd remembered and found on a map in the glovebox. Amy Jo would need to be separated from her friend before he could see her again. It wasn't worth the risk to confront her with him, whoever he was. He was of no consequence.

"I'll visit Miss Amy Jo at her home and catch her by surprise." He smiled. "Then... heh heh... then it's back to Apalachicola to visit Gina and Ben. Maybe a quick check on Cat." His internal psychosis began to churn again. The wheels spinning faster and faster as he became wound tighter and tighter. "Ethan fucking Kendricks. It will soon be your time! It's almost time to fulfill my promise to Miss Cali Lea Jenkins. What a poor young broken soul she was, bless her heart." The wicked smile seemed to twist into a saddened frown as his memory trailed off to the moment he'd found her alongside the road. Nearly naked and incoherent. Shaking and frazzled, lost, and stoned on some mind-numbing potion she was dosed with by Ethan and his sick perverted buddies. *He'd pay for that sin. Yes indeed. Old Roy boy paid for his part of those atrocities—and of course for raping his wife, Cat and creating that little shit, Darrell Lee. Calling that bastard mine for all of those years. If it's the last thing I ever do, Ethan, you will get your just desserts, just like Roy did. At my hands.*

Jay pulled over and checked his map a couple of times as the late afternoon sun began to sink lower, painting another beautiful sunset across the Florida sky. As he looked out across the slowly dimming heavens, a passerby would likely have seen him and taken him as a tourist having made a wrong turn. He stood outside his car recalculating his coordinates and appreciating the beauty of the pink and orange colors mixing with the blue to make a shade of purple impossible to duplicate in any other place across the country.

The truth was, in some crazy fashion, Jay was like that sunset himself. At times he was a pallet of a very strange example of beauty stirred into a mixture of innocence and horror. In rare moments his evil was merely a conglomeration of gray clouds and rainbows haunted by a past storm he'd held no control over. Billy Jay was a product of his surroundings every bit as much as a devilish tornado formed from hot and cold air mixing. Devastating, but by no real fault of its own. Jay hadn't been given any kind of a chance to be anything different unless he would have allowed himself to surrender to the power of a faith like Ben and Gina had accepted. *But I can't do that yet. I still have business to settle first. Then we'll see about surrendering my soul to an entity who denied the innocence of a mother and her son.* Those were the last

THE CALL HOME

thoughts that blanketed his mind as the darkness began to tuck those beautiful Florida colors into the blackness of the evening.

31

"Goodnight, Malcolm. You do know how much I appreciate you, don't you?"

He stepped closer and gave Amy Jo a hug. "Yes, yes, I do. I just hope you'll listen to what we talked about. Take some time. You have plenty of vacation built up and I think you need the break. Your book drained you. That crazy psychopath burrowed too deep into your head. But you're past all that now. Bury it and take some time to recuperate. Dig up that boy from your high school days—the one Georgie reminded you about. Who knows?"

"I'm actually working on that now."

"Good, so I can stop my worrying about you a bit?"

Amy Jo punched Malcolm's bicep. "Yes, big brother! You can slow your worry!" She giggled. "I've permanently derailed all attempts to ride the Georgie Rovaria train and have redirected my focus on Cable Lee Johnson. After all, we share a blast from the distant past and that has to account for something—right?" She laughed.

"You're crazy, Amy Jo. But it's why I love you so much, I reckon." He paused a moment. "How's that going? I mean, are you two back on common ground you can share without too much awkwardness?"

"We're fine. I have to admit, she definitely put some pretty warm steam in my engine that I never expected. But we're good. I've never been kissed like that before. Do you think there's something wrong with me?"

"There's nothing wrong with you, Amy Jo. You're horribly lonely. But you've been so busy that you refused to accept the fact you're still human. You need companionship. You more than me needs that. I don't see how you live alone out there in your museum. I mean, it's beautiful on your orange tree farm, but it's so remote and—well—lonely, way too full of memories from your grandparents. I mean, I get it, but—that's coming from me, and I don't seem to know shit! I'm almost forty and I still live in the shadows. And I thought maybe we finally held even more in common!"

"A leopard can't change their spots—or at least that's what they say."

"Meaning?"

"Oh, come on, Malcolm! You're an editor for crying out loud! Read between the lines! It's obvious."

"I get it, you're not going to change any more than I am, but it doesn't mean you can't change your habitat! Branch out from the old storybook memory you're living in and cling too desperately—that's all I'm saying. Don't wither into the grandparents that raised you without living your own life first. The rocking chair on the porch doesn't look good on you yet!"

"I'm an orange tree farm girl, Malcolm. I'm a loner, I'm not lonely. What spots are you wanting me to try to re-arrange? The spots that made me who I am? I can't do that. I won't out of respect of what I was given. I said I'm searching for Cable; I can't promise any other attempts at conceding to change! That in itself is huge! Almost as huge as kissing a beautiful Spanish woman and hoping she kisses back!" Amy Jo laughed.

"You got me there. At least you're finished with Billy Jay Cader."

"Yup. Finished. The only other blast from my past that still haunts me is...."

Malcolm waited for Amy to continue. "Well? You have my curiosity peaked now."

"The letter in the box on my mantle...."

"So—would you like me to come over and you can open it and read it with a good friend sitting next to you with a warm shot of bourbon and a shoulder to cry on?"

"Sometimes—I wish someone would steal it, so it wasn't lying there with that call that occasionally taunts me. She doesn't deserve the right to have that strong of a hold over me. Does she?" Amy Jo's mood changed as if the light buzz from the drinks had now passed with the cool night breeze that lightly chilled her. "I do wonder why she gave me up so easily. Why she let my father do those horrible things to me." She paused again, glancing around the sidewalk, appearing as if she wanted to go back inside and sit back down at a table. "I want to know how she could explain that to me in a letter, or if she even tried. Part of me feels as if I'll never let that question go if I don't open the goddamned thing." Amy Jo paused. "... but the other side of me says not to dare open it and give in. What do I do, Malcolm?"

"I can't answer that for you, Amy Jo. I can be there for you anytime you need me, but I can't make that decision. You have to do that. You'd never forgive me if I suggested what to do and it turned out bad." He reached out and touched her arm softly. "You know I love you like a sister. You know that don't you? We're family even if we don't share blood."

THE CALL HOME

"I know. This is why I usually stick to wine and stay away from the umbrella drinks." She smiled. "Rum brings out the blues in me."

"Want me to take you home tonight? We can leave your car and I can pick you up in the morning."

"No, I'm not drunk. I just know myself better than to drink anything other than wine." She leaned in and gave Malcolm a peck on the cheek. "I'll be okay. What doesn't kill you makes you stronger! I'll see you in the morning. Thanks for—being you and being in my corner."

"Always, Amy Jo." He returned the light kiss on her cheek. "How about a quick call or page me when you're safe at home?"

"You got it. I'll just page you with 1234 like I have in the past. Home safe and sound. 1234."

"Don't forget!"

"G'night Malcolm. Love you." Amy Jo smiled and winked before she turned and made her way to her truck. *What song would Grandfather magically place for the radio to play tonight?*

*****

Amy Jo's drive home was melancholy. She was unsure why the damned letter from her mother was now on her mind so much lately. She'd managed to keep it in the shadows for so many years. She always felt if she gave in and read it, she would be betraying all the love her grandfather and grandmother had given her. They'd been able to somehow write off their daughter, so why shouldn't or better yet couldn't she? But there it was. Tempting her to break the seal, the pact, and taste the forbidden fruit by reading it. Much like she'd tasted the forbidden kiss of another woman. A crazy comparison but she knew temptation was one battle she could fight for only so long before caving in. Was tonight the night her foot would step over the line in that sand she'd drawn so many years back? The line that had felt a hundred miles away for so long. Why was life throwing these attempts at changing her core being?

She was so deep in thought she never took notice of the Buick parked down the road from the entrance to the farm. She had visions of cracking a bottle open once she'd paged Malcolm with 1234, then she'd tackle the odd seduction of that damned letter that lay yellowed and brittle—nestled in the wooden box on her mantle.

*****

Jay watched the headlights moving down the nearly vacant highway towards him as they began to slow. Was it finally Amy Jo? Or had someone in the small house to the west of the main house call for the police to check out the car parked along the highway? When the headlights slowed enough to make the turn onto the drive, he dropped down below the seatback so he wouldn't be noticed.

Once turned, he lifted up to survey the car moving to the main house which was only lit by the single porchlight as if it were a beacon leading strangers to safety. The smaller house, nearly a hundred or so feet away, held lit windows with dancing shadows of people inside moving about. He'd been watching and deciphering the lay of the property. It wasn't much more than a minute after the car door opened when he noticed the shadow of someone making their way towards the main house from the other. Amy Jo exited the car and slowly made her way to the porch, entering as the front door breathed the life of brighter light. A couple of seconds later, the silhouette of a woman stood at the front door. Almost instantly, the door opened and closed as the shadow of the woman passed over the threshold before the doorway dimmed again to only the porchlight's faint glow.

"Damn the luck! Who in hell is that?" Billy Jay questioned aloud as he bumped his fist on the steering wheel. He reached up and removed the white plastic cover of the dome light before twisting the bulb loose from the socket. He would carefully investigate closer so he could lay out a plan to execute.

32

Shadows dimmed the soft lighting that barely escaped the internal space of the house. Jay stood in the darkness avoiding any of that light from reflecting back from his silhouette. He saw who the figure had been that beat him to the door. It was a brown-skinned woman who stood at what appeared to be a bar separating the kitchen from the rest of the room. His heart felt strangely odd when Amy Jo's face turned towards him from the opposite side of the bar that the neighbor stood. So, this is where Amy Jo grew up. A far cry from the hell I knew. This appeared pleasantly—happy and cozy. Billy Jay shook his head as if clearing away any memory that battled to distract his attentions from the moment at hand. He hadn't held his normal luck today. Twice his plans needed to be re-evaluated and updated. He continued to watch the two women as Amy Jo poured what appeared to be wine into two glasses. They smiled and conversed together.

*****

"Oh, Amy Jo! I'm so glad to hear that! I'm sure you won't have any problems finding him. You are a very talented

THE CALL HOME

investigator. You should be a cop!" Georgie giggled as she reached across to meet the glass being slid her way.

"I don't know about that, Georgie, but I do have some hopeful leads on Cable. I talked to an old friend up in Volusia County that says they are reworking the bridges over Spruce Creek. She swears one night when she was eating in New Smyrna Beach that she overheard a table of guys wearing orange safety t-shirts talking. Cable Lee was a name spoken several times. She says she remembers it because the name seemed very unique." A smile grew and began stretching her lips wider before she sipped from the glass and then returned her gaze to Georgie. "Wouldn't that be crazy if it was really him? I mean, that's only what, an hour or so away?" She said as she pulled her glass to her lips and tipped it again.

Georgie's smile matched her friend's. "That would be perfect! Let's both cross our fingers on it. Not that I'm really superstitious!"

The two moved over to the couch and chair in the living room. Amy Jo sat in her favorite chair and Georgie on the couch to her left. Both women's faces were visible through the window off to the side of the front door where the corner barely caught a glow from the dim porchlight that still remained on.

*****

Billy Jay began slowly edging over towards the door, drawn to the entrance like a moth to the flame. His eyes were as dark as a raven's. He never hesitated as he stalked across the porch stepping from the shadows and into the canopy of light that subtly lit the front door. His pupils quickly shrank as if cowering in retreat, back into the darkness, when in fact, it was anything but that. He lifted his hand, shaping it into a fist, before bringing it to the door and wrapping it three times in rapid succession.

*****

Amy Jo's and Georgie's heads snapped quickly to the front door.

"I wonder who that could be?" Amy Jo questioned as she looked at her wrist at the small silver watch. "It's after ten."

The light through the front window dimmed and brightened with movement. "You weren't expecting anyone?" Georgie asked.

"Maybe it's Malcolm? I just parted ways with him in town before coming home." She pulled herself up and out of her chair, a small groan escaped her as she landed flatfooted onto the hardwood floor. She walked over and twisted the deadbolt to the left, unlocking it before twisting the knob open and pulling the door inside. "Malco..." Her sentence screeched to a sudden stop mid-word, his name quickly morphing into, "... oh shit!"

The air was suddenly sucked from her lungs as she stood in shock of who stood in her doorway. Georgie's face frozen, appearing her open mouth was ready to release a scream if her throat would only allow it.

Jay drew his finger to his lips displaying the common sign of "staying quiet." The whites around Jay's eyes grew more prevalent as he stepped across the threshold into Amy Jo's personal space as she slowly backed away from him.

"Amy Jo Whitenhour..." His gravelly voice quietly spilled her name from his lips like the slight sound of a hummingbird's wings whirring as it hovered over a succulent flower. "... it's—wonderful seeing you again. There's been—so much that has happened since—our last conversation." He twisted his face slightly over to Georgie. "Are you able to remain quiet and calm young lady?" He nodded his head up and down as if coaching her into answering the way he wanted her to.

"Are... are you... you're... not... not going to hurt... her... us... are you?" Georgie sheepishly quivered her words.

"I don't plan on doing any such thing, but it will, of course, depend on you and how you react. I was hoping to catch Amy Jo alone, so we could—catch up on—life—and things."

"I... I... can... I won't..." She looked over to her friend, Amy Jo. "... I won't scream or... or cause any... trouble."

Jay smiled. "That's a good girl. Please don't move unless you ask." He turned his attention back to Amy Jo. "Amy Jo, my sweet friend, you haven't changed a bit. Still as radiant as that first day I saw you sitting nervously with moist hands clasped together—prim and proper like the investigative reporter you were born to be."

"What are you doing here, Billy?"

"Oh, Amy Jo—please tell me we aren't back to that. You know my friends call me Jay and that I detest the name of my—my sperm donor of a father."

"Why are you here? Everyone thinks you're—you're dead. Maybe you should stay hidden in the shadows, so they keep thinking that?"

"Oh now, Amy Jo, those aren't the words I was expecting to hear from you when we saw each other again. You surely knew I wouldn't be able to leave things the way they—were ended for us—by—Warden Willy—did you?"

Amy Jo looked over at Georgie, concerned with how she was dealing with their predicament. The danger she'd unwittingly placed her in. The skin tone in Georgie's face had lightened to a shade that didn't fit her complexion. She appeared as frightened as the doe who'd just looked up in time to see the headlights bearing down upon her.

Amy Jo's stomach suddenly felt queasy as it twisted and rolled inside her gut. She knew this may not play out well for either of them. Georgie, or herself. The odd closeness she once shared with Billy Jay or the comparison of him to her grandfather was now long gone. All of those things had been filed away back in her mind's attic almost as soon as her book was turned over to her publisher. She was onto the next chapter in her story having placed the past part of her life deep into the recesses as lessons tried and learned. Apparently, Amy Jo hadn't taken all of those lessons learned as they needed to be. She found herself standing in front of the man who had felt like her teacher for a four-month class concerning murder, mayhem, and it's cause and repercussions. A teacher who had supposedly died at the hand of his next students in line. Fellow prisoners, men also responsible for horrible crimes against society and then captured, judged, and the sentence carried out. Sure, she'd certainly been fooled by his well-guised performances of compassion and caring. But now—now seeing him standing in front of her, uninvited in her home—she felt none of those past feelings of pity for his growing up under the fist and rule of the devil to whom he'd been born. She only felt the tremble of what may happen next to her friend and possibly her.

33

Joyce's first day couldn't have been any more difficult. Certainly, her boss had taken everything in great stride and shown compassion and care, but she really needed the comfort of her daughter now that it was over. What she didn't need was what awaited her. A lonely first night after this difficult first day. Now sitting alone in a low budget room equipped with dirty and depressing furniture, which was the only place she'd been able to afford. She pushed the door open and quickly closed it behind her as if someone might see what she'd lowered her standards to. She hadn't mentioned anything of her temporary accommodation to Mitzi or Darrell, knowing they would attempt to have her drive the hour and a half from Tallahassee back and forth to Apalachicola. No, she wouldn't be doing that. She could bear the month or two living like she'd just moved out from home after college before she'd found employment. It was a far cry from the rental she and Mitzi had moved into when they first arrived in Apalachicola. It was a more abrupt and mind-numbing change from the beach house she was forced to leave after finding out about Ethan's now apparent dark world he'd kept hidden from her.

She fell back onto the couch after turning on the small television that sat across from the coffee table. The table which apparently served as a hiding place for the palmetto that now scampered across the dusty floor. Her eyes attempted to tear up, but she fought them back and instead prayed for her world to be salvaged. She was strong and resilient. She wasn't new to starting over or the hell that always brought it on. She'd experienced many different flavors of the cause, but realized it always tasted as if the key ingredient were men. Joyce had felt every bit as lost when Roy didn't work out, and she was pregnant then. At least that wasn't the case this time. The difference back then being her parents were alive with open arms to give her refuge. Now, she just felt completely alone.

Joyce had felt hungry at the end of the day but now, as she sat completely drained, her hunger pangs seemed to have faded. The TV dinners in the freezer no longer appealed to her. She got up and walked over to the window to spread the drapes and let the last of the daylight in to aid in knocking away any of the depressing mood she'd slipped into. It was Monday evening and that had always brought the NBC Night at the Movies. Hopefully it would be a good one tonight. She reminisced about the days before Darrell when she and Mitzi would pop popcorn and spend the evening together on the couch watching. Now she thought about her family and how Katie was likely wobbling around in their living room vying for Mitzi B and Darrell's attention. She already missed them terribly. She wondered if Katie was old enough to understand the feeling of missing her. She settled into the couch by scooting her feet underneath her and pulling the thin blanket, that lay draped over the back, around her shoulders.

*****

THE CALL HOME

There were times in this life that Mitzi felt very connected to her mom. The two of them had been through so much together and alone. Mitzi never knew what life was like actually living with Roy. He'd left once he found out about her. He wasn't a kid-type person. He wasn't much of a person at all. She'd felt relief at finding out he wasn't really her father. The problem was that left her wondering who her father really was. Joyce had always claimed the only possible father was in fact Roy. He was the only man she'd ever slept with. There was a boyfriend back in high school, but that was long before Roy. Then after finding out about Ethan, it all began to make sense. The little sex games Ethan, Roy, and Charley Bingham played. Their sick little sex club of drugging girls and sharing them.

It made Mitzi sick to her stomach, but she'd accepted the only possibility of her birthfather was now Ethan. His interest in her and her mom and some statements overheard pretty much sealed the deal and closed that chapter in her life. Knowing how sexual of a person she was and how nonsexual her mother was—instilled the fact that Ethan was indeed her birthfather. It no longer was of interest with her. She had Darrell and Katie, but her mom, and the fact she was now mentally lost, alone, and over an hour and a half away, brought on the sting of missing her. She was worried too. She knew what she faced this morning and what she was going to talk to her new boss about.

Yes, this evening, she felt very connected but torn. She felt like she should drive up and spend the evening with her. Pull her into her arms and let her know she wasn't alone, and everything would sort out and get better. This too shall pass. While Darrell would tell her that wasn't a smart idea and that she needed to conquer some of this on her own, "Mitz! She's a sought-after paralegal who was headed to law school with Ethan. Please don't go—give her some space—call her." And he was likely right in the end. Instead, I'd go to the high school in the morning and see if I could drop my load of concerns off with our old counselor, Debbie. She was mine and Darrell's anchor when we were drifting out to sea with all the Billy Jay shit that was going down. *God, I'm glad that psycho is dead and gone.*

"Hello, Mom. How are you holding up?" Mitzi asked. "You worried me, four rings before you picked up. I was about ready to call the Tallahassee Police to do a well check."

"Oh, Mitzi B. Don't do that. I'm okay. The first day was a bit of a doozy, but Jim seems to be a caring and concerned boss. He's not a fan of Ethan, I can tell you. Of course, I guess I was about the only one of those besides his office admin, Addi, that was. Anyway, I survived today, and Jim says he will be glad to help me. There is something about him though. Something familiar. I guess it's because of all the circumstances I'm dealing with."

"What do you mean, Mom?"

"I can't put my finger on it. I guess maybe all these defense attorneys are built with similar genetics inside them. The way they hold themselves or the looks they carry across their faces. It's just—funny in a weird kind of way. But I'm doing fine now. I did stop and buy a bottle of wine after work and I'm getting ready to watch Monday Night at the Movies. I wish you were here to snuggle in like the old days." She quietly laughed.

"I hope it's a good one tonight. Don't watch if it's sad—or scary—or about love—or...."

"Hey, kiddo! You're whittling away all of my options!"

THE CALL HOME

"I love you, Momma. Katie, Darrell, and I miss you already. You can come back—you do know that don't you?"

There was an awkward silence and Mitzi swore she heard a muffled sigh. "Mitzi B, I'm the mom—you do remember that don't you? You're Katie's momma. I need to figure this out on my own. I know you love me. I know you and Darrell are gracious enough to put up with me if I need that, but...."

"I know, Mom. I just want you to know that you always have a home here. You've been the best mom ever and have trained me well by example. I just want you to know I love you and I'm thankful I was lucky enough to be yours."

"Now you are gonna make me cry, sweetheart. Seriously. I love you too. I'm so happy to see who you've become in spite of all the circumstances you were faced with. Hey, girl, my movie is starting."

"Okay, Mom. Call me if you need anything, okay?"

"You got my promise. Love you, and tell Darrell thank you for being who he is—and give that sweet little girl some lovin' from her grandma, okay?"

"You got it, Momma. Love you."

CLICK.

34

Addison lightly knocked on Ethan's office door as she slowly pushed it open. "Ethan—are you in here?"

"Addi, darling—what are you doing here so late?"

"I saw the light on as I left the Coffee Caper. I wasn't sure if you were still here, or maybe forgot and left your light on."

"I have this damn appearance in the morning, and I've just wrapped up the arguments. Would you like to share a libation with me?"

Addison Charmaine slowly sauntered over to his desk, putting her palms down on the top of it forcing her biceps to push her ample breasts tightly together billowing her cleavage out through the neckline of her shirt. "Is that all you have time to share tonight?" She batted her brown eyes and softly giggled, causing her breasts to jiggle.

"Oh, Lord, sweet Addi. You certainly do know how to entice an older gentleman attorney into becoming a bit of a younger at heart lumberjack." He grinned as he settled into his high back leather chair with his crotch suddenly stretching the pleats of his trousers tightly. "I just do not know how to refuse such an offer. The devil does hold my reigns, although he never seems to pull back on them in dismay."

THE CALL HOME

Addison kicked off her shoes and bounced around the desk as Ethan spun his chair to meet her jiggly bouncing body. "Addi, just when did you start wearing these absolutely ravishing outfits? Surely, I haven't been so blind and distracted as to not have noticed you before now?"

Addison's hands moved to Ethan's face and gently cupped it within her palms before she pulled his head towards her, pushing his cheeks tightly against her fleshy chest. "Ethan—I've been attempting to seduce you for years in my own quiet and less than confident ways. It just seems I hit the fortune of finding your penchant for my excellent office management skillset—finally!" Addi's hands moved slowly and methodically down his chest to his lap until she found the lumberjack's wooden axe handle and lightly gripped it.

Ethan's groans quickened as his thrusts became more focused toward a finale. His brow wet with perspiration, his heart pounding out a rhythm that would challenge even a much younger man than he. He opened his eyes to see Addison's breast rotating in tethered circles around her chest as her back lay on the walnut desk, her legs open and jiggling and then tightening firm between thrusting towards him and then momentarily relaxing, matching her lover's cadence. She squealed and then screamed just before Ethan's forward movements abruptly stopped. His entire body fell limp as he grabbed for his chest and then tightened back up as if clinching in sharp pain. Their eyes locked briefly before Ethan's red face tightened in a painful grimace then fading into a ghostly pale white. He clutched his chest hard with his right hand as he released Addi's soft side, attempting to grip the slick finish of the desktop as he fell to his knees, mouth open and eyes quivering like a cockroach's legs in his last moments of life.

Addi pulled herself up to a seated position in surprised shock as she attempted to peek over the edge of the desk to spy what had just happened. Her moist flesh now relaxed and shaking as the reality of the situation became apparent. Ethan was suffering a heart attack. *Have I killed the man I finally succeeded in attaining?*

*****

An hour later, Addison found herself in the ER waiting room of Weems Memorial Hospital, pacing back and forth praying Ethan would survive and not hold her responsible. She was very antsy and tried not to replay the moment over and over as she fought the memory of seeing the look of frightened pain spread across his face while he gasped for air. It was horrible. It was nothing he deserved and then again everything he likely deserved. She wasn't foolish enough to believe he was a man of innocence in any sense of the word. She knew he'd not only saved wicked perpetrators of horrible crimes from due reprimand, but he also was responsible for a multitude of illegalities himself. She'd heard all the rumors of the private club he and friends had started. Phuck-House. Supposedly a hidden party room at Ethan's beach home where they would entice young high school girls out and drug them before doing unnatural things to them. Paying them off to keep quiet if any memories returned, which was seldom. She'd been abhorred herself at the quiet whispers shared at the Piggly Wiggly or coffee shop between women likely curious of such lewd things. Or possibly out of anger over losing a case or jealousy of his money and power. But now, after finally experiencing him... well... she felt her face redden as she continued to pace, thinking about what

THE CALL HOME

had happened. He was inside of me sharing pleasure like I—and then....

She felt horrible thinking of such things at a time like this. She was so confused and conflicted. She also mixed in thoughts of how this would all play out in town. In the paper. Would her name be in print if he lived or—died? Would anyone else show up here at the hospital? His two best friends were already gone. Charley and Roy. And Joyce? Did she care enough about him still to come see him?

She hoped not. It was a selfish thought, but she still didn't want to ever see her again. She was glad she'd heard the talk of Joyce leaving town. Who would get his beach house if he died? What would become of the firm? Her job? She had to push these thoughts from her mind. He would be okay. They would be together again. Someday, a long time from now, it would all be hers. Someday. Not yet though. He's such a great lover.

"Ms. Addison Charmane." A nurse called out. Addison turned sharply and saw a doctor had just pushed his way through the swinging door and was headed to the front desk of the nurse's station. Addison quickly and nervously rushed over to answer her page.

"Yes, I'm Addison Charmane. How is Mr. Kendricks? Tell me he's going to be fine, please...."

"Doctor Talbert is... oh, Doctor Talbert, this is Ms. Charmane, I was just about to tell her you wanted to see her."

"Ms. Charmane, I'm Dr. John Talbert, the heart doctor that has been assigned to Mr. Kendricks. Can you follow me to the consultation room please?"

"Yes, yes of course, but—he's going to be alright, isn't he?"

"He is stable right now, but let's talk in private. Does he have any family or are you able to help with medical decisions?"

"I'm not family, but..."

"Does Mr. Kendricks have family close?"

"Ethan has no family. I'm his admin assistant at his firm and friend for... well... for my entire career... years." Addi's face became fixed on Doctor Talbert's, concern washed across her eyes like a tidal wave of fear. "This is sounding... um... serious. Is Ethan going to live? I have some... um... some... feelings... some guilt... I mean... we... we... were...." Addi's words stumbled from her lips. She didn't want to tell the doctor what they were doing, but she wanted him to know in case it would help with his treatment. "... we were... we were making love when... things became... they were just awful... Doctor. I thought he was... was dying right there with me... under—him."

"He's going to live, Ms. Charmane. I'm confident of that. Nitroglycerin is a... vasodilator... or in short... expands the blood vessels which helps with the angina pectoris, or chest pain. Mr. Kendricks has some arterial blockage. He is going to need a stent inserted, possibly a bypass. We won't know for certain until we can get him into surgery. He is stable and free from the chest pain he was suffering at present."

"Oh Lord. Surgery? Is this... dangerous?"

"There are always risks involved, but in order to stop the atherosclerosis, a disease process that clogs the coronary arteries, I'm confident a stent will be adequate along with some changes in eating habits and of course alcohol consumption which can stretch the heart muscle from alcohol-induced cardiomyopathy."

"Ethan practically survives on bourbon. He's an attorney with stress. I'm afraid he wouldn't be able to stop drinking. He's probably a functioning alcoholic."

THE CALL HOME

"Like I stated Ms. Charmane, Ethan will need to have therapy after the stent or stents—and make some major life changes if he doesn't want to be back here again. This is very serious. I believe we can help him recover from this, but it will take efforts on his part to do so."

"So, how soon will he be in surgery?"

"I'd like to schedule him for first thing in the morning."

"Please take care of him, Doctor Talbert. I love him. I'll do my best to help him recoup on my end any way I can." She looked up at Doctor Talbert with serious eyes. "Can I see him now?"

*****

"Ethan—sweetheart, how are you feeling?"

Ethan turned and opened his eyes slowly, "Joyce?" He asked.

"It's me, Ethan, Addison. Do you remember what happened?"

"Oh, Addi, I'm sorry... I... I'm kind of... I... I think I've had... too much... too much to drink tonight."

Addison smiled at him, slightly hurt he'd called out Joyce's name, but she moved in and kissed his lips lightly. She dodged the oxygen tube dangling from his nostrils. "You're in the hospital, Ethan. Do you remember anything?"

A hollow emptiness washed across his face as he appeared to struggle searching his memory for what she asked. "Addi—sweetheart—I'm in the hospital?"

"Yes, Ethan, you were taken here by ambulance. You and I were up in your office... together... do you... do you not remember what we were doing?"

A slight smile stretched his lips wider as he appeared to recollect at least some of what had been happening. Addison smiled and began to blush a bit.

"I remember you... you... I was... you and I were...."

"Yes, Ethan, we were making love in your office, and you suffered a heart attack...."

His face became puzzled. "A heart... heart attack?"

"Yes, Ethan, you scared the hell out of me!"

"Did I... did I at least... wait til you finished?" A smile crept across his mouth, cheek to cheek.

Addi lightly tapped her fist on his bicep. "Ethan William Kendricks! I thought you were dying! I... I... thought... I'd killed you. Don't be a fucking comedian now! We're gonna get you fixed up and then you have some life changes to make. I don't wanna lose you. You're everything to me."

Ethan stared at her. "Life changes?"

Addi leaned in close, "Yes, Ethan, life changes. I don't want tonight to be the last time you're inside me. You have to take better care of yourself."

"Changes like... like what?"

"Like all of that bourbon you pour down your throat! You need to learn to practice moderation."

"Oh, for crying out loud, Addi. You can't teach an old dog new tricks. I was hoping you'd snuck a bottle of my finest here from the office! I need a quick snort." He grinned.

"You are a tiresome mess, Ethan." She leaned down again and whispered. "Surely you can get used to just fucking me whenever you're thirsty for a double? I'm better exercise for your heart too." She ran her hand down the topside of the sheet he lay under until she felt a slight movement. "See? You're already improving." Addi grinned wickedly.

THE CALL HOME

"Is there anything you need me to take care of at your home? I locked up the office tight."

"Will I be here for long?"

"Surgery in the morning. That's all I know."

"The keys are in my pants pocket. Feel free to stay there. Help yourself as if it's yours, and Addi—thank you, sweetheart."

Addi looked into Ethan's eyes and smiled. "I'll take care of everything. You concentrate on getting well." Her hand cupped his as she leaned in and kissed his forehead. I'll be here in the morning before you go into surgery."

"I suppose I'll be here, unless I break out and go back to the office for a nightcap."

"Damn it, Ethan, remember what I said." She reached back and patted the sheet where a lumberjack keeps his wooden axe. "See you in the morning."

35

"Hello, Mitzi! What a great surprise!"

"Hello, Mrs. Thomas."

"Mitzi, you're not a student anymore, you graduated, honey, it's Debbie to you now, young lady." She smiled.

"Okay, Debbie." Mitzi giggled. "That just feels strange, calling you by your first name!"

"It feels a little strange knowing that one of my favorite students is now practically married and has a baby girl! Of which, I am very happy for you and Darrell." Debbie stepped in and hugged Mitzi. "So, what brings you here today?"

Mitzi's head dropped just a little sending signs that a school counselor would be privy to seeing and understanding it wasn't just a cordial visit. "Mrs. Thomas—I mean, Debbie, I have some slight worries in my life and... and... I always felt very comfortable with talking to you...."

"Mitzi, feel free to come see me anytime! I'm just a school counselor and not a licensed therapist or psychologist, but I'm a friend that is always available to have you bounce things off of. I'm glad you feel comfortable talking to me. I certainly miss seeing you in the hallways and in my office. We shared some kind of crazy times, didn't we?"

"Yes, we did. I don't really have anything in particular about me, it's my mom that I'm worried about. I guess in a way, it's other people's troubles that are weighing in on me. And the occasionally wondering if my birthfather is Ethan Kendricks." She nervously smiled to hide the things that were gnawing at her.

"Speaking of Ethan, I heard some information through the grapevine this morning. I'm a little hesitant to share it with you, but—I also think I probably should."

"If you tell me that you got hold of a blood test of his and can tell me for certain if he's my father or not—I guess I'd want to know one way or the other." Mitzi sidestepped on her legs back and forth as she slipped each hand into a jean pocket anxiously. "Is that it?" Her eyes searched Debbie's with intensity.

"No, Mitzi. Maybe we should sit for a moment." She pulled out a chair from her round table where they'd sat before when Mitzi and Darrell met with Principal Bingham and her. Mitzi slowly meandered over and hesitated before she decided to sit. She scooted into the table's edge as Debbie did the same. Mitzi blankly stared at the wall of previous years of students that filled the long-painted cinder block expanse.

Debbie drew Mitzi's attention when she reached over and cupped Mitzi's hands with hers. It was a gesture that brought a tone of seriousness immediately. The air in the room seemed to change its consistency from light and airiness into a thick and heavy fog. All with just a human touch of her palms enclosing Mitzi's hands, instantly warming them. Again, it wasn't a warmth that felt entirely welcoming. It felt more like it was an act of calming tensions before they had the chance to rise. The pictures of students quickly blurred into each other and were instantly unrecognizable. Even if it was last year's grouping she'd been concentrating on.

"There's no other way to start other than just put it out there for you to take in. I'm not sure how this will make you feel and again, I had no intention of being the one to tell you, but I guess in retrospect, I'm glad I am since you are so comfortable with me and—since your mother is now in Tallahassee—isn't she?"

"Um—yes. She... um... she left Saturday so she could be ready to start her job with Jim Bollard, the attorney she just started with yesterday."

"Jim Bollard—that name seems familiar—anyway, since she isn't here to be the one to tell you, I suppose it's better coming from me in this setting than hearing it at the coffee shop like I did, or God forbid, Piggly Wiggly or the gas station." She tried to smile warmly, but again, the gesture felt out of place and uncomfortable.

"Just spit it out, Mrs. Thom... I mean... Debbie... sorry... but, you're beginning to freak me out."

Debbie's hands squeezed Mitzi's a bit tighter as she let out a sigh before continuing, "Ethan Kendricks suffered a heart attack last night at his office. He... he... was taken to Weem's Memorial by ambulance and is undergoing surgery this morning. Probably as we speak. At least one stent is expected is what I heard."

Mitzi's eyes remained steady like the cemented orbs of a statue. Not so much as a tremor. A moment or two slipped by, only broken by the sound of the second hand clicking one tick as the hand jumped from segment to segment. She hadn't noticed the sound before hearing the news, but now it became thunderous. A quake began in the toes inside her shoes before it worked its way up her feet and through her ankles, growing stronger and more visible until it shook at her shoulders in a very noticeable eruptive tremble. It was as if it were hot lava being cast from her interior. She sucked air with an audible gasp until she couldn't absorb another wisp of air into her lung cavity and then she slowly let it back out with a quiet hiss as if a balloon had formed a tiny hole. "I wish he would have fucking died right there. A wretched tormenting death that burned like a thousand matches being lit at one time, scorching his skin, and stinking of sulfur." Her head dropped as her hands pulled away from Debbie's like a snake slithering under a small crevice at the edge of the table.

*****

In all her years as a high school counselor, Debbie had never experienced a reaction quite like Mitzi's. And she'd seen a lot. Loud screams of denial when one student was caught smoking marijuana in the restroom. Another's loud and threatening outburst when a student was accused of touching a female student inappropriately, cursing so loud it could be heard throughout the first floor while grabbing the security officer and wrestling him down to the ground after a fight was broken up in front office. Yes, Debbie Thomas had seen a lot in her tenure, but Mitzi's reaction came out of nowhere much like quiet water being drawn to a boil and then abruptly becoming ice without any plausible explanation. Debbie wasn't sure how to react. Afterall, Mitzi was no longer a student. She was a friend.

"Mitzi—" Debbie quietly and calmly called out in close to a whisper. "Are you okay?" She waited a few seconds. "Is there anything I can do or say?" No response other than hearing Mitzi breathe as she stared at the wall of photos blankly as if she never heard a word spoken to her.

Debbie watched as Mitzi's blank stare flashed to a look of curiosity. It drove Mitzi to abruptly standing and then quickly walk towards the wall, her attention completely swallowed by something there. She stood in front of the photos of the class of

1950. Several seconds went by and before Debbie could make her way over beside her. Mitzi turned and simply stated, "Oh my God! I've got to call my mom."

36

Detective Tony Rawlings strolled down the boardwalk and upon finding a bench overlooking the pier, sat back on it. He relaxed and rested, taking in the mixture of sun and partial shade. It was almost homey. A quiet little spot barely off the path and shielded by the scorching sun's rays by two long-reaching limbs from a giant Live Oak tree. He'd seen the Tanner House quietly perched above the boardwalk and across the street behind where he sat. He imagined it being like a hungry wolf staring at him as if he were its next victim, waiting patiently for the correct moment to attack. Stalking and planning his attack. His guilt began flooding over him. He couldn't make himself turn around and look behind and up to the second-floor apartment on the left. That was the place that changed his world forever. Merely the brief gaze at the front door of the apartment on his way to the bench, which remained closed as it had been, caused his right hand to quiver while he mentally replayed the moment shots had rung out. He swore he felt the heated singe of his bloodied appendix just as it had burned that day as the bullet entered. Tony's wrist shook ever so slightly, but the tremor was there and noticeable. The sight of it forced his eyes to track down and observe his trigger finger, mentally daring it to show even one sign of quaking. His stare brought the coolness of the handgun's steel straight to the bone just from its memory in his grip. Had Chief Finney been right? Tony silently asked himself. *Was I too close to the case to be safe and effective?* Those were thoughts that quickly followed. He began to wonder if what he was doing was indeed too risky. Was it worth losing his badge over? What about Hank? Would his partner praise him or not be able to forgive him if he'd been right about Billy Jay returning and he ended up killing him. Not in self-defense, but twisted into that for the cost of taking his partner's life?

The devastating memory of that awful day began to play out once more in his mind no matter how much he attempted to squelch it in its tracks. He could see the look on Sam's face as clear as vodka in a glass as he quietly closed in on Billy's front door. He knelt poised and at the ready, waiting to hear the whistle of a bird call, the sign for all clear. Both knew all hell could break loose at any time. It was part of the price paid for being a detective. One never knew for sure which way it would go on attempts to question a possible perp on their own home turf. Especially a suspect to be questioned about a law enforcement officer being murdered.

Tony could almost feel the wind blow over his shoulder the same as that day he squatted down next to the window at Billy's upstairs apartment in the Tanner House. He carefully peeked in as the light breeze quietly billowed the drapes, parting them inward into the room and allowing a partial unrestricted view of its interior. It had appeared empty, but no bird call had been made yet. And then—there it was, the whistled tune of a non-specific Aves that sounded slightly out of the ordinary. He'd felt a quick breath of relief. The sign signaled that all was quiet and clear.

THE CALL HOME

BAM! BAM! Two quick bursts of gunfire followed by another loud BANG! The last had brought an instant burn to Tony's side. Things went from quiet to chaos without warning.

The third shot had zinged through the curtains of the open window and quickly dropped Tony to his side. He could remember the details although he wasn't positive the sequence was exactly as it had always replayed. He was told by the department's shrink that the human brain can twist these memories to help mend any mental torment after a traumatic event. Tony had played the game of answering any questions the way Ms. Wallace, the head shrink, would want to hear them, but he thought it was all mojo monkey bullshit. It had gotten inside his head and made him question, though. This had always pissed him off. He was fine and he did remember Billy Jay rounding the corner where his partner still lay dead to any movement. Likely the results of unwittingly catching lead from the first two rounds he heard being fired.

Tony tried to push the memory back watching his partner raise the barrel of his revolver to take his shot at Billy Jay once he passed over him. He refused to relive the visual of Billy Jay turning and executing Sam, not allowing the memory to guilt his eyes again. He slumped back onto the bench where he sat. Out of breath, even though he'd been sitting idle for several minutes. It felt as if he had just returned from a past that should never have happened. A nightmare. That's when he felt it. Chief Finney and his partner Hank were both wrong. He not only should be here to avenge his partner, but he had to be. He owed it to Sam's wife and son, Jason. He by God, owed it to Sam. Maybe his conscience would allow him a reprieve from the guilt if he could only bring Billy Jay back to face the death sentence he'd been judged, convicted, and sentenced to. But would he allow himself to leave it to a system that had already failed at dealing out that justice once?

Tony sighed and again washed his thoughts away by staring out across the expanse to the pier. Making note of others doing their daily tasks of whittling away time. All of which was what had actually brought him here to begin with this morning, killing time and relaxing—and of course—waiting.

It wasn't long before he noticed a woman who appeared to be in her late forties or maybe mid-fifties slowly walking towards him. She stopped and hesitated several times as if she were a bit confused or possibly lost. He turned occasionally to see if she was still moving his way. She looked attractive from his vantage point. Thin but shapely, nicely dressed in a light blue and white cotton dress that screamed summer was here.

Tony didn't really care too much for most people, but he always had felt drawn to observe attractive ones, watching their actions from a distance. Surveilling people was a trained skill, but he'd always naturally loved watching people from an early age. He also enjoyed seeing the coast, even if it were only boggy-like bay water. Put beautiful female bodies scantily clad with sand and water in the background—well, he could retire to a place like that. Not this one. This little one-horse town held bad mojo, besides the view this place sported wasn't really what came to mind when he thought of going to an ocean or a beach. This was more like big lakes up to the northwest. There wasn't much motion of rolling waves or surf; no children playing in the water's edge, or any sun worshippers laid out sunning half-naked bodies stretched across towels. Much too much fear of a gator leaping from the water to taste what wandered too close to shore. Only the movement of fishing poles dipping and rising oddly in and out of sync with each other along the sides of the pier as they cast lines over the wooden rails. The water below, almost dead calm. Instead of the surf, only the sounds of the wind brushing fishing boat cables and gear that

THE CALL HOME

clanked out in brief hollers calling for business so they could motor from the boring slip. Restless and ready to be captained out to sea.

Tony turned and looked behind him once more, acknowledging the Tanner House, but choosing not to stare, and instead, he purposely steered his thoughts to Terri Duncan, the beautiful cop who'd somehow ended up picking him out of the bar crowd and going home with him the night he drank himself to a trashed state. He imagined she now wondered why he'd felt the need to leave on vacation within days of meeting her. He'd probably left her thinking he was like the typical guy, skating out on any possibility of a relationship. But that wasn't the case with him this time. Of course, he hadn't given her the full story. With her also being a part of the police department that had just forbade him to do exactly what he was now doing; he didn't know how to tell her about the guilt he felt with the joy in meeting her. He wanted to tell her that those last few nights sleeping with her had him questioning himself for the first time since his divorce and that he may have the feelings of actually falling in love with her. But not now, not with what he was responsible for. Sam's widow now having no one to do the same with her. He wasn't ready to talk too much about all the baggage he still carried closely and heavily protected, as if it were a treasure instead of a sentence condemning guilt. He was sure she'd heard some of the gossip anyway. All the talk about how his partner he'd lost in a gunfight and all because he placed him at the door where Billy Jay shot and killed him first, with no time to react. He couldn't explain how his dead partner had left behind a wife and young son because of a choice he'd made in laying out the failed tactic they'd used. How could any fellow law officer allow themselves to trust and put themselves in their care for any kind of real relationship after failing their partner so badly? He definitely couldn't talk about Chief Finney removing him from the case that wasn't really even a case anymore. Nor could he share the fact the chief was forcing him to take time off in order to cool down and recollect his thoughts and take control of the emotions he was trying to drown in alcohol instead of seeking the help of therapy. He couldn't tell her he had basically gone rogue now and was retracing the scene of the crime in hopes Billy Jay would pop back up so he could get redemption for himself under the guise of being there for his partner. He could of course, preach the fact he was a good cop—but he couldn't deny he was also chocked full of so much mental despair that he was unsure any woman could or would ever be willing to deal with him once the true Tony was revealed. This entire thing now had him questioning if he was even a good cop anymore, or ever was? Or had he become a dangerous individual who was hellbent on curing his own mental anguish through catching and rehanging the devil who'd somehow had escaped justice? Had he himself become a version of Billy Jay Cader? Justifying his vigilantism by any means possible? Judging and convicting others by his own set of rules with his own way of doling out the punishment?

Tony was battling these twisted rationales woven together into the loosely knitted mental mess he'd become aware was encasing him. Dominating his thoughts to the point of leaving himself too entrenched to see in front of his own nose. He came back from his lack of attention just in time to notice the woman who appeared lost, was now just a few yards from him. She was still moving rather willy-nilly and slow in his general direction, and she did appear very odd compared to any of the others within his sight. But it was tourist season and Apalachicola held some attractions that drew all kinds of tourists who loved to flock to the otherwise quiet spot as compared to other Gulf Coast towns.

"Do you know you're sitting on the bench where I met my husband."

Tony looked up and the woman he'd been watching was somehow now standing directly at his side. His eyes were immediately drawn to her shapely curves normally hidden beneath the sky-blue and white linen sundress that was now boldly pressed against her body with the assistance from the airy breeze blowing down the hill.

He instantly questioned himself. How can I call myself a good detective after letting this beautiful older woman just meander right up on me without my noticing? But he smiled and slightly shook his head to himself before answering. "Sounds like a story you're wanting to share, ma'am." He slid to the opposite edge of the bench and gave her a flirtatious wink, only because her attractiveness drove him to act like a typical man before consideration. "You can sit if you like—and of course, don't mind sharing the bench seat with me."

She smiled and turned to sit. After getting comfortable, she sighed under her breath, never turning to meet his eyes. She folded her hands and placed them on her lap after resting her purse on the ground beside her. "I used to like to meet new people and chit-chat."

Tony grinned to himself. "Used to?" He questioned.

"Why yes, now-a-days, I don't get out too often. I live over with the Reverend Watkins and his wife, Gloria. They say I had an accident and now I can't always remember things right. But I remember I used to like to talk to new people. And I met my husband right here, right where you are sitting."

"Where's he at? You're still married, right?"

She nodded her head quietly and remained looking out towards the fishing pier. Quiet as if she were mulling the questions over inside. Tony had just about written off getting an answer and was actually thinking about getting up and walking up to the Tanner House to face the taunting wolf that still remained sitting on the hill above, but she slowly turned to him and broke the uncomfortable silence that had lingered between them.

"You know, I don't really know where he is. He's been gone quite a while. Billy Jay was a good man for a few years, but something changed inside him and—and—I don't know where he went. He ran. He took one of the people I loved most and left me here alone." She attempted to force a quiet smile across her lips, but Tony could sense a painful past that had a strong hold clutching onto her from her own shadows, trapped within her somber words. "Life can be funny like that, don't you think? Kind of odd how people just—just change sometimes." She finished with a hush and looked back to the pier as if the question she'd asked didn't really have an answer or any need for one. It's only purpose to be words filling the void between her thoughts. Merely sprinkled about like a peppery seasoning to ease a gentle segue into the next topic.

"What's your name by the way, if you don't mind me asking." The woman questioned.

"Ma'am, my name is Tony Rawlings. I'm on a bit of a vacation break. What's your name, are you from around here?"

"Catrina Anne Cader, but my friends always call me, Cat."

Tony felt a chill blow through him as if a cold breeze came up from the salty water and surrounded him whole, straight to his bones while bypassing the skin and meat.

Cat turned back to Tony and smiled. "It's nice to meet you, Tony Rawlings. I hope you enjoy your time of relaxation. Every man needs a bit of that, I believe. Don't you?"

"Yes, ma'am, Ms. Cader." The name soured as it slowly crossed over his tongue. All he could think of, was the burning question, was this woman Billy Jay's wife.

"You can call me Cat. Can I call you Tony?"

"Why yes, yes you can, Cat. Tell me about this missing husband of yours."

She turned away from the pier and again looked at Tony. Focused deep into his eyes and drew a breath. Tony felt as if one hell of a story could possibly spill out onto his lap. He also felt an odd attraction that she seemed to radiate towards him.

"Well..." Cat paused, Tony watched her profile, examining her eyes and mouth for any telltale signs as if he were interviewing a suspect in the interrogation room. "I guess the start of a story is always best from the beginning, isn't it?" She turned and smiled. "It's quite a long tale, are you sure you have the time?"

"On this beautiful day, ma'am, here on my first full day of resting and relaxing, Cat—I have all the time in the world. And if not today, there is always tomorrow." He couldn't believe what he was saying. Was she getting to him, or was his hunger to find her husband's possible whereabouts—taking control to the point he would use her to get to him?

Cat's shoulders rose and fell as if it were a sign of excitement that he would take the time to talk to her. He never gave any clue of why he really had such an interest in her husband. He just returned her smile and said, "Yes, the beginning is always the best."

Cat began as if she'd scheduled this chat like an appointment with a therapist. She appeared to be comfortable with Tony from the moment she'd sat down. "I met Billy Jay right here. On this exact bench. He was such an interesting mess of a human soul. Hungry and lost looking, much like a rain-soaked puppy needing a new friend." She nestled in as if the bench gave her a familiar feeling of home. Her eyes lit up, and then dimmed slightly. "Oh, have I already mentioned this? I get forgetful sometimes these days."

"No, no, Cat, you just take your time and I'll let you know if I've heard something already. How long ago did you meet him? Your Billy, that is."

"Oh, it seems like such a long time ago now. We have a son, Darrell, he's... let me see... I think... hmmm... he just got out of school not too long ago. Darrell is nineteen, I think. And he's my youngest. Billy James was four years older, so...."

"*Was* four years older?" Tony asked as he leaned forward and rested his elbows on his kneecaps, turning to look into Cat's eyes.

The tone in Cat's voice began to change as she started to answer him. "Yes—Billy James was older than Darrell Lee." She pulled her purse up from beside her and opened it, digging through until she pulled a hanky up and dabbed her eyes before sniffing and touching it to her nostrils. "Billy James is gone. Such a long time ago now. I surely do miss him. I can still picture his sweet face. But... but I... I just can't remember what his precious voice... sounded... like... I try. I try really hard to search the shadows and corners of my mind—and put the sound—to the picture I see when I close my eyes, but—." She sniffed and lightly touched the handkerchief to her face again. "I'm sorry, Tommy. I just get teary-eyed when I think of my oldest boy and how he left this world. It was... it was just... just horrible." She turned and Tony could see the glimmer leave, taking the sparkle away from her blue eyes that were likely once very dazzling and brilliant. He tried to picture her face 20 years younger.

"I'm sorry, Cat, I... I didn't mean to...."

"Oh, it's okay Tommy. How would you have known and how could I tell the story without talking about him?"

"I hate to correct you, but I want you to know whom you're talking to, ma'am. My name is Tony, you've called me Tommy now twice. Was there a Tommy in your life at one time?"

Cat looked up towards the puffy clouds and a sternness entered her expression for a moment before she brought her focus from the sky back to Tony. "My father's name was Tommy. Tommy Wayne Dobbyn. I'm sorry. I guess you kind of remind me of him. I miss him on sunny days like this."

"Is he still alive?"

"No, no he is not. I was told he died when he attempted to stop a robbery here in town at the Gibson Inn. A young man only twenty-five. I was only twenty-three when the young robber shot and killed my father. Daddy was a police officer across the bridge in Eastpoint."

"I'm sorry Cat. That must have been a difficult thing to understand and accept at that age."

"He wasn't even on duty. Momma said he'd stopped at the Gibson Inn to get a room for her and my father as a surprise because they'd been fighting." She began to frown. "She disappeared not long after the funeral. It turns out she hadn't really been trying to surprise my father..." She looked into Tony's eyes. "And he didn't really believe the young man was robbing the place. It seems the two, my mother and the man, were having an affair. My father, Tommy, suspected something was going on and barged into their room. Room 213...."

Tony's eyes widened and Cat must have noticed. "Room 213 at the Gibson Inn?" Tony questioned, hardly believing the coincidence of it all. Tony was a cop who didn't believe in coincidence.

"Why yes, why?"

He wasn't sure if he should answer or just change the subject nonchalantly. He thought a moment and then surmised, what the hell have I got to lose? What difference would it make. He somehow believed Cat either didn't know Billy Jay's whereabouts—or she was playing some kind of a crazy game with him and the peculiar way she portrayed herself. "Well," He began. "You're either going to think I'm lying or believe this is somehow some kind of divine control over us meeting here today."

An expression of confusion lay ruffled across her face like a veil made of tulle had been laid over to conceal something. "What do you mean, Tommy... I... I mean... Tony?"

Even her question matched her look. He just couldn't define if it were true uncertainty—or manufactured. "I mean, Cat—I'm staying in Room 213 at the Gibson Inn—and..." He kind of let a nervous snicker escape before continuing, "...and, you won't believe this, but I'm also a cop..." He uncrossed his leg to let the blood begin to move back through as the discomfort suddenly agitated him. "I'm actually in Apalachicola for a reason. A very specific reason. I'm breaking command in doing so." He hesitated. "I'm looking for an escaped convict. One who may not even be alive." Tony had no reasonable explanation why he'd just revealed all of these things to the woman he'd just met, but in all truth, it gave him a feeling of solace. He shook his head slightly as if doing so gave a path to an explanation. Which it didn't. All he knew was that he wasn't supposed to be here, he'd somehow stumbled into the wife of Billy Jay, the man he was looking for. And now—well, now all of this bizarre shit was encircling him like buzzards flying overhead, impatiently waiting for the stench of death to call them in for the feast. And here he sat on the same bench she'd met Billy Jay some twenty years ago, below the

THE CALL HOME

Tanner House, where he'd been bushwhacked by this woman's husband. *What in fuck are the odds on that?* Tony thought. "This town is batshit crazy ain't it?" He asked Cat before he could catch that big fish and reel it back in.

    Cat turned as if to answer him. But any words he would have given dollars and donuts to hear—just lay hollow and silent, trapped on Catherine Anne Cader's lips.

37

Mitzi turned and faced Debbie as she stood looking back from Apalachicola High's wall of alumni. She appeared pale white, at least three shades lighter than mere seconds ago.

"Mitzi? Are you okay? You look like you've just seen a ghost."

"Do you see this school class of 1950, Mrs. Thomas?"

Debbie moved towards Mitzi's side and pulled her glasses down to the tip of her nose as she squinted and peered over the top of the rims. She maneuvered her eyes quickly at first across every face but began to slow down as she caught notice of Charlie Bingham's photograph. She felt a sudden sadness as she remembered part of his remains being found all the way up at Alligator Point. A chill passed over her. Goosebumps formed and traveled up her arms. She continued to pass over the black and white faces of each kid, taking notice of Roy Burks photo briefly as she scanned. So many horrible recent events involving several classmates from this graduation year. After thinking of how Roy had perished that night and what had happened to another pair of favorite recent graduates, Kyle and Vio. She kept dragging her finger over each photo in the same manner until she stopped once more. This time her nail rested on Ethan Kendricks' photo. He was a handsome boy—even back then, she thought to herself. That's when it hit her. It was like a streak of lightning way out in the distance. The kind of summer heat-lightning you watched as the multiple bolts feather out like tree roots dug into the black sky, enjoying the scene knowing it's so far away that you're safe from its reach. And then, out of nowhere—the loud sharp crack of the thunder you weren't expecting. The jolt hits you as hard as a blind-sided punch to your stomach, jarring your conscience enough to retain that tiny speck of a memory to retrace what you'd just been shocked into remembering.

Mitzi stood quietly as if stunned into silence as Debbie's finger touched the first image in the framed grouping, Margaret Daisy Anderson. She began the labor of slowly tracing her finger again over each picture but this time she mentally read the students' names as she studied their faces more closely. Becky Barnes, Gregory Bassett, Charley Bingham, Salley Bixler, Sue Anne Bixler… That's when she stopped in the queue. Debbie's finger touching the face of a name she'd somehow seen before but forgotten, yet recently heard it again. James T. Bollard, or Jim. The name and image rang a mental bell. She'd seen him in the paper. He'd defended some slime-ball up in Tallahassee. He was a defense attorney along with Ethan Kendricks. James's picture showed a smug smile that emanated full blown entitlement. He wore the look of an attorney even in his senior picture. His pinstriped suit coat and wide dark necktie. She had an instant distaste for him. Her shoulder rolled to her left where Mitzi still stood, just a hand reach away.

"See, Mrs. Thomas! How can that be? My mom has no idea that Ethan and Jim were classmates—I just know it! She's in the middle of a damn snake pit waiting to get bit but has no clue of the danger awaiting!"

"What do you mean, Mitzi? I'll admit it's quite a coincidence. A small class of fifteen that year and having two of them become attorneys and practice law in towns only an hour and a half apart. I would think they'd surely bumped into each other in court occasionally, but snake pit?" Debbie asked.

"Mrs. Thomas...."

"It's Debbie, Mitzi."

Mitzi put her hands on her hips and responded, "Debbie—that's not what I'm thinking about..." She lifted her hands and opened them out in front of her in a jerky motion. "Don't you get it?"

"What am I missing, Mitzi?"

"I'll bet they were close friends. Look at them and then look at the others in the photos. One doesn't look anything like the other. Ethan and Jim both look like birds of the same feather. Rich little spoiled shits. They both already wear the appearance of wealthy attorneys before even graduating. Of course, they hung out together." She sighed as if she couldn't believe that Debbie wasn't catching on. "Ethan is an oversexed dirtbag. He possibly killed two women in Springfield, Missouri." She stopped instantly.

"What are you talking about, Mitzi? Ethan killed who? Where?"

Mitzi's face turned another shade paler. "I forgot I haven't told you any of this. My mom and I think we figured out who my birth father is. None other than Ethan William Kendricks...."

"What? How did you come to this conclusion?"

"It's a long story, Mrs.—I mean, Debbie." Mitzi smiled briefly. "I'm never getting used to calling you Debbie, Mrs. Thomas."

"So, Ethan may be your father? I'd heard Joyce and he were possibly seeing each other, and I knew she worked for him, but...."

"I know, it's crazy—and it gets sick. Like makes your stomach queasy kind of sick. Disturbing, disgusting, and perverted stuff."

And he may be your father? I mean..." She shook her head and then grabbed Mitzi's arms. "... What can I do to help? I'm... I'm at a loss."

Mitzi looked at Debbie and shrugged. "I have no idea, but I know my momma needs to know they at least knew each other back then. My mom is working for Jim Bollard now and has dumped a load of Ethan problems on him on her first day because I pushed her to."

Debbie saw the whites of Mitzi's eyes grow larger. "What Mitzi?"

"What if Ethan and Jim are still friends and he wants to protect Ethan from all of this?"

"What? Mitzi! You have me completely baffled with what you are inferring? I'm lost!"

"I need to call my mom—now! She could be in danger!"

38

Jim Bollard wasn't expecting to hear a story like the one Joyce Bonham told him—the poor damsel in distress, was what came instantly to mind. He'd heard nothing about any of this. *Was it true Ethan was possibly keeping something from him?*

Jim let a less than friendly smile drift across his face. While it's true he desperately needed help in his law office, he had found very special humor in "snatching" Joyce out from under him, so-to-speak. It was also true he'd instantly found Joyce to be very attractive and never understood how Roy Burks could have ever persuaded such a woman to marry him. Even now when he thought of those two paired together and twisted up naked like a pair of pretzels into one—it sent shivers up his spine and the need to vomit.

When Jim heard about Joyce's parents passing away and her leaving Birmingham to move back to Apalachicola, something clicked inside of him he didn't exactly understand. He wasn't sure if it was her beauty and youth, the smile he'd remembered, or just knowing she was coming here, which was closer; he only knew something inside him grew in heat and that the route of that warm feeling—had been her.

THE CALL HOME

He now knew he needed to see Ethan and hash things out between them. He was far too old to return to those days—and those kinds of games they once played in their past. In the world today, it would be far too dangerous to justify its risk. Ahh, but those were some days he thought quietly to himself. His memory began to drift back to a different time bringing a stiffening down in the older toolbox he still carried. The way that evening ended brought another flashback in history that tied the knot in his throat as etched recollections of an outcome he never saw coming. He also swore he'd never forget. Ethan fucking Kendricks, you foe who played as a friend—under the guise of deceit. I'll have my day—and the woman you loved and lost.

James T. Bollard would win in the end. This is what he told himself. He'd bring Ethan to his knees—all while enjoying another round of casual unwitting sex, well, on her end anyway.

39

Cat felt very awkward at Tony's question about the town being "batshit crazy." She was born and raised in Apalachicola and a part of her felt as if she should be offended by his crass statement. Another part of her wasn't certain why she should be—or even why she cared. Her life here, after all, seemed to feel like a sharp mixture of both; very happy and—and—well, batshit crazy painful.

Cat looked up at Tony and forced a grin. She studied his face and could tell by his look that he wasn't sure how to respond. She suddenly felt like a cat and mouse game had developed between them.

"Cat—I'm... well, I'm sorry. I'm the visitor in this town and my calling it batshit crazy was simply wrong and I apologize. Will you accept that I am sorry. I have a genuine interest in you and your husband, I really do. But..." Tony paused. "... in order for me to know how I should proceed, I need to know if you and Billy Jay are still—together, or... or if you... know where he is, or how I could find him."

Cat instantly wore a confused look across her face. She appeared as if she'd missed part of the conversation or something. She hadn't really told him very much about Billy Jay. And now the question she wore made it seem to Tony that he was talking to her like their entire conversation had always been surrounding her husband. Her face instantly gave away that she'd put it all together. Tony realized he'd blown his bluff when he saw she hadn't even worn a true poker-face. Her knowledge of what he needed from her had trumped any cleverness he thought he'd held over his new "friend."

"Tony?" Cat pushed from her lips as if it were a paste her tongue was tripping over and attempting to get rid of. "I think I better go now. Maybe we'll bump into each other on another day before your vacation ends...."

"Cat! I'm sorry if I offended...." He spoke. But he knew she held no intention of coming back to talk. That ship had sailed.

"Have a good day, Tony Rawlings." She pushed herself up with some minor struggle and immediately turned to her left as if she were a robot programmed to make the maneuver as she walked at a leisurely stroll back in the direction she'd come.

Tony watched her slowly disappear into the distance. He knew immediately he screwed the pooch. He'd been quickly moving towards the inside scoop on Billy Jay. All it took was one insensitive verbal slip and he'd been swept to the curb, losing every opportunity he'd been given in one very peculiar moment. What he did next was what every other gumshoe would have done after such a snafu. He got up—and followed her from a distance. He attempted to blend into the scenery and watched the interesting and somehow captivating woman's every move. He'd at least find out where this preacher Gibson's place was where she claimed to live. *Billy Jay—I know you'll be back. You won't be able to stay away only to die a quiet old man—and I'll be waiting for you, I'll help you into that next unknown level, you son-of-a-bitch.* His thought remained inside his head as he dodged in and out of cover like a mouse following the "Cat."

40

"Mr. Kendricks." The doctor scanned the folder in his grip, his eyes moving systematically as he viewed the papers he held. "You're a lucky man today, sir." He looked away and smiled. "You must have an angel watching over you. If you had been brought in any later, the outcome would have been totally different."

Ethan's eyes were a bit dull but still held a sharpness that managed to pierce past the medication he was under to calm his chest pain. Doctor Talbert would soon catch a glimpse of Ethan's personality through hearing his stubborn tendencies toward suggestions of working on health issues. "Ethan—can I call you, Ethan?"

Ethan nodded in agreement.

"I see in your file that you have a penchant for rich, fatty foods and alcohol—do you smoke?"

A knowing smile grew across Ethan's lips as if he had already surmised where the doctor's questions were leading. "Only the very finest of cigars—It's John William Talbert—isn't it?"

"That is correct, it has been ever since my mother labeled me with it the day I was pushed out of her nurturing assembly plant." He smiled, attempting to bring a bit of humor to the conversation he'd been told would head in the direction of some form of courtroom banter.

"So—can I call you John? Or do we have to go through the formalities of calling each other by our titles?"

"John is fine. I must warn you though, I have been forewarned that speaking with you about these kinds of matters, will bring the aggressive... um... big dog down from the porch... were the exact words used to describe the scene." Again, Doctor Talbert smiled, showing no compulsion to back away from what needed to be said from his professional stance.

Ethan attempted to sit up straight, obviously feeling as if he were in an unfavorable position like being poised beneath the judge's bench instead of at an equal face-off between two attorneys, which is where he placed the doctor's level of education to his.

"I know your—educated suggestions—will be that I—change my lifestyle, much like you would have your wife, change her outfit if it didn't fit your—expectations."

"Ethan, Ethan...."

"Do not address me as if I were your child, sir. I know the drill and I'll live the way I've chosen to live—until I live no longer. Asking me—at this stage and schedule of life—to give up everything that I've worked hard to enjoy—well, it's just not—in the cards I'm holding."

"You've heard the old adage that you can lead a horse to water...."

"I've heard such bullshit my entire life and I've avoided drinking in what others have suggested to wit's end and I thank you for clearing my internal plumbing, but I'll not rebuild the entire structure because one part of it momentarily stumbled."

THE CALL HOME

Doctor Talbert snapped the folder he held, closed. He did it with a look of disappointment mixed equally with the look of a fortune teller at a carnival, knowing the future but also aware the receiver held no belief. "You'll need to stay another couple of nights so we can monitor your recovery and then of course, you'll need to enjoy a time of rest and relaxation and several scheduled sessions of rehab therapies—where you'll tirelessly listen to some of the same line of preaching that you've just shunned." He stepped to the bedside and held his right hand out to shake Ethan's. He acted a bit hesitant already guessing Ethan may not bring his hand out to meet. He had misjudged that prediction as Ethan's palm tucked into the doctor's and squeezed a very light grip. Not one expected from a bulldog attorney such as Ethan was known to be.

The doctor increased his grip, challenging Ethan to do the same, but no words were spoken from the doctor's challenge between the two. Ethan did notch up his tightened grip as it began a tit for tat, which Ethan would quickly lose because of his lack of strength.

"You'll regain both your power and stamina—if you do what I've instructed and follow the plans the therapists set. You can overcome the challenge you've met, and you can also conquer it. It's all entirely up to you, Mr. Kendricks." He smiled. "If I were in a courtroom facing some horrible accusation—I would want you in front, leading the charge. But if I were in your shoes facing the hurdle you've met and were forced to overcome it, I would want someone exactly like myself to lead that charge." The doctor loosened his grip and removed his hand from the sweaty palm he'd been gripping. "Words to think about, Mr. Kendricks. Words to indeed mull over and consider." He turned to leave the room only to almost bump into Addison Charmane as she stood appearing stunned in the doorway, apparently overhearing most of the conversation.

*****

Addi stood still, waiting for the tension in the room to vacate along with Doctor Talbert as he passed beside her. He whispered a few words to her, "Good luck with that one, Ms. Charmane, he's as stubborn as a cantankerous old gator hungry and cornered but refusing to eat while being watched." The words had fallen from his mouth into the air as soft as a feather wafting delicately to the ground. She looked down into the opening in her purse to see the flask Ethan had ordered her to bring. She dropped her hand into the bag and shuffled some items, pushing the metal container lower, burying it amongst a woman's clutter.

"Good morning, Ethan?" She greeted with a question mark dangling at the end. "I take it you got the not-so-good news."

"You knew about Talbert's ending summation, I assume?"

Addi wanted to dodge the question because she knew what the next would hold and it would have everything to do with the contents in her purse.

"Did you bring—my medicine, darling? The medicine the 'doctor' attempted to ban me from."

And there it was. No thank you for being here, sweetheart or him saying, 'darling I want to get healthy and live so we can share our passion forever.' No, it all boiled down to, 'where's my bourbon, honey.' Addison may as well have been nothing more than a barmaid with sexual benefits because he acknowledged nothing but his thirst for his goddamned whiskey like an addict would to his cocaine dealer.

THE CALL HOME

It appeared this morning had brought unwelcome life revelations to both of them. Addison reached in and dug through the clutter until her fingers felt the cold smoothness of the flask. She wrapped her grip tightly around it as if she could choke the hold that it held over him as she pulled it from its concealment. Addison watched her boss's eyes as they gleamed at the sight of the silver container. She held it within his sight long enough just outside of reach for his eyes to leave their surveillance of it and draw up to meet hers with the look of relief that she'd feared from him. That was all she needed for her heart to finish breaking. He was an alcoholic, and she already knew that. But what she had hoped but found untrue, was that his love for the poison which was responsible for delivering him to where he now lay—held far more importance and power over him than whatever he'd ever share with her.

Addison Charmane forced a smile from her lips that stung as if her hand were being gnawed on by a deadly coral snake chewing and oozing its poison into her bloodstream. The burn of losing something you unexpectedly find out you never really held. It had all been an illusion. Ethan truly was the snake. Being within his reach was every bit as dangerous as that deadly but beautiful orange, black, and cream-colored Florida killer.

Ethan didn't even look stunned as she tossed the flask onto his bed and turned to walk away. She fought every urge she could to look back at him when she reached the door. The torment flooded over her like a huge tsunami wave swallowing her in its momentum and rolling her up the shoreline before robbing her ability to breathe as it pushed her deeper and deeper into the abyss. Before she passed the room's threshold, she lost her battle not to glance back at her boss and recent lover. What she saw was unfortunately just as she suspected. His eyes didn't hang in question on what had just happened, instead they were closed tightly together as his head tipped back, the flask's lid twisted open and held to his burning lips dousing the desperate thirst for its contents.

Addison had lost her first case. She turned and walked away, feeling as if she were doing the dead man's dance to the gallows. She clutched the wall as her legs wobbled without control, reaching for anything to grasp onto to slow her fall to the ground. She sat on the floor drowned in tears like an unwanted puppy leashed to a tree with no other future in sight but to be alone and pitiful, tethered to a dead-end career, her dreams crushed by a metal flask of distilled grains.

41

Amy Jo looked again at her friend, Georgie. She attempted to show confidence through eye contact, assuring her that everything would be okay.

"You know, Ms. Amy Jo—we never did finish that last discussion—no answer to your last question before you... well... ended our interview that night. There were prices to be paid by both of us I suppose—."

"Billy... I mean... Jay... is there really any need to retrace the past? Your answer came eventually with your conviction. And while I can't pretend to understand the why's or how's of how you could perform such evils, I certainly don't see what the relevance would be in doing so now."

"You've changed, Amy Jo and maybe—maybe I have too? I'm not sure your change necessarily suits you, though. You've—grown, I don't know, maybe more—callous since our last time together."

"Why are you here, Jay? You're surely not imagining that you and I had or have some kind of—thing, do you? I mean, I made mental comparisons between you and my grandfather, but..." Amy Jo attempted to use caution in her wording. "...but we don't have—anything. You weren't honest with me back then and I demanded insinuation, Amy Jo. That's never really been a part of me. I could have raped Gina a long time ago when she barged in on Ben and I and his conviction and sentence being played out. I could have raped the whore he'd invited into his home as I lay hidden waiting for them to finish and her to leave. Again, not my personal devil to deal with...."

"What about those poor seven girls, Jay? What did they do to deserve your wrath and sexual deviations you forced upon them?" Amy Jo knew she had said something she shouldn't have. It was the demon she and Billy Jay had shared in their past. It had been the one thing that instantly broke her. Now it became the terrifying elephant in the room once again. She now regretted ever bringing it back to the surface while Georgie was trapped here with her. *Have I just given us our death sentence?* She contemplated. It was an odd thought; she didn't feel scared for herself although she knew her friend was terrified of what may come.

"I thought that was of no importance to you now?" He questioned.

"I don't want to play these games, Jay. I want you to leave and let Georgie and I finish our evening together—as if you'd never shown up here. I want you to disappear back into the shadows and... and just die the death that will eventually catch up to you. You've been hurt and you've passed that hurt to many innocent souls that didn't deserve...." Amy Jo stepped the few steps it took for her to reach out and touch his hand. "... I want you to seek that peace and accept handing over your will. It's your only hope Jay."

"You have no idea what I was dealt, Amy Jo. My words that I told you could never really paint an accurate picture. There's no way you could see things like I see them. The pain I endured

THE CALL HOME

my entire life growing up until that last evening I gained a tiny shred of retribution for my mother and I." He turned silent.

"How did you get retribution, Jay? Tell me…."

It was quiet again. You could have heard a palmetto scamper across the hardwood floor, had there been one.

Jay coughed, clearing his throat before continuing, "…when I beat that wicked son-of-a-bitch to death before taking every fuckin' dime he had stowed away."

Amy Jo looked at Billy Jay blankly. "To death? You think you killed your father?"

"I left him barely begging for his life in words so broken and bloody, they were too unrecognizable to decipher. His face was smashed in by two swings of a sock filled with his own goddamned change."

"You didn't kill him, Jay. I… I… I met him…."

The air became heavy in Amy Jo's living room. Silence shattered any quiet that had already hung in the room over them. It felt like an emptiness somehow swallowed each of the three of them. That's how Amy Jo felt and assumed they all did by the lack of any responses and the looks upon their faces. Amy Jo watched as Jay's face seemed to wither. It felt as if something sucked every feeling and emotion from the room and then left, leaving it hollow and jingling in an odd quiet sound like a broken wind chime blowing in a windless vacuum. It was unexplainable, impossible for her to decipher in the vague moments left afterwards. The only thought Amy Jo could muster was one repetitive question that played in a loop inside her head. *Where does this go from here? What happens next?*

42

Billy Jay kept his composure. In the past sudden changes in his expectations would throw him into frantic episodes filled with rants and pacing wildly. In this moment though, he was completely lucid and calm. His eyes were the only part of him that seemed capable of movement. He stood statuesque in the middle of the two women while his eyes traced back and forth between them. Not in a maniacal way. He remained silent as he attempted to decide just why he had come. All he really knew was that he'd been driven to see her from the moment he realized she'd been taken from him. He'd worried about her ever since he'd seen her fall, ending up lying cold and lifeless on the concrete floor of the visitation room at the prison. He was handcuffed to the desk, so he knew the bulls were aware he'd done nothing physically to cause the accident. He knew however what it was that had caused the episode. It was the question about his involvement with the seven young girls they'd found, their remains stuffed in those blue barrels out in the cistern on a piece of property where he and his family had lived. Somehow Warden Wilkerson had put together he and Amy Jo were talking about those girls when the incident happened. He erased her from his existence from that night forward. She'd been his Shangri-la for

THE CALL HOME

sixteen Saturdays and then 'poof' one night, that Shangri-la was removed from his life forever.

Those nights and days had been hell on earth, but he would not surrender the information Warden Willy demanded from him. He was forced to spend day after day in exile from every other soul and left to suffer in his own dark madness alone. Held in a dark musky cell in the basement solitary confinement. Forgotten. He conspired to create a list of wrongs that would need righted. But tonight, upon seeing Amy Jo again, he now wondered if this silent world he'd been forced to exist in along with being hung— had somehow stolen a part of him and killed it, leaving only an empty vessel void of the anger he'd been filled and surrounded with his entire existence up until this very second. Why had he killed those girls? What force was trapped inside his soul that caused the callous evil that drove him to do the things he'd done. Could he always hold his father to the fire in blame?

His eyes continued to cut through the emptiness like swords slicing through thin air. His prisoners, for no other definition, sat in silence likely wondering what their outcome would be and when the horror would begin. Only one thought fought within his mind now to spirit him away. That single thought now became Catrina, his wife. What had happened to her in his absence? Could she still love him like she had so long ago when she'd walked up to that bench overlooking the pier in Apalachicola? Did she still have the magic inside her that could calm his internal storm and bring peace?

The quiet was broken in a hushed call that fell from Billy Jay's lips like a baby slipping through its mother's arms unexpectedly and by mistake. The mother attempting to reclaim the grip she'd held only seconds before on the baby before it hit the floor with a thud; only to end with an even scarier silence. "Cat... I...."

"Just go, Billy Jay. Please. Run and don't look back." Amy Jo called out. She'd remembered him telling her about those very words in one of their conversations during an interview session. His wife Cat had called them out to him. Begging him to just run after he'd accidentally killed his only true-blooded son. Amy Jo now hoped he would do exactly what he'd done all those years back, which had ended any chance of normalcy he'd ever held.

Amy Jo looked at Georgie as they both sucked in a deep breath of relief when the front door quietly shut, ushering in the feeling of being saved from something that could have been devastating. Several minutes passed while both of them sat stationary, attempting to come to grips with what had just transpired. Georgie on the couch, Amy Jo now back in her favorite chair. Both hoping the beast had really run, deciding never to return.

After hearing a car engine start and seeing the glow of headlights pull into her drive and then back out exiting after turning around, Amy Jo finally planted her feet on the hardwood floor. She pushed herself up to walk the few steps to her friend who was still perched on the couch as if nailed tightly to its cushion, unable to move. Their arms found each other, and Amy Jo pulled Georgie into her bosom. It was a familiar gesture they had shared under much different circumstances in their recent past. This time the emotions were entirely different. This time they hugged each other very tightly without the awkwardness of any sexual inuendo. They both broke down in unison, flowing with tears and bodies shaking from the release of adrenaline they both had held tightly within until it could be released.

THE CALL HOME

"I'm so sorry for putting you in danger, Georgie—I never...."

"It's okay, Amy Jo. We're alive. It's okay, I love you."

"I love you too, Georgie. I'm just so, so sorry. I have to make a call to the Tallahassee division of the Florida State Police. To Tony Rawlings."

"The detective who lost his partner?" Georgie asked.

"Yes, I have to let him know where Billy Jay is headed."

"How do you know that, Amy Jo? He didn't say anything about that."

"He let it slip, Georgie, he's going back to Apalachicola."

"Why in the world would he go back there? They'll be looking for him, won't they?"

"They think he's dead, like I did."

"Okay, but why—why would he go back home?"

"To see his wife, Cat. To say goodbye. I think he's planning on exiting this world in a fire-filled blaze of retribution."

*****

"I need to leave a message for Detective Tony Rawlings, please."

"I'm sorry but Detective Rawlings is out of the office for an extended period. Is there anyone else I can transfer you to?"

"Is his partner still Detective Hank Robbins?"

"Yes, ma'am. I believe Detective Robbins is in his office this morning too. Can I see if I can put you through?"

"Yes, ma'am, please do."

"Your name and what this call is related to?"

"My name is Amy Jo Whitenhour...."

"The woman who wrote the book about Billy Jay Cader?"

"Yes, ma'am, that's me and Mr. Cader is the subject I need to discuss with the detective."

"I'll put you right through, and by-the-way—your book was very fascinating. Very informative. Thank you for writing it. I can't imagine spending so much time with such an evil man."

"Thank you, there were some challenges in doing so."

43

"What the fuck do you mean Rawlings is vacationing in Apalachicola? And who told you Billy Jay is alive?"

Hank stepped up closer to Finney, broaching his personal space, almost within smelling distance of the morning's coffee on his breath. "Amy Jo Whitenhour, from the Orlando Beacon."

"That crazy bitch that wrote that book almost feeling sorry for him?" Finney shook his head as he held his hand out in front of him, resting his palm on Hank's chest and easing him back from his space. "I wanna know why in hell Tony is in Apalachicola. You knew about this?"

"You told him to take some R and R, sir. That's what he's doing. He took his fishing gear and told me he was going to fish."

"Fish for trouble is what he's likely doing, and he by-god has found it!"

"Sir, it may be lucky he's already there. Amy Jo believes Billy Jay is on his way there to...."

"So, this reporter is now playing detective for the Florida State Police Department, is she?"

"This 'reporter' more than likely knows more about the inner workings of Billy Jay than any other person alive—other than his wife, whom Amy Jo believes he is going to say goodbye to before he clears his list of repayments on those he sees hurt him. I think Tony's in trouble."

"Why is that, other than the trouble he's in when I see him?"

"He's at the top of Billy Jay's list, that's why. And he is there having no clue of the storm that may be brewing as Billy Jay makes his way there. Ms. Whitenhour says he has a car. That's less than a six-hour drive. He left last night. He may already be there, sir."

"You go check things out, Hank. And—you better stay in very close contact with me. I want you to be on me like white on rice—got it? Stink on shit, buddy."

"Thanks, Chief."

"Let me know when you contact Tony. Good luck and..."

"I know, Chief, white on rice, stink on shit."

Hank hit highway 267 south and once he was clear from traffic, heavy-footed his pedal pushing his plain-dressed squad car, the police version of an '86 Impala, to its limits. Built on the 404 horsepower 383 motor mated with a 4T65-E-HD transmission, it had a top speed of one hundred and thirty-nine miles an hour. Hank held the speedometer's needle to the far right as his interior police lights flashed on and off from the front and back red and blues. His light silver-colored Impala smelled hot as he pulled into Apalachicola, just over an hour later. He'd shaved about a third of the normal time off with no problems. He knew Tony was staying at the Gibson Inn where he would have eyes on the Tanner House at all times. That's where he pulled into and quickly exited, heading to the front lobby desk.

*****

THE CALL HOME

Billy Jay's head was jumbled. The long five-and-a-half-hour drive towards his home in Apalachicola gave him plenty of time to wrestle all the turmoil between the demons in his head. Damn Amy Jo for having company that night. Damn him for not having the patience to wait for a clearer opportunity. Not that anything would have turned out differently. He knew she couldn't love him. He knew he shouldn't love her. Cat was the woman he owed. He'd taken her first son from her, not that it was entirely his fault, but he *had* been the man who killed him. He'd also left her holding the bag as he turned and ran like she'd begged him to do. And then the day Darrell had tried to shoot him when he'd come back. All the killing he'd done during the years between marrying Cat and now. Not that some of them didn't deserve what they got. Roy Burks in particular, for raping his sweet Catrina while he was out on the road driving. That fat awkward buddy of Darrell's who fucked with him by leaving the Mason jar tiles scattered around his apartment. He deserved being fed to the sharks. No regrets with him. But those seven girls—he'd made false reasons in his head for killing them and Amy Jo had caught him with it.

It dawned on him what she'd said. It was almost a turning point for him when he heard her statement. Somehow her words had gotten lost between hearing them and now translating what she'd really said.

"You didn't kill your father—I met him." She'd blurted out in a tone as if he'd been crazy for thinking he had. Words as if he'd known he wasn't dead, and it would actually have changed anything in the world he'd created afterwards. It wouldn't have, would it? He questioned himself.

As he steered the stolen Buick just under the speed limit down highway 98 past Lanark Village, memories of Chubbs re-entered his thoughts. Sharp reflections of guilt needled him as he became haunted by the memory of the fat kid's fear. The teen had worn a look of shock and question in his eyes just before he'd swung the tool iron down hard onto his neck where it met his shoulder, dropping his clumsy blubbered body to the pavement. Billy Jay looked to his left as he passed the gravel road that he'd driven down towards the beach that night to dump the body. The moment the kid had struggled to free himself from the plastic tarp he'd wrapped him in to keep Ben's van from becoming a mess with bloody evidence. The memory of reaching into his pocket, pulling the folding knife, and dragging its razor-sharp blade from the chubby kid's throat, spilling his blood into the dark salty waters of the Gulf before pushing him away to disappear. The dark depths swallowing the body to be devoured by the creatures below.

    A cold chill caused Billy Jay to slightly jerk the wheel of his car, pulling it towards the empty lane of traffic to his left as if being called to return to the scene of the crime. He knew better than to answer that call. He was already living at great risk returning home to finish uncompleted business. His skeletons were definitely alive and rattling their bones at him. He was very aware of each action he'd taken on this journey back to answer his call home. Like he was merely a piece of metal and Apalachicola was a powerful magnet. He was succumbing to the calling force, unable to resist its pull. There was no avoiding the grip it held until he heard and felt the loud slap of the two metals slamming together, locked in place unable to be pulled apart until the magnetic field was drained clean with his wrath.

44

"Momma, I don't know how to tell you this, but...."

"What, Mitzi B? I don't understand the worry in your voice. Is Katie, okay? Darrell?"

"They're fine, Momma, it's you I'm worried about. Are you in your office?"

"Mitzi, of course! It's only my second day. I'm not gonna be late on my second day! What's wrong? You're scaring me!"

"Is your boss in?"

"Yes, of course he is, he's in his office, why?"

"I want you to make up an excuse to leave, can you do that?"

"Mitzi B! I'm *not* going to do that. Why would you even ask such a thing?"

"He can't hear us, can he?"

"Mitzi! What is going on with you? And no, I don't imagine he can."

*****

Jim listened as he heard Joyce's end of a conversation she was having as it became louder. He'd pressed his ear against the wall to try and listen. He didn't want to be forced to open the door. That's when he decided to listen in on her call. His phone system was set up where he could do that if he ever found the need to home in on a client's private conversation with someone as they used his phone. He knew it was shady, but an attorney needs every advantage at his fingertips at all times. There may be a slight click, but as long as he had his end muted, the client would remain unaware of the intrusion.

*****

"I want you to listen to me, Momma. What I'm about to say may cause you to... to show signs of worry to Jim. You don't want to *do* that."

A small click sounded into Mitzi's earpiece of her phone. "Are you still there?" She thought maybe they'd been disconnected.

"I'm still here. Just what in hell is going on here? Why the clandestine talk?"

"I went to talk to Debbie Thomas earlier today. My old counselor that was so helpful to Darrell and me."

"I don't see how this affects me or where you're going with this. I'm very busy, Mitzi. I don't have time for this."

"Hang on a minute, Mom. I'm getting to the part you need to hear. I was there and I happened to glance on her wall of photos. Different pictures of the different years of senior graduates. Pictures dated all the way back to when the high school first opened."

"Again, I don't see where this is important enough to break me away from the mountain of work I need to get up to date on."

THE CALL HOME

"1950 graduates from Apalachicola High, Mom. The year Ethan Kendricks graduated along with Charley Bingham and Roy...."

"Why are you bringing this up? I already knew they all went to school together."

"Did you know Jim Bollard graduated from Apalachicola the same year? Alongside those three other sick bastards?"

There was silence on the line.

"No, I guess I didn't know that, but why the tone of seriousness? What could that possibly matter?"

"What if Ethan and Jim were close friends like he was with Charley and Roy?"

"Again, so what?"

"Mom! Think about it for a minute. What if they are still friends? You've talked to Jim about what we know with Ethan and his watch and those girls in Springfield, right?"

Joyce's head began to tumble and mix like a cement truck stirring the rock powder and water into a thickening product. "Oh my God! What if Jim wants to protect Ethan instead of nailing him to the wall for what he's done?"

"Exactly! But one more scary thought—."

"What Mitzi?"

"What if Jim was involved with the things that we now know Ethan was. Like Phuck House."

"Phuck House? I don't care to hear that word come from your lips, young lady. What if Katie hears such things?" Joyce questioned in a tone filled with a hint of disgust. "Why would you even say such a phrase? Makes no sense."

"It's what Ethan called his little club of sick perversions. Debbie told me all kinds of stories she's heard from around here through the years since she's lived here."

"You mean, small-town gossip that can be based on biased opinions and untruths to malign the character of attorneys that may have failed representing angry clients the way they feel they should have been? Finding their way of revenge by spreading such ugliness, such as rumors like—Phuck House?" The tone of Joyce's voice was accusatory with a hint of 'what the hell have I gotten myself into.' There suddenly was a mild shakiness in her voice.

"Momma, I don't wanna risk you doing nothing giving "the benefit of doubt" to any attorneys from this back-woods town or surrounding area. You're all I have left, and I don't wanna lose you because you still have a blind saint living inside your heart. Besides, I have one other scary thought to share with you. I wanted to wait until we were face to face, but this possibility may be the one thing that will motivate you to listen and act quickly."

Another moment of quiet hung over the phone line between them as if her words travelled as slow as a bug swimming in molasses.

"And what's that notion, Mitzi B?"

"Don't hate me for what I'm going to say—okay?"

"I wouldn't hate you if you ran a shive into my side. You're my flesh and blood."

"Okay, but—what if by some crazy act of the perverse—I'm also a part of Jim Bollard's flesh and blood?" Mitzi waited for the bomb to explode. She swore she heard her mother's mouth fall to the floor in a splat before any words found their way through the awkwardness of the horrendous seed she'd just planted inside her mother's ear.

"Oh, my Lord, Mitzi! What a... what... a... God... I think I'm going to be sick...." Mitzi heard first the sound of possibly a trash can being pulled in the background just before the sound of her retching followed by coughs and the sound of a person quietly spitting. "Ptoohey...." It was obvious her thoughts had hit home as bad as she felt about aiming for the fence and swinging for the home run that would force her to run from home base and round them towards her real home.

"I'm coming home, Mitzi."

"When?"

"I'm leaving now."

"Don't stop for anything, Mom. Grab your purse and leave without explanation. Please."

"I hope you're wrong and Mr. Bollard is a forgiving man...."

"You have a home here with us, no matter which way it goes.

45

Joyce clutched her purse in hand as she began to pull the front door open to Mr. Bollard's practice. Jim's office door opened, and he hollered out to her as if he hadn't known the circumstances for which she was leaving. "Are you going out to pick up supplies you've found you need? I can call and have them delivered."

"No, I have a personal errand I need to run, I'm sorry, it came up suddenly...."

"You'll be back, won't you?" he asked, fully knowing her motive already. He hadn't expected his plans to fall through as fast as a sandcastle melting back into the ocean at high tide.

Joyce turned back to the door, answering only with, "Sorry," as she continued without any further explanation.

Jim thought about following her out and confronting her further at her car, but what good would that do other than draw unwanted attention to himself. No, he thought to himself. I'll regroup and plan another direction of approach to the problem. This is nothing different than finding the need to change strategies five minutes before court. I've done it a thousand times with the outcome I needed in the end.

The one thing Jim hadn't even dreamed of—was the possibility of being Mitzi's birth father. Yes, Roy had shared his

THE CALL HOME

girlfriend a time or two with him. He'd told him it was club rules. In fact, he'd had to reciprocate the deed, match for match, by bringing Doris, his girlfriend, over to Roy's apartment. He scratched his head as he reminisced, hmmm, Roy never had any children other than... oh well, no matter who the father was, me or Ethan, I'll make sure I'm never accused... All it would take, he surmised, was a good game strategy. Let Joyce run back to her daughter. Letting Ethan take the hit for those girls in Springfield by cluing them into the fact of whose watch they were in possession of, and he could devise a plan to be shed of Joyce and— his possible daughter. No, Doris must never become privy to the possibility of all this. I love her family's money far too much to lose that cash-cow this late in the game.

46

Tony walked back towards the Gibson Inn. By now he was conditioned to quietly observe the Tanner House too. He was able to tune out the bad memory most of the time to a light annoying hum in the back of his head. Kind of like tinnitus in one's ear. You always knew the background noise was there, but most of the time you could convince yourself it was gone. While he knew that buzz in his ear and heart would never leave, he prayed catching Billy Jay being stupid enough to return would hopefully go a long ways towards curing his symptom of the horrendous sin he'd committed by letting his partner's life be taken.

Tony crossed the street and was about to step into the Gibson's parking lot when he saw the silver cop edition Impala. "What the fuck?" he questioned aloud as he ran his fingers across his partner, Hank's vehicle. "What in hell are you doing here, Hank?" He headed to the lobby to see if he was there.

No sooner than the door opened, Hank rushed up to him with the look of excitement written across his face. "Tony! You're alright, thank God!"

"Hey, I'm happy to see you, too, I guess, but what's with the 'I'm alright' routine?"

"You're not gonna believe this, Tony...."

"What? The last time I saw you this excited was when Sarah from Robbery rested her hand on your..." He smiled. "... um... what she thought was your concealed weapon!" Tony laughed out loud. "Of course, it was—well, the small, soft fleshy one, that is!" He punched Hank's arm. "Hey, snub-nose, by the way, has she ever called you back?"

"Thanks for the memory, partner, but this is serious shit."

"Serious enough to risk your career by being seen in this town with me?"

"He's alive, Tony. I have confirmation." Hank put a hand on each of Tony's shoulders in case he needed steadied. "He's headed here as we speak..." Hank slapped Tony's shoulders. "... if he isn't already here."

"Confirmation? From whom? Who's the source?"

"A very reliable one, Tony. Amy Jo Whitenhour."

"The reporter we talked to that wrote the book that almost appeared to condone his actions?"

"The one and only. Seems that Billy Jay became close enough to her to show up at her house last night."

"Showed up where last night?"

"Amy Jo's farmhouse she grew up in, just outside of Orlando. An orange tree farm her grandparents left her. If you'd read her book, you'd know that." Hank smirked.

"So, Amy Jo actually saw him? Talked to him? I mean, how does she know he's headed here?"

"She's an investigative reporter, Tony. A bit of a gumshoe, herself. Apparently quite good at it. She said she got Billy Jay to slip up and mention he wanted to see his wife, Catrina, or Cat as she's known around there. And yes, a friend of Amy Jo's was at her house with her when Billy Jay showed up. Georgie Rovario, the next-door neighbor, daughter of the couple Amy Jo rents the farm rights to." He smiled. "Seems you were right, Sherlock, when the rest of us doubters like Chief Finney, were dead wrong and calling you crazy."

Tony's head snapped up, "Who called me crazy? I want names, Hank!" He held the stare as long as he could before cracking a smile.

"Seriously, Finney started out driving hard, but he's in your corner. I could tell he was even worried about you. I'm supposed to keep him updated— 'white on rice, stink on shit' were his words." Hank looked over when he realized if anyone was nearby—he'd just blurted out things that shouldn't be public. He quickly scanned the room and it appeared free from anyone within earshot. "Do you think we should call for back-up?"

Tony snapped back immediately without hesitation, "Hell no!" He fired back. "In fact, I want you to head back to Tallahassee. You've delivered the word; I want this arrest alone and on my own. Billy Jay is not escaping justice this time." He spat the sentence from his mouth as if the taste of the words passing over his lips tasted like a dog's ass might if he licked it himself.

"No way, Tony. I'm not leaving so you can either die by Billy Jay's hand this time or let your stubborn ass torch your career by touching a lit match to the stick of dynamite you'd shove up his ass by doing something that I know in my heart isn't who you really are." Hank's face carried a seriousness and determination that Tony realized he'd never seen before.

"I appreciate you, Hank. Really, I do, but you've never lost a partner because you didn't think things through before acting on them."

"Neither have you, Tony. You lost a partner whose time was called. It had nothing to do with anything you did or didn't do. I've seen all the reports, I've heard all the talk. The facts just don't match up to your claims. You're just wrong, partner. Why won't you accept what everyone else in the department sees? There's no need for you to try and die a martyr. The department has already lost enough good men. We're the under-gunned good-guys against the over armed and unrestricted by the rules bad-guys. Of course, we're gonna lose at times. It sucks it happened during yours, but let it go, not your cross to bear."

"Let's go up to my room. We can continue this banter upstairs where I can at least keep a watchful eye."

"I'll agree to that, Tony. I'd love to share a beer too but..." He winked. "... we need to keep all of our wits about us. Uncluttered and sober. Terri says hi, too. She wanted me to pass on a kiss, but I declined."

47

"Oh my God, Amy Jo!" Malcolm exclaimed. "Why are you even in the office today? You need to go somewhere safe and make sure that psycho isn't following you!"

"He's going to Apalachicola, Malcolm. He all but told me so. But..." Amy Jo's head tipped down like a child just about to either ask a question they expect a no to or positioning themselves to be scolded. She slowly looked back up to meet his gaze. "I think I've found him."

"Him? I think he found you."

"No, not Jay. I believe I've found Cable. I'd like to take a week—maybe two."

"Amy Jo! Of course, I want you to take some time and explore where life is tugging you. Please, don't even think about my saying no! Go, I hope your bags are already packed and in the truck. You might even think about renting a car!"

"Oh, I'm taking the truck. I need to listen to my grandfather's words of encouragement on the way there, so I don't turn around before I get there!"

"How in the world can you hear your grandfather's words in that old truck?"

THE CALL HOME

"The hum and purr of the engine, Malcolm. His voice is in the swipe of the windshield wipers during a rainstorm, the music from the radio that causes my leg to bounce to the rhythm. I know every tick, click, and squeak of that truck. I've learned to listen for them. They become audible in their different sounds and volumes at just the right times when I ask questions." She smiled. "I know—you think I'm crazy, but—that truck is our vessel in sharing conversations with each other. He steers me safely all the time. It's unexplainable if you don't have faith, Malcolm. I can recite incident after incident, conversation after conversation where questions were asked and answered through the hum of the tire, a click of a piston rod, or the whir of the cooling fan."

Malcolm sat relaxed in his chair and smiled. "Amy Jo—Amy Jo—you certainly are a one-of-a-kind, young lady. And this Cable Johnson will be one fortunate soul if you find him, and he succumbs to the magic you hold inside your heart. And thank God, Billy Jay steered his devastation in the opposite direction and you're not begging to go dive into the middle of it. You did alert the authorities about him, right?"

"I got word to the lead detective's partner. He told me he was on it. My feelings aren't quite as—as...."

"Fucked up as they were in the recent past?" Malcolm stated it only because he could read her like a book and knew what word fit. But one she would refuse to fill in herself.

"Yes. While I stand by my original prognosis, he is the enigma that still makes me wonder. He's a hurting—okay, a fucked-up hurting soul that's wrapped up in an evil that was brought on by environmental circumstance and far from his control."

"Just be sure to avoid wandering too closely again. I need you, Amy Jo. And—I expect frequent updates while you are away on this adventurous journey."

"You know I will. You're like my only big brother I never had. You and Georgie are my family."

"Love you, Sis. Always and forever."

"Back at you times ten, big brother!"

Amy Jo turned to leave his office and as she stepped through, she turned again before letting the glass door slowly swing closed and quietly said, "Seriously, Malcolm. I hope you know how much you mean to me. I love ya to the moon and back."

"You too, Amy Jo. Talk to you soon and..." He held his crossed fingers up in front of his face as he finished his sentence, "... good luck building that new bridge."

48

Amy Jo knew the truck would keep a steady conversation with her. It seemed as if she'd been away far too long from talking with her grandfather. The regular weekly conversations she'd mentally kept on her trips to and from her interviews with Billy Jay as they sat in the depressing interview room had been left vacant for far too long. Memories of those dull, chipped painted walls of that urine scented room at the table he was shackled to that they shared had always drawn depressed feelings from the moment she'd entered until she exited. The stark differences between those quiet drives and the tense conversations with a man who was chained to the floor as they sat at the metal table talking, always seemed to make her ask life questions to her grandfather on the drives back home. After those trips ceased, her attention seemed to immediately segue into Georgie and her attempts to decipher what kind of a relationship they may develop. Today though, she missed her conversations with Grandfather, her hero.

"I'm sorry, Grandfather. I've missed you. I'm glad you haven't given up on me. I know I've probably been a bit of a disappointment to you and Grandmother of late. I've been living in confusion. It seems no matter how many years older I grow—I still don't seem capable of maintaining and nurturing any real knowledge on my own—without you helping nudge me in directions I should take. The wind has been blowing me off course and my sheets constantly flail in those stiff breezes without catching any of the breath to take me where I needed to go. I'm still not ready to captain my vessel on my own. I'm not sure I'll ever be capable without you on the bridge." And there it was, even in her subconscious. Bridge.

The thing with "talking things over with Grandfather" was that it always brought an instant blur to her vision. Tears of joy or from the sorrow of missing the man who saved her, always flowed during her drives as she emptied her heart out on the inside of the truck cab. She would almost always look to her side in hopes of seeing him sitting there. His knowing eyes and loving smile. Even the hopes of glimpsing a light airy vision of him would suffice. While she was never fortunate enough to actually witness any apparition that could be logically tied to him, she always caught a sound or picture, maybe a quick flicker of focus on something that felt oddly out of place for the moment, but enough to collect her attention to absorb and acknowledge it. She always attributed those instances as his way of letting her know he was indeed there by her side. His form of answering—directing her where to go or what to do.

"I'm not crazy am I, Grandfather? Believing that you are really here beside me? I know there is a thin line between our worlds. I believe you have somehow managed to keep a slight rip in that layer that keeps us separate from the possibility of feeling touch or hearing actual words, yet still together—but I know it exists, I feel you here." She wished for some kind of sign letting her affirm his presence as she reached for the radio knob to break away from her thoughts. It was in that instant her finger twisted the

THE CALL HOME

volume up to overcome the sound of the wind that she got her answer as clear as expensive crystal. The song Fly Like an Eagle was playing and the lyrics Tick-tock, doot, doot, do, do rang out loudly from the speakers in that familiar tune. It was an old favorite of theirs from the Steve Miller Band, circa 1976. She caught a large blur of movement swoop down as she left the bridge over Lake Monroe on highway 4. What she saw in that instant was the answer she'd sought to the plea she'd just made. It was no coincidence. That would be more unreal than the idea of it being her grandfather's way of letting her know he was indeed always a thought away from her. A beautiful large Bald Eagle dropped from its nest and dove down, gliding just above the lake's surface running parallel to her as she drove. She swore its face turned its head and gave a wink from its golden eye just before it changed course and veered off back across the lake. It then turned a complete circle and performed another fly-by as if to say, "That's right, sweetheart, I'm with you." It all happened in a fluid action taking less than the time it took to say thank you. She pictured the smile across her grandfather's face, which likely mirrored hers the first time he took her on his sail plane demonstrating dramatic maneuvers mimicking what this eagle had just done. Miracles truly do exist if you invest the time and energy to open your eyes and ask, followed by focusing for the answer.

Amy Jo wore the look of a young girl on Christmas Day. Joy sparkling in her eyes as if she'd just opened that one gift she had spent the entire year wishing for with all her heart, and then seeing it in the unwrapped box on her lap. Nothing could take this moment away from her.

It was 5:30 pm when Amy Jo's truck pulled into New Smyrna Beach. As she wandered around driving the streets, she saw several Johnson Bridge Builder's trucks parked in the parking lot of a bar called Just One More. It appeared to be a little local dive bar. Several contractors in bright yellow shirts and vests milled around the parking lot as she turned down Barracuda Blvd just off Causeway North. She admitted to herself it looked like a good place to find trouble if one wanted. She, however, was just hoping to find a memory. Cable Lee Johnson.

After pulling into a parking spot, Amy Jo twisted the key left, killing the engine to grandfather's truck. She smiled, feeling his presence in the air surrounding her. She knew the sun beaming down through the windshield was the likely source of heat that warmed her bare shoulders exposed because of the tube top she wore. But deep down, she believed it was the warmth of her grandfather's hands resting on them in assurance. She almost felt a gentle squeeze as if he were giving his precious granddaughter the feeling that everything was going to work out. Amy Jo believed in her heart that she was being steered like a vessel to a familiar harbor. She'd managed to weather some storms and some rough waves, and while she had felt alone at sea at times, this was the calm after the front had passed. She'd somehow even made it past Billy Jay showing up at her front door unexpectedly. Life was surely about to make a turn back to some form of normalcy. "I'm ready for normal, Grandfather. It's time to dock the bow in the slip, leave the bizarre world for someone else and come back home to the comfortable." She spoke aloud to herself as she drew back on the moment the eagle glanced over at her in flight and winked as if they'd shared a moment together cutting through the wind.

Amy Jo sat in the driver's seat, lost in thoughts, and maybe feeling a little apprehensive of what may come from stepping out and walking into the middle of a little local bar, the "Just One More." She pulled herself upright by gripping the steering wheel in each hand, tightening her biceps, and arching her back. She twisted her body to the left and then right, feeling the tension release with a couple of little cracks speaking out. Shrugging her shoulders upwards to finish the ritual of stretching to ready herself, she wiggled her legs to aid in adjusting her cutoffs. She then grabbed her purse and pulled up on the door handle. The hinges creaked a bit, she chose to take it as a groan of good luck from her hero, and she stepped out from the cab sucking in a deep breath. "Here goes!" She quietly said to herself as she looked to the blue sky above before finishing her thought, "...I'm here, it's all up to you now, Jesus. You giveth and taketh away. I'm praying I receive just a bit of your Grace of the giving today." She swung her purse over her shoulder and adjusted her sky-blue tube top by pulling the top edge up and then cupping her breasts and pushed them to a comfortable position before walking towards the unknown inside.

49

Joyce twisted the key to the Volvo expecting it to fire up immediately. When it didn't, she pumped the pedal a couple of times and tried again. It growled like it wanted to start, but then faded into a few clicks before even those sounds hesitated. She turned the key back and then twisted it to the right again. Nothing. Her hands gripped the steering wheel as she glanced up at the office door. Good, Jim isn't following me. She comforted herself. She rested her forehead down on the steering wheel attempting to calm herself back to a point before Mitzi had called. Please, Lord. Please. She lifted her head and stared back down at the key dangling from the steering column. Glancing back up to the door, she swore she noticed movement just inside. Sure enough, there was Jim standing at the entryway looking out at her. Joyce looked back down at the key and placed her fingers around it as the front door of the office began to open. "Holy, Jesus, please start..." She twisted the key and mashed her foot down to the floor. Jim cleared the doorway and was on his way towards her in the parking lot. "Jesus Christ, please!"

Jim's foot was about to step down from the curb when the Volvo kicked over and roared to the sound of a spooled-up aircraft engine. Joyce let her foot off the gas and shifted the car into reverse

THE CALL HOME

then stomped the accelerator, screeching the tires as she backed out almost clipping her boss's Mercedes. She gave an awkward wave as she straightened up the wheels of her vehicle and then stomped on the gas again, chirping the rubber on the pavement and bouncing the rear wheel over the curb and onto the road. A sigh of relief ended quickly as she looked up at her rearview mirror and saw Jim standing at his car door getting ready to climb in. Is the bastard going to follow me? She asked herself as she pushed the pedal harder against the floorboard and sped off.

Joyce's mind was filled with scrambled thoughts mixing in and out becoming a jumbled quagmire of fear, wonder, and worry. Could he be Mitzi's father? She started to picture the sordid possible act in her mind before her stomach began to tumble again. Breakfast rushed up into her mouth before she forced herself to swallow it back down, too afraid to pull over to let herself freely release the bile begging to exit. Did those sick pricks drug me up and pass me around taking turns riding me like a fucking merry-go-round? The thought of Roy, Ethan, and Jim—and maybe even that slick dick principal Charlie all doing sick sex acts with her while she lie helpless in a drugged vegetative state. She was forced to pull over and swing her door open, hanging her head out just clearing the interior and heaving until her stomach was completely empty. Nothing but dry heaves left. She hurt. She couldn't think. Could she ever recover from this?

That's when she looked up and saw a black car coming up on her in the distance. Holy fuck! It's him! She said before pulling the door shut and jamming her foot back on the pedal, swerving back onto the highway just as he was pulling off behind her. She looked again in her rearview mirror and watched as he too pulled back onto the road behind her. She saw the small piece of what looked like scrambled egg hanging onto the corner of her lip. She wretched again, only heaving with nothing else left to spill out. Her head was perspiring as she swerved left than right before semi-straightening the car and speeding back up until it screamed. Seventy... eighty... ninety miles per hour. Jim was on top of her rear bumper. Every time she took the chance to look into her rearview, she saw what appeared to be a madman hellbent on saving his ass. "Get off me, you fucking jackass" she screamed at the top of her lungs as if he could hear her harsh anger and would follow her command. Which he did not.

*****

As if by some stroke of coincidence, a silver Buick was heading towards Apalachicola in the same direction Joyce and Jim were going. It was Billy Jay heading back home to finish up some affairs. He recognized the Volvo as it shot past him erratically, a black Mercedes on its tail damn near nudged against it. They had to be doing every bit of eighty, he thought. "What the fuck is going on here, little Joyce? Just who in hell did you piss off?"

Billy Jay pushed the Buick to its limit but wasn't having any luck catching up with them. He didn't let up on the gas no matter how loud the stolen car whined in agony.

*****

"Come on, Joyce! Slow up just a bit..." Jim clutched the wheel of his Mercedes as if he were racing in the Grand Prix. He pictured his life racing down the shitter at Mach speed if he didn't stop Joyce. She was figuring out way too much of what he and his high school buddies had done upon graduating college and meeting back up. They'd ruled this fucking town while playing crazy sex

THE CALL HOME

games with any girl they'd wanted as if they owned their little part of the pond. I can't lose what I've worked so hard to build—and enjoy... not over some doped-up sex doll, no matter how fun she was. No way in hell could Doris find out about any of this. She'd leave me for sure... she'd leave me destitute, taking all of her family's damn money with her. No way in hell was that going to happen."

Jim looked down at his speedometer. Eighty-five miles an hour. They were past Lake Munson and traffic had been practically non-existent. Not too unusual at this early morning hour on a Tuesday. He pushed the Mercedes a little harder, tapping the Volvo and causing it to swerve before Joyce managed to straighten it back up. He edged out to her driver's side of the car and gave his vehicle more gas, creeping slowly up just past the rear wheel.

*****

Joyce's fingers were stark white with red blotches from gripping the wheel so tightly as it shook from the strain of the motor. Her eyes darted constantly from her rearview and side mirrors to the windshield in front of her. She'd never driven this fast before and she felt tight knots filling her intestines as her shoulders became weak from being hunkered so tightly with fear-filled tension.

"What the hell are you trying to do, Jim?" She frantically yelled as tears of fright began to blur her vision. "Leave me alone!" She screamed as her body shook with trepidation. Her Volvo's front end wobbled towards the centerline and then back to the rough edge of the gravelly side. She cried out for help at the top of her lungs as Jim's car edged closer towards her driver's door. She turned to catch a glimpse of the mad man stalking her. Herding her like a rabid dog snarling at her ankles as she poured every ounce of any unspent energy into getting away from its hungry gritting teeth.

In an instant everything changed. One breath and the entire scenario evolved into the unimaginable. The hunted became nothing more than a twisting rolling victim, as if tackled to the ground in a fight for the kill.

*****

Jim's car hood was almost even with Joyce's door. The road was leading them over a bridge with railings on the side and a thick row of trees and foliage beyond. He wasn't sure how far the drop-off was on the other side of the thin railing, but this was his chance. She surely couldn't survive crashing over the edge at this speed. Jim grasped the Mercedes's wheel like an experienced racecar driver and quickly twisted it to the right, nudging Joyce's Volvo to quickly veer to the left before she managed to turn it back to the right. Her car suddenly turned sharply to the left again and then was overcorrected back to the right before nailing the curb causing it to lift from the ground and continue quickly plowing through the guardrail as if it were a sheer paper airplane rising before—plunging out of sight in a flash below the bridges surface.

Jim continued driving, but gradually slowed down and blended back to a normal speed. He knew he'd need to stop and survey the damage to his car. And hopefully, if it wasn't too noticeable, turn back around to see if his act had been successful at solving his problem.

*****

THE CALL HOME

Joyce's hands released the steering wheel as the force of hitting the curb sent her vehicle airborne, disorienting her completely. Upon crashing through the railing and impacting the shallow marshy waters below, the magnitude of impact threw her into the windshield, shattering it and flinging her limp body end over end several feet ahead, skipping across the water's surface like a stone thrown from a child's hand before submerging below the surface, leaving nothing exposed but her bloodied face and upper torso twisted in an unnatural way on the muddy bank.

*****

Billy Jay couldn't believe what he'd just witnessed. "Holy shit!" He said aloud as he slowed the Buick down to a speed he could take in the scene before coming up on the point of impact. His eyes focused on the skid marks that painted black streaks back and forth until they disappeared through the railing's crumpled and flattened ends of the section now missing. "Damn! This looks a lot like the bridge Kyle messed up the night ole' Roy Boy met his maker!" He snickered a wicked chuckle before he let the image of what Joyce was likely left in. "Bet there won't be much left of that hot little mess of a momma."

Billy Jay's vehicle slowed to a near stop, but he kept his need to pull over completely at bay. He couldn't afford to get caught up in the law asking him questions. *No, that would fuck up my plans completely.* He spoke as he internally began thinking to himself. *I reckon you're surely gone, Ms. Joyce. Maybe after I wrap things up at home and I make my exit from this world—we can meet up later and have a fiery time together in hell.* Other cars began to take notice of a possible accident and began pulling over on both sides of the highway. Billy Jay slowly sped up and moved down the road towards Apalachicola. It wasn't but a few minutes later that he noticed the black Mercedes parked in the far corner of an empty gas station parking lot.

"I'll be jiggered! That looks a lot like Ethan's buddy, Bollard." Billy Jay slowed again and put his turn signal on as he turned the wheel and headed to the opposite side of the lot. "Well, now. Looky-loo, what to do, what to do." He smiled. "Seems you've got yourself in a bit of a jam there Jimmy boy." He circled his car in a wide loop and instead of pulling to the opposite side of the lot, he changed his direction and slowly pulled closer to the Mercedes.

Billy Jay reached over and snagged his hat before perching the fedora on top of his head, pushing his greasy, scraggly hair back around his earlobes before exiting his car. He took his time watching Jim Bollard inspect his car as he slowly and quietly walked towards the man who surely had just murdered Joyce Bonham. *Oh my, my... how little Miss Mitzi is gonna cry... not expecting her pretty momma to die, not without saying goodbye.* Billy Jay shook his head in a twisted kind of enjoyment at what the day had brought so far. *A person just can't make this shit up*. He thought to himself as he stepped ever closer to the sweat-drenched old balding lawyer kneeling at the front end of his Mercedes rubbing his head as if he too were wondering... what to do, what to do.

50

Mitzi waited with anything but patience. Her world sat on pins and needles as she attempted to rock Katie in her lap. She was happy it appeared her mother took her call serious, but she also knew how her thoughts would build and twist in her mind on the drive back home.

"Darrell, are you sure it's okay that my mom moves back in with us? I know it's tight here, but...."

"Oh my god, Mitz—of course it's okay! I love your mom! She's been through hell, and I never wanted her to move out to begin with. If it wasn't for her accepting me..." He looked over at the mother of his child, the first girl he'd ever fallen for. "... if it wasn't for her—well, none of this would have ever happened with you and me."

"I know. And now I can't believe all the shit she's gone through in her life. Thank you for being there for her—for me..." She looked down at her baby and then looked back at Darrell, "... and of course, Katie. She looks just like you! You do know that don't you?"

"She looks like us, babe. Both of us."

"I wonder who I look like?" She sheepishly asked Darrell.

"I know it's gotta be hard not knowing for sure who your father is. I'm sorry, you know I'd jump through fire to find out for you if I could."

"I know. It just seems like every option of the who—doesn't really matter because they all seem like sick and evil perverts. Is that why I'm so... so... horny all the time? I'm sorry, but my sex drive seems to match the possibilities of where I came from, no matter which of the possible choices it is. I'm not some sicko to you, am I?"

Darrell sat down beside Mitzi. He touched her shoulder and began running his fingers lightly over her back. "I don't want you to change a thing about you. It doesn't matter to me who you came from. I love you completely for who you are." He lightly squeezed the back of her neck and leaned over and whispered, "...and, by the way, I love your sexual side too. I can't imagine you any different. I love you."

"I love you too, Darrell. Forever and then more." She smiled and let her hand fall to his lap. "I'm the luckiest girl alive. I hope my momma can get some of my luck in her life."

"When she gets here, we'll make sure she feels the desire and need we have for her to stay."

"How in the world did I ever get lucky enough to find you?"

Darrell laughed, "I think maybe it all started with me checking out your ass... at least... that's how I remember it from your perspective! And a note found by the Coffee Caper!" He laughed.

"I hope I catch you always checking out my butt."

"If Katie were to take a nap today... you know... before your mom gets here..." He winked.

THE CALL HOME

"You ready for a nap, sweety pie? Momma and daddy could use some snuggle time...."

51

Billy Jay walked up on Jim without his noticing. He was too busy kneeling down on the pavement looking at the scratches and dings on the passenger front end of his car.

"Well, now Mr. Bollard—have ya been busy playing bumper cars today?" Billy Jay hissed an odd cackle after asking the question.

Jim looked back behind him with a startled stare. He started to reach into his jacket pocket...."

Billy Jay pulled out a blade and quickly countered, "Now, now, Jimmy boy, you wouldn't want to be putting your hands anywhere I can't see 'em. It would be a downright shame to stick a liar... I mean... *lawyer* with a blade like one con would to a con with a shiv. I mean, we got some hashing out what just happened a few miles back before we begin thinkin' 'bout presentin' your case before the court." He smiled a toothy grin.

"Presenting my case? Before what court?"

"My court, of course! Now I won't be demandin' any highfalutin terminologies like makin' you call me 'your honor,' or nothin' like that, but I do believe there be enough evidence to bring up charges against yourself."

"Just what are you talking about Mr. Cader?"

"Oh, Lord, Mr. Bollard, you aren't trying to make me believe I didn't see what I saw back there behind us, now are you?" Billy Jay shook his head in disbelief. "... you can say I'm not the smartest kid in class—but my eyes are pretty keen, and your automobile seems to show some proof of bein' a part of all that hubbub a few miles back. I reckon Ms. Bonham is likely gator bait by now. Poor little Mitzi ain't gonna be seein' her momma no more. Thanks to your bumpin' her off into the swampy waters at eighty mile an hour." He chuckled. "Some expert drivin' for certain though, from such a pompous old fart, I must admit."

Jim shook his head and began to get back up onto his feet. "Maybe there's something we could work out, Billy Jay? I rub your back; you rub mine kind of proposition?"

"Sounds like you're admitting some guilt in this whole mess."

"I can get you cash, Billy. A sizable amount. Enough you could disappear into some distant town where nobody knows anything about you. You could start fresh. I won't say a thing." Jim looked up with hope in his eyes.

"Now Jimmy, you think I'm interested in—startin' over? That actually makes me wanna laugh." He guffawed before ending with a chuckle. "I'm here to clean up some accounts here before I turn in my judge's robe, so to speak. I reckon after practicin' a few more rounds of the Mason jar punishments, I'll be more than ready to finally meet my maker. I'm actually startin' to believe there's something to all this bible and faith stuff." He paused. "Makes me wonder just what's inside your belief box, Jimmy? You believe you'll be forgiven for what you did to that pretty little lady?" Billy Jay asked.

*****

Jim realized in this moment that he was truly in dire straits. He was a smart man who reads the tone in people's voices for a living, and he could sense Billy's enjoyment at seeing him squirm was not gonna disappear no matter what he offered. He could see the devil in his darkened eyes, and it suddenly scared the shit out of him. His heart had just begun to settle down before he got ambushed by Billy. "You can't think of anything we could come to terms with together—any arrangement we could work out that lets me climb into this car and drive off?" He lifted his head and glanced over with his pathetic eyes at the man he knew held judgment and power over his life at this point. He wore broken hope across his face, and he knew it. He also sensed inside his wired mind that his life was likely boiling down to only minutes. He'd seen the same look up at the bench from judges he'd dealt with his entire career. He could read a jury like a court docket, a prosecutor's eyes that intuitively perceived they'd won the case upon closing arguments. "Anything, Billy Jay? I'll do anything. I'm not ready to meet my maker. My wife... my kids and grandkids...."

James T. Bollard barely got his last word out before Billy Jay coldly stared into his eyes and nonchalantly shoved the blade into Jimmy's throat. He removed it twice more after inserting it repeatedly in his neck while Jimmy's eyes opened wide showing the whites all the way around his pupils.

Jim gasped two words as blood gurgled up and poured from his mouth. "Tell... Mit... zi..." He sucked deep for air as he clung onto Billy's arm, trying to stay standing but slowly sliding down to the pavement.

"Tell Mitzi what?"

THE CALL HOME

"... I'm..." His eyes showed the mental and physical strain it took to fight getting his message out. He tried to wipe the fluid from his lips, smearing bright red blood across his light gray jacket sleeve. "... sorry..." As he sat leaning against his Mercedes, his eyes and hands searched to evaluate his wounds. His fingers fumbled, unable to see how bad his punctures were. His head fell back against his front fender and rolled to the left, resting on his shoulder in an unnatural way as the life slowly faded from his face, his breaths became shallower and less frequent.

"Let go, Jimmy. You've been judged and found guilty. Sentenced to death and served. Let go now and... face your maker...."

*****

Billy Jay stood over James Bollard's body and quietly stared, close enough to hear the last gasps for air slowly die away until his fight for life surrendered. He wiped his blade on the tail of his coat and then turned and walked back to his car and opened the door, calmly slid into the seat, removed, and tossed his fedora onto the passenger's seat cushion as he started the engine. After pulling up to the highway, he looked both ways and turned right as he continued on towards Apalachicola. Billy Jay apparently could find no reason to drive back by the scene of the crash. He knew he'd hear all about it on the radio or in the paper soon enough. The little town would be all a buzz, but this time, it wasn't on his account. Not entirely, anyway.

52

When Jay pulled into town, it was early evening. The sky was beginning to darken as he drove slowly down the road scanning the area for anything that drew his attention. He first drove by the Gibson Inn and rolled past it, looking up to the Tanner House, to the upstairs apartment he once lived. Memories of his last moments of freedom in this little town of Apalachicola before the damned pair of state lawmen attempted to ambush him. That scene played out in his head as his eyes scanned the place. His front door where Sam fell bleeding at his feet, and then to the railing where he and Tony locked eyes before pulling triggers.

There were lights on at the two bottom apartments, yet total darkness upstairs where he once lived and where Joyce and Mitzi had moved into. He wondered if Mitzi had heard the news yet. "Poor little girl. Mommy ain't comin' home, not tonight, baby girl." He shook his head with no particular expression on his face. The only sorrow he felt was the fact he hadn't been able to toy with her. The memory of going through her drawers when she rode in the ambulance with her daughter that night so long ago. "Yeah, I had me some expectations back then, Joyce." He shook his head as if in disappointment. "One fine, sweet ass. Both you and your little daughter."

THE CALL HOME

Billy Jay felt an odd disjointedness as he continued to cruise throughout Apalachicola. It was as if he'd crossed back into a world that was familiar, but somehow no longer his. Like watching a movie he'd seen before but not holding complete memory of how it ended. He passed the Tanner house again, feeling as if he were trotting along on a hamster wheel, moving in the circles of memories, trapped and unable to stop the perpetual motion. He felt worn out, mentally spent, and removed. He couldn't explain it, but as he thought about the past, waves of electricity hummed throughout his body just underneath his flesh. His fingertips even tingled with tiny sparks.

Billy Jay pulled the Buick into a parking place next to the docks. It would be easier to survey the area on foot. He felt drawn to his old upstairs apartment. He called it home and in some odd way, this little shithole of trouble was just that—home. He exited the car and quietly closed the door, nothing more than the quiet click of the latch catching. No "thunk" of the door slamming.

He slowly started toward the Tanner house. An instant warming of his heart hit him when he noticed the bench in his peripheral vision. The bench where he'd sat surveying a target, an easy mark to rob before a beautiful woman in a sky-blue dress he managed to impress, sat down next to him. "Awe, Catrina. You were such a surprise to me. So wholesome and delicate. Like a flower I'd never noticed before." He quietly spoke under his breath to himself. Before he reached the bench, he saw one light turn off and another slightly dim in the bottom right apartment. "I wonder who lives there now?" He questioned. There were still no lights or signs of activity in any of the other two apartments.

Billy Jay turned his back on the Tanner place and scanned the boardwalk and pier before he sat in that once very familiar spot. He nestled in and placed his right arm on the bench's back, reminiscing of that first late afternoon. The one he finally felt comfortable enough to put his arm around Cat's shoulder. "Lord— if you're really out there... and... you really have created me like Ms. Cela says you did... why... why would you make something like me so damned broken and filled with evil? Why would you let someone you created suffer like you let me suffer as a small child? Why would you place an angel like Cat in my path, and then let me rebuke her so easily and take my only son's life by my own hand?" His heart seemed to overtake his senses, steering them into reflections of his past. His momma, daddy, Ms. Pasternack and Cela Moses. "Why would I believe in you? Why do Ben and Gina believe..." He questioned aloud. "Why do you give in one moment, and take away the next, if you love all of your creations?" Billy Jay shook his head back and forth. "If you can't believe in me, one of your supposed handiworks, why in hell would I believe and accept you as my... savior? You haven't saved me from nuthin'! In fact, if you really exist, you're the one who gave me the desire to be who I am. I'm nothing more than a lost soul, clay in your hands, not mine. Lost because of the lack of your direction from day one."

Billy Jay's heart rate was building. But right after he suggested the possibility that he was designed to be who he was, the growing anger seemed to be vanquished in an instant. A calm once more began to set in over his mind and body. He began to think about his life in the beginning with Cat. He breathed in a big deep breath and let it slowly leave his lungs in a drawn-out exhale as he looked out watching the calm gulf water in front of him. He sighed. "I did love you, Cat. I believe you've been the only bright spot in this life I've ever lived. I'll miss you the most, even though you cheated on me with that nasty, dead dog, Roy. Picturing you and he tangled together gives me rage! Satisfied rage now at the memory of gunnin' that waste of life down on the bridge."

THE CALL HOME

On the tail end of that thought, another blossomed up from the depths. Kyle and Vio and the twisted mess of metal of that Chevelle they were encased in. "I do wonder what's become of those two kids? Did they live? She deserved to, that beach hippy, though—another pompous waste of human flesh."

Billy Jay sighed. "What to do, what to do?" He shook his head slowly. "Oh, I got my list of what needs to be done, done… before…." His eyes dimmed in the moonlight as he scanned the pier, the place he once fished regularly with preacher Gibson. He began to quietly speak, "Cat—we had some good times, didn't we?" he questioned as he turned to his right, as if she were sitting beside him. "You're the only woman I've ever loved. The only woman that was without sin in my eyes… at least… at least until Darrell. You shoulda known you couldn't fool me forever. I knew from day one. I didn't want our world of happiness to end—you do know that don't you?" He glanced away as if he didn't believe her unspoken answer. "I'm sorry about that day at preacher Gibson's church. I didn't mean that. I hope you know that too."

The moon's reflection across the still Gulf waters began to lull Billy Jay into a comfortable state of mind. His eyes began to slowly close as if the lids were heavy lead being pulled together by shear lack of energy to hold them open. It wasn't very long before his arms slid down to his sides and his chin dropped to his chest. Slumber stole him away from consciousness.

53

Hank knocked on Tony's door. "Hey, old man! Wanna get some coffee and breakfast?" Not getting a response as soon as he wanted, he reached up and started to knock again before the door swung open.

"What the hell?" Tony asked, his eyes still filled with sleep fog, his hair messed up and standing up in every direction. "What time is it, for god's sake?"

"It's 7:30 in the a.m. Time for cops to be downing coffee and shoving donuts down our gullets!" He laughed. "There's a little diner around the corner called the Coffee Caper. I was just heading there. Throw some clothes on, tame that hair doo down and let's go!"

Tony stepped to the side and let Hank push the door wider open as he stepped forward. "Good lord, Hank, bring the excitement down a notch or two."

Hank eyed the half empty bottle of Wild Turkey. "Tony?" He questioned as he shook his head in slight dismay. "You gotta keep your head clear, friend. He's coming home, you're on his turf. You gotta be on point in this. It's playing for keeps buddy."

"You sound like maybe you're practicing to be Finney's secretary..." He shot a glare that was meant to sting. "... well, you

THE CALL HOME

have the nagging drone down pat, but your tits are way too small for me to take you with any seriousness." His sneer morphed into a smile.

"I'm serious, Tony. I like you as my partner. I'd like to make sure I keep you."

"Okay, okay." He answered as he threw his shirt on and then slicked his hair back with his wet hands from the bathroom sink. "I get it. I had a weak moment last night. I still think of Sam and the fact it shouldn't have been him...."

"We've gone over this a hundred times already, Tony." He said as he stared at his partner's reflection in the mirror. "None of us are promised that it won't be us. Sam knew that and although I didn't really know him that well, I'd bet my last dollar he felt the same way, knew the risk, and would rather take one for you than vice versa."

Tony's eyes glanced to Hank's, "Thanks, friend. I'll overlook the fact that your chest is flat and hairy, and I'll take heed of your sage advice. Even though I'm old enough to practically be your dad."

"Thanks, Pop!" Hank laughed. "Now get those old bones moving so we can get some coffee going."

The two headed out the door and Hank glimpsed across the street towards the Tanner house, spying an older guy who appeared to be sleeping on a bench. "Looks like that guy shared a little too much whiskey too." He laughed.

Tony didn't even look up, too focused on not letting his feet trip on the stairs and picturing a plate full of bacon and eggs. "You going for sausage or bacon?"

Hank looked back. "Come on, if you can't answer that question on your own—I may need a new partner after all."

"You're stuck, buddy, and bacon it is!" He laughed.

The two rounded the corner both dressed more like tourists than detectives from the state police unit out of Tallahassee.

*****

Billy Jay stirred bringing his hand to the left side of his neck and began rubbing it. He opened his eyes and suddenly came to the stark realization he'd fallen asleep on the bench, and it was morning. He quickly looked around before standing up and moving towards the Buick. It was still quiet out and he decided to leave and find something to eat. Somewhere out and away from town. Away from the local cops who may recognize him even though he felt fairly well disguised. That's when he thought of a house. A house on the beach. A house owned by someone he still had business to deal with. A judgment coming that was long overdue. Ethan Kendricks. He thought of a silent promise he'd made to a pretty young girl a long time ago. He could kill two birds with one stone up there. Billy Jay opened the door to his "borrowed" Buick and smiled as he climbed in and turned the key he'd found so easily when he'd stolen it. The luck of having opened the door of a tired old man's car who had the bad habit of just dropping the keys to the floormat as if no one would ever dare use them to go for a joy ride.

He realized in this tiny moment in time that his life wasn't always filled with bad luck only. He was actually spared troubling challenges several times throughout his journey. After all, he'd even survived being hung. He laughed out loud. "I'd even been able to pass judgment and sentence on the sonovabitch that was responsible for the malfeasance brought against me at the end of a sheet wrapped with an extension cord." Billy Jay loved using words that the likes of the Ruby brothers would be left clueless of their meanings. "But I got my vengeance when they got their just desserts!" He laughed again as he steered the car east on Highway 98 towards the bridge. The bridge he owned justice over Sheriff Roy Burks, the man who raped his wife and gave him his bastard son, Darrell. "Yes... yes indeed, this time on this earth is filled with oddities, cruelties, and... and... yes... even—pleasures... of sorts. Depending on how and when one views back on them." His gravelly voice cackled aloud to himself as he drove down Main Street Apalachicola. Past Kendricks's law office and the Coffee Caper among many other little shops for little tourists to waste their time and money in.

    Billy Jay was too deep in recollecting the past to notice Tony Rawlings walk out of the Coffee Caper's door onto the sidewalk full of the morning hustle and bustle of this forgotten little shithole of a town. Had he noticed, his morning would certainly have played out in another way and the entire outcome of this visit might have turned out totally different. But he remained lost in his past instead of looking to how his immediate future with Ethan may turn out as the tires underneath reeled him ever closer to the nest of the snake he planned on exterminating.

54

"So Tony, do you think Billy Jay is in town yet?"

"I have no idea. You were the one telling me he was headed here from the Orlando area. That's not that far. I sure as hell haven't seen any signs of him."

"That reporter, Amy Jo Whitenhour sure thought he was in an all-mighty hurry to get here."

"His estranged wife didn't let on knowing anything about it. Of course, she didn't really show any interest in talking to me about him either." Tony reiterated.

"Small town here. He'd be crazy to show his face around here too much. Have you got any agenda figured out why he'd bother coming back?" Hank asked as he lifted the last of his to-go cup of coffee to his lips.

They continued to walk down the main commercial commerce area on their way back towards the pier, Tony continued, "I know he still has a son here."

"According to Amy Jo, the boy isn't Billy Jay's. He raised him... well... for the first part of his childhood until he killed his oldest son in the 'accident'" Hank spouted off. "The way she tells it, Billy Jay just terrorized him as a child and didn't do much different when he showed back up the last time. The boy was

THE CALL HOME

actually the son of Sheriff Roy Burks from—raping Cat, Billy Jay's wife. Supposedly while he was out on the road, something about Sheriff Burk giving her a ride home when he saw her carrying groceries. He invited himself in and when she offered him some lemonade—he decided he deserved more than fresh-squeezed lemons."

"None the less, I plan on talking to Darrell. Might as well do that today. Maybe he's heard something from the psychopath." Tony paused in their walk, stopping, and turning towards Hank. He looked at him with question for several seconds before saying, "Did Finney okay you just staying here with me?"

"Yup."

"Interesting—for how long and in what capacity?"

"After hearing from the reporter who wrote her book and hearing Billy Jay is indeed still alive and possibly headed here—he pretty much said to stay and watch out for you... even... uh-hum... help you catch this guy without killing him."

"So, you're on the timeclock?"

"Yup."

"But I'm on vacation? Just how in fucks-sake does that work?" He turned back and started walking again, not waiting for his partner to answer his question. He did turn back to see if Hank was following behind, which he was, about three steps with his head down. "He can pay for a room for you too. No more couch time in my room... you know, buddy... the f'ing room that I'm paying for myself because 'I'm on administrative leave,' or... vacation, or whatever the hell Chief wants to call it."

"Still grudging I see." Hank snickered.

"Wait 'til you see his face when I haul that psychopath's ass into the station handcuffed and gagged after he said he was dead or long gone."

"Yep. Still grudging. Speaking of that, Terri told me to tell you to hurry and get back too. Seems she needs something she thinks you have." He snickered. "Nothing but limp, tired and hanging to the left is what I told her you had."

Tony's face reddened, followed by a sparkle in his eye. He looked over at his partner as if he'd been caught with his hand in the cookie jar. "She really said that. She misses me?"

Hank smiled. "Oh, she misses you. Believe me. Every single time we bumped into each other after you left, she asked me if I've heard from you. 'Has he asked about me? Do you think I have a chance with him'" He snickered. "She's practically got you bagged and tagged, my friend."

"Okay, Hank, this conversation needs to cease and desist. Back to the reporter, she insists he's coming back here, right?"

"She said it was practically straight from his mouth."

"He'd surely come back to the scenes of his crimes. His apartment upstairs in the Tanner house and on the bridge where he killed Burks. Maybe his old house to see if things have been disturbed in his old shop."

"Don't make me go back there, Tony. I can't stomach that cellar or cistern, and that old man's gutted wild pig... no thank you, very much."

"I didn't ask you to come, buddy. Those are exactly the places I plan on going. Along with a preacher and his wife's place."

"What?"

"It's where his estranged wife lives. It's where Darrell lived too. Before he shacked up with a girl he met in high school, that is."

"I'll go, but I make no promises of not puking my guts out."

Tony laughed as they made their way back towards the Gibson Inn.

55

It took several seconds for Amy Jo's eyes to adjust from the bright sunlight of the parking lot to the dimmed ambiance of the bar. She felt the weight of several stares from the strangers spread out across the room even though she couldn't see well enough to focus individually on them. The crack of a cue ball breaking the cluster of balls at one of the tables sounded like thunder booming before the silent wait for the flashing bolt of lightning to flare.

Conversations seemed to suddenly return, filling the room as if she'd passed muster and was no threat—that or looked like too much of a snarky bitch to approach for conversation. Amy Jo scanned the room looking with hope for the familiar face of her past. She wasn't certain she'd even recognize him after all of the years that had rolled by. If her eyes happen to wash across his sweet face, would she even know it? She continued scanning as she walked up to the bar through the sea of bright yellow t-shirts and the aroma of hard-working contractors mixed with cigarette smoke and stale spilled beer.

"What'll you have, Miss?" A deep gravelly voice called out.

"Um," she hesitated, "I'll just have whatever beer you have on tap."

"PBR okay?" He asked.

"Perfect..." Amy Jo hesitated, "... you don't—um, happen to know a guy named—Cable, do you?" She asked with a strong hint of hope which seemed to quiver within the syllables she pushed out.

He nodded to his left, towards the pool tables. "I imagine he's over that way watching out for his employees, so they don't drink too much or lose all their paycheck to the local sharks. It's payday, so he's on watch so they show up on Monday!" He laughed in that same rough and crusty tone. He finished drawing her beer from the tap and handed it across. Amy Jo reached in her purse and started to pull her wallet out. "Keep it, ma'am. First one for new pretty customers are always on the house." He winked. "Lookers like you are good for business!" He winked again as he scooted the glass to her.

"Why, thank you! Hopefully I can help out by recouping your money!" She grinned.

"If you stay for more than ten minutes—I'll quadruple my investment, sweetheart. You can bank on it!"

"Thanks—I didn't catch your name. Mine is Amy Jo."

"Vince. Nice to meet you, Amy Jo. Cable is a lucky man to have a beautiful woman like you asking for him. Hope he deserves your search."

Amy Jo sheepishly smiled and turned to see if she could pick Cable out from the group of guys around the pool tables. "I imagine I'll be back for another." She turned and slowly waded through the growing crowd towards the game room side of the bar.

It didn't take long for her face to begin to blush. She saw a familiar face that had definitely aged and tanned, but still held that magic glow of the young boy who had done the only thing he knew how at the time, to "save" her from the torment the other kids were doling out. It was him, though. Cable Lee Johnson, right there, not thirty feet away standing in the flesh and as gorgeous as she remembered him to be.

Amy Jo stood in the shadows and leaned against a column, taking in the sight, and reliving some memories of high school. He was still very handsome. He'd held up well. His hair was lighter than she remembered, probably from working out in the sun so much. She felt the stretch of her lips from the smile caused by her memories. She watched as he stood leaned over the green felted table, eyeing the target he'd drawn on the freshly racked balls. The stick being pulled and pushed, back and forth as he lined his shot up for the break. His eyes tracking from the one ball then back to the cue. It appeared as if he were about ready to strike, drawing all the way back and then stopped short and pausing. His eye wandered a bit, and she felt a flash of warmth.

Cable Lee started to move the pool cue back and forth again, readying himself for the break. It was almost like watching a pitcher go through his mental windup, readying himself to throw a fast ball. Again, it appeared as if he were about to launch the cue ball in its attack, but just before the stick came rifling forward, he stopped. He lifted his gaze away from the table and moved to the left side, letting his stick slap down on the tables outer rail top. He shook his head back and forth and smiled a boyish grin. The smile grew wide enough that Amy Jo could see his white teeth glowing from his dark-tanned face. His eyes moved upwards before instantly looking over and locking onto hers. He looked down at the table and then back at her. Another smile followed by a head shake before he walked over to his opponent and shook his hand. He reached down to the bills laying on the rail top and scooped them up in hand before folding them and slapping the cash with a slap into his hands. Cable patted his opponent on the shoulder and gave him a fist bump. He grinned a boyish grin as he redirected his attention back to Amy Jo. He shook his head looking down to the floor and then back up, his face slightly redder than it was seconds ago. He turned his gaze back to the table like a young frightened teenage boy might in order to buy a few more seconds mustering the courage to take that long walk towards the girl he was about to ask out.

Amy Jo's heart pounded with each step that brought Cable Lee closer, as he maneuvered in and out through the sea of patrons blocking any straight and direct path to her. She held mixed emotions, almost enjoying the extra time it was taking him to make his way, but it also built more tension and excitement as she stood shakily bringing the glass of beer to her lips. The seconds felt like minutes as their eyes seemed to play together in the closing space between them in an awkward dance of disbelief, surprise, and seduction.

Her immediate attention carefully searched the left hand he held his beer with. She nonchalantly investigated for a sign of any wedding band or untanned lines from one removed before coming in. None. She quietly sighed with relief. Her smile grew and the electricity between them seemed to spark even brighter.

Cable set his beer down on a table near her and in an almost rehearsed and orchestrated maneuver, her glass hit a table beside her just as their bodies closed in tight because of the crowd.

"Amy Jo Whitenhour—" Cable Lee softly spoke as his arms opened wide enough to invite her into them.

"Cable Lee Johnson—" She countered as she stepped into his waiting arms. He pulled her in tightly and nestled her into his chest as he slowly squeezed her into a warm bear hug with his biceps growing as his arms folded around her.

THE CALL HOME

Amy Jo's arms instinctively wrapped around him in reciprocation as they both drew in together even tighter yet. She tilted her head back, her short hair still pushed back behind each ear as she took in his smiling face before she felt instantly compelled to step up on tiptoes and lay her head down on his shoulder, nuzzling her chin into his neck and taking in his aroma. She felt a comfort that was like being at home again, reliving her high school days with the one person who had stepped up to the plate for her when no one else seemed to care.

"Oh, Amy Jo—" He pushed his mouth to her ear. "I've thought about you so, so many times throughout these years apart." He pulled back to look at her as if he were checking to make sure it was really her.

Amy Jo lifted her head and turned to meet his as if they were both being pulled by the puppeteer's hands at the strings attached to each of them. "I've thought of you too, Cable." She paused, not wanting to make herself too vulnerable too quick. She quickly threw caution to the wind. "I'm not here by chance though, Cable. I've been searching for you."

He squeezed her sides tighter. "I'm glad you found me. I wanted to look for you—but—I told myself you were surely happily married and wouldn't want to bump into a blue-collar working guy like me."

"Honestly, I'm not sure the timing would have been right before now. How's the 'timing' for you right now?" She asked almost too afraid to hear his answer, wishing she could draw the question back in and bury it with small talk.

He loosened his hug so he could lean back and see her face better. He studied her for several seconds. It appeared to make Amy Jo feel some discomfort. "Can we maybe go to dinner tonight? Somewhere with less going on? Quieter and better ambiance for two long lost friends to catch up." He asked.

"Absolutely, Cable. You name the time and place."

"Let's leave these beers on the table and sneak out now."

Amy Jo's hands squeezed his sides as she loosened her hug and began to pull back. "I'm all in for that."

The music continued and the rumble of chatter and laughs continued as Amy Jo and Cable walked out the door and into the late afternoon fading sun, letting the bar door close behind them. There were hollers of, "Where ya going, Cable?" and "Woohoo... look at Mr. Lucky... bang one in for us!"

He looked over at Amy Jo and apologized, "I'm sorry, Amy Jo. You know that's not me. It's what one gets in a contractor's world. They don't really mean to offend."

She looked up and grinned. "I'll bet you'll just tell em you got into my panties like you told those jerks in high school! Not that you really did get into my panties back then!" She punched him in his arm.

"I sure wanted to, Amy Jo. I won't lie, I daydreamed about that quite a lot!" He sheepishly grinned.

"You still interested?" She laughed and smacked him. "Cause you may have a better chance nowadays!" She pushed him away and then pulled him back.

"You gotta let me buy you dinner first—it'll make me feel more like the gentleman I want you to see me as."

"Oh, you're gonna buy me dinner, Cable Lee. And not any ole' McDonalds or Kentucky Fried Chicken!" She giggled.

Cable stopped suddenly in the parking lot, causing Amy Jo's arm to stretch back behind her until she too stopped.

"What? Did I say something wrong?" Amy Jo asked.

THE CALL HOME

There was a pause between her question and his answer. "Is that your grandpa's truck?"

Amy Jo's face wore a look of shock. "You remember my grandfather's truck? Really?"

"Amy Jo—you have no idea what memories of you I have kept and revisited all these years. I don't want to scare you off, but... I almost left my parents because of them making us move..." His face changed from an easy-going care-free look to one that appeared to almost mask what she was looking at. "... it... it truly broke my heart. I thought about even trying to emancipate myself from them."

Amy Jo's smile faded into a struggling question mark. "Seriously?"

"Seriously, Amy Jo."

"Because of me?"

"Entirely because of you. I know this is a lot to... just... drop on you, but—I really cared about you. I had daydreams of you and I dating and getting serious after high school. I never planned on moving. I sure as hell never planned on working for my dad and then taking over crews for him. That was his dream, not mine."

"Why didn't you ever tell me any of this? Things might have... might have turned out so much different for... for... both of us?"

"I was just a stupid kid. I told my mom and dad. They told me I'd get over you that I was young and that I'd fall for ten more girls before it was all over."

There was a moment of silence that overtook them both as he walked her to her grandfather's truck. They stood close with a quiet nerve-stumbling pause, Amy Jo struggled for words. Words she never would have expected to speak. At least not so quickly after finding him. She never really expected to find him in the first place. It was a big world, even the state of Florida was too large to have expectations of finding someone that was "who knows where." But she now felt a need to respond with care and not just haphazardly speak.

"Cable—I need to think this through before just spitting something out. Let's go sit down and get reacquainted. This is kind of overwhelming. I didn't really expect to even find you. I had no idea of any feelings you had for me back then. I've been through a lot recently and I'm still dealing with some of it. I want to move with tempered caution, for both our sakes. Okay?"

"Is there someone else?"

Amy Jo couldn't help but allow her lips to widen into a smile. "No, it's nothing like that. I'm single. Hell, I've always been single. That's part of my problem. I don't know how well I share. I mean—I dance to the beat of my own drum. I've not been kept under anyone else's rules or expectations—ever. Especially since my grandparents passed. I've been a loner—buried in my work. I have my weird routines that are ingrained pretty deep, but... but... let's not try and solve this here... not here in the first twenty minutes of seeing each other. Not in the parking lot of Just One More! I think we deserve a nice quiet restaurant to catch up with each other, don't you?"

"A voice of reason... and just when I thought we were gonna hop right into the sack! Damn me for bringing up dinner first!" He grinned. "Of course, we should do that! I know a quiet place that will be perfect. Wanna follow me just in case you want a quick escape?"

"I'll follow you, but not because of that reason. Where are you leading me?"

"I've got a quiet little apartment where I can grill some fish and we can sit and catch up in the nice cool air-conditioned comfort

THE CALL HOME

of my home." He smiled. "You can trust me, Amy Jo. You can leave if you're uncomfortable in any way."

"I ain't gonna lie, that sounds perfect, Cable. Just promise you won't change your mind and lose me on the bad side of town!" She grinned.

"No chance of that." Cable smiled. "I'll pull around, I'm in a white work truck, be right here in a minute."

Amy Jo climbed into her pickup and watched Cable walk away. She shook her head in disbelief of how this impromptu adventure had turned out so far. "Grandfather—? Give me some clues, some advice. I just need a sign if I'm doing what's right for me." She sat waiting for a white work truck to pull in front of her. When it did, she started her vehicle and instinctively reached for the volume knob of the radio. John Cougar Mellencamp's Jack and Diane was playing. Amy Jo wasn't sure if this was the work of her grandfather or not. It was a story about two young lovers, but it didn't fit as well to circumstances like in the past. She pulled behind Cable and followed as they wound around unfamiliar streets to her. She found her left leg bouncing to the beat of the song, smiling as she took in the scenery. It was the next song that felt like an answer, but not one she would expect from her hero. It was Marvin Gaye's Sexual Healing. She grinned. From everything she'd just been through with Georgie, she felt like she truly needed a "sexual healing" of some kind. Maybe an awakening? After all, she was still technically a virgin. Well, from someone she had made a personal choice with. Rape as a child didn't count. She'd never asked for that.

The awful thought suddenly reminded her of something she hadn't yet dealt with in her life. A thing that no matter how she'd buried it in her past, seemed to always push its way back into her presence. Hidden away in a small wooden box on the fireplace mantel back at home. The letter. An unopened letter that was sealed and tucked away in a long-yellowed envelope addressed to her from her mother. A mother who should have known and cared about what was happening to her at the hands of her own father. Suddenly her stomach felt queasy.

As she continued to follow the friend of her past, one who had revealed teenage feelings for her she would have never guessed from so long ago. Amy Jo began feeling like she should run. She suddenly felt trapped between feelings of hope and fears of how she could handle those feelings when mixed with those of her past. Her nightmares. Was it even fair to place Cable in the middle of what she now felt was a recall on a fucked up beginning she'd never settled?

A sexual healing was exactly what she needed. To be touched by someone who held "real" feelings for her. Not just some twisted need to wield a perverse power over a child to gratify their own internal demons. She began to shake, feeling as if she should just veer off on a side street and quickly twist and turn through other streets in order to lose Cable and save him from the huge mistake of becoming involved with her, one he seemed so willing to unknowingly take.

Cut and run—or ride out the squall and hope for a soothing calm to come from this crazy circumstance she'd set out to discover originally?

The brake lights in front of her made the choice for her. It became obvious as Cable pulled to the side of the road, that they were at his home. It was too late to coyly escape. She wondered now if she'd missed the point of her grandfather's silent hint and he'd taken control and led her to the answer she failed to comprehend. She pulled over and behind Cable's truck with shaky fingers. After she twisted the key to the left, killing the motor, she realized—that was that—she'd now ride the storm out and see if the calm would indeed come. Could she pretend nothing had happened to her psyche on their way from there to here? Or would it be etched across her face like a headline in The National Enquirer.

She breathed in a deep breath and slowly released it in a long exhale. "Calm down, Amy Jo." She quietly said to herself aloud. "This could be your salvation you've been searching for."

Her hand lifted the handle on the door, and she pushed it outward, hearing the metal against metal squeak that she was so used to hearing.

She looked upward to the sky as if her grandfather were hovering above waiting to hear her thoughts. "I got this."

56

Ethan Kendricks sat on his front porch staring out at the grove of Torreya trees. They were becoming endangered in and around Apalachicola. His were in good shape, some as tall as nearly forty-five to fifty feet in height. Their needle-like leaves filtered sunlight in shining tiny rays as they illuminated the bright green needles covering their cone shaped bodies. Ethan thought they were beautiful, their sight every bit as gorgeous to him as his ocean view on his deck out back. Their odor smelled like a stinkier version of cedar when the branches were cut or bruised from wind gusts, but Ethan enjoyed the scent, smelling very woodsy. It mixed well with the salt air breeze.

  He was really only able to get out to either the back deck to his favorite chair, or the porch swing on the front. Joyce had loved to sit here so much. His lackluster energy after his heart attack left him making one choice or the other most days, tiring out too quickly to do much walking around.

  This life of sitting was difficult on Ethan. He was a man who usually needed very little sleep, being known for late nights out or in his office back in town. With Joyce moving out fairly recently, he'd already gone through a lot. Not that he wanted anyone feeling sorry for him. He'd been hurt and almost taken his

THE CALL HOME

own life, reaching that point where it seemed to be the only answer. Was it that which had brought on the heart attack? His heart telling him that if he couldn't manage the job on his own, his heart would take care of the task?

If he was honest, it was likely the wild sex his office manager had been offering up after Joyce left and nearly shooting himself at his desk in the office. Addi was the type of woman to do whatever it takes to keep him going. All the way up until he'd pissed her off, that is, by choosing the bourbon over her sexual advances. He'd always assumed she'd known the fact that whiskey in any form was the one thing in his life he held no intentions of ever relinquishing. *My God, I've collected different bottles of it my entire life! A man doesn't just give up what brings him happiness and comfort, even friendships were brought on by my love of libations,* he thought as the swing silently moved back and forth at a slow cadence kept up by his leg movements.

Awe, he thought again, the friendships, births—and of course the deaths of friends that came. So many memories. Roy—Charlie—and those two beautiful... his thoughts halted for a brief moment before the pause in the movement of the swing woke him from the blankness. Those two gorgeous girls in Springfield. The unseen straw that came tumbling down on the unaware camel who suffered a broken back. He shook his head in dismay with himself. *How did I let two pretty—very sexual adventurists—become the ruin of me and my world?* He asked himself. It didn't seem to matter that their actual lives had ended at his hands. Certainly, they held some of the responsibility of their demise. They had after all dosed him with some likely experimental drug of her father's company. He wouldn't have been culpable of what happened had they not given him that magic drug gone sour. They'd still be alive and just a pleasant memory from the trip. Now, they'd been a liability, a hidden secret he had to bury deep enough to never rise back up to the surface. But that wasn't able to happen. No contingency plan made and then to leave behind his fucking watch. Joyce was catching on to his ruse.

What else could I do but keep her in the dark and then let her go? If only I'd been able to complete that final task in my office. Of course, then there was Addi. Ethan smiled as he reminisced of the rough and tawdry fun they'd shared after—again, drinking bourbon together and building their relationship. My God man, bourbon was the catalyst of getting us together in bed! Why would she, of all people, want me to give it up? It's what drew our desires together, dropped our inhibitions! He shook his head as if he were suddenly just too damn stupid to figure women out. Oh, the days of his and his buddies' playtime with girls too young and fool hearty to know any better than getting high and losing all their inhibitions. *Damn! They do grow up and figure ways to hold our desires hostage to them when they become women.*

He began pushing his legs again and the swing answered by beginning to sway. He wasn't sure he'd be able to sit still much longer. Even if it were doctor's orders and limitations on energy spending. There was no one around his home to hold rank over him. He reached over and grabbed the handle of his walker. The swing slowed back to a stillness as he steadied enough to pull himself up and begin making his way to his liquor cabinet behind the bar. It's time for a celebratory drink. *I deserve it!* He smiled through a painful groan as he slowly hobbled, his walker aiding his short journey where he felt seriously drawn to go.

Ethan poured a tall glass of Pappy Van Winkle's single barrel. After all, it had been a while since he'd served up a tasty libation. He found it difficult to make his way using the walker while holding a drink. The decision to leave it at the bar and head

THE CALL HOME

to his back deck was made easier with the thought. It was for all intents and purpose, a closer travel back to his bottle from there. He backed up to his chair and tried to sit back into the cushions as easy and slow as possible. He did spill a dribble or two on his chest, *but what the hell?* He internally told himself.

He took in a deep breath of the salty early afternoon air. The waves quietly sang their wispy cadences as they rolled up the shore and began turning back after giving up the fight for ownership of the sandy beach they attempted to conquer. Ethan drew the glass of fine-grained bourbon to his nose in order to sniff in the aroma. "Awe, one of life's richest pleasures. I do so love a memorable bourbon. Like a beautiful virgin girl. Savor her while her youth is yours, rue the day when she's grown and nonconformant." He lowered the drink to his lips and slightly tilted it, allowing a good swallow to enter his mouth and rest upon his tongue before finishing the well-practiced ritual. "Joyce, Joyce, sweet taste I was able to hold and enjoy for much too short of time. I wonder if there is anything in this cold world I could offer up to retrieve and keep you as mine once again?"

He closed his eyes as he drew his glass back to refill what he'd just swallowed. He let nature's sounds of the ocean and seagulls fill the hollow canyons of his consciousness, hoping to let it drown out his memories and lull him into a mild drunkenness. "If I were a poor man, I suppose my misery of this loneliness would be tenfold. I can't imagine how a person could go on without at the very least—" He opened his eyes slowly and recaptured his sight of the beauty in motion before him. "—without this. Life would be much too dreadful and vacant of any purpose."

Ethan continued to sip his bourbon, each sip becoming a bit fuller and more abundant than the one before. The effects of his self-medicating began to weaken his hardened heart and leave him more and more vulnerable to reliving the actions leading him to where he was. Memories of that first night with Joyce began to infiltrate his silent thoughts in harmony with the ocean orchestra playing its well-practiced concerto. It wasn't the first memory of him and Joyce. It was the one here. Not the evening in his bedroom while Roy lay drunk and passed out downstairs in the club room. No, the evening when Joyce came to his bedroom by her own accord. Her own needs craving to be fulfilled. The night he laid all his cards on the table, risked his entire hand, bluffing his way to victory. That's what he'd always done. Bluff. When one can't win by holding the necessary means, a true winner learns how to lie his way to a triumphant outcome. Ethan had learned that valuable lesson at a very young age. He became quite grand at it. He supposed, as he took another sip of Pappy's, while his acquired ability to dominate others with his quick decisive words without defeat—actually became the catalyst for his desire of becoming an attorney. He continued his thought out loud. "Why not be compensated well for one's talents at bullshitting with elegance and deceitful demure." His thoughts and comments drew a smile that obviously battled its way through his forged wall of hidden secrets buried deep inside about who he really was.

Ethan wasn't a fool. He wasn't truly a sociopath. That thought even scared himself. He'd learned manipulation of other's pains, fears, and sorrows like lessons from a master. He knew exactly what and how he did what he did. He refused to let watching others crumble in defeat at his hand leave any type of scar on his skin. This was what made him a truly wicked person. And he knew this. He'd learned to accept this fact about himself and even enjoy his talents. "I am a smarmy, deviously evil sonovabitch. I do indeed deserve this loneliness and sentence of a physically weakened heart, if there truly is a God who allows us to lord over him with our own will." He shook his head. "It's far too late for this self-evaluation of my soul and what it holds. Even far later to attempt any change in my personality. I've taken too many spoils from it and enjoyed them far too much to attempt any false forgiveness of such." A slight tear formed in the corners of Ethan's eyes. They felt foreign and uncomfortable to him. He couldn't remember ever experiencing tears. Not even when he'd accidentally caused his younger brother to die. Most certainly not when his parents died.

He set his drink down on the table and drew his hands to his face, the index finger of each hand wiping away any sign of wetness from underneath each eye. "Tears are for men with tendencies towards female weakness." He spoke coldly as those tears wetting his fingers were quickly wiped away on his trousers. "Joyce—I miss the hell out of you. If anyone or anything in this dark world could bring me to the point of a heartfelt cry—or if it could bring you back to me..." He retrieved his drink again and studied the condensation droplets on the outside of the crystal glass. "... well, I might allow a sign of weakness, like a tear, slip down my cheek without wiping it away in shame..." He brought the glass to his lips and gulped every bit of the light tan liquid down. "... but we both know that'll never fucking happen." He looked at the empty glass for a few seconds as he recollected his thoughts, making them stern in his mind once more. He then, without any sign of emotion, threw the glass against the railing, shattering it and showering broken shards across the deck and down the wooden steps leading to the sandy ground. The place he'd taken his lifelong friend's life. Charlie Bingham. Just before he loaded him into the wheelbarrow and rolled him into the shallow rising tide. And until this very moment—had never thought again about it.

The phone just inside the sliding glass doors of Ethan's home rang. He sat, believing it would stop after three or four unanswered rings. But it didn't stop. It kept ringing with unrelenting urgency. His hands gripped the arms of the chair he sat in and he began to attempt pulling his weakened and slightly sottish ass up. "Goddammit! I'm trying to get up to answer you, you impatient fuck!"

57

Billy Jay's stolen Buick made its way towards Ethan Kendricks's home. He decided it was time to begin implementing his agenda. Ethan was at the top of his list. The memory of making a promise to Cali Lea Jenkins, the girl who at the time was just a young teen he'd found near naked lying in the ditch near the highway. The memory of that Friday evening as he drove his big rig towards his home. The irony, as he pulled over to check on her wellbeing, that he actually had a girl's dead body wrapped in plastic and tucked in a cardboard box in the back of his trailer. He admitted to himself again as he drove by that spot, that he had actually contemplated adding her body to his already collected one, but something snapped inside his psyche when he knelt down at her side.

"Cali Lea Jenkins—I don't understand it at all, sweet baby girl, but you..." Billy Jay's eyes began to blur unexpectedly as he stared at the exact spot, still etched in his memory as clear as if it were happening today. "... but you, you were somehow special. You were my one good deed—grace instead of judgment. A brief serendipity in the life of... of all this fucked-up disjointedness. I know that makes no sense. I don't understand it myself. Not even after all these years of it settling into my brain and resurfacing time and time again. I just don't fucking get it—but there it is—blurred as raindrops sliding down a window, yet bold as the shiny brass on a trumpet players instrument." He shook his head. "I guess it don't really matter at this point. Somehow, you've either been able to forgive him after all this time—or you're still patiently waiting for me to do what I said I'd do. Well—sweet baby girl, this evening—will be your evening. This one is for your retribution. I'm only sorry it's taken me so long to get 'round to it. I'll make it nice and lengthy for you though. Painful and memorable. I just wish you could join me and savor every groan and holler for him begging me to just finish and let him die. He'll be begging like a little girl for that baby doll on the store shelf." He cackled out with the sudden giddiness of a happy child.

The memory of Joyce came back over him. First picturing the two of them, Ethan, and Joyce, as they both squealed in pleasure while he cased the house out that last time he was at Ethan's. He'd planned on taking care of Ethan that night, but Joyce's being there spoiled it. Well now—now he could spoil Ethan's evening. First by telling him what he'd seen. Joyce's car flying over the edge of the bridge and landing upside down in the water after Bollard's Mercedes nudged it off the road at eighty miles an hour. "Oh, the look of shock and terror that pretty little bitch's face had to be wearing just before her last moments. Ole Jim was chasing and playing with her like a schoolboy wanting to touch her privates, but her having no part in it." He laughed maniacally; his laughter only dulled by the wind noise blowing through the open windows.

Billy Jay was becoming jazzed by what was to come. Working himself into the frenzy that would soon become Ethan's worst nightmare. He fidgeted in the driver's seat as one memory morphed into the next. Chubb's was another past flashback.

Another body wrapped in plastic that had unwillingly accompanied him along this route. A tire iron to the head in Apalachicola had forced Billy Jay to load him into his work van and drive what he then believed was his dead body. He'd just passed the side road to the beach where he'd dumped the fat teenager's body into the shark infested waters. "That little bitch didn't know who he was playing with when he started leaving punishment tiles in front of my door as if he knew what I was doing." His eyes began showing more whites around his dark pupils and iris' as the past became fresh in his mind, as if it were happening for the first time now. "Poor little misfit couldn't find a girlfriend like his other two buddies." He laughed. "The things dumb kids do to gain clout in a group of kids prettier and more popular, but of course without realizing any possible cost. Well, I guess he learned his lesson—just a little too late!" The image of Chubbs still being alive after unrolling him out of the plastic and dragging his fat carcass into the rising tide almost brings a tear. Billy Jay didn't realize he wasn't dead until he heard his gurgling begs to help him. "I answered you Chubbs, didn't I? My trusty Buck knife sliced you ear to ear ending any pain in this world you were feeling before pushing you out into the deeper shark-filled currents."

Billy Jay reveled in his celebration of his past accomplishments, much like taking in souvenirs pulled one by one from a veiled treasure box and then soaking in the relived magnificence. Billy Jay was regressing back into the man unable to manage himself and keep control.

The sun glimmered through the trees making shadows of flickering light. It seemed to draw Billy Jay back to the present, stealing those past memories and tucking them back into the corners of his mind. He smiled to himself. "Ethan William Kendricks, that's right, you bastard, your time of judgment is coming nearer with the setting of today's sun." He looked up to the sky before him as he continued driving.

*****

Ethan managed to grab the phone from its cradle and pulled it to his ear, "Hello, this is Ethan." He answered gruffly.

"Hello, Ethan..."

"Addi? Is that you?"

There was a brief silence that hung over the line between them.

"Addi... darling? Are you okay?"

"I'm... I'm doing... okay. I'm afraid though... I fear you won't be once I tell you what I need to tell you."

"What are you going on about, Addi?"

"I have some... some bad... no... likely some... devastating news that I would rather tell you in person—but...."

"Just spit it out, Addi."

"Can I come see you?"

"Addi, darling, you are always welcome to come see me anytime... but... this... this hesitation in your voice along with your hint at devastating news has me on edge...."

"If you will, I'll wait, and we will talk when I get out there. I'll leave in just a bit if that's okay?"

"Addi, darling, whatever you feel is best. That will give me some time to prepare myself."

"If you mean by preparing yourself by having a few more drinks—please wait, I think you'll want a few after we talk."

"My God, you're not going to inform me that your pregnant are you now, honey?" He half laughed ending with a choked chuckle.

THE CALL HOME

"Oh, my no!" Addison tried to smile to herself, but she knew what this news would bring to Ethan. It wouldn't be any kind of laughing matter. She'd known since that day she'd found him alive in his office and somehow managed to bring him out of his depression enough to share their first time naked together, that it was Joyce he really wanted. Not her. She'd imagined as he was making love to her that he was more than likely picturing her in his mind. She knew this news of her death would come as a very painful shock to him. She also knew that he would likely turn to his whiskey for comfort instead of her. While this broke her heart, she knew she couldn't just walk away from him and stay gone. She'd tried that the day at the hospital. The lure of him in her mind had been a struggle not to call and beg him to give her another chance already. He was a bastard, no doubt. Horrible to people, women especially. Wine them, dine them, bed them down and then slip away leaving them in shame. *But damn it, I don't care. I want him*, she told herself internally.

"No, Ethan, I'm not pregnant. It's nothing like that. I'll see you in a bit." She paused. "Please don't be inebriated when I get there. Please."

"My God, Addi, you make it sound as if I have no control over myself. I'll be here when you get here." Ethan drew in a breath before finishing his statement. "I'll be here... and... and I'll be sober. You have my word."

After he hung up, he pushed the walker into the corner by the bar. "I don't want her see me appearing like an elderly invalid." He spoke aloud as if he were explaining to guests his decisions. He spied the open bottle of Pappy's on the counter. He never even hesitated as he reached up and grabbed another glass and poured the caramel-colored liquid half-way to the rim. He held it up and stared at it as he swished it around in small circles, stirring up its aroma, before holding it to his lips. He inhaled its oaky scent before tipping his head back and swallowing its entirety.

"Just what in hell kind of devastating news could Miss Addi be delivering to me? What else could tumble to demise in my life right now? What in hell have I done to deserve this uncertainty—and at this stage of life?" He set the crystal glass onto the bar top with a clunk and then lifted the bottle again for one more little drink. This time, he filled it much closer to the rim before retrieving it and making his way back out to his deck chair. He slowly stammered in small steps without the aid of the walker and then softly sat into the overstuffed patio chair. After a sigh, he sipped this time from the glass and took in the view of his own private scene of perfection. A view filled with nothing but rolling waves, a beautiful slather of puffy white clouds painted across a blue sky that were beginning to fade into a one-of-a-kind sunset full of pinks, lavenders, and oranges. The dark ominous night sky beginning to swallow up the colorful beauty before him and stealing it away to the depths of the ocean's abyss.

"I believe if death called my name right now—I just may well be ready for it." He then pictured his office manager's naked powder-white voluptuous body, her full breasts held in hands as she sat upon his lap sliding back and forth to the chorus of waves splashing up the shoreline. "Well, I guess I should be careful what I say aloud. I guess I'm not quite ready for that final day." He smiled to himself as he pulled the glass once more to his dry lips and wet them with its contents.

58

"You know, Hank..." Tony began before stopping a second or two. "I've been wondering..." He paused again. "Who would Billy Jay be willing to risk his freedom to come back and see?"

"I would think Cat would be on top of the list. If he's any kind of normal guy at all. I mean, it's probably been a while since he's—you know—got him some skin time with a woman.

"If he really is here already, why hasn't he been there?"

"Maybe he has, Tony. Or maybe it's Darrell or..."

"Joyce Bonham! He could be wanting to see her. He lived next door to her and Darrell. They had their share of... incidents... that was in Sheriff Burks' files. Hell, Roy, I believe he was the one who ended up being the biological father of Darrell. That was Billy Jay's reasoning for gunning him down. He apparently raped Billy Jay's wife years back while he was on the road." Tony shook his head. "I can't believe I'm just now putting this together! Revenge makes people do crazy shit. And Billy Jay is all about forcing redemption from people who have hurt him. His M.O. is judging people and convicting them!"

"True, Tony—but how does this correlate to where he might be?"

"Darrell lives up at the Tanner house. Below the apartment Billy Jay lived. Joyce lived upstairs with her daughter before all this went down. They had several tiffs where Roy had to go settle arguments between them."

"Does she still live up there?"

"I don't think so. I saw somewhere in the files that she was living with a local defense attorney. I'd heard his name before. He's known for getting some really bad cookies out of and free from trouble."

"Let's go see this, Darrell guy. He may actually be in danger."

"Right under my nose and I didn't even smell it. Maybe Finney is right. Maybe I do need to take a break from this game."

"No, Tony, you've been the one that has uncovered every bit of valuable information we've gotten so far. You are the one who found those girls' bodies and gave closure to their families. You found Billy Jay and put him away...."

"What I did, Hank, is put my partner in unnecessary danger and made his wife a widow."

"Bullshit, Tony. Again, with this same song. Sam knew what he was doing and what the risks were. Sometimes good people lose. It's life, it's not your fault."

*****

"You know I don't usually do this kind of thing." She stumbled over her jumbled thoughts. "I mean—I've never done this...."

"Done what? Have dinner with an old friend?"

"I've had dinner with a friend, but I've never gone to a 'friend's' home that I haven't seen in... what... how many years?

And a man at that!" She smiled. "I'm a reporter and I know better than to leave myself vulnerable." She laughed.

"You know I'm not a dangerous threat, don't you?"

"What I know is that you told your friends all those years ago that you got in my pants!" Amy Jo continued to laugh.

"Yes, I did. I admitted that I did. I also said I did that only to help you out—granted, in retrospect now, it seems like it wasn't the best choice, but...."

"I'm kidding Cable. It actually changed my entire school life. You were the only person that 'got' me. You seemed to see right through my hurt and loneliness and cured a lot of it. Even if it was experimental therapy!"

"I always hated that I had to move away before we got to know each other better. I also mentally beat myself up for not telling you how my feelings were growing for you. Stupid kids, right?"

"So, are we gonna spend the rest of the evening here at your doorstep—or are you going to invite me the rest of the way in?"

"I'm sorry." Cable reached out and held Amy Jo's hand as he ushered her into his living room. "Stupid kids, right? That's what I feel like right now." He grinned.

"That's a shame, Cable, because right now—I feel like a young adventuresome woman." She suddenly blushed, wishing she could snag those words up quickly and reel them back in.

Cable smiled. "Why Amy Jo... are you coming on to me?"

"I'm sorry. I don't know what I'm doing. My mouth and brain connection is all tangled up. Don't listen to what I say, I'm far too giddy to be held accountable for anything that spills from my lips."

"What is that line you guys always say when you're interviewing someone? 'Can we put this on record?'"

"So... what's for dinner?"

"Nice segue...." His lips widened across his face showing his beautiful pearly white teeth.

"Can we start this interview over? I mean... I don't know what in hell has taken over my brain!"

As the front door closed, Cable pulled Amy Jo closer in and said, "I'd rather start back where we left off all those years ago—you know—before we could see what might have happened. Maybe fast track to this moment and assume everything went perfect and that our chemistry just now finally lit up."

"Are you going to kiss me, now?"

"Yup, I sure enough am." Cable pulled Amy Jo tighter into his chest and she willingly tilted her head back slightly opening her mouth to invite his mouth to contact hers.

Several minutes passed as they explored each other through the unseen fireworks that seemed to be exploding all around each of them.

The moment came when they each retreated their tongues back into their own mouths and they slightly separated from each other enough to look eye to eye.

"You're dangerous, Cable Lee."

"I was thinking that you were the dangerous one in the room, Amy Jo."

"You know what I'm thinking, Cable?"

"I'd give anything."

"I'm hungry—but not for food. But...."

"But?"

"I don't know what you know or think you know about my past, but—."

"We all have pasts, Amy Jo. What's in yours that you want me to know? It will be off the record and never revealed—I promise."

"It could be a mood killer, but—I really have to tell you."

"It's okay, Amy Jo. I wanna know everything about you. In a weird kind of way—I've been saving myself for this moment right here."

"Really?" Amy Jo's eyes appeared relieved. "Can we sit down? I'll make this as quick as I can."

"There's no reason to rush. This is just a first step. We can walk, we don't have to run."

They both moved to the couch as Cable flicked the table lamp to a dimmer setting.

"How's that?" He asked.

"Perfect." Amy Jo hesitated.

"Take your time. I'm a patient person."

"I think I already knew that, Cable." Amy Jo drew in a deep breath, letting it out slowly as she built her psyche up and laid out her risk that could change everything. "I'm... I'm... I don't know how to start...."

"Amy Jo! I'm not judging and I'm not going anywhere. You could tell me you planted a bomb in my house and I'm staying as long as you do." He grinned. "A horrible analogy I know, but you know what I'm saying—right?"

She took another deep breath and then smiled as she let it out. "I'm a virgin, but then again—I'm not." She shook a bit, and her voice began to grow shaky. "I've... I've never been with anyone... I mean... anyone that I invited...." She looked down to her lap.

"You've been—raped? Is that what you're saying? If so, that's not your fault, Amy Jo."

"I was... sexually abused by... by... by my father."

Cable leaned over and took Amy Jo into his arms.

"My God, Amy Jo. I'm so sorry. So, so sorry. It's not your fault though. That... that doesn't change a thing about how I have felt or feel for you right now. I always wondered what made you so... so withdrawn. You were so beautiful and smart...."

"My grandparents rescued me."

Amy Jo caved into Cable's arms and began softly sobbing.

"I've never been made love to, and I don't know how I will react—I've not known how to deal with men in anything that involves—those kinds of feelings. I've just never had those feelings before, but—I want you. I know I shouldn't just say that. We've just gotten reacquainted, what... less than a couple of hours ago? But I actually crave to be with you. But—I have no idea what kind of reaction could be spurred by attempting to do just that."

There was a quiet calm in the room. Only slight sobs and Cable holding her, telling Amy Jo that, "it's alright." That he was there with her and wanted to be with her too.

He squeezed her tightly, holding her as if he'd never get to hold her again. He kissed the top of her head and began running his fingers through her mid-length dark hair, lightly caressing her scalp. Amy Jo snuggled in tighter and slowly looked up to see his eyes. Their lips were drawn together once more like the pull of gravity.

59

Tony knocked on the door. Hank and he both stood on either side leaving it clear. A natural safer way to avoid any gunshots from an unseen perp.

The door slowly opened and a very young woman in tears holding a young toddler stood to greet them. "Can I help you?" She asked as she sniffed.

"I'm Detective Tony Rawlings and this is my partner, Hank Robbins. Is Darrell available? We'd like to talk to him."

"Is he in some kind of trouble?"

"No, ma'am. We just have some questions. Are you okay, ma'am?"

"No, not really. I just found out my momma died."

"I'm so sorry, ma'am."

"Darrell is in the other room getting ready to take us up to find out just what happened."

"Are you Mitzi?" Tony asked.

She nodded in affirmation.

"Then, it's your mother, Joyce who passed?" Hank questioned.

Again, she nodded, yes, more tears poured down her cheeks. "I just know it had something to do with James Bollard... or... or Ethan Kendricks."

"I hate to bother you at a time like this, but it may be a life-or-death matter. Could we ask you a few questions?" Tony asked.

Mitzi dabbed the handkerchief over her eyes. It was obvious from the redness that she had been crying for some time. She nodded as she opened the door wider to allow them in. She pointed to the sofa.

Tony continued. "Thank you, Mitzi. Can I call you that?"

She sobbed, "Yes. And you're welcome."

Those are both attorney's names, correct?"

Mitzi nodded affirmatively again.

"So, would either of them have ties to Billy Jay Cader?" Tony asked.

Mitzi's eyes immediately opened wider, giving both detectives cause to look at each other with affirmation that she did indeed have some kind of tie with possibly both of them.

"Momma worked for Ethan, I never trusted him, and they began dating. He cheated on her and possibly killed a couple of girls over in Missouri. She left him and went to work for James Bollard." She paused to wipe her eyes again and fidgeted with her daughter who was beginning to stir. "I just called her when I found out that James and Ethan went to high school together and knew each other. I was told they were both slime balls. I warned my momma and told her to get away from James and move back home with Darrel and me."

"And this was all recent?" Hank questioned.

"I called her this morning, and she told me she was leaving immediately! I just got the call that she died in a car wreck. I know James Bollard had something to do with it. I just know it."

THE CALL HOME

Darrell came out of the bedroom with surprise across his face.

"What's going on here, Mitzi? Who are you guys?"

"They're detectives asking questions about Billy Jay."

"He's dead, right?" Darrell asked.

Hank looked at Tony and they both turned back to Darrell.

"No, he's alive." Tony stated. "We have word that he may be headed back here—he may already be here. You need to keep your eyes open and be careful."

"Why would he come back here?" Darrell asked. "He hates me and doesn't want anything to do with me—nor I him."

"We're just saying to keep an eye out and on your family. He may have a motive to come back and get revenge."

Mitzi looked at Darrell. "I thought this was all over! I thought our new dilemma was Ethan and... and James, now."

Tony looked at them both after Darrell walked over and sat next to Mitzi and took the baby into his arms.

"It may somehow all be twisted together in a bizarre knot." Tony spoke as he started to get up. "I know you two... or three... have to get somewhere to take care of... things. Be careful, and can we talk again when you get back?" Tony pulled out a card to give him.

Darrell got up and reached for the card that Tony was leaning forward to hand him. "Of course, Detectives, we'll give you any help we can."

"Do you have an address for these attorneys? Residences and businesses?"

Mitzi got up and walked over to a small telephone table and opened a drawer. She got a sheet of paper and a pencil and began writing addresses from a small rolodex. "Here." She handed it to Hank. "Here's both their home and office addresses and numbers.

Please get back with me. I have some things I want to share with you after we...." She began crying again.

"Yes, ma'am. We will. Again, I'm very sorry for your horrible loss. And we will be in touch to listen to what you have to share." Tony said as they walked towards the door. "Thank you both."

*****

As the two detectives walked down the hill and towards The Gibson Inn, Tony said, "What a crazy stroke of luck—I mean—sad luck, of course, but...."

Hank nodded his head in agreement. "I think we need to head to Ethan's office."

"Indeed! Just what I was thinking. And it's just around the corner basically. Let's get my car, though, just in case we need to head out to his house. Looks like it's a ways out of town."

"Gotcha, boss!"

"I smell a rat. A big fucking rat." Tony said as he picked up his pace.

"We may have found a pair of em. I never did care for liars—I mean—defense lawyers." Hank retorted.

"We're gonna catch that bastard. And when we do—I'm gonna make him bleed, Hank. You may wanna stay here and out of the way. I don't need you risking your career, buddy."

"I'm with you like white on rice, Tony. Orders I was given. I'm here to make sure this goes by the book. You don't need to throw your life and career away. Billy Jay's got a chair waiting for him. Crispy-fried Billy Jay."

Tony looked at Hank with a seriousness Hank had not remembered ever seeing from Tony's cold steel grey eyes. "Or hot lead. He's not escaping this time. No way in hell. I'm ready to put this case to bed, forever."

60

The Buick Century pulled off the highway and onto the winding drive leading towards Kendricks' home. He found a little narrow path the car would barely squeeze through the trunks of a grove of Torreya trees that would hide it perfectly. The pine needle-like leaves quietly brushed against the sides of the car as the dimming sun fought through the tangled limbs to shine down and illuminate Billy's path through the forest. He idled further and further now wondering how he would ever back out in the dark. For that matter, even the light of tomorrow morning—should he choose to punish Ethan that long.

Billy Jay smiled. His luck must be with him this fading afternoon. A circular clearing lay ahead appearing to allow him to turn around with some crucial maneuvering. "My years of living behind the wheel of a long-haul truck will aid in my facing the automobile in a more favorable quick getaway when needed.

As Jay exited the car, he glanced around the area making certain he held his plan to his best ability. He'd felt his rear passenger side tire feel as if it had dipped or sank in some soft dirt. He walked around surveying how the car sat. "No need for surprises should I need to quickly vacate the area. I still have—heheh," He cleared his throat before finishing his statement. "...

uncompleted—business dealings." He grinned again. "And of course—a pleasurable one. With Joyce now—gone, and Amy Jo showing no interest..." He smiled wickedly again. "... there's always Gina. Ah yes, Gina, you sexy, confused, and sexually unsatisfied woman. Well, I can titillate you in unimaginable ways, Gina, honey. After we take out a certain 'too busy for one's wife's needs' kind of a husband."

As he walked around the front of the car, his foot closest to it sank a bit in the stack of needle-like underbrush. He stooped down on one knee and examined the ground closer, brushing the vegetation away until he found dirt. Soft dirt. "Hmmm..." He mumbled aloud. "...looks almost as if someone has been digging here fairly recently." His smile changed to a more thought-filled look mixed with confusion. "Tweedle-dee, tweedled-dee just what hell this could be." He began to stand up and he saw something that glimmered as his body moved. It caught his eye, but then he lost it after changing his position. He squatted back down and focused more on the area where he had spied the sparkle. As he began his slow ascent to his feet, the area glittered again from a ray of sun hitting it just perfect from that one angle which gave it away. He kept his eye on the area as he crawled towards it. It was about three or four feet away from where he spied it when he was searching through the softened dirt. His hands now lightly brushed over the fallen leaves raking his fingers through the dry scrub until he felt something foreign that didn't seem to fit the area. Running his finger through and around a piece of what felt like wire, he carefully lifted it up. The sparkling glimmer grew and stretched as the dirty ornate chain kept getting longer the more that he lifted it from its resting place under the leaves.

Just as the chain broke free from the soil and leaves, a tiny gold cross escaped from its hiding place and swung freely back and forth clinging onto the chain which it was tethered to. Billy Jay drew it closer to his face and cupped it in his hand, blowing what dirt he could from it. His eyes grew colder as he studied what dangled in his grip. He stood to his feet and turned, opening the passenger door, and reaching in for the thermos of water. He twisted the top and poured some of the liquid into his cupped hand and swished it over the piece of gold jewelry as his eyes grew colder and colder with anger. "You sonovabitch, Ethan!" A small tear began to ooze from the corner of his right eye. "You motherfuckin' cold-ass, spoiled, sick, mother..." He couldn't finish his sentence, suddenly caught up with an emotion he wasn't normally familiar with. Sorrow. He'd buried emotions like that away a long, long time ago. "Why? After all this time, why?"

A redness in Billy Jay's flushed face would have been a dead giveaway of his anger taking hold had anyone been there to see it in the slowly darkening evening. He was ready to fulfill what he'd come here for... plus extra for what he'd uncovered. "I'm parked on a goddamn grave site aren't I, Ethan? And one not covered up too damned long ago." Billy Jay had recognized the necklace. He'd seen it once before, but now he realized his promise was coming too late to be realized by the person he'd given it to. "There will be an extra and extended price for you to pay, Ethan William Kendricks. An extremely painful price at that."

Billy Jay walked around to the trunk and popped it open, reaching in and lifting out a tire tool. "I'm pretty handy with one of these Ethan. Maybe you can talk it all over with Chubbs if you see him. Of course, if one believes—I imagine he's been past the pearly gates, while you will never catch a very lengthy glimpse of that entrance to your new awaiting home." With that said, Billy Jay quietly closed the lid and began retracing his path back to Ethan's driveway, a tire tool in his right hand—a fragile golden necklace

THE CALL HOME

swinging from his left. The small gold cross still reflecting a glimmering with what little light that occasionally glinted from its smooth shiny surface as it swung back and forth in time with each step he took forward.

Ten minutes later, Billy Jay was standing at Ethan's front door. The porch light backlit his lanky silhouette as he quietly opened the storm door and wedged the tire iron in between the front door and the jam. One quick powerful pry and the door was opened. He pushed it back out of his way and stormed the entryway with abandon. A quick glance to his right gave away Ethan's position. His head just above the chair in which he sat looking out to the ocean. Apparently, he hadn't heard a thing.

Billy Jay walked to the sliding door that led to the outer deck. The floor creaked a sound that brought Ethan's rough and dry voice to call out to whom he thought stood behind him. "Addi, my dear, is that you?"

"You were expecting company tonight?" Billy Jay asked as he stepped through the doorway.

With a shocked look across his face, Ethan answered. "What in hell are you doing here? I thought you'd be long gone, hiding in broken down barns or dumpsters where you belong."

"I found something, Ethan. Something you were hoping to leave buried in your past." He held up the necklace, the tiny cross swinging back and forth. "Tying up another loose end?"

Ethan's eyes appeared to open wider at the sight of the piece of jewelry. His head quickly turned away as he reached for his glass of bourbon and lifted it to his lips.

"My Poppa had that same problem, Ethan. Not killing young ladies like you seem to enjoy—he took his anger he held packed deep inside and used me as his punching bag." Billy Jay stepped around and stood in front of Ethan's seated position, allowing him to see the tire iron held in his grip. "No, the problem I was talking about—was that bottle of poison you continually fill your glass with, enjoying it as if it were a cool lemonade on a hot summer's day. But it's really only poison that twists and turns a person's heart into a broken glass that can never hold anything but sorrow and regret." Billy Jay stared intently as Ethan merely sat sipping from his glass. "The only thing is—it pickles your brain to a point you don't even know what the fuck you'd care about if you weren't a slave to it. You just keep feeding the monster it turned your soul into—crushing and killing the ones you should love."

Ethan held the glass up for a second gulp. "That's some really deep shit, Billy Jay. Would you like to pour yourself one and see just what more it brings out of you? It'll settle those angry invaders you hold on to. Might even make you likeable—who knows?"

"The thought makes me want to do one thing..." He stepped up to Ethan and raised the hand holding the tire tool. He locked eyes with Ethan as the memory of his final confrontation with his drunken father while he lay in a stupor on his couch, just before he left home for good. The moment of reflection passed quickly, and he brought the tire iron down to the side of Ethan's head and shoulder. Much like he had with Chubbs, only with less force. He didn't want to kill Ethan. He just wanted to subdue him while he searched for a means to hold him in place. He also brought it down with less force than he had swung the sock full of change down on his poppa's face as he lay passed out. He was full of the emotions of knowing Ethan had snuffed the life out of Cali Lea Jenkins. But he somehow kept the pent-up anger at bay enough to withhold a force to kill, and only knock Ethan to unconsciousness.

His heart raced with adrenaline. His soul reacting to a feeling of the vindication to come. He looked at the broken whiskey glass at Ethan's feet. It's funny, but in that violent moment, he hadn't remembered even hearing any kind of crash. Just the sound of something hard contacting something less hard. A thump like a baseball bat hitting an overstuffed pillow. It was quiet. A silence so void it felt as if it should have been ear-piercing.

Billy Jay sat down on the chair adjacent to where Ethan sat slumped, blood oozing from the small open wound at the point his ear connected to his head. The skin from his ear had ripped away. He just sat watching blood slowly slip out and slide down his neck. That's when he heard the sound and depicted it as the loud roaring silence it had been. He looked out to the ocean and saw the moon tilting as if pouring its contents into the sea. The sound of each wave pushing its way, with all its might, back up the shore before giving in and retreating back from where it had come. The sound suddenly became so loud that it felt as if it were swallowing him. It became harder for Billy Jay to suck in the air he needed in his lungs. It felt like he was being pulled under by the waves, drowning with the sound that would not cease. He didn't know what was happening. This wasn't the way this was supposed to be. He must force himself out of this state of—internal chaos.

"Ethan!" A woman's shriek and sudden movement toward the man who sat next to him was the catalyst of stealing Billy Jay back from the tumult he was temporarily held hostage.

"Oh my God, Ethan, are you okay?" The woman had rushed past Billy Jay as if she hadn't even noticed him. He carefully laid the tool iron on the ground and scooted it underneath the chair he sat. "What happened to him?" She cried as she attempted to awaken him. "Did he fall in his damned state of drunkenness and hit his head?"

The woman held no clue that Billy Jay had brought on the entire incident. *Lookey-loo, what to do, what to do?* He thought to himself. The flashback to a similar scenario with Ben and Gina after he'd broken into Ben's home, had him tied up and bloodied when Gina let herself into the scene she had no right to be involved in. Shear bad luck and coincidence. How he'd let her take control of his mental faculties after letting his guard down eventually ending his entire purpose of being where he was. He couldn't let that happen again. Look where it had gotten him. Riding on a trail of hopeless repeat.

"I'll go get a wet towel and some ice." He spoke in a rattled tone as he stood.

"Ethan, darling, please open your eyes. I... I ... love you, Ethan." Addi blubbered uncontrollably.

Billy Jay opened cabinet drawers searching for what he needed to control the situation. He grabbed a towel and put some ice in it, then opened a drawer and spied an ice pick. He grabbed it up and kept opening drawers before finding a roll of duct tape, which he grabbed. He quickly walked back out and handed the towel with the ice to the woman whom he had no clue of or what she was to Ethan. He'd heard her proclaim her love to him, but other than that, he knew nothing about her. She took the towel and as she grabbed it up, she obviously noticed the duct tape and ice pick.

"What? What are those for?" She cautiously questioned.

"I'm gonna have to ask you to take a seat over here and let me—tape you up to the arms of it."

"What? But—Ethan is bleeding and—and he hasn't opened his eyes...."

"We'll see to him after you comply to my wishes—my—demands. I must insist, ma'am. Ethan and I were in the midst of the beginnings of his—trial—so to speak when you inserted yourself into our courtroom.

THE CALL HOME

"Courtroom? Trial? Just what in hell are you talking about?"

"It's a complicated story that you can witness after..." Billy Jay hesitated, "... get your pretty little ass over to that goddamned chair like I asked you to do. Does that clarify the situation with a little more detail?"

She quickly stood back up and began to move toward the chair Billy Jay had designated for her to sit. She glanced back and forth between Ethan, Billy Jay, the chair, and then back to Ethan. She nervously sat back as Billy Jay stepped closer, pulling a length of tape from the roll. The action created a memorable screeching sound from the stickiness releasing the grip from itself.

Billy Jay stepped behind her as he pulled one hand around behind her then wrapped the tape around her wrist.

"Why are you doing this? What did Ethan do to you? Was he your attorney and lost your case?"

Billy Jay laughed his wicked laugh. "No, Ma'am, I'd never trust that slick snake oil salesman to represent me. Do you know what kind of a snake you've crawled into the nest with? Any clue at all?"

He pulled her other hand around back and continued duct taping it. After finishing and checking his handiwork, he stood up and looked down on her from an elevated position. He couldn't help but notice her milky-white cleavage. Her soft appearing flesh pushed together tightly and looking as if it would bust the seams of her top in an attempt to escape from the thin cloth assigned to keep things in place. Billy Jay guffawed. "I can see what he sees in you, but—I am at a total loss of what you would see in him. Well, other than this expensive and exclusive Shangri La lifestyle. Are you just a gold-digger with big tits, honey?" He asked as he stepped around to watch his attempt at digging at her.

"I'm not going to dignify that with an answer." She worked up enough gumption to lift her head upward and look into his dark black eyes. That's when it came to her. She knew who he was in an instant. "I thought you were dead. We all did. I guess the devil really is difficult to kill." Her breasts bounced within the tight confines they were held.

"You ever sleep with a devil? Well, other than the obvious one..." He tilted his head towards the silent man still slumped in his chair. "I'm surprised that demon over there is ever sober enough to get his sword drawn hard enough from its sheath to make a stab of any kind." He laughed like a cackling warlock.

"You've got me secured, I'm not going anywhere—please go take care of Ethan and make sure he's alright. Please."

Billy Jay turned and walked over to Ethan and placed one hand on the arm of the chair and pulled another strip of tape away from the roll and began wrapping it in place around the chair arm. He looked back at the woman shackled to her chair and asked. "What's your name and just who the hell are you to Ethan?" It came out in an almost normal unthreatening tone. He turned back and repeated the same procedure to Ethan's other arm.

"Addison Charmane. I'm his... his office manager. I have been for years."

Billy Jay smiled. "Then you are very aware of the evil this man is capable of and very active in doing."

"That would be the pot calling the kettle black, wouldn't it Mr. Cader? Now could you please check on him?" She asked in a pleading softer tone.

Billy Jay looked at Ethan lying to his side like a sleeping baby. He looked back at 'Addi' and smirked. He withdrew the ice pick from his back pocket and first slapped Ethan on his cheek. No response. He looked down at the top of Ethan's hand laid out on the chair's arm and held by the tightly wrapped tape. Billy Jay then raised the ice pick above it, watching Ethan's expression of shock grow. Ethan's eyes widened just before Billy Jay drove it down with a quick force, pulling it back out quickly as Ethan screamed out in pain. He looked down at Ethan's opened eyes and asked him, "You remember me, don't you?"

"Good God, man. What in hell are you doing?"

"Say my name, asshole, so I know you know who I am."

"Billy..." he groaned as he looked down to his hand seeing blood flowing from a small puncture. "... Billy Jay Ca... Cader, you worthless fuck!"

Billy Jay turned to Addi, "See? Everything is good. The trial can continue.

"Please, Mr. Cader, you—you don't have to do this. We won't say a word about you being here. Just let us go and you run. We won't call the police or anything, will we, Ethan?"

Before Ethan could say a word, Billy Jay pulled the necklace from his pocket and dangled it in front of him. "You know whose this is—right?"

Ethan nodded his head with affirmation.

"That gravesite just west of your house out in the grove of trees is where you buried her, isn't it?"

Ethan hesitated with contemplation.

Upon not answering his question quick enough, Billy Jay twisted to the right and plunged the ice pick into the top of his other hand and withdrew the bloody pointed spike. "Didn't you?"

Ethan held his eyes tightly closed in what was certainly immense pain. He groaned loudly under his breath as Addi screamed out in tears begging Billy Jay to stop. Billy Jay lifted his ice pick clad hand over Ethan's hand again. "Answer the question truthfully Ethan or you'll feel what Jesus surely felt on the day of his crucifixion. You are a believer of the Bible aren't you, Ethan?"

"God damn you, Billy Jay, yes! Yes, that's where I buried that little bitch! She was threatening to expose me, damn it. I had to do it." He turned away from Addi's staring eyes, unable to face her with what he'd just admitted to.

"How did you do it, Ethan? No bullshit answer, I wanna know exactly how you killed her. What you did before she died and how you got her out there. The entire fucking story."

"I can't." Ethan begged. "Not in front of Addison. I won't."

Billy Jay lifted his sharp spear again as if he were a taunting Roman standing at the cross of Jesus. "This can go quick—or you can die in agony—it's your only choice of which way it will happen."

Ethan's face was a stress filled gray, his eyes spilling watery fluid. "I'll tell you; I promise—can I... can... can I please have a swallow from that bottle on the table? I swear, I'll tell everything for a drink."

Billy Jay laughed. "You're fucking pathetic. You don't ask me to promise to save your woman, but you'll ask for a swallow of poison. You make me sick. I'm gonna give you that drink, but first I'm gonna see just how much you 'love' this woman who declared her love for you."

Billy Jay turned away and stared at Addison with eyes that planted even more fear and loathing in her brain. He walked around behind her and began massaging her neck before slowly moving down to her shoulders. Addi pulled her shoulders forward attempting to avoid the touch of his hands upon her. In doing so the action pushed her breasts tighter together, exposing more flesh pushing out from the top of her blouse. Billy Jay shifted his gaze from Ethan down to the voluptuous sight below. His hands rounded down and past her arms before running his fingers lightly over the white flesh that was now shaking in small waves. He looked back up to surmise Ethan's demeanor at the show he was giving him. He saw little care in Ethan's face. Billy Jay continued to push the fingers of each of his hands underneath the blouse's fabric. Harden nipples began to push against the cloth from underneath. He continued to watch Ethan's expression, searching for some kind of reaction. Addi's breathing bounced back and forth between loud heaves of sucking air into her lungs and silent moans when she wasn't breathing at all.

"She's petrified of what I'll do to her, Ethan. Which is it? I stop here and you answer all the goddamned questions I ask or—I continue, and you wait a little while longer until Addi and I are finished. Then I'll get you that drink you asked for before we continue the questioning. It's all up to you. I know what Addison is hoping for. While she'll never get to experience what she got with you, I promise if you choose her over the drink—" Billy Jay paused, letting the question truly sink into Ethan's pain-filled brain and body before finishing. "... I'll not lay a hand on her, after you and I finish our business, I'll leave and—and send help for her. She'll get to live without sharing her precious gift with me against her will." Billy Jay gently tugged on Addi's blouse with each hand's fingers. The pressure obviously tempting the buttons retaining her breasts to concede to the pressure and begin to allow her trembling fleshy tits to burst forth exposing them in all their glory. "Well, we're both waiting with anticipation of your choice, Ethan..." Billy Jay looked down, almost hoping he chose the drink. He then looked at Ethan again. "Bourbon and Boobs... or save the woman who loves you the embarrassment and experience of what the wrong choice will bring to her? You get to be the judge instead of the defendant for this girl's sentence. What say you, Ethan? Her clock is ticking, and I must say—my ability to refrain from having my way with her is swaying. Ms Addi—I can just imagine how wonderful that pretty little mouth is with those thick, red-glossed lips. Hmm-hmm. Tick, tick, tick...."

61

Darrell held Mitzi tightly in his left arm as Katie snuggled in unaware of what her mommy and daddy were going through. Too young and innocent to feel the pain or realize the consequences life can unexpectedly dump on a family. Mitzi trembled as she sat listening to how they found her mother's body and what the scene was there at the bridge and then further down the road where James Bollard's car and body were found.

    The officer could only make assumptions at this point, but the evidence was appearing as if there had been a high-speed chase between the two of them with James' car nudging Joyce's into the bridge railing and into the water. Afterwards, James possibly pulled over to examine the damage to his vehicle and someone who had witnessed it had judged and convicted him, giving the punishment instead of letting the justice system take care of it.

    Mitzi cried violently, but managed to speak, "It... it... had to be... be... Billy. Billy Jay Cader. He must have... have happened onto...." Her ability to continue ended. Her sobs heaving evermore as she pulled away from Darrell in order to catch her breath. She struggled with the task of filling her lungs with the much-needed oxygen.

A woman officer walked over and held out her arms to Darrell, offering to hold Katie so he could comfort his wife without restrain. He lifted his somehow still sleeping daughter to the female cop's hands. She was obviously very experienced as she quickly tucked her into her bosom and swayed back and forth. Katie never batted an eye.

Darrell leaned over to his devasted wife and pulled her into his chest. His lips moved to her ear, and he whispered, "I'm so sorry, babe. I love you—our baby loves you. We'll get through this, as a family. Your mom is in a better place now, Mitz."

She sobbed and drew a deep breath that seemed to aid in calming her psyche. "I wasn't ready, baby. I don't wanna lose my momma." She sniffled. "Katie won't remember how special her grandma really was or how much she loved her."

"Yes, she will, Mitz. We'll make sure and teach her along the way, tell her stories of her, keep pictures around the house and in her room. She'll remember through us, baby. I promise."

Mitzi suddenly looked up and pulled away from Darrell's hold. "I wanna see her." She stiffened. "I'm ready to see her. Her body."

"Don't do that, Mitz. You don't wanna remember her this way, sweetie. Wait until she's—cleaned up and closer to a state you'll not have to fight that haunting image every time you think of her."

"Darrell Lee, I wanna see my momma right now. I wanna see how that sonovabitch left her. I don't want to forget what he stole from me, from us, from our daughter. I only wish I could kill him personally. More than I'd want to see Crazy Jay die in the chair."

THE CALL HOME

Darrell moved back toward his wife and reached for her arms, pulling her back into his body. "Trust me, Mitz, you'll thank me if you don't do this."

Mitz looked over at the detective. "Take me, goddamnit. I'm ready."

The detective looked at Mitz, then Darrell. Darrell nodded to him with a look of "okay" and then he looked at the officer holding his daughter.

"Will you watch our Katie while we do this?"

She looked at her captain, who immediately nodded yes.

"Okay, Mitz, let's do this. Just remember, it is against my better judgment."

"You don't have to go with me, Darrell."

"You surely don't think I'd let you do this alone on your own do you? We're in this life together—forever, no matter what we face. I love you."

Darrrell and Mitzi followed the detective down several halls and doorways until they were standing in front of closed double doors that read in large capital letters. It brought a chill just seeing it spelled out before them, all in bold, black letters, LEON COUNTY MORGUE-TALLAHASSEE, FLORIDA. A cold chill washed across Mitzi, and she shivered.

Darrell squeezed her hand and whispered. "Are you sure you wanna do this?"

Mitzi hesitated, drew in a deep breath, and answered, "I'm sure, Darrell. I don't really want to—but I need to. It's my momma and she's all alone. I need to let her know I'm here and I miss her and love her and will always remember her." As the door was held open, more tears slid down her cheeks. She knew Darrell was likely correct. She would regret seeing her this way, but she would eventually hold herself accountable for not going in when she had the chance. She needed to feel her touch and reassure her momma how she felt at this moment. She had to tell her that her little Katie would grow up knowing how wonderful her grandma was and would have loved to be around her.

"This way Mrs. Cader." Mitzi and Darrell were led through another door with a very small window in the center. The temperature immediately dropped once they crossed the threshold. She could feel the death that surrounded them the instant the door closed behind. There was a wall of what appeared to be locker doors on the opposite side of the room and to her left and right. There were names on small placards on each door that held a corpse. The county coroner, Dr. Max Conner, had a nondescript appearing face. A man who appeared devoid of emotions concerning death, pointed to the side of the room they were to follow him to. He stopped midway down the wall and motioned them to stop in front of door 12, Bonham.

Mitzi's eyes were blurred, and she attempted to wipe them dry with the sleeve of her shirt. She almost felt like changing her mind purely on the feeling she was getting from the coroner's demeanor. Dr. Conner glanced at Darrell, Mitzi, and the detective, waiting for the nod to open the door and slide the steel gurney out that rode on steel ball bearing glides. The detective nodded and Dr. Conner placed his rubber gloved hand on the levered handle and pulled down, releasing the catch, and opening the door to the left. He placed both hands on the black handles of the gurney and with a slight tug, the ball bearings began spinning, humming in quiet whine as they eased the gurney to slide smoothly from the darkened drawer it had been held. There was a white sheet pulled up over and tucked under the padding on the bottom on two sides. The sheet clung tightly that outlined the body that was lying beneath it.

THE CALL HOME

Mitzi now doubted if she was truly ready to see her momma under these conditions. She felt obligated as if her mother was somehow floating invisibly above her, yet longing for her to see her how she was. She turned to Darrell.

"I don't know if I can handle this, Darrell. I know I should, I feel like she's calling out to me."

"It's your decision. I'm going to be with you no matter which way you choose."

Mitzi looked up at the coroner. "Okay, but..." She hesitated. "... will I be able to have a couple of minutes alone with her—once you've—pulled the sheet back and— revealed her?"

"Of course, Mrs. Cader. We'll accommodate whatever we can to ease your time with the—with your loved one."

Mitzi nodded and leaned into Darrell. "Could you give me a few minutes and then come back in? I wanna do this first part alone. I just feel like I'm supposed to. Is that okay?"

"I understand, sweetie. I'll be just outside. Holler out if you need me." He pulled back, giving her some space. "I love you, Mitz. Always and forever."

"I love you too, Darrell. Thank you." She forced a slight smile and then nodded again for the coroner to pull the sheet back as Darrell and the detective turned and began walking towards the door.

As the sheet was pulled over her momma's face, Mitzi drew in a loud breath followed by a huge painful sob. Darrell turned, poised to run back, and try to save her from her torment, but he trusted her to call out his name if she truly wanted him by her side. He fought the urge to run her way but forced his feet to walk him past the threshold and allow the door to swing closed. It showed on his face that it was one of the hardest things a person could do.

The detective had seen his look and reached out touching his shoulder, "Sir—you did the right thing. I know it has to be tough. She'll get through this. I've witnessed this kind of thing before. She'll respect you for giving her space with her mother."

*****

Mitzi sobbed as she ran her fingers through her momma's hairline. Her lips looked blue and cold and of course her eyes were closed as if she were asleep. Mitzi longed to see her momma's beautiful eyes, but it wouldn't matter in the state she was in. There was no false look of life still within her body. Her forehead and cheeks were horribly bruised and swollen. She had obvious cuts and abrasions. She was cold to the touch. Her skin wasn't hard or stiff, it just didn't feel natural because of the coldness. "I love you momma." She sniffled as her fingers ran across her hairline again. "I don't know if I can make it without you. I'm not ready for you to be gone." The tears flowed and as she leaned closer, wet salty droplets fell from her cheeks and chin and landed on her mother's. Mitzi laid her head on her mom's chest and quietly spoke to her as if she were merely asleep. "I promise you that Katie will always know who you are—I mean—were. You've been the perfect mother and now grandmother. I'm so sorry how your life was and how it turned out. You deserved so much better. I promise I'll live a life you'll be proud of. Please look down on me often and talk to me in any ways you can." She paused as if she were waiting for her to respond. The entire time she was alone with her was surreal. Mitzi fell in and out of the reality of the moment. She lost track of how long she held her momma's cold hand and whispered promises of keeping her in her daily life.

THE CALL HOME

The door quietly opened, and Darrell walked softly towards her. Mitzi turned to him, her face showing the emotional wreck she now was. She pulled the sheet up as if hiding her mother's naked body from Darrell. It wasn't meant to be anything; it was a natural reaction of protection. She also knew Darrell really didn't want to see her in the state she was. She sniffled again and quietly spoke. "I... I... think... I think I'm... ready to...oh Darrell!" She broke into loud sobs as she reached for him to hold her. "My momma's gone. She's... she's never coming back. She won't be here for me to talk to or laugh with..."

Darrell pulled her up and over to him. "I love you, Mitz. I'm sorry. I'm sorry I was wrong in telling you not to say goodbye. I...."

"Shhh..." She put her cold finger to his lips. "It's okay, you were trying to protect me. You really do love me, don't you?"

"You don't ever have to question my love for you, Mitzi. You have every bit of it. You and Katie both. I promise."

"I promise the same to you, sweetheart. I love you." There was a moment of eerie quiet between them as Mitzi turned and slipped the sheet just low enough to whisper, "I love you, Momma. We all do. I promise to see you again one day." She pulled the sheet back up and turned to Darrell, "Please take Katie and me home now. I need to lie in bed with the both of you and cuddle until I fall asleep."

"You got it, babe."

The light rain became heavier before they made it home to Apalachicola. Kyle and Vio were watching out their window waiting for them to come home. The sky over the coast became a light show of lightning, with booms of thunder intermittently shaking the windows with their roars. It was as if the entire coast was upset with what had happened to Joyce. The sky's raindrops crying tears of sadness across the entire forgotten coast. At least that's how it felt to Mitzi as she ushered her very good friends and neighbors to her door and said goodnight. She watched them walk the thirty or forty feet under the cover of the upstairs deck and then she shut the door. She and Darrell stood, turning off the porchlight and living room lights and stood outside watching the flashes of lightning and listened to the clang of fishing boats rocking in the docks with the crack of each clap of thunder in the distance. Mitzi felt a storm coming. Not necessarily the one at present. She felt something much darker and far more sinister coming her way. She wondered if at any point in her momma's last days, she ever felt the call home, her heavenly home.

62

Tony asked Hank, "Did you read the map correctly? We're out in nowheresville, middle of the sticks. I can't imagine the famous defense attorney, Ethan William Kendricks, living out here in the middle of this gator swamp in nowheresvilles."

"Nowheresville? Boss, the ocean views in this area are only available for multi-millionaires and are to die for. And I'm telling you, it's just out here a bit further and off of the highway. I swear, I read the 'goddang' map correctly. If you don't believe me—trade me places, I'll drive, and you can navigate."

"It's gonna be way past friendly house calling time if we don't get there quick."

"Since when did you give a fuck about any friendly house calling time when calling on scumbags?"

"Since Sam and his family paid the price for my not thinking anything about it when we went to question Billy Jay."

"First off, it wouldn't have mattered what time it was when you two went to question that psycho serial-killer. And second, let's stop going down this road...."

"Oh! So, you admit reading the map wrong—what road do we take?"

"You know damn well what I'm referring to—and it ain't no wrong damn road that we're driving on. It's the one that you tirelessly take when you ride the blame train for Sam's death. Blame the asshole we're hoping to find tonight. Blame him. Just don't gun him down in cold blood like he did Sam. I don't want to have to visit my friend and partner in the glass house to hear about the skin games you're forced to play with ugly tattooed cyclops with overly large dicks. Got it?"

The car went quiet for a couple of miles. Hank looked over at Tony who was staring intently on the road, but he swore if he could concentrate hard enough, he'd surely be able to read Tony's thoughts. He knew he was running through different scenarios of every possible way tonight could go down—should Billy Jay really be at Kendricks' for any reason at all. He knew one thing for certain. Tony would insist on taking point and being the one at the front door. He admired him for it but was also a bit pissed. If it weren't for the fact, he trusted Tony more than any other detective, he'd give him his opinion on it when he called it.

"Slow down, I think the turn off is just up ahead." Hank said.

Tony responded by letting his foot off the gas and coasting.

"There it is, that's it." Hank said quietly. His heart began pounding a little harder. It always did when making unexpected house calls. That was the most dangerous call of duty there was. Especially domestic abuse calls. You never knew what you would run into on the other side of that door. Sam had found that out the hard way.

"I'm taking point on this one, Hank."

He turned and nodded. "I already assumed so." Hank responded as Tony made the slow turn off the highway and onto the narrow drive, dousing his headlamps.

THE CALL HOME

"I'm going to pull off to the side just up ahead there between those two trees. We'll walk from there."

"Good call."

As Tony gently pulled the car to the right, Hank reached up and popped the interior light cover off and removed the bulb. "No need to light us up as we get out." He smiled.

"Good call, Hank."

They both exited the vehicle and silently shut their car doors. Tony walked around and met Hank just in front of the car.

"Here's what we do. We go to silent mode from here on. I'll cover the left, you the right, on the way up. We case the perimeter of the home before we knock or make an entry. I want to know who all is in there and just where they're positioned, if possible, before we confront. If it comes down to it, cover yourself first. You're by-God not dying out here tonight, Hank. Got it?"

"Got it. But you're not dying either." Hank winked.

They walked in silence, not so much as a twig snap or a leaf crunched. It was as if they were walking on marshmallows. They began to hear faint voices up a short way and off to the right through the trees. Dim lights began to twinkle through the tree limbs. Tony looked over at Hank and signaled to stop and listen. One of the voices got louder, almost a shout. It sounded like an argument.

"So, what is it, Kendricks? Goddamnit—the clock is ticking! I can't wait all fuckin' night! Make your choice, damn it! The woman or the whiskey!" The conversation they heard was as clear as water.

"You sonovabitch, Billy! Just kill me! I can't make that choice! There's no need to hurt Addi, she's not a part of any of this."

*****

There was quieter mumbling that neither could make out. Both Tony and Hank picked the pace up, realizing that the possible perps were outside, likely making it much easier to make out how many and their positions. Tony also now realized that Billy Jay was likely there. Something bad was in the middle of going down, but Billy Jay wasn't escaping tonight.

The two made it to the house which appeared void of anyone inside. They maneuvered around the structure's far side and made it underneath the deck where the conversation was taking place more loudly above them by a couple of feet. Tony made out three separate voices. It appeared to be Ethan, Billy Jay, and an unknown female. It sounded as if the woman and Kendricks were either tied up or incapacitated in some way. The boards creaked overhead and the person they assumed was Billy Jay, was moving around a chair where the woman was seated.

"Ethan, I'm not gonna kill you just yet, buddy. There's a court proceeding we're in the middle of here. I do, however, need you to make your choice so we can know how to proceed."

Ethan groaned in pain, his voice weakening. "I'm... I'm... so sorry... Ad... Addi... but, I... I... just can't think without... without... a drink."

"Ethan! You bastard! I loved you. I really loved you, for—for all these years. You... you're... giving me up... for... for... a fucking... drink of whiskey?"

"Well, well, lookey-loo, what to do—heh heh..." Billy Jay chuckled. "I somehow knew your answer would be whiskey the minute I offered up the choice, Ethan. You're just too damned predictable, and I don't even really know you. I'll get you that drink—right after I have a lookey-loo at this sweet little abundantly packed package right here... you know, the one you're trading to me for a snort." Billy Jay's fingers tugged at the edges of the fabric barely holding Addi's breasts within its confines. A brisk pull from each of Billy's hands abruptly freed Addison's large milky-white breasts as they spilled freely from behind the gray lacey top that had defied gravity by retaining them in the first place. Her white fleshy breasts jiggled as Addison's nervous embarrassment and trembles of fear from what was likely next to happen overtook her. Her nipples were perked as if it were chilly outside, and they appeared hard as nails.

"Well, now, Ethan. One can definitely understand your enticement to work hand in hand with such a bountiful beauty. I myself would have chosen the lady over the whiskey—and forgot that need to wet my whistle. But I do wonder if the sight of me enjoying this little gal right here in front of you—will make you want to recuse yourself from watching and maybe even change your mind?"

"Please, Mr. Cader, please don't do any of this. I'm begging..." Addison tearfully pleaded while the fear screamed from her demeanor.

"I am so sorry that you have stumbled into this judgment and unwillingly become the defendant's collateral damage—but—as the presiding judge in this trial—I can't just deviate from a set decision without some kind of—counteroffer. There are set rules and procedures, darlin'. You do see my dilemma, don't you?"

"You could let Addison go, Billy Jay. This is between you and me. I'm sure she can keep all of this to herself and say nothing to anyone."

Billy Jay reached down and cupped Addison's breasts within his grip and gently squeezed. He looked up at Ethan, as Addison attempted to pull herself back in repulsion.

"I do believe the young lady is quivering with anticipation. I can't just let her go. She was part of your plea deal to delay the proceedings while you enjoy your libation and I as the judge take a momentary break and—well—release some tension from my bench. I believe I'm practically forced to enjoy her—by the courts standing—alone." He said as he slowly released one breast, running his finger over her nipple as he pulled his hand to his back pocket where he slowly drew out the small ice pick that he had pierced Ethan's hands with, leaving small bleeding holes in his flesh.

"Oh, don't do this, Billy Jay. I confess, I killed Cali Lea. I'll admit it. I had to. She knew too much. Please let Addi go—I'm begging you."

Billy Jay pulled the ice pick up and held its point close to Addi's neck. "Hold still pretty lady...."

He pushed the point lightly against her neck, sending chills that created little goosebumps that popped up all across her neck. She began to hyperventilate mixed with muffled sighs fearing she was just about to die.

"Billy Jay! Goddamnit! Put the fucking ice pick down! Don't do this!"

*****

Tony had already drawn his revolver and was holding it pointed up towards the deck boards in an attempt to draw a bead on the target. He needed a clear shot, but the shadows moving between the cracks of the deck boards made homing in on a safe shot almost impossible. He needed to be certain to at least incapacitate Billy, but not harm the woman. The barrel of his firearm traced the silhouette of Billy Jay back and forth as if magnetically tied to him as he moved. Hank too held his weapon tightly in his grip, waiting for either Tony's lead or on the ready to react to any situation that would quickly transpire.

Hank whispered very quietly to Tony, "It's justifiable, take the shot when you can...."

It wasn't two seconds later that there was a loud bang, sending a body stumbling to the deck as splinters of wood sprayed down on Tony and Hank.

"Jesus! What in hell?" The body above screamed out.

Hank quickly led the way underneath the deck to the steps about fifteen feet away, Tony on his heels. They scampered up the steps, guns still drawn and pointed ahead of them, and once rounding the top step, turned, and found Billy Jay rolling on the floor in confused agony. Addison screamed shrill cries, and Ethan was leaned over in the chair he was taped to. Tony kicked the ice pick away, out of any possible reach from Billy Jay as Hank surveyed the inside of the house in tactical movements from room to room. Tony rolled Billy Jay over and yanked his arms behind his back as his captive yelled out.

"What the fuck are you doing here?" He hollered.

Billy Jay's eyes contacted Tony's face as Tony cuffed each hand squeezing his wrists with the steel bracelets as tightly as possible.

Through gritted teeth, Billy Jay began to mutter, "Well, I'll be jiggered, lookey, lookey at who it is. I believe I gunned down your partner! Made a poor widow a single mommy too. Poor little boy without a daddy. Makes me wanna fuckin' shed a tear." He giggled a sick laughing sound. "And now you caught the boogie man once again but couldn't kill him." He grinned a most wicked grin, his eyes showing bright white surrounding each dark iris and pupil. "I would have thought your aim would be better! 'Course, it wasn't that good last time, was it? I'm surprised they'd send a damned rookie again to catch me."

"I suppose you feel the misfortune now of me not killing you with that shot—since you'll be going back to prison now—for a much shorter stint this time at least." He dug his knee into Billy Jay's wounded leg and ground it into the deck as he quickly turned him around so he could get really close to Billy Jay's face. Close enough that the spit from his words sprayed Billy Jay's eyes with mist as each hard punctuation of his spoken words were sharply launched. "I didn't kill you on purpose, you motherfucker. I want to watch those devil eyes of yours—explode from their sockets—when the electrical juice shoots through your worthless and detestable soul. I've been living for this day, and I'll be there Billy Jay—I promise you that. Your death will be my show of a lifetime, and I'll toast a shot of whiskey to my partner Sam once you're slumped over and sizzling like bacon in the chair—basted in your own pile of shit and piss." Tony grinned.

Billy Jay continued to laugh out loud as the blood streamed from the bullets path that shredded a trail up his leg and into his groin as if he felt no pain whatsoever. "You can't kill me—I'm the goddamn devil. You won't be able to hold me behind bars. You already tried that foolishness once!" He continued cackling like a crazed animal.

Hank was on the phone just inside calling for backup and a couple of carts, or ambulances. After hanging up, Hank rushed over to Addison and removed the tape holding her to the chair before checking her vitals and then quickly going back inside to find a blanket to cover her with.

*****

THE CALL HOME

Addison sat trembling, black streaks of mascara running down her cheeks with the streaming pools of tears. She just stared vacantly at Ethan while they removed the tape from his wrists and wrapped his wounds.

Addison caught Ethan staring back at her as he mouthed the words— 'I do love you, Addi' while wearing the most scared and sheepish look she'd ever witnessed from the man she'd once thought of as the most handsome Pitbull of law. Tonight, though, he just appeared a pathetic drunken vagrant while she watched him beg the detective for a little nip of the bottle of bourbon sitting all alone on the table. "It's just to help with my pain and calm my mental state, of course." He whined.

Addi called out to the detective, "Cuff that lying bastard, he's guilty of killing some girl named Cali. He admitted it too. To Bill—Mr. Cader, that—that beast that was going to kill me."

"I'm no killer. I only agreed to the crime to possibly get you free, Addi. I'm a goddamn attorney, I'm no killer."

"You're a drunk fucking coward who was going to trade letting that psychopath rape and kill me right here in front of you—and just for exchange of a drink of your damned overly priced whiskey. Kiss my ass, Ethan William Kendricks. You had me and threw me away, handing me to the wolf from hell."

Hank did cuff Ethan Kendricks before aiding his partner in separating each of them until the county wagons could pick them up.

Once the cavalry arrived and hauled Ethan and Billy Jay away in separate ambulances and Ms. Addison Charmane in a squad car, Hank looked at his partner and grinned. "You sure know how to close a party down, buddy." He winked before continuing. "You got him, Tony. You by God got him by the book, fair and square." He then looked at him with question. It was almost painted in bright red across his face.

"I know what you're wanting to ask, Hank."

"You do?"

"You want to know why I didn't take the kill shot—for Sam and his family...."

"I must admit I'm curious, especially since as your friend, partner, and witness, I gave you the 'all clear.' It would have been a perfectly justifiable and legal shot."

"Justice over vengeance, my friend. I didn't realize until that very moment of pulling the trigger—if I really believed I held that inside me or not. I guess I do."

"Yes sir, I guess you do, Tony."

63

Tony knocked on the door while looking down at the black penny loafers he was wearing. He smiled to himself quickly as he glanced down toward the docks across the street. His gaze then moved to the calm salt water that lay placidly flat as a pancake all the way out until the water ended, and the sky began. *I'm on the frickin' coast,* He guffawed, *I should be in sandals and a bright flowered aloha touristy shirt, not black loafers, trousers, and a sport coat...* he said to himself internally as he brought his hand back up to knock again.

Hank headed back up to Tallahassee first thing this morning to investigate Joyce Bonham's and James T. Bollard's deaths. Tony knew he too would head back as quickly as he could to help. But he still had unanswered questions about Billy Jay and Ethan Kendricks and just what was going down last night at Ethan's.

The door opened and Detective Rawlings hadn't even noticed because he was too deep in thought. So much happened so quick after months of the case being completely stagnant. Hell, Finney had all but called him crazy for believing Cader was even still alive... I guess he....

"Hello." She spoke quietly.

Tony quickly looked up; he was jolted back to reality.

"Hello, Mitzi, you don't mind if I call you by your first name, do you?"

"No, Detective Rawlings, I don't mind."

"Please, just call me Tony. No need for these formalities." He attempted to smile at her, but it somehow felt lost in translation. "I'm sorry to bother you, Mitzi, but I remember you telling me something about a watch of Mr. Kendricks that was left at a crime scene in Missouri?"

Mitzi's eyes began to water. "Yes, that's correct, Mr. Rawl... I mean... Tony, sir." She sniffed a couple of times. "I'm sorry, really, I am. I think about how my momma was chased down—like a rabbit and—run off and drowned... murdered—like— unwanted puppies bagged up in the creek."

"I'm really sorry to confront you and bring this kind of thing up, really, Miss...."

"It's okay, I suppose life has to move forward and... and... if what I can tell you will help speed up putting that crazy fucker away for good." She dabbed at her eyes, wiping back the beginning stream with her fingers. "Yes, they have Ethan's watch, a watch that supposedly once belonged to Al Capone. He practically worshipped that gangster according to my momma. Springfield City Police found a watch with A. C. scribed on the back at the murder scene. I guess Ethan paid a fortune for it and almost never took it off. At least, that's what momma said, and quite frankly, I don't think I ever saw his wrist without it either."

"Thank you for helping clear this question up for me. You've given me just what I needed to have the reason to go there myself and see what's going on, have a talk with the detectives over there. You've given me that, Mitzi, thank you."

"You're welcome—Tony. I'm glad I could help."

THE CALL HOME

"Take care, and here's my card if you think of anything else or have any questions. And know that my partner is investigating the other end of your horrible loss at Lake Munson."

"Thank you. I... I... really appreciate you doing this."

"We'll keep you updated as we can."

*****

"How's it going there Hank?"

"It's looking cut and dry as far as what happened. Bollard's car and Joyce's car definitely traded paint. It's the "why" it happened that may be tough to finalize. It was just the two of them at his office it appears. Bollard followed her it looks like."

"What about the scene where Bollard was found?"

"Three knife wounds to his neck. He bled out. Coroner says the weapon was likely a 4-to-6-inch blade, half inch in width. Like a Buck folding knife. Like the one found in Billy Jay's stolen Buick."

"Have you talked to Cader yet?"

"Not yet, Tony. How did your conversation go with Mitzi Cader?"

"Good enough to head to Springfield, Missouri and talk to detectives about a watch they found at the scene."

"When you leaving?"

"In about twenty minutes."

"No time to see Terri?"

"Not this time. Is she asking?"

"Call her Tony, good Lord, she isn't gonna wait forever if you don't talk to her."

"She's on my list, buddy. I'll see you—and Terri—when I get back."

"Be safe, partner."

"You too, Hank. Tell Terri, I miss her, and I'll be back as soon as possible."

"Chief gonna fly you there, or are you driving?"

"I'm flying, even though if God had of wanted me to do so—I'd be sporting wings of my own."

"Never thought of you as someone afraid of floating at 35 thousand feet in the air!" Hank laughed.

"Thanks, Hank. Give Billy Jay the finger for me when you see him."

Hank snickered. "You got it. Give Ethan the finger and Terri a big sloppy wet kiss."

*****

Springfield, Missouri

"Detective Rawlings, this is Chief Adner."

"Nice to meet you Chief, I hear you may have some evidence that I can possibly tie to a suspect for you in your double homicide. A watch."

Chief Adner's facial expression suddenly changed. "Let me stop you there, Detective...."

"Okay...."

The chief cleared his throat and fidgeted a bit in his chair. One of the wheels squeaked as he scooted closer to his desk and folded his hands together into each other. "We have a problem, Detective Rawlings...."

"Okay, just what is that problem?"

THE CALL HOME

Adner cleared his throat. "The watch."

"Yes?" Tony questioned.

"We—huh—we no longer have possession of it in our evidence room."

"Who has it?" Tony had never seen a chief's face change color so quickly. The chief's demeanor became sheepish, losing all strength in his voice. "Chief?"

"It seems a—a detective Osborn checked it out from evidence—and—hasn't returned it yet."

"Meaning? I mean, just get a hold of him, and have him bring it back. I may have the owner of it—which gives you the likely suspect in your double homicide...."

"There's a problem with that, Detective Rawlings...."

"What could possibly be a problem with closing a case with the perp we presently have locked up for another possible murder?"

"We don't employ a Detective Osborn."

The chief's office suddenly became cold and silent.

"You've got to be fucking kidding me...." Tony's head dropped, matching Chief Adner's. "How in hell did that happen? And when?"

"I'm going to let you talk specifics with our lead detective, Ray Gallum. He's been lead since the morning the first body was called in. As far as this Detective Osborn, I'm embarrassed to say, I don't know how this got by our evidence removal protocols. We have cameras that capture video at the evidence counter, but we haven't evaluated the footage yet. We just realized the watch was missing when we got the call you were headed this way. I'm horribly sorry, Detective Rawlings. This kind of shit just doesn't happen under my watch. I can't yet explain this, but I will personally get to the bottom of this and see what we can do to recoup the evidence."

"My thought is that it's long gone. Our suspect likely set up this evidence grab. He's a wealthy attorney with a penchant for shifty behavior. I just hope he doesn't skate out of these murders or the one we have tied him to in Apalachicola."

Chief Adner picked up his phone receiver and held it to his ear, "Rebecca—get Gallum up here to my office, ASAP."

64

Amy Jo nervously pulled Cable's t-shirt up and over his head exposing a lightly hair-covered chest, muscular abs, and very muscled arms. Her heart pounded with a new anxiousness.

Embarrassment almost eclipsed her as that first memory of Georgie fought to overtake her. Her hands moved down Cable's back as he led her towards his bedroom, the trail of their clothing strung out from the front door down the hallway as if leaving a path for later rescue.

Amy Jo didn't want to be rescued though. Her insides tingled and ached to be held tightly in Cable's arms, his heated body warming the surface of her skin as he pressed in closer to her.

"Are you sure about this, Amy Jo? I don't want you to do anything you're not comfortable with."

Without hesitation, her hands moved down to his boxer shorts, "I'm certain, Cable. I've never wanted anything more." She sat back onto the edge of his bed as he stood facing her, her hands moved from his back side around his hips and to the bulge in his underwear.

Amy Jo's breathing became stronger. Cable leaned into her, his hands now resting on her shoulders as he slowly laid her back onto the still made bed. She sighed, keeping her eyes open as

Cable's mouth moved closer, his lips making soft contact with hers before his tongue began tickling the inside of her mouth, searching and probing. She tugged down on his boxers, pulling them as low as her arms would reach, exposing part of his manhood.

"Are you still, okay?" He asked quietly.

Her smile grew as her hand touched him caressingly. "Yes. I'm perfect. I want you."

Cable rolled to his side and completed pulling his boxers off as Amy Jo wiggled out of her panties. He looked down at her neatly trimmed patch of soft hair and ran his fingers softly around the area. He leaned in, pushing his lips up and to her ear before whispering, "Amy Jo—you have no idea how many times I've fallen asleep daydreaming about this exact moment. I didn't believe it would ever actually happen."

"What's going to happen afterwards?" She hesitated. "Wait—don't tell me. We can worry about that later—okay?"

Cable lightly breathed into her ear before he gently pulled her legs apart and climbed between them.

Amy Jo's eyes rolled up inside her head as she moaned and cooed in pleasure. She never hesitated or regretted her actions. She made no mental comparisons of the things she'd suffered or been through in her past with the feelings she felt now. Everything was as if it were meant to be. Cable seemed to sense every action she craved, and he answered to it with careful and loving passion.

They made love two more times before deciding to come up for air and dinner.

*****

THE CALL HOME

Cable Lee looked up from the grill as he flipped the steak. The smile he wore was almost ear to ear. He looked back down when he noticed Amy Jo caught him looking at her.

"What Cable Lee? Surely you don't mind sharing eye contact now." She grinned, her cheeks beginning to blush. "After all—I've seen your..." Her cheeks blushed with even more red. "...everything."

"My everything, huh?" His smile stretched even wider somehow. "So just how was—my everything? Up to snuff and all in satisfying order?"

Amy Jo walked around to where he was standing, her beer lowering from her lips as her hand reached out and touched the spot on his pants that held what was inside her just minutes ago. "I could get used to your 'everything' very easily, Mr. Cable Lee Johnson."

"I'm glad to hear that." He put the grill tool down on the table beside the grill and closed the lid before reaching down and pulling her into himself. "I'm definitely ready to spend a lot of time with you and—you know—everything." His lips touched hers, the taste of the Pabst Blue Ribbon still fresh on her mouth. So, how's the orange farm? You still live there?"

"Yeah, I live in Grandfather and Grandmother's house. The farm is rented out to a sweet family who live in the guest house now, along with my best friend, Georgie."

"Hmm. I don't think that name rings any bell. From our school days?"

"No, they were new to the community when I leased the farm and guest house to them."

"So, what do you do these days?"

"I'm a reporter for the Orlando Beacon. Investigative reporter."

"That sounds exciting."

"Not as exciting as crawling around hundreds of feet above water and concrete building bridges!"

As the evening progressed, the two shared a steak and then drank beers and talked about old times. Amy Jo couldn't take her eyes away from Cable's, afraid if she looked away and then back—he may disappear. She most definitely didn't want that. Between the laughs and conversation, she felt hints of sadness as she attempted to block out the worries of how a relationship between them could be tackled while overcoming all the barriers that would impede. She tried to dismiss those thoughts and retain the happy and provocative ones. She couldn't help but keep refreshing her visual of his tanned and muscular body twisted up with hers, while he was inside of her, as one.

How could this feeling she had now—be so polar-opposite of the fear and dread they brought back before Grandfather came and rescued her? She pushed the thoughts out of the way and concentrated on how things felt when you wanted to give yourself to a man instead of being taken. She'd been so afraid all of these years that those "spectacular" feelings her female friends had shared with her of what love brought, would never fall upon her. But tonight, as she blushed and laughed, smiled, and looked into eyes that were clearly feeling the same—she felt applauded and rewarded for putting everything out on the line. She knew as a reporter that all the facts hadn't been collected. Not enough evidence to proceed with a story based as fact. But—she had put effort into investigating and was ready to do all the homework it would take to authenticate her findings as documented testimony. And what a beautiful subject matter she thought, as she continued to take in and visualize what she and Cable would likely continue later.

THE CALL HOME

That time did finally come.

"I know this is a stupid question, Amy Jo..." Cable looked sheepishly at her before continuing, "... you are planning on staying here with me—aren't you? I mean, I don't want to take the chance of you leaving...."

She punched him softly in the arm. "I was kind of hoping you'd invite me. I was beginning to wonder, though!"

After even more incredible lovemaking, Amy Jo finally spooned into Cable, and he fell asleep. As she listened to his light snores, her mind was far too wired and tangled with internal thoughts sparking and arcing off each new possibility, to let go and fall asleep. She softly changed positions by slowly turning over and just stared at her man's face, dimly lit by the moon's light shining in through the window. "You're gorgeous, Cable Lee. Just like I remember but even better." She spoke aloud quietly. "Is this what love for someone other than family really feels like? Because—it's wonderful." She grinned both outside and in as she kept her eyes wide open watching Cable until they finally closed involuntarily as she fell asleep.

65

Tony boarded the plane full of disappointment. Sure, he'd found a connection with Roy Gallum that he could share information back and forth with on the case, but the agony of them losing the evidence was devastating. He knew deep down that just by what he'd seen, he was almost certain Ethan Kendricks was involved in the deaths. He was now wondering just how many other shady dealings and acts this slimeball had been involved in. He knew one thing—he never grew tired or bored of digging holes. He'd continue digging until little Chinese children rained on top of him from underneath him. He knew the thought made no sense and was just wrong in every kind of way, but it showed his undying determination once he'd caught the scent of a dirty rat.

The flight seemed much longer coming home than it did going. He dreaded telling Hank that the evidence had been lost—stolen more likely. It then hit him on the head. He'd need to tell Mitzi, and that would break her heart. He did have the scent though, and that was the important part of beginning a battle. Desire, scent, and determination. He would assure Mitzi that he was aware there was something, and he was not giving up until the fat lady had sung the final note.

THE CALL HOME

*****

The wheels from the aircraft landing hadn't had time to cool before he saw Hank standing at the gate waving at him.

"Well? That was fast! It's either great news—or I don't wanna talk about it..." Hank searched Tony's demeanor following his statement. "... damn! I'm not liking what I'm picking up in the air between us. Feeling like a stale fart of some stranger's crop dusting just before we crossed tracks with em."

Tony looked at his partner. "You won't believe it when I tell you."

"Hit me with it, Tony."

"They lost the fucking watch. Poof! Gone."

"How in hell did they do that?"

"A Detective Osborn ordered it out of the evidence room."

Hank scratched his head. "So, tell him to shag his ass back to the station with it. Problem solved!"

"Not so fast, Speedy Gonzales." Tony replied.

"What do you mean? It's the obvious answer. Damn, did you need me to go with you?" Hank asked with a bit of smarminess in his tone.

"Springfield police don't have a Detective Osborn on their payroll, nor any of the outlying towns according to Chief Adner."

"You've gotta be kidding me! Someone just waltzed in and withdrew major evidence from a double homicide? And no one questioned it?"

"Yup. That's just about what I heard."

"Well, this hurts them as much or more than us—doesn't it?"

"What it means is—we're gonna have to dig deep on his supposed murdering a girl named Cali Lea, a crime he says he admitted to only to save Ms. Addison Charmane from Billy Jay raping and or killing her."

"And Billy Jay isn't talking—at all. He just looked at me with every question and smiled. No pleading the fifth or telling me to fuck off. He just sat and stared—and laughed when I offered to come up with an agreement if he cooperated with us."

"I figured as much. I mean, he's already sittin' on death row awaiting them to fire up the chair. The states execution board is likely already testing it out on watermelons. They aren't gonna want to wait too long after already losing him once."

"Damn. Back to square one—again." Hank said as they walked out through the airport doors.

"And I have to let Mitzi know how we no longer have access to any evidence we could tie to Ethan Kendricks."

"Ouch. Hadn't even thought of that angle yet. I can say for certain that it was Bollard's car that bumped Joyce's into the lake. It appears to be homicide. I think somehow Billy Jay stumbled onto the entire scene and took out Bollard. Of course—he wouldn't deny or admit it. Just laughed at me as he stared with those crazy black eyes surrounded by white. That guy scares the bejesus out of me. I'm thinking he could very well be Satan, himself."

"At least I'm gonna watch him fry like bacon soon. It may be the only consolation, but I'll be there with popcorn in hand."

*****

Tony and Hank worked relentlessly for six months talking to Billy Jay, Ethan Kendricks, and Addison Charmane. They were relentless in attempting to clear up the details of all the last incidents from the recent past. Beginning with the escape and finding the Ruby brothers dead, their naked bodies intertwined as

THE CALL HOME

if they were incestual lovers, to the deaths of James Bollard and searching for missing person Cali Lea Jenkins. Occasionally Tony would hear from Detective Roy Gallum from Springfield, Missouri, but no loose ends on any of the cases could be cinched up and closed. The "watch once belonged by Al Capone" that was said to be Ethan's and was checked out of evidence by a fictitious detective—was never returned of or heard of again.

    The day came when Billy Jay Cader's execution date was set. This would likely close with finality any luck of solving much of anything they still had on their plates. It had come down the ranks to Tony and Hank from the lips of Chief Finney.

    "They're getting ready to toast Cader, Tony. I know it's bittersweet but take solace in knowing you did your best and the devil is at the end of his judgment, sentencing and soon final execution."

    "There's not much sweet about it, Chief. Tell that to Mitzi Cader. That's not gonna bring back her momma, or to the families of those two young ladies in Springfield. I've been looking back at cases that were closed or not even considered to be active homicides like Chubbs Deeks and Charlie Bingham, both found in ocean water and torn up by sharks. Shady circumstances each and every one." Tony drew a deep breath. "What the fuck is wrong with the people in this town? What's wrong with the state having more taste for blood and vengeance than solving crimes for families left without answers other than agony?"

    "Tony Rawlings..." Chief Finney spoke before hesitating. "... who in hell are you today? You've wanted nothing more than retribution for Cader killing Sam. That day is finally coming down the pipe and you're changing your M.O. right before my eyes?" He questioned.

"Chief—don't get me wrong, I want to witness Billy Jay becoming cooked Cader con carne more than anyone else... but..." Tony paused. "... I want justice for these other families who have suffered loss with no answers. I know Billy Jay can give us at least some of those answers. There was something going on between Kendricks and him that night. I wish to God that woman wasn't about to be brutalized so we could have finished hearing what was going on. But that didn't happen that night. I think with some time and persuasion, I could get some of those answers out of him. Hell, just give me 20 minutes in a room with no cameras, I'll get answers, then the state can blow his eyeballs outta their sockets in a sizzling simmer-filled grandioso."

"They won't go for it, Tony. It's been signed, sealed, and delivered to all the media outlets. Ain't no backing it up now. Besides, Billy Jay has refused any representation and hasn't asked for anything but a last meal of a T-bone steak dinner and a big slice of pecan pie."

"Well, isn't that just hunky-frickin-dorie." Tony said with strong sarcasm. "As long as the killer gets his galldamn T-bone and a big ole slice of pecan pie with cool whip." He finished with a big guffaw. "So, Chief—when is the celebration day?"

"Two weeks from tomorrow, 11:59 pm." Finney responded.

"Two weeks? Shit! Get me in to talk to him, Chief."

"Oh, he's already asked to see you. In fact—you and two other people are the only ones he *will* see. He says you owe it to him, and the others are friends."

"I owe him?" Tony laughed and shook his head. "Who's the other lucky people that made his special list of attendance?"

"Amy Jo Whitenhour—and—Gina Dane."

"Who is Gina Dane?" Tony asked.

THE CALL HOME

"Ben Dane's wife. They were the couple from New York that Billy Jay broke into their home and held them hostage." Hank said.

"How did you know?" Tony asked.

"I've been researching all of the records and files on Billy Jay Cader. Those names were in Sheriff Burks' files. And of course, I read Amy Jo Whitenhour's book about him."

"Why would he want to see her? And more importantly, why in hell would she go see him?" Tony questioned.

"It's a long sordid answer. I've actually talked to her on the phone. Billy Jay actually—raped her about eight months ago." Hank answered.

"What the fuc...."

"She's about to pop a kid out. She's worried as hell it may be his and not her husband Ben's." Hank explained.

"This story and town just get crazier and crazier. Her husband knows this possibility?"

"Yup. He's of course hoping Billy Jay isn't the father, but...."

"Oh, Lord. I can't take any more of this place. I feel like the crazy is like a bad cold and I'm prone to catch it...." He held his hands to his head. "Chief—tell me we aren't all three going to meet with him at the same time? Like a psycho-pity-party."

"No, not all at once. You're up first, then Gina, and finish with Amy Jo. His request."

"Well, let's by God, give the serial killer what he wants—even if he won't give us what we ask for. And by the way, what about his wife Catrina Cader, she didn't make the list and I did?"

"She doesn't want to see him. She denied the invite. And who knows, Tony, maybe he will give you something at the last minute." Finney responded.

- 333 -

"I'm not waiting til the last minute, Chief. Get me in tomorrow or the next day. I'll save the last minute for—later, I may just have a bargaining chip."

"What's your bargaining chip, if I may ask?" Chief Finney questioned.

"His wife, Cat. I talked to her in the park by chance when I first got into Apalachicola."

"He may not give you the option of seeing him." Hank said.

"He's in fuckin' prison Chief, you know, the glass house, the slammer, the place where they have to do everything the warden and guards tell him. It's not the Beverly Hills Hilton Hotel where the concierge makes suggestions." He turned and made a what-the-hell face. "I'm pretty sure he doesn't really have the option of turning me down, Hank."

66

"No, Vio, the detectives can't prove Ethan has done a thing. The evidence was taken from the police station."

"That's horrible. What a wicked, wicked man. I'm so sorry, Mitz." Vio pulled her best friend into a loving hug.

"My mom looked just awful. I can't help but think of the fear and panic that was her last thoughts before...."

"I'm sorry. I don't know what to say. I wish I did; I wish I could make it all where it didn't happen."

"I know you would. Detective Rawlings told me he isn't giving up. He said there are loose ends that are bound to unravel if he keeps poking and pulling. I think the worst thing is that Katie will never get to know what a wonderful grandmother she had." She knew she had to change the subject before she fell back in the rabbit hole. "How's Kyle doing?"

Vio grinned an evil grin. "He's doing really well. He's... he's climbed back on the horse—like a pro if you know what I mean." She snickered. "I'm gonna have him back to walking if he keeps things—up! So-to-speak!"

"Good for you two! And that would be wonderful if he can. Is that really a possibility?"

"His doctor actually thinks it may be. He says he can't believe the progress he's making. Can you imagine? Kyle actually walking again?"

Mitzi hugged Vio. "You guys deserve this. You have my prayers, girl."

"You have mine, Mitz. I can't imagine what you're going through. I knew CJ was trouble that first time I saw him, and you never did like Ethan, did you?"

"No, I never felt everything was good with him. I didn't trust him. Detective Rawlings is going to see Darrell's mom this morning to convince her to go with him to see CJ, Crazy Jay."

"Why?"

"To help convince Jay to give up any information he knows about Ethan or Bollard." The mere mention of Jim Bollard's name brought the beginnings of tears to Mitzi's eyes, realizing he was the one who killed her mother.

*****

"Mrs. Cader, thank you for agreeing to see me."

"Please, Detective, just call me Cat. That's what everyone has for—forever. And you're welcome. I don't really see what I can do?" She asked.

"Well, your husband—or, estranged... I'm not... I'm not sure how I should...."

"Detective Rawlings...."

"Tony, please, Cat, call me Tony."

"Well, Tony—I don't really know what I can do to help you with—Billy Jay. We aren't together anymore—haven't been for years, I mean, he attempted to—to patch things up, but...."

"He wants to see you before... before his sentence is carried out. I think he may want to get some things off his chest... confess his sins to you."

Cat laughed a quiet laugh. "I really don't think he sees the things he's done as sins—Detect... I mean, Tony." She fidgeted in her seat a bit. "I think he's incapable of seeing the harm he's done. It just ain't inside him—his heart is completely incapable of those kinds of feelings. His past...."

"Yes, ma'am. I know he lived a horrible childhood and...."

"It was far, far past horrible. His father was a monster. And what does a monster make? Another monster. Darker, deeper withdrawn... a killer with no sense of morality. That's what Billy Jay was born to be by no choice of his own."

"I think something broke free with him. I think he wants to talk. I think he wants to be remembered for something other than his gruesome past."

Cat guffawed. "Detective Rawlings!" She exclaimed. "A snake doesn't shed his skin instantly... and a monster doesn't grow a conscience overnight! I loved him. I lived with him—I bore his child... the one he killed. I forgave him because the good Lord commands that I do just that. But I don't have to believe he's changed. He could—change—if he'd ask his Maker's help and forgiveness, but I don't see Billy Jay ever asking. I believe if he even acknowledges Jesus—he considers himself his equal. He believes his mission is to judge everyone else's inequities and sin. His responsibilities were diminished by his father's unjust punishments in his mind."

"Am I to take this as you won't go see him with me?" Tony asked.

"No. I'll go. I suppose deep down I want him to humble himself to the Lord and answer his call home. But I wouldn't be puttin' money in the bank expecting it. That's all I'm sayin'. And I don't believe one snake has ever given up another for nuthin'. Especially not for just bringing a discarded old woman back to tell him goodbye for good."

"Thank you for agreeing to come with me. I hope you're mistaken about the situation."

"Oh—and—Tony..." Cat waited until Tony turned his eyes towards hers before continuing. "... it's okay to despise him like you do. Forgive him for what he did to your partner. Not for his sake, but for yours. You won't heal completely until you do."

*****

That day was finally here. The morning before Billy's midnight execution. News teams had assembled all over downtown Apalachicola's main street. The sidewalks were full of people as if it were the opening of tourist season. Tony was up earlier than usual. Terri, his new girlfriend, had surprised him the night before by showing up and knocking on his door at 10 o'clock. He was pleasantly surprised when he was greeted by her covered only by a very sheer sundress—no undergarments underneath. Just warm soft skin aching to lie nestled into his. There was hardly time for a spoken hello before he sensed what was on her mind. And— it happened to be the exact thing on his mind and just what the doctor ordered to loosen his tight muscles.

This was the morning he was to meet the other women who had made Billy Jay's list. Tony had contacted each one asking for all to get together and discuss how this oddly requested meeting would go. None of the three others, all women in Billy's life in assorted ways, had any inkling of how or why this was going down. They'd all agreed to meet discreetly at Gina and Ben's restaurant,

THE CALL HOME

Apple on the Bay, before heading east to Raiford, Florida, to the Florida State Prison where the event would take place.

Gina, of course, was the first one there to answer the door at the restaurant that overlooked the bay. She was very pregnant and appeared ready to give birth at any moment. Ben, her husband, introduced himself and shared a few minutes of conversation before he excused himself to the office in back. Gina led Tony to a table next to the bank of windows that overlooked the water. A gorgeous view that he commented on more than once.

"So, here we are Detective...."

"Please, Mrs. Dane, call me Tony."

"Only if you agree to call me Gina."

"Of course." Tony smiled. "So, when's the due date?"

"Wednesday is the official day, if I make it that long!" She chuckled.

"I imagine your husband is excited—and scared as hell too!" He grinned.

"If you only knew the half of it, Tony." Gina pulled a chair to sit. "My back is killing me, so I hope it's okay to sit."

"Perfect! I only wish I was here for food and the view!"

"I have coffee coming out to us. Black? Or cream and sugar?"

"Black is perfect."

She smiled and then that smile faded as if she had something to say but didn't know how to broach it.

"You can tell me anything, Gina. I'm not here to judge you or demand anything."

She hesitated before starting, "You mentioned my husband being nervous and scared about this baby..." She looked down at the table and fidgeted with the silverware laid out. "... well, he is very scared. It's probably because of Billy Jay wanting to see me.

You see—about nine months ago..." Her head moved to the coastline, her eyes appeared to focus on the horizon and the clouds hovering just above. "... Ben and I were, well, the business was just getting started and... and... Billy Jay was an employee of ours. Long story short, we went out of town for the day to pick up some artwork..." Her hand rose from the table and with her pointing finger, she moved it around aiming it at several pieces of large works hanging on the walls. "... he was driving me in our work van to pick them up. Our discussion led back to New York when I stumbled onto him, Ben tied up in a chair and bleeding. I asked him why he hadn't raped me when he had the chance." Her eyes maneuvered back down to the table in an embarrassing retreat. "...to shorten this story up, we had sex. I'm not sure if it could actually be called rape or... I mean... I had said no... but... I also brought the circumstance on myself. When I found out I was pregnant... I held off telling Ben until he... until he knew something horrible was happening inside my head. I guess when I just blurted it out to him one night expecting to lose him over my words and actions, I was surprised. Becau... because Ben is a very... a loving and... very special man. He's stuck with me no matter what the outcome. I'm not sure if my baby is my husband's... or... or that monster's." Gina's eyes lifted from the table and stared deep into Tony's. "I used to be a stripper in New York City. I wasn't the nicer woman I've grown into. I don't want to break my husband's heart and I know that is why Billy Jay wants to see me. To gloat and twist the blade in a little deeper, a little harder into me... and... and Ben. He wants me to tell him that the baby is his... before he dies. I know he wants to know he has a legacy left... he... he killed his first... first son."

"It's none of my business, but—do you think your baby is his?"

THE CALL HOME

"I have no idea. I've never been pregnant before. I don't know if some of these sharp pains are normal or if they are driven by the demon who may have planted his seed inside me that's growing and wanting out."

"I'm sorry, Gina. That has to be an awful lot to have to think about, through a time that is supposed to be filled with joy. Don't give him the satisfaction of controlling you. It won't change the outcome and Billy Jay doesn't deserve to gain anything from you. Nothing. In less than fifteen hours—he will be gone from this earth forever, nothing but a nasty memory and only if we allow that to him."

"I'm sorry for what he did to your partner and his family. I truly am very sorry. Ben and I thought we were doing what God wanted us to do by bringing him back to face his past. He fooled us into believing in him. He's brought nothing but pain to us and this community. And for that, I'm very sorry." Her hand reached over and touched Detective Rawlings hand.

"Thank you for that, Gina. It's not necessary but thank you."

A woman brought in a tray with cups and a full pot of coffee, setting it quietly on the table before leaning down to Gina's ear and speaking quietly.

"It appears your other guests are here; can I have Kanita show them in?"

"Certainly." Tony spoke, sliding his hand out from underneath Gina's.

Gina nodded to Kanita and then reached for a cup to fill for Tony.

As the two women made their way between the tables to where he and Gina were seated, the two stood up to greet them.

"Hello, I'm Amy Jo Whitenhour, from the Orlando Beacon."

"I'm Catrina Anne Cader, but y'all can just call me Cat. Everyone does."

All four sat down and Gina poured two more cups of coffee and slid them to each one of the guests before picking hers up and slowly sipping it.

"I'm detective Tony Rawlings from the State Police Task force. I along with my previous partner, Sam Hayden, were tasked to work on the murder case of Sherriff Roy Burks. We went to talk to the suspect, Billy Jay Cader, and question him when a gunfight ensued and took the life of my partner Sam. Billy Jay has been my case ever since. I appreciate all of you for agreeing to meet in advance of our scheduled meetings tonight with Billy Jay. I'm not entirely sure of what to expect, but I've learned it's always best to be prepared in advance so chances such as mine and Sam's, don't happen again."

Gina spoke up. "Will we be in any kind of danger?"

"No, ma'am. Billy Jay will be secured and unable to harm. My statement was merely to point out, being prepared is far more beneficial than being caught by surprise. I have no idea what Billy Jay hopes to gain from this other than showing his control he still believes he has by getting us to give him an audience."

Amy Jo began to speak, "I don't know if any of you have read my book, Snapshot into a Killer's Mind, but I spent sixteen weeks going out to the prison he was in and interviewing him for the book. He's a charismatic individual with the ability to persuade outcomes you would never expect to give him. I gave him the benefit of all my doubts up and until I found out about the seven girls that..." Her eyes and demeanor changed upon even the short mention of the girls. "... the girls he brutalized and killed. Before

THE CALL HOME

that came out, I have to admit I was sucked in and held compassion for him. I still believe if he were not made to grow up in the circumstances, he was in, that he would be a completely different person. Nature versus nurture has always been a theory I hold interest in."

"I loved him deeply. But I saw brutality worse than I could have imagined. He tortured my boys with his damned Mason jar punishments. I loved him and hated him all at the same time. He was like a dark spell cast over me. One that took years to break. More difficult than giving up the booze I am addicted to." Cat spoke in tones of quiet reserved reflection.

"I suppose we all have our skeletons that we bare from Billy Jay's actions." Gina answered as she looked down and ran her fingers in tiny circles around her belly.

Cat looked over at Gina's actions and contemplated the look across her face. "Is he responsible for your baby?"

Gina smiled an odd smile before answering. "I wish I could say for certain that he wasn't, but only time will tell." She said in a monotone voice holding mild hope.

The four sitting around the table continued talking and sipping coffee until Kanita returned with another worker carrying in trays holding breakfast plates and began placing them in front of each guest.

"This smells absolutely wonderful! And totally unexpected!" Tony boasted.

"Serendipitous!" Amy Jo added.

"I haven't eaten here yet, I'm ashamed to say." Answered Cat.

"I've been told the eggs are reminiscent of yours, Miss Cat." Gina replied. "This recipe is from my mom. Born and raised in the Bronx, New York, although I was told by Jay that it was the south's way of cooking them." It was the first statement about Billy Jay that held no tones of negativity hidden within.

"Of course, I was told that after he'd broken into Ben's home and held him hostage. He told me he was hungry and asked me to cook him some breakfast, which I did out of complete fear. He looked a complete mess. Greasy messed up long hair and scraggly beard, that captured spilled scrambled eggs, dirty clothes. Looked just like what one would expect to see a homeless man looking like." She suddenly stopped talking after noticing the blank stares from everyone's eyes. "Anyway, I hope you enjoy them. Sorry for rambling. That damned man still deals out moments of normality as if he were never the raving lunatic that he truly is."

67

Addison wasn't able to get much sleep lately. Her world was tipped topsy-turvy ever since Joyce's disappearance. She'd certainly gotten to make the move towards Ethan after finding him in his office alive when she'd expected a horrible scene of his bloody death instead. But Ethan never returned to the demeanor he had before that day. It was as if he'd lost his mojo. His game off-kilter with Joyce's absence. And now, possibly facing horrible charges of things she knew deep down he was very capable of, but refused to let the suspicions totally overtake her perception of what she wanted him to be. At least all the way up until this last night out on his deck with Billy Jay Cader.

  She'd gone out there to give him the news of Joyce's death in the car wreck, hoping to console him and woo him back. Seduce him for another round of passionate lovemaking that might sway him towards forgetting and accepting Joyce was gone for good. But that hadn't happened. She realized she'd not only lost him to Joyce, but the power of his drinking held much too strong a hold over him to force a choice between whiskey or her undying love. The alcohol had long been his best true friend, able to be there with nothing more than a twist of the cork and a crystal glass. The desire much easier to swallow and fall into that type of ecstasy than dealing with the hard to control emotions of a woman who knew him all so well.

The thoughts and memories were there though. Her body ached to be twisted into knots with his. Him on top ravaging her as if she were his prize. The smell of bourbon infiltrating her nostrils as he heavily breathed into her ear as he thrust his hips forward, driving his lust deep inside her. She found herself lying under the sheet, legs open apart widely as her fingers caressed that special spot, she knew all so well. She'd spent hours dreaming of what finally had happened to her. Years of playing secret roles with her boss in scenes performed on top of her desk, the front door locked, or in the conference room, or like what finally played out for real. The black leather couch in his office, the large bull shark dangling overhead by thin wires. Backlit by subtle lighting giving the appearance of the alpha predator lured in closely to what may have been seen as a seal in distress, circling to decide to strike and give in to a feeding frenzy or evade a meal determining the risk too great. That first time was intense. She'd only imagined the outcome for years previous, never expecting to actually live it out in reality. The recent memory now overtaking her reality as she replayed their first time together. Addi's fingers plunged deeper, her coos and sighs becoming less restrained.

"Oh, Ethan..." She cried out, almost instantly recognizing there would be no returned response. There was no odor of whiskey surrounding her, no groans of satisfaction being growled into her ear. No moving hot, sweaty flesh grinding against hers. Nothing but fingers of her own searching the cavity of her body. Emptiness overwhelmed her as her fingers withdrew, her hand moving up to her stomach as it suddenly felt the pangs of loneliness. "Will I die alone? Will I be known as Apalachicola's

THE CALL HOME

lonely old spinster who conceded herself to a Pitbull holding dark secrets and only caring for himself—and expensive libations?"

Suddenly those passionate feelings fell sour, leaving her full of self-disgust at what she was doing just mere seconds ago.

The date suddenly entered her mind. It was execution day for Billy Jay Cader. She knew Ethan would want to be there if they allowed him. He'd, after all, at one time offered to represent him. Would the outcome of the scene on his deck have changed his ability to do so? They hadn't found any evidence to keep him locked up. Would he somehow slither away from any culpability of the young girl's disappearance that he and Billy Jay were beginning to discuss before the detective stopped Billy Jay from possibly driving the ice pick into her brain right in front of Ethan?

She had heard through the legal grapevine that he had been chosen as one of the twelve citizens invited to view the execution by the warden who had the decision-making authority. Amy Jo Whitenhour was chosen as one of the media, Billy Jay's estranged wife Catrina Cader was allowed as family, as was Darrell should he choose to go, even though Roy Burks was his biological father. Ethan Kendricks, Detective Tony Rawlings, and Gina Dane by choice of the warden. She imagined the warden had chosen some of the twelve allowed at Billy Jay's request although she had no official facts to confirm that. Only through Ethan's past experiences on cases he'd worked that ended in such, which were very few because of his extraordinary record of seldom losing. She imagined he would be attending if circumstances had not changed. He would likely enjoy watching this particular case come to a final close due to recent developments. His future may well depend on it closing in silence.

Addison Charmane threw her sheets back, exposing her naked powdery flesh. She climbed from her bed, making her way to the bathroom where she peed and immediately climbed into her shower hoping to scrub away the memory of—well—everything. Especially her moment of weakness she'd caved into. She'd go to Ethan's office and check phone messages and see if there was any sign of him being there. After all, one cannot just remove the muscle memory of "showing up" to one's only career for so many years, no matter what the circumstances had brought. It was bred into her like a daily prayer taught to be consistent. It was habit. It had been her entire life up to this point. Old habits die hard.

    The warm water dribbled down Addi's skin as she ran the soapy washcloth over herself attempting to scrub away unwanted memories. There were still moments she seemed to fight, drawing attention to the areas Ethan was drawn to. Her mind was a mess, and she feared this internal battle was one of permanence that would cling to her no matter how much she mentally attempted to eliminate it.

    After drying off, she studied herself in the mirror. She would be forty-five in a few short weeks. Would she ever find a man who would be interested in her? Technically, she was likely unemployed, never married, no children, and lived in an apartment she would soon not be able to afford when the paychecks ended. She had lived very humbly and had a bank account that would take care of her for a while, but not indefinitely.

    As she stared into the mirror at the face looking as intently back, she asked herself aloud, "Should I start searching for something far away from this place?" Her hands moved light fingertips over her nude body, causing tiny goosebumps to swell and appear over the trails she laid. "Is there a man in this state with the appeal of Ethan but the heart of someone much kinder? Would I even be attracted to such a man if I were to stumble into him? Am I some kind of sadist when it comes to the opposite sex? My

THE CALL HOME

uncontrolled needs to be dominated and abused yet given the freedom to run an office like I have Ethan's?" The goosebumps disappeared as quickly as they'd popped up and she decided it was a sign to get dressed and head to the office.

An hour and a half later, Addison found herself unlocking the office of Ethan William Kendricks, Defense Attorney at Law. She flipped the lights on even though the sun shining through the windows was more than adequately doing the job without their aid. She set her purse on her desk and began to roam throughout as if it were her first day and exploration was needed to acquaint herself. She moved down the hallway and peered into what was Joyce Bonham's office for a short time. The nameplate was still there. The memory of welcoming her and showing her the office fed the feelings of excitement Joyce had shown upon stepping in and seeing her name on the door and then walking across the threshold and being totally taken off guard at the huge desk and bookshelves surrounding the walls. "You gave it all away, honey. I wonder if you ever had regret. I don't believe I could have done what you did, just walk away and never look back. Of course, see what it got you?" She ran her hand over the leather covered desktop, papers still stacked neatly in the tray from the day she left, as if they were there for her to pick up and continue completing the needed work. Ethan had all but stopped practicing law after that day. Clients were still calling, and she'd done everything she could do to complete what Joyce hadn't. Life at the firm had all but come to a stop since then. Joyce's office frozen in time as if a harsh winter had fallen, covering everything in a cold frost.

Addison backed out of the office and turned, staring at the door immediately across the hallway from her. Ethan's door. The quick memory of jumping up and running to it that day she heard the sound of a single gunshot from behind it. She suddenly felt the same chill as her hand reached for the knob, wondering if she could, or even should twist it to the right, allowing the door to swing open freely.

The call to explore her recent past overtook her will to leave it buried. She grabbed the doorknob and slowly twisted it until the mechanism clicked, allowing the door to begin its opening. Upon stepping across the threshold, the large bull shark looming overhead was the first sight that her eyes gravitated to. Her gaze then fell to the black leather sofa below before taking in the pool table and to his collection of expensive bottles of bourbon that donned the shelves lit by the blue lights above. "Damn you Pappy Van Winkle and your poisonous venom that aided in bringing the man I loved to his knees.

Her head then turned to his desk. The place she'd found Ethan a few seconds after the shot. A cold black steel revolver still in his hand, empty crystal glass sitting beside his other hand resting on the leather clad top. She looked over at the gigantic original painting by Steven Bassett, the artist who painted the creation that Ethan was drawn to paying whatever price he asked in order to have it hanging in his showplace. The colors red, black, white, and yellow melding to oranges over the thin blue line. The painting still held the tiny hole where Ethan's decision to end his own life had suddenly changed and turned the barrel of the gun to the black and red explosion. He loved that damn painting, she thought to herself as she stared so intently. She didn't notice the door open a bit wider, or the shadow the sun cast through Joyce's windows and the glass pane of her door through his.

"Addison, my dear...."

She turned startled as her hand naturally reached to her cleavage in shock. "Oh, my Lord, Ethan. You scared the hell out of me!" She stood silent for a moment searching for further words to say. "I'm... I'm sorry... I suppose... I should... should turn my keys back in... I know... I probably... don't... don't work here anymore. Habits... are... are hard to break." She stumbled end over end with her thoughts and words.

"Bullshit, Addison!" Ethan shot back. "You will be here I hope, as long as I am. Hell, I've left the business to you after I die. You've been the most faithful friend and employee I have ever had."

"Ethan—other than Joyce—I've been your only employee you've ever had, so I'm not sure what value that makes me other than foolish at this point."

Ethan sauntered in closer with a limp, his cane in hand, his eyes appearing as if they'd aged twice as much as his recently broken body had. Once he had hobbled close enough to touch her, his hand reached out and waited to see if she would move in for a hug or stay at bay.

"Oh, Ethan. How do you still keep this control over my will? And why?" She said as she moved into his personal space and widened her arms to accept him into them.

"Addi, my dear, I'm a lost cause and you deserve so much better. I'm... I'm falling... failing... falling apart. Age and circumstance are swallowing me down like a bitter pill."

"Bullshit, Ethan. You seem to forget some physical activity we recently shared—right over there..." She pointed towards the leather couch. "You aren't too old. You're a fucked-up individual... but... somehow... somehow... I am always... drawn back in." She reached around and gripped his back, letting one hand slide down to his ass before giving up the restraint she thought she held from letting her desires take over and moving her fingers to his front side and searching out what she'd daydreamed earlier this morning. "I've always had the desire to please you,

Ethan. More than I should, I know." She looked up to his face as she nuzzled into kiss him, her hands now fumbling with his belt buckle. Her tongue left his mouth as his trousers dropped to floor from the weight of his pockets. She slowly lowered herself down to her knees as she tugged his boxers down past his erect penis.

"Oh, Addison, my darling. You needn't..." He hesitated. "I have no willpower either..." He groaned as the palms of his hands cupped her head while she slowly bobbed back and forth. It wasn't a minute later, Ethan groaned a final moan as he looked down and watched his special friend look back up to him, wearing a look of self-disappointment as she wiped her lips of any seed that had spilled out and began to stand back up.

"Would you ever consider... giving up your whiskey—for me?" She stared into his clouded eyes with a look of hope in hers.

Ethan bent down to pull up his boxers and trousers. "I want to, Addison. I really do... but...."

"Don't finish your answer, just consider the question for a while. It's an important answer to me, Ethan. Not one you should make a snap response to." She looked at him as he cinched his belt. She patted his now flaccid crotch softly and quietly finished with, "I'm gonna go for now. You have an execution to get ready to view... and... and... I have some... thinking to... to do." With that she turned and stepped around him as she headed towards his doorway. She stopped and looked back at him as he quietly stood watching, words apparently trapped within his mouth. She smiled briefly at him as if she would never see him again, never take in the sight of him in his office, before sighing and gently pulling the door softly closed. *Things will never be like I want them,* she told herself as she laid her office keys on her desk and fixed the entry door to the office to lock on her way out. She suddenly felt okay with leaving. The feeling had dropped down upon her shoulders

THE CALL HOME

like a bag of soft fluffy feathers, with just enough weight to realize a decision had been made. She made her last walk down the stairs from the second-floor entrance of the Office of Ethan William Kendricks-Defense Attorney at Law.

68

Tony and the three ladies broke apart and went their separate ways around noon, making plans to meet back up at 2 pm for the three-and-a-half-hour trip to Raiford. They were to meet with Billy Jay Cader for a quick 15-minute meeting at 6:45 pm. Detective Rawlings had gotten special arrangements through the warden begging for a chance to eke out some possible information to aid in locating the body of a local missing young lady, Cali Lea Jenkens.

*****

Tony opened the door to his room at the Gibson Inn to find Hank sitting in the chair talking to Terri.

"Hey, Hank ole buddy." Greeted Tony.

"How did it go with the other contestants?" He asked with a bit of grin.

"I'm hoping but not counting on anything. We'll see. We're meeting back up in about an hour and a half to drive up to FSP for our meeting." He said as his voice dropped a bit. "Would you mind giving us a bit, Hank. I haven't seen much of Terri for a

THE CALL HOME

while, and I want to—talk—with her a bit before I have to go again." He winked.

Hank grinned back, "Gotcha, boss. Just be careful on your drive over and back. Good luck, partner!" Hank was smart. He didn't kill any time heading for the door. As it closed behind him, Tony said, "He's a great partner..." He winked at Terri then continued, "... the man knows how to read between the lines." He grinned. "I'm gonna just shower off to cool down really quick..." He gave her an evil smile. "... see you under the sheets in ten minutes for a round of catch-up love-making?"

"I'd be cuffing and stripping you down myself if you hadn't offered willingly!" Terri quipped back. "I don't know if you have to have a pow wow with that thing to have him ready for some spelunking or what... I won't ask, just know the tight cavern will be open and ready!"

Tony's voice could be heard laughing occasionally over the water splashing in the shower. Terri did her part to be ready, the sheets open and her legs parted for when he poked his head out from the door. She giggled to herself realizing how lucky she was to stumble onto such a great man who appreciated her humor—and of course—knew how to handle his firearm beautifully. Including how to holster and retrieve it in a beautiful rhythm. She laughed at her thought so hard, she snorted which drew her stark-naked man out of the bathroom and into bed that much quicker.

*****

Tony pulled up to the Apple on the Bay about twenty minutes late. All three women were outside waiting.

"Leave it to the man to be late!" Amy Jo quipped.

"I hear your girlfriend is in town." Gina added.

"Do you ladies know what color my bowel movement was this morning too?" He laughed before he realized these weren't fellow police officers and he turned red in embarrassment.

"It's okay, I'm a retired stripper, remember?" Gina laughed.

"Retired? When? Don't men like watching women with child, stripping?" Cat said. "I'm sorry. I know that's horrible. I apologize. I blame all off-color comments on my permanent brain damage my husband gave me."

"Let's load up before this gets any further down the alley." Tony replied.

"Are we gonna make it in time?" Amy Jo asked.

"I'm a detective, I have a car with lights and sirens—I think we'll make it." He chuckled.

Once loaded, he flipped his lights on and chirped the tires pulling out onto the highway.

As Tony pulled underneath the steel arched sign of the Florida State Prison, the amount of Constantine wire fencing and armed tower guards present, showed the seriousness of the security it maintained. There were already news vans and anchor crews set up along the highway at the entrance along with the parking lot just before the guarded entrance gate.

"Oh my, my husband's execution is making quite the brouhaha." Cat surmised. "I had no idea of the spectacle someone being put to death drew."

"It's like the Roman Coliseum." Gina chimed in.

After parking and checking in with the warden's secretary, the four were ushered in through the double lock-down doors where one door completely closed before the other began opening. You were like a caged rat with no cracks to slither underneath until

THE CALL HOME

the guards were ready for you on the other side, whichever it may be—coming in, or checking out.

Guards ushered them through several more lock-down doors and hallways until they stopped and unlocked a room with a round table and a steel loop on the steel tabletop, another on the floor.

Amy Jo looked around. "This brings back some haunting memories."

Tony glanced over, "You gonna be okay?"

"I'll be fine. It just reminds me of the last time I saw Billy Jay. Well—other than opening my door at home in Orlando to him being unshackled and standing in front of me for the first time ever."

They all sat down in a semi-circle around the table. The guards stated they would knock before bringing Billy Jay in and that once locked down, they would be just outside the door. "It'll be about ten minutes until he's brought down. He's going through rules and expectations now with the warden." One of the guards stated. "Any questions before we step out? Oh, and just to warn you ladies who may not be experienced in pre-execution interviews with cons—be careful. Some will try and break your heart, some will attempt to con the shit out of you, and others will be like 'the lights are on, but nobody is home.'"

"Thanks, guys. I'll take care of 'em." Detective Rawlings answered.

As the guards were closing the door, the four heard a comment by the one who had seemed to be helping. "There's always the one who thinks they fuckin' know it all...." And then the door closed with a loud metallic bang.

Ten minutes later, the sound of chains slowly became louder and more apparent from Tony's and the women's room. It was surely the chains clinking together that held Florida's next recipient of the three-legged chair, Old Sparky, built in 1924 by inmates and used regularly since that year. The sound grew louder but slowed to a snail's pace until it halted at the door, all sound but human chatter ceasing.

"I know the Goddamned rules, Baker. I ain't no new meat. Hell, I'm damned near dead meat."

69

Amy Jo recognized the voice. Her heart began beating faster and she didn't know why. Sure, she had wondered why he requested her visit, yet, deep down, she did hold an inkling why. They had built a relationship together that had abruptly come to an immediate and unforeseen end. Warden Willy had made certain of it. The friendship or at least understanding they'd come accustomed to was shattered overnight. She wasn't certain which way her feelings would go when he walked through that door.

Baker came in and made a statement. "Billy Jay would like to see each of you separately for five minutes and then as a group for ten minutes. Warden Taylor has agreed to allow that if y'all agree."

The four looked at each other and nodded simultaneously in agreement.

"Mr. Cader would like to see Miss Amy Jo Whitenhour first if that is suitable with you Miss Whitenhour."

"Yes sir, that is fine with me." She answered before she'd even thought the question through. Her gaze turned to the heavens, even though she was held in a maximum-security state facility, she knew her grandfather would be watching over her. She quietly thought to herself an internal plea to him. Please, Grandfather,

Give Grandma a big hug from me and... and... please give me the strength I grew up learning from you... to... to tackle this test. Please give me the strength to give Billy Jay the words I want him to hear.

"You ready ma'am?"

"Yes, sir."

"I need the other three to line up against the wall over there to the right of the door. Once we lead Mr. Cader into the room and secure him, I'll ask you to step out of the room without delay. We will bring you in the order requested for your turn. Are we clear?"

Amy Jo's heart was throbbing. This procedure brought back the memories of her first visit, watching Billy Jay's eyes as he stood behind the guards while they seated him and locked him to the table and floor. She remembered how degrading the entire act was. She knew he was dangerous and had killed, but she also saw him as being treated like a wild animal. And it bothered her then. Knowing he was going to be put to death very soon, it bothered her now as they led him like a steer to be slaughtered. This was just one step before death that they dangled in front of him.

Her eyes followed his. She was shocked at first to see his bald head. She'd never seen him without his curly and unruly dark strands. He looked older since he'd showed up in Orlando at her home. He no longer appeared dangerous. He was almost pathetically thin. His eyes sunken in and his cheeks showing jawbone.

After the guards had secured him, they turned and said, "Just holler out if he gives you any troubles, we are two seconds away."

"It'll be fine. I don't believe this one wants to hurt me. He had that chance recently and left when I asked him to."

THE CALL HOME

The man she'd heard called, Baker, nodded at her and as he left, the heavy metal door made that loud sound that said the outside world was far from this place.

"Jay...." Amy Jo quietly spoke.

"Oh sweet, Amy Jo." He answered in his raspy voice, less volume and growl in it tonight. "I'm glad you came. I really wanted to be able to say a proper goodbye to you. I'm... I'm really sorry... sorry for showing up unannounced... but... but really... I'm so sorry for that night. I'm... I'm sorry for the things I done to them young girls. No... no... no one deserved that wrath. I hate how you... you... found out." He finished in almost a hushed whisper, his will almost too weak to spill words.

"Billy Jay, we don't have a lot of time together. I have something I feel called to tell you... can... can I do... can I do that?"

"'Course you can, Amy Jo. I'll listen."

"I know you know about the Bible. You told me about Miss Cela Moses trying to reach your heart. I just want you to know...."

"Awe, Miss Amy Jo, it's far too late for that. Ain't no creator wanna deal with a broken soul like mine."

"I know you've read the bible, Billy Jay." Amy Jo reached over the table and put her hand on top of Billy Jay's. "Have you read about the two thieves hanging on crosses to the left and right of Jesus? The Book of Luke?"

"I've read it, one was sorry for his sins while the other didn't join in and question Jesus."

"That's right Billy Jay. The repentant robber asked Jesus to remember him when he entered his kingdom." She wiped away the tears that began spilling from her eyes. "... You can be like that man, Billy. Salvation for you isn't too late if you choose to believe."

Billy Jay smiled. "Amy Jo—I've been struggling with that whole concept since Miss Cela started telling me 'bout it. I just don't know if I can believe a king could forgive someone who has done the things I done. There are things you don't even know, Amy Jo. Horrible things." Billy's bald head dropped, the wrinkles on his forehead looked damp and Amy Jo seemed to see fear emanate out from them. She knew it didn't make sense, but he wasn't the same man she'd seen even a month ago. He looked like he was scared but had accepted this was near his time to leave. With that look of distant fear, she saw resolve. She hoped he'd listened. That was her mission for this trip. She wanted him to repent and go to heaven. As evil as the deeds he had done, she felt he was still redeemable. Made to be evil by a lack of nurture. Torture, both physical and mental. God hadn't created Billy Jay to be what he'd become. The devil took advantage and did. And she'd met the devil and faced him down.

"I wish I could go tonight—knowing I'd see you again, Miss Amy Jo. Up in heaven someday."

Amy Jo looked into his eyes. What she saw was far different from the first time they met. He didn't intimidate her anymore. He'd lost that power he once held. She looked around the room for the camera. She knew she was being watched at the least, likely recorded for posterity. She leaned forward, placing a hand on each sunken cheek and cupped his tired face. "I have a belief, Billy Jay. It's strong and it was given to me by my grandfather, long after I'd given up on my own life. I think I probably felt much like you. I actually preferred the thought of death instead of what my father was doing. What my momma ignored in her drug induced escape." Her hands held Billy Jay's face, not letting go even when he attempted to look away. "My grandfather taught me the importance of believing in our creator. He gives us hope in something better." Amy Jo moved her hands from holding his face, down to around his neck. She hugged him close, showing compassion for the man who had lacked showing it to anyone else in this world. "I need to know that you will do what I ask. I need to know I'm right about you, Billy Jay. You *are* worth saving. I feel it in my bones. I see that young boy in your eyes, the one that never had a chance. Please... I want to bump into you just past those pearly white gates that have the path lined with gold."

The door opened and Baker stepped in with two guards. "It's time Miss Whitenhour."

She nodded and then turned for one last look before he'd be led to that awful moment. She pulled him close one more time and whispered in his ear, "Promise me that you'll be there to greet me, Jay."

As she pulled away Baker held her steady by her arm. Billy Jay winked at her, as a tear slid down his cheek. He whispered five simple words. "Free your skeletons, Amy Jo." And the door closed with the sound of permanence.

70

Gina entered the room after passing by Amy Jo who was wearing a tear-soaked face. She saw herself in a way as they passed. Just like that day at the prison when they first met nearly bumping into each other. Amy Jo's tears changed Gina's fear into worried compassion. She almost backed up to leave, but Billy Jay's eyes caught her, and she became the fish ensnared in the net being drawn in. The man had an irrefutable power. She slowly sat, resting her roving hands on her belly.

"Boy or girl?" Billy Jay asked.

"He's a boy." Gina answered.

"Is he ours?" He asked.

"I can't say for sure, Jay. I'm scared if he came from your seed... from... from that... that day. I need you to tell me that you didn't plant your demon seed inside me."

"Gina—I only know of one woman I fathered a child with and that was Cat. Our son Billy James. He weren't evil in any kind of way. Darrell wasn't from my seed. Sheriff Burks raped my wife when I was out on the road. He raped her after giving her a ride home with two arms full of groceries. It's why I killed him." Billy Jay drew a deep breath. "My son Billy James was a good boy. I treated him horribly and I killed him in defense when he'd finally grown tired of me and my ways. But he was a good boy." He dipped his head, and it began to rock back and forth. "I'm sorry for what we did... what I did that day. It wasn't right. I'm sorry if that boy inside you is from my seed. I know neither you nor Ben wants it to be. But Gina—I never meant to bring you any harm. You're the only other woman besides Cat that I ever loved. I know it was wrong to lust after you. I know I'm payin' a price for that sin and many, many others. I just hope you can forgive me one day. I hope Ben can forgive me like he's forgiven you. You can tell him how I feel if it ever seems right to do so. I'm not a man used to sayin' I'm sorry, but I'd tell you a hundred times over. I imagine it will be you I'll be picturing in my mind when they hook me up with that lid and all of them wires. You'll be the last thought before I die, and I'll be telling you I'm sorry."

"Damn you, Jay for telling me that. I wanna hate you for all you did to me. But... but... I... I can't seem to force myself...."

"If that boy looks like me..." Jay took a deep breath. "... would you tell him I loved him for the short moment I thought he was mine?"

The door opened and Baker walked in. "Times up, Mrs. Dane."

Gina looked over at Jay. There was about 10 long seconds of silence as Gina mustered up the voice to answer. "I... I... can't promise to tell... to tell him that. I'm sorry. I... I won't do that to Ben... ever." Gina quickly stood up and rushed out through the door like a rooster with his tail feathers on fire.

71

It was Catrina's turn. She slowly walked in and sat down and bravely looked into the man's face she'd fallen in love with so many years ago.

"I knew this day would come, Billy Jay. Felt it in my bones for a long, long time. I'm glad I don't know what all you've done to others. Lord knows you did enough damage to us. Your family. What can you possibly say in five or ten minutes that can change any of the pain you've caused? Billy James ain't gonna come through that door. That woman's baby out there won't suddenly be guaranteed to be her husband's instead of yours. The same actions taken by you that you crucified your family for. I didn't, by God, make love to that damn sheriff that raped me that day you shoulda been home. I bet you were rapin' one of those young girls and killing her the day you could have saved me from the hell I lived. And killing my boy! I don't know why I let that detective talk me into coming here. Ain't no good gonna come from it." Cat's eyes contained not one single tear. No muscle so much as twitched as she sat and faced the man, she fell in love with that became Satan himself to live with. "If it weren't for my son, Darrell. I wish I'd never met you. I know Preacher Gibson and his wife Gloria have taught me that Jesus commands us to forgive—but I can't bring myself to do it again. I can't. Every time I try to do just that—my baby boy Billy James's face appears in my mind. The memory of his body lying on our living room floor—that knife stickin' straight out from his heart. And all I saw of you was your back side runnin' down the porch steps, your clothing disappearing into the night." Her body tensed up; her face reddened. "All I got to say to you, is go to hell, Billy Jay. Make that fire down there burn a little hotter. You ain't nuthin' to me but a dying ember, a flash in the pan and you're gone and forgotten." She attempted to get up and failed, leading her to holler loudly, "Get me outta here! Get me away from this son-of-a-bitch!"

Billy Jay sat calmly as Baker quickly opened the door with expectations of needing to beat Billy Jay down, his Billy club out clutched in his hand and almost looking disappointed when the need wasn't there. He quickly ushered Mrs. Cader out through the door.

twice the man you are, and she dresses herself in panties instead of boxers like you probably wear."

"Is this why you wanted to see me, Billy? You really want to spend your last hours—getting one over on the cop whose partner you stole from him? I don't care about that. I want the Jenken's family to know what happened to her, where her body likely is."

"The Jenken's family don't give a shit. That's just it. They wrote her off just as soon as they found out where she'd been. No matter she fought like hell to get away. Left for dead in the ditch. All drugged up and raped by three of Apalachicola's most honored citizens. Phuck House. It ain't that hard to find this shit out—detective." Billy Jay coughed, gagged just a bit. "I saved the young lady. She was alive before I ended up in jail. She worked at Pappy's. Figure this shit out on your own, Detective Tony Rawlings. That's what the good people of Florida pay you for."

"Where's her body, Billy Jay. Go ahead and give me shit about it but make it easy for us to nail that prick for what you say he did."

"Look where you found the Buick I stole. Should be a cross on a necklace somewhere near the deck from that night. Ethan killed Cali Lea. He had to; she knew too much. He's killed every other person involved in Phuck House. Their little sex club of sickery. Ain't it suspicious that his buddy Principal Charlie Bingham ended up dead in the Gulf? He was part of it. Of course, I took care of Roy Burks, another key figure in their club. Cali Lea escaped. I saved her and told her I'd pay them back some day. I was distracted and late on my promise. I guess Ethan decided to take things into his own hands again."

"Do you know anything about a special watch he wore?"
"The one Al Capone supposedly owned?"

"Yeah, that one."

"I thought he'd already told everybody in every county in Florida."

There was a knock before the door opened. Baker stepped in. Time's up. Warden says Cader needs to be taken back to his cell."

"Billy Jay—." Tony paused. "Thank you for the help."

"You forgive me?"

"I'm not sure I can do that just yet, Billy Jay. Whatta, ya say, I'll work on it."

"It's all a guy like me with limited time can ask for. For what it's worth, I'm sorry. It's been quite a last evening for me. My legs are getting' shakier' by the minute. I was hoping to walk out to that chair on my own accord but that may be a battle I can't win. As long as I ain't cryin' like a baby, I imagine I can face it."

"Thanks, again, Billy Jay."

In this moment, it appeared something changed in Tony. A small piece of his insides—softened. He wasn't sure why and in truth he somewhat worked at denying anything happened. But deep down, he felt different. He knew evil was still evil, and compassion was a word he'd never embraced, but as the door closed with that steel sound of finality, and he looked at the three ladies he'd come here with, compassion was a word he now felt he'd been introduced to. It would take time to sip it in and get used to its taste. There would be no deep swallowing of it, but he'd let it simmer instead of immediately spitting it to the floor like before.

73

The room was cold in appearance. Amy Jo wasn't sure what to expect it would be like. She'd never attended an execution. She knew Malcolm wouldn't press her, but she knew he would love to be surprised with a good article about her experience. He'd told her she had the ability to take a tragedy and by telling it from her unique perspective, bring an entirely different point of view to light. The writer inside her began to take over her thoughts. She was reminded by all the times she'd played the reporter as a child, interviewing her grandmother. A smile came to her. It felt very awkward, and she quickly tried to hide it, deeming this room, with the old wooden chair of death being the centerpiece—was no place to display a happy memory on her lips.

    Amy Jo quietly scanned the room, slowly taking in the blank stares worn on the seated faces. This was nothing like being the audience awaiting a concert or movie. *We are going to see someone die in front of our eyes.* She thought to herself. There wasn't the excitement in the air of attending an opening play. There was instead the weight of dread. She could see it everywhere. Gina's eyes bore a sadness and uneasiness as her hands continued to drag her fingers lightly around her belly as if caressing and calming her baby, maybe attempting to cause drowsiness so he wouldn't sense what was about to happen to a man that could be his father.

Catrina just stared blankly ahead at the chair. She couldn't read her thoughts. It was possible her brain had temporarily shut down. She had been told the head injury had changed her. Another bad thing tied to Billy Jay, although an accident he'd claimed. One man tied to so much destruction and sorrow. Billy John, Billy Jay's dad, suddenly popped in her head. She'd much rather be here to witness his being publicly electrocuted. That devil seemed far more deserving. A quick sad and almost terrifying thought came to Amy Jo. What if Billy Jay refused to make peace with Jesus? What if he instead goes to hell and... and his father is there to greet him and begin his torturous dominion over him again and again? Over and over like a sadistic nightmare. A sudden pain shot down into her gut and she thought she was going to be sick. She glanced around to see if anyone noticed her mood change.

Gina looked over at her and quickly lifted one hand from her tummy and reached over cupping one of Amy Jo's hands. It was warm and the action brought immediate comfort. Internally, she began to talk to her grandfather. *Be with me, Grandfather. I need you to be that rock for me. I'm afraid. I suddenly don't want to be here. I don't want to witness this cruel dog and pony show of retribution. It's like the Mason jar, but from a different form delivering evil. It's as if it's okay if the state deems it. It's still murder.*

Her deep begging contemplation was interrupted by sounds filling the room. A staggered dragging sound drew her attention and forced her eyes to Old Sparky. My God, they named it like it's some kind of state monument to be proud of.

There he was. Billy Jay. His slippered feet shuffling, almost being dragged along as a guard on either side ushered him towards the contraption. His head hung low towards the floor.

Someone broke the rules and hollered out, "Burn in Hell, Billy Jay!" Likely a family member of one of the girls he'd brutalized. Guards quickly moved towards the area the voice cried out.

Amy Jo continued to watch as they seated him in the chair and began strapping his legs and wrists with what appeared to be leather straps. They removed his slippers and then all movement stopped. The warden's voice came out over the speakers. "Does the prisoner have any last words?"

Billy Jay Cader jostled a bit in the seat as if attempting to settle in. His bright orange jumpsuit rustled until his movement stopped. He cleared his throat as his statement pushed through in a dry raspy tone. "I've... I've done things... I... I... now regret. I... I... didn't set out to be evil." His eyes scanned the small room where the twelve to fifteen visitors were seated. "I'm sorry. I... love you Cat, Gina, Amy Jo... all for different reasons. Forgive me." His eyes found Amy Jo's and he locked onto her eyes. He smiled, likely each woman believing he was smiling at them as they sat so close together. His gaze went skyward, and his last spoken words were, "Forgive me, Jesus. I'm broken. Please accept and heal me, my soul is handed over to you."

And then silence fell upon the small room as only the sounds of final preparations were heard. An electrode was strapped to Billy Jay's left ankle and a very large sea sponge that was so soaked with saline water it poured over Billy Jay's face as they placed it first on top of his freshly shaven head and then the copper lined helmet strapped on top. He appeared like an early football player with frightened eyes. They then put what appeared to be a

THE CALL HOME

black canvas veil snapped onto the helmet that hung down just past his chin leaving the last image they in the viewing room would ever see of him alive.

The microphone crackled before Warden Taylor's words soberly sounded out. "It is now time for Inmate Billy Jay Cader's sentence to be carried out. The time is 11:59 pm."

A guard plugged a cord into a junction box at the base of the chair as Billy Jay sat quietly. It appeared as if he were attempting to wave as his right hand lifted from the armrest as high as he could bring it. The sound wasn't loud like they expected it to be. It was sudden but just slightly louder than the sound of a mechanical whoosh, like an elevator moving from one floor to the next. They all witnessed Billy Jay's body suddenly lift with a jolt, but no words or groans came from under the hood covering his mouth. His body remained stiff and raised as far as the straps would allow for about fifteen seconds and then the sound vanished suddenly, letting Billy Jay's body drop back to a slumped position in the uncomfortable wooden chair. About ten seconds later, the same sound again came alive in another mechanical breath, and while Billy Jay's still clenched fists tightened once more as his body heaved upward, it remained held statuesque until the sound ceased once more, dropping Billy Jay's limp body back into the seat. This time as his body lay slumped, his hand remained unclenched and lying lifeless, his fingers lay draped over the edge of each armrest.

A black curtain was dropped down from the ceiling covering the chair and Billy Jay's body. About five minutes later the microphone crackled a short burst once more before Warden Taylor's voice was broadcast over the room once more.

"This concludes inmate Billy Jay Cader's execution. Time of death is 12:09 am. Please exit at this time."

And that was it. Billy Jay left this world with no fanfare. No fiery shootout, no dramatic event at all. He was there and now he wasn't. Amy Jo's heart just felt empty. Two things came from what she experienced. She'd quickly concluded upon the dimmed lights brightening, that she could indeed hold onto hope that Billy Jay was now standing before the Pearly Gates of Heaven, possibly greeted by her grandfather alongside Saint Peter as he was now finally one of God's children. A decision he'd made on his own. The other thing—she knew was it was time for her to let go of the last bit of hate she still held. When she got home to Orlando, to the home she'd grown up in after being saved from her parents—she had a letter to read. It was time.

74

As Amy Jo sat quietly in the back seat of the detective's car, she stared out through the window into the clear dark sky. A storm had just passed through this area, but it hadn't been the kind with lightning and thunder. No raindrops or flooding. No dark black thick clouds swirling in ominous circles, little hook clouds dropping low teasing the ground below with the threat of tornadoes. No, this destructive storm had come in the form of just a man. An innocent boy born into a devilish world he held no choice in. It had taken years of torment to brew into something people could foresee and fear. And now, now that storm had been vanquished in a way it would be unable to build back up in its original way. Yes, there would be storms to pop up in the future. Some weaker, some of the same strength, maybe even harsher. But this storm, Billy Jay Cader, had been snuffed out with little fanfare once its winds were caught within the net.

Heat lightning briefly lit up the interior of clouds far off in the distance. Possibly opposite of the sign a rainbow brings. Quiet flashes of light from the heat reminding any observing it, that a dangerous cold front can sneak in silently at any moment, unsuspecting.

Amy Jo smiled, too dark in the car's interior for anyone to notice. She thought she wasn't seen by Tony's eyes watching her through the rearview mirror as he steered the vehicle down the long barren straight highway. The smile that escaped her mind was exposed across her lips and was the thought once more that she had somehow said the right sequence of thoughts and words to tempt Billy Jay to seek forgiveness and accept a Savior who was forgiving enough to give grace even to a diabolical killer if he gave himself to Him. She'd helped be the sedative he'd needed but not realized, to help calmly usher him into his next life. And in return, he'd given her the need to close some doors quietly to a few rooms that held a darkness she hadn't been able to hide well enough or shake. Maybe now a healing could begin. She'd found a man she could now see herself sharing a life with, Cable Lee Johnson, but she needed to sweep out a few cobwebs that had clung on far too long.

Forgiveness. Such an easy word to fall from one's lips, but so difficult sometimes to take that word and turn it into action. She wanted life to start fresh though, and to do that one must let go of the past. Remember it, acknowledge its presence, forgive, and turn the page to the next blank white sheet ready to be written with a new chapter.

She hoped the others gained the same knowledge and need that this experience had given her. There had been some good come from the bad. One must certainly be willing to do some soul searching to find the shiny treasure buried hidden within, but there almost always is a silver lining to every dark cloud if you look.

When she was finally dropped off back in Apalachicola, and everyone had said their quiet goodbyes, she leaned into Gina's arms and placed her hand on top of Gina's that still touched her belly in soft circles and whispered, "I think your little boy will be beautiful. I also think no matter who the biological father is, you and Ben will nurture him into a fine young man. I see it in your eyes, Gina. I feel it in your heart. I want you to call me and stay in touch. Please?"

Gina nodded, her eyes appearing to allow a calmness in Amy Jo's sincerity.

"I will, Amy Jo. I promise. I kind of feel like I finally have a best friend in my life. Thank you."

"No need to thank me, I feel like I'm the lucky one. Come visit me soon, okay? Call me when you have your baby. I want to be there for you."

"I will."

As Amy Jo opened the door to her grandfather's pick up and pulled herself up and in, she looked out towards the others one last time and waved her hand goodbye before pulling out and back on the highway to home. She did what she most always did once she was rolling. Amy Jo reached for the radio and twisted the knob to the on position. There was a favorite playing, and she wasn't surprised. Angel Falling Too Close to The Ground by Willie Nelson. Again, her grandfather was somehow able to give her the tune she needed to hear as the wheels rolled ever closer to home as the sun began to show the first signs of climbing out of the horizon and into the morning clouds.

"I love you, Grandfather and Grandmother. And I'm going to read my mother's letter as soon as I see the porchlight lighting our front door. Thank you for everything."

*****

The truck finally pulled down the road between the two fences that led to Amy Jo's home. The light was on just like it always was. Georgie's parents' house appeared to be empty. They must be out. It was just as well. As much as she'd like to see Georgie and tell her all about Cable Lee, she wasn't ready to rehash Billy Jay just yet. She'd start her article for Malcolm after sleeping, but first things first.

    She twisted the knob to the front door and entered, taking in the aroma of the home she hadn't realized just how much she missed. Any tension that still remained within her muscles, both from the event and all the driving, soon began to release. She immediately opened the refrigerator door and reached in that familiar part of the shelf and pulled the bottle of Moscato out. Like muscle-memory she simultaneously reached up and grabbed a wine glass from the cupboard. The clock on the wall showed it was only 9:45 in the morning. "Oh well..." She spoke aloud. "... it's 5:30 in the afternoon somewhere." She made her way to the couch and set the bottle and glass on the coffee table. Before sitting down to relax, her eyes made their way to the fireplace mantle. She stared at the small hand carved wooden box that held a few special things within. This included a certain letter that she had held in her possession for over eleven years mostly untouched—but never breaking the seal.

    Amy Jo almost ignored the feelings brought on by her experience earlier to open and read that letter she'd all but refused to even acknowledge. Her tired body began to lower to the couch she knew would allow her to sink comfortably into and enjoy relaxing with a glass of wine. Just as her hips almost touched the cushion—her legs locked; her muscles began to raise her butt back up. She couldn't turn her back on those earlier feelings of—forgiveness. The word now felt like a contract she'd signed with Billy Jay. He'd kept his end up and now it was her turn to reciprocate and do the same. The box now drew her over as if it held a magical pull to the rings, she wore on three of the fingers of her right hand.

As Amy Jo's fingers hovered over the box's lid, her hand began to quiver. She drew the glass held in her left hand that she'd filled almost to the rim with Raspberry Moscato before making the few steps back to the couch, box in hand. Amy Jo raised the glass to her nose and slowly sniffed in the fruity aroma and then closed her eyes and rolled her neck around in circles. She heard the pops and cracks as relief began to radiate throughout her body. She looked at the lid, her right hand now resting on top of it. Her fingers spread out and with her thumb on the front edge, she rolled the lid open, exposing a smooth but tattered yellowing unopened envelope. She hesitated but picked it up clasping it between her fingers as she let the lid flop closed and sat back onto the couch, plunging deep into her favorite place to relax. The letter now lay on her lap as her free hand reached up and twisted the switch to the reading lamp.

75

Ben Dane paced back and forth in the waiting room. His brow was wet with nervous perspiration. The door opened and Darrell, along with Mitzi, hurried over to him. He fell into Darrell's arms, his head dropped onto his shoulder.

"Gina came home and almost immediately fell on the floor." He pulled his head up and away enough to see Darrell's face. "Her water broke. She's... she's in with the doctor. She's having our baby, and I'm scared."

"I know Mr. Dane...."

Ben put his hands around each of Darrell's biceps. "Mr. Dane? Really? I'm about to be a father and you call me that after all this time?" He let a smile slip through, letting Darrell off the hook.

"I'm sorry, Ben. Everything's going to be fine—right?"

"A nurse just came out and told me everything looked great, she was brought in in perfect time."

"That's a good sign! It wasn't too long after a nurse gave me that same news that they told me to come in and meet my new daughter!" Darrell said.

Mitzi stepped in and gave Ben a hug. "I'm glad she's here and in good hands."

THE CALL HOME

A smiling nurse came through the double doors and walked towards Ben. The nurse saw Mitzi and smiled, bringing a matching grin on Mitzi's face. "Now this pretty little lady I remember! Momma to a beautiful little girl with some reddish blonde curls!" The nurse paused. "Mr. Dane—you're a daddy now! A handsome young boy with your beautiful eyes! He looks just like you!"

Ben's face flushed. "He's okay, right?"

"He's fine, in fact, he's a chunky little boy! Very vocal too! Wanna go have a look and maybe hold him?"

"Oh my God, yes! Yes, I do! Is my wife okay too?"

"Both momma and son are perfect. Your wife's smile is gorgeous. She looks like one happy momma."

Ben opened the door after going through a hand scrubbing lesson with the nurse. The first thing he noticed was his sweet wife's grin, ear to ear, as she held their son across her chest. She looked up as he came in.

"Oh, Benny—he's so beautiful—and—and he looks just like you, his eyes, his chin... the little dimple matches yours."

Ben moved closer and leaned down kissing Gina's forehead. He then turned and studied Benjamin Robert Dane's tiny little arms and hands, his fingers wriggling as Gina cooed and talked to him. He reached over and gently touched his boy's chin then his fingers.

"He's unbelievable, Gina. We made a very handsome baby boy, didn't we?"

"Yes, we did. Have you called your brother yet?"

"He's on his way."

"So is my mom." Gina said and then looked back down at little Benny. "I had to let her know she was gonna be a grandma. She told me she was just thinking about me and wishing she would hear from me."

"God is good, Gina."
"Yes, indeed he is."

76

Amy Jo lifted her glass again just after refilling it. The unopened letter was still sitting on her lap. She put her glass down on the table and then picked up the letter. "I guess there's nothing like ripping the band-aid fresh from the wound." Amy Jo said aloud, and then she carefully tore the end of the envelope open, lifted it to her lips and blew between the front and back, causing it to billow out enough so she could grab the folded papers with her fingers. She held it for a moment just staring at it, looking at the cursive writing through the backside of the paper. She sucked in a deep breath and began to unfold the two or three pages that had been sealed inside and kept inside the box like a buried body.

She laid the papers onto her lap, picking up the glass and gulping a quick drink before reading the first words:

My dear daughter,

I don't really know how to start to try and explain my mistakes in this life and with you. I don't have any right to ask for anything from you.

The handwriting was so perfect. And while some of the ink had apparently gotten wet in spots, which made it difficult to read at times, her mother was correct. She had no right to ask her for anything or for that matter to have even reached out to try. She imagined the now the dried blotches of faded and splotchy ink marks stained in tiny circles—were likely tears that had dropped onto the pages by her mother as she wrote them. Was she sober at the time? Her handwriting made it appear she likely was.

Amy Jo continued, her eyes up to this point completely dry, her mind mentally closed to letting the written words affect her in any way. It was almost too difficult for her to even mentally picture what she looked like the last time she'd seen her. After all, her grandfather had whisked her up quickly that day after telling her to go outside while he confronted her parents. She continued reading,

I can't even imagine now the kind of pain and mental anguish you were forced to endure with what happened. I'm so sorry, baby girl, that I ignored what your father was doing to you, what my lack of protecting and saving you, did to you. It's unforgivable, yet I pray you can find it in your heart to do just that. I know you hate both of us and you have every right to. I wish I could explain everything and why my body and mind were numb and void of anything. It's no excuse, baby. I will never be able to give you any valid excuse. All I can say is that my mind was so sick and tired that I felt as if I were walking dead. My hunger for getting high in any shape or form had been out of my control. I was a slave searching for any escape. I hate myself now for leaving you and not stopping Frank from doing what he was doing. It's so ugly and horrible for me to imagine. I wish I was dead most of the time now. I knew Grandma and Grandpa were the best thing for you. It's why I didn't fight to keep you. I knew you were at least safe with them. Life got really hard after you were gone. Frank would hit me and tell me it was all my fault because I didn't love him. I guess he was right, I didn't love him. I hadn't for quite a long time. I felt so betrayed that first time I actually realized what he was doing to you. When he came out of

THE CALL HOME

your room, I confronted him and told him I would tell the police. He laughed at me and told me I was nothing without him. Nothing but a worthless waste of air, that he could kill me and bury me and you out in the swamp, and nobody would ever care.

    Amy Jo's eyes were still dry. The memories of her father forcing her to take her clothes off in front of him had begun to become clearer. The not knowing or understanding of what was happening and why. The fear of no longer trusting and the inability to speak out those fears. And then the touching. Each minute causing more lack of understanding and the vileness of being penetrated in places no one, let alone someone who had been trusted at one time to keep her protected. Her body and space being violated in every unimaginable way. And now—reading words from the woman who had given birth to her and was given charge to love and protect her—now giving worthless excuses that she'd apparently believed would cause a painful wave of forgiveness over her inactions and ignoring. Pretending she hadn't seen and known what was going on. The acts had been repeated many times, not that if it were even once—would be forgettable or forgivable. But that's what she was being asked after all these years of keeping her feelings locked up tightly in a box, pretending to herself that it was all a mistake wrapped up in a bad nightmare.

    Amy Jo, I do love you. I know you may never believe those words, no matter how many times I would say them over and over if you would let me.

    I'm not messed up anymore, Amy Jo. I'm clean and sober now for just over a year. I'm not with Frank anymore. That's another story, but not one for writing on paper. Let me just assure you that your daddy can never hurt you ever again. I was way too late in aiding you from the horror I looked away from. But that horror is no longer a threat.

I'm praying that after reading this, that maybe, just maybe, you would allow me to see you at some point when you are able, so I could speak face to face and beg your forgiveness. I don't expect this. But I do pray that God will let you see that I'm not the mother now who deserted you back then. I can't compare the evils you suffered, but I did suffer some darkness too. But I also know you wouldn't have been made to suffer anything like you did, If I had been the strong, loving mother the Lord expected out of me. The Lord's forgiven me now. It took a long time, a difficult journey, but He walks with me now. All I can do now is pray that you still have a relationship with Him too, that grandma and grandpa have kept you strong in faith and full of grace and forgiveness in your heart.

I now live in a small apartment with two other mothers who were once as broken as I. The address is the one on the envelope, here in Birmingham, Alabama. I pray this letter finds not only your hands and eyes, but your heart and that you believe my words I'm writing and how truly sorry I am for what I allowed to happen. I pray you know the meaning of forgiveness and grace that I have learned. Ain't none of us owed that gift. But I have learned to forgive myself, Jesus taught me I must do that so I can be a child of his again. Unforgiven self-regret will do nothing but open one's heart up to the devil to do his due.

I pray you are happy. I pray you haven't put the memory of me so deep in a dark hole that you can no longer see my face as it once was when my heart was healthy and full of love for you.

I'll always love you Amy Jo, even if you choose to never forgive me, I'll always love you and hate for being any part of breaking you.

Your Momma.

THE CALL HOME

Something in those words finally broke through into Amy Jo's psyche and opened the floodgates of tears. The glass of wine on the table was no longer able to erase the pent-up pain from coming out and being exposed for the first time in many, many years. She sobbed and wailed.

"Why, Jesus? Why?" She cried out through wet lips and blurred eyes. "What do I do? I know I'm supposed to forgive—but how can I forgive an evil man like Billy Jay—and still hold my momma accountable for the shit life she gave me?" Amy Jo buried her face in her hands as she lifted her feet to the couch and tucked herself into a ball into that same couch she used to snuggle up in between her grandparents and cry sometimes—laugh at other times and watch movies together or listen to Grandpa's records. There were tears shed there too. "What do I do, Grandfather? Tell me, please—I'm begging you...."

The phone rang, breaking her mind away from the drama of the letter she'd promised herself she'd never open.

"Hello." She answered in a quiet tone that would cause anyone who knew Amy Jo to question what was wrong.

"Are you okay?"

Her sniffles followed by a cough, caused the person on the other end to respond again before she could answer.

"I'm headed your way, Amy Jo. Hang on. I'll be there as quick as I can."

"You don't have to do that, Cable."

"You sound down, I'm headed there."

"I... I don't...."

"Nonsense, Amy Jo. I'm headed out the door now. Is this from the... the execution?"

"Sorta. I—um, I read my momma's letter. And I haven't slept since I don't know when."

"Crawl into bed and go to sleep. I'll be there when you wake up."

She smiled. "That sounds wonderful. But I hate you feeling like you have to—but—I love that you feel like you *have* to." She wiped her nose and then cleared the tears from her eyes with her shirt.

"I love you, Amy Jo. I always have."

"Don't ever let me go. You promise?"

"I promise."

"I had no idea forgiveness was so difficult and held so much power. My world is forever changed. I'm glad I have you to hold and cherish. Life is so precious and so unpredictable, isn't it?"

"Yes, it is, yes indeed it is."

Amy Jo and Cable Lee hung up. She decided to snuggle in on her favorite couch covered up with one of her grandmother's handmade quilts. She closed her eyes knowing her new man, a boy who had helped her way back in high school, would be with her when she woke up. She laid her head down, thankful she finally took the step to heal a hidden pain she'd held onto for far too long.

"I forgive you, Momma. I do love you. I promise I'll find you. I promise." Her eyes closed and the sound of soft snores followed shortly after. Tomorrow would be the start of a new beginning.

*****

Life can be filled with a struggle that can outweigh any happiness. Life can give us just enough of a fragment of *that* happiness to give us reason to answer the need to be fulfilled. The urge to recall the past or dole out retribution for the suffering given to us.

THE CALL HOME

That strong, stubborn and silent need to go back.
The call home.

THE END

thank you,
Eli Pope

Made in the USA
Columbia, SC
02 August 2024